PRASE FOR **LES ROBERTS** AND
THE MILAN JACOVICH MYSTERY SERIES:

"A clever plot, a vibrant Cleveland and rural Ohio setting, and a realistically drawn hero make this series one to watch. It exudes much the same sort of charm as the early Spenser novels did."
—*Booklist* (on *Pepper Pike*)

"Roberts handles the private-eye format with aplomb and takes full advantage of his Cleveland scene . . . Best of all is his Slovenian sleuth, vulnerable and fallible, whom we are likely (and would like) to see more of."
—*San Diego Union* (*Pepper Pike*)

"Fast-paced and smoothly narrated."
—*Washington Post Book World* (*Full Cleveland*)

"Another smooth page-turner from Roberts, who keeps the action moving and still fits in some wry observations on parenthood, teenagers, and marriage."
—*Kirkus Reviews* (*Deep Shaker*)

"Roberts combines a strong character and a clever plot with the ethnic diversity that Cleveland provides. He proves that Midwest private eyes can hold their own with the best ones from either coast."
—*Des Moines Register* (*Deep Shaker*)

"There's an affection for Cleveland and an insistence on its ethnic, working-class life that gives vividness to the detection. Roberts writes with sharp wit, creates action scenes that are drawn with flair, and puts emotional life into a range of people."
—*Washington Post Book World* (*The Cleveland Connection*)

"Roberts is one of the best crime writers around, and *The Cleveland Connection* is his best effort yet. The plot has all the right ingredients—danger, suspense, intrigue, action—in all the right amounts; Milan Jacovich is the kind of guy we want on our side when the chips are down; and Roberts even makes Cleveland sound like a swell place to live. Don't miss this one."
—*Booklist*

"Packed with unusual heroes, villains, and political twists and turns . . . a mystery that defies predictability."
—*Midwest Book Review* (*The Lake Effect*)

"A real treat . . . If you've somehow missed this series, definitely give it a try . . . If you're already a fan, this book will delight you even further.
—*Mystery News* (*The Lake Effect*)

"A corker of a whodunit...Gritty, grim, humorous, sentimental—a perfect 10." —*Chicago Sun-Times* (*The Duke of Cleveland*)

"The characters are vivid, and the plot goes in unusual directions, but ultimately it's Cleveland that captures our hearts." —*Pittsburgh Post-Gazette* (*The Duke of Cleveland*)

"Roberts affectionately weaves in the history and rich ethnic mix of Milan Jacovich's Cleveland turf." —*Publishers Weekly* (*Collision Bend*)

"Roberts is a wordsmith of high order, and *Collision Bend* is a terrific novel of the mean streets." —*Meritorious Mysteries*

"Roberts certainly creates a sense of place. Cleveland rings true—and he's especially skillful in creating real moral and ethical choices for his characters." —*The Plain Dealer* (*The Cleveland Local*)

"Jacovich [is] one of the most fully realized characters in modern crime fiction...Roberts is a confident writer who knows his character well and who has made him complex enough to be interesting." —*Mostly Murder* (*The Cleveland Local*)

"[Roberts] tells his tale in spare and potent prose. His Cleveland stories get better and better, offering far more than regional insights and pleasures." —*Publishers Weekly* (*The Cleveland Local*)

"A series that gets better and better...strongly recommended for those who like their detectives cut from the classic mold." —*Booklist* (*A Shoot in Cleveland*)

"[Milan Jacovich] is a hero one can't help but like. Roberts's polished prose, inventive plots, and pleasantly low-key style add extra appeal to his long-running series." —*Booklist* (*The Best-Kept Secret*)

"Page turner of the week...narrative comfort food...a nifty spin on a classic P.I. formula." —*People* magazine (*The Indian Sign*)

"Brilliantly plotted, with a powerhouse climax." —*Booklist* (*The Dutch*)

"[A] roller coaster ride of a mystery...Roberts speeds the reader through an investigation offering plenty of delicious twists and turns without ever compromising credibility." —*Publishers Weekly* (*The Irish Sports Pages*)

THE IRISH SPORTS PAGES

The Milan Jacovich mysteries
by Les Roberts:

Pepper Pike

Full Cleveland

Deep Shaker

The Cleveland Connection

The Lake Effect

The Duke of Cleveland

Collision Bend

The Cleveland Local

A Shoot in Cleveland

The Best-Kept Secret

The Indian Sign

The Dutch

The Irish Sports Pages

THE IRISH SPORTS PAGES

A MILAN JACOVICH MYSTERY

LES ROBERTS

GRAY & COMPANY, PUBLISHERS
CLEVELAND

Gray & Company, Publisher
1588 E. 40th St.
Cleveland, Ohio 44103
www.grayco.com

Library of Congress Cataloging-in-Publication Data
Roberts, Les.
The Irish sports pages : a Milan Jacovich mystery / Les Roberts.
p. cm.
ISBN-13: 978-1-59851-013-3
ISBN-10: 1-59851-013-4
1. Jacovich, Milan (Fictitious character)—Fiction.
2. Private investigators—Ohio—Cleveland—Fiction.
3. Swindlers and swindling—Fiction. 4. Slovenian Americans—Fiction. 5. Cleveland (Ohio)—Fiction. 6. Irish Americans—Fiction. 7. Women judges—Fiction. I. Title.
PS3568.O23894I75 2006
813'.54—dc22   2006000951

Printed in the United States of America

10 9 8 7 6 5 4 3 2 1

For Nick Orlando

THE IRISH SPORTS PAGES

CHAPTER ONE

The atmosphere in the bar seemed to actually be humming, or rather vibrating like a well-played violin string, with a purity of tone and pitch worthy of a concert hall. Whether it was in anticipation of great food or the promise of something yet unspoken, I didn't know. You won't find a better-dressed, better-connected, or better-looking crowd in all of Cleveland than at One Walnut, the upscale restaurant on the corner of Walnut and East Ninth Street. An awful lot of the area's beautiful people show up on any given night, but especially on Fridays, which is the week's most important time for networking. It's the kind of place where everyone makes an entrance, even if they're not important at all.

On this particular evening, longtime leading morning-radio personality John Lanigan, of the *Lanigan and Malone Show* on WMJI, was looking at his reflection in the enormous circular art deco mirror behind the bar and chatting with flame-haired Melanie, who is something of a bartending legend around here because of her killer martinis. The air crackled.

After I'd said hello to them both, I was led down a wide hallway into the main dining room, where Cathleen Hartigan awaited me for our dinner engagement. She was far and away the most elegant-looking woman in the place.

I didn't spot her immediately, because she'd been seated in a little alcove to the left of the entrance, her back to the soft gray wall, and when I approached and she raised her face for a kiss, it fell into that limbo of something more than a hello kiss and something less than anything else. I wondered if any of her lipstick had been transferred to my mouth during the exchange.

"You look sensational," I said. I didn't lie. Her fair Irish good looks seemed to glow, and her gray silk dress shimmered when she moved. I hadn't seen her in a while, but I thought she'd allowed her blond hair to grow a bit longer, and she was wearing it more softly around her face. Her perfume, rising up to enchant me, was subtle and expensive.

"You're looking pretty good yourself, Milan," she said in that lilting voice that could be a clarion call in a courtroom and a soft, low purr anywhere else. "It's so good to see you. I really appreciate your coming."

"The pleasure's mine," I said, and truth to tell, it was. I'd been pleased, but more than a little surprised, when she called me and invited me to dinner. She had suggested I bring along one of my standard agency contracts, so I was fairly certain that this time we were only going to be talking business. You could say that Cathleen Hartigan and I have a "history"—one that goes back about seven or eight years.

I suppose some clarification is in order here. I spent some time in Vietnam in the military—an MP sergeant—and then several years as a Cleveland cop prior to becoming an industrial security specialist and private investigator. That stint with the police is probably what got in the way of my ever getting together romantically with Cathleen Hartigan. Because long before I met her, she was the sometime girlfriend of a man named Victor Gaimari, who is number two on the depth chart of northeast Ohio's biggest crime family, right behind his uncle, Don Giancarlo D'Allessandro. And early in my relationship with Victor, I broke his nose, and he subsequently had me pretty badly bruised by three of his employees.

Here's irony for you: since that time, Victor and I have become friends, sort of. And his uncle, the don, seems to think I walk on water. We've done each other a few favors over the years, which isn't as bad as it sounds, and even though I hate the way he makes his money, there's no gainsaying that Victor is a charming, affable guy—a pretty good ally when the chips are down, if it comes to that.

Back when he introduced Cathleen and me at a party he was giving, naming her my "dinner partner" for the evening, I think he'd gotten it into his head that since he liked me and he liked her, we would probably like each other. And we did. But their past romantic involvement had been problematic for me. I knew she was no gangster's moll, no fluff chick. She was a successful attorney, and her mother was a judge, her brother was a congressman, and her late father had been a state senator. But I couldn't get my nineteenth-century morality past the fact that she and Victor had once been lovers.

That's the reason our relationship never amounted to much— a mild flirtation and a few quasi-innocent kisses is about as far as it ever got. And that was my fault.

I'm in my forties, and everyone my age or even close to it has a past, but in my shortsightedness and self-righteousness—traits that have been pointed out to me by more than one person in my life—I perceived Cathleen to be in some way tainted goods, and I walked away.

Stupid me. Stupid me again when I ran into her at another Victor Gaimari party last year. Before that she'd been married for a short time to another lawyer, a cheapjack shyster from the west side. She subsequently divorced him when he got disbarred for suborning perjury in a workers' comp case. I drove her home after the party that evening and kissed her good night rather passionately—and then didn't do a damn thing to follow through.

I've been on my own for a long time now, both businesswise and relationship-wise. I have my own agency in the Flats, the born-again riverbank neighborhood a hop-skip away from downtown. Milan Security, in case you want to look it up in the telephone directory. That's my first name, Milan, with the accent on the first syllable—*My*-lan. Europeans say *Mee*-lahn or even Mi-*lahn*, but my parents wanted to be regular Americans, so they always pronounced it with the long *i* sound. And if you think that's difficult to say, try bending your tongue around my last name, which is Jacovich. Pronounced *Yock*-o-vitch. It's Slovenian, because Slovenia is where my parents came from. There are more people of Slovenian descent in the Cleveland area than anywhere else in the world outside Ljubljana, which is the capital of Slovenia. And if you're geographically challenged and don't know where or what Slovenia is, look it up in an atlas.

I'd been surprised to get the dinner invitation from Cathleen Hartigan that afternoon; there are only so many times a woman can get rejected before she figures out that she's wasting her time. So I knew this dinner get-together was more of a professional meeting and not a date. Not personal.

I sat with her and ordered a drink, and we chatted for a while about this and that, comfortably, the way old acquaintances do. We didn't reminisce about old times, because we really hadn't shared any. I imagine she was wondering as much as I what might have been. And then she sat up a little straighter in her chair and unconsciously moved her drink away from her and said, "My mother is going to be joining us this evening, Milan. I hope that's not a problem."

And all of a sudden I was a little bit less at ease than I'd been five seconds earlier. Maureen Carey Hartigan is a former Cuyahoga County prosecutor and currently a judge of the Common Pleas Court, with a tough-on-criminals reputation that makes defense attorneys quake at the knees. I couldn't help but wonder why Cathleen was bringing the two of us together.

I wasn't even certain the judge would remember me, but I certainly remembered her. I had been called twice as a prosecution witness in her courtroom, including once when I provided damaging testimony against the misbegotten son of a bitch who killed my best friend, and who Judge Hartigan had sentenced to life imprisonment without the possibility of parole. My best friend, Marko Meglich, was a cop; cop killers get short shrift in any courtroom in the country, but especially in Hartigan's. She had been tough and professional and fair on that occasion, and sympathetic, too, and I'd developed a healthy respect for her.

"Of course it's all right," I answered Cathleen's query. "I know her from court, but I've never met her socially." Then I looked at the way Cathleen's usually full lips tightened into a line, and I amended, "I have a feeling this isn't exactly going to be social, either."

"Let's wait until she gets here, Milan. I'll let her tell you about it." Her general attitude was a bit too mysterious for my comfort.

When Judge Hartigan arrived five minutes later, the buzz in One Walnut suddenly resembled the sound of a Beverly Hills restaurant when someone like Tom Cruise walks in. Cleveland judges get their faces on television a lot, and Maureen was more photogenic than most. Owner-chef Marlin Kaplan came out of the kitchen to say hello, and virtually the entire restaurant staff greeted Maureen by name, as did several customers as she made her way through the dining room. Not unusual; the restaurant was close enough to the courthouse and the glittering high-rise law offices downtown, so I supposed she knew practically everybody in the place. Unlike New York and Chicago, where it's fairly common to spot entertainment celebrities everywhere, from the most expensive restaurants to the supermarket to strolling on the sidewalk, and give them little attention, in Cleveland luminaries from all walks of life are treated as such, and while it's rare that anyone actually bothers them in public, they are invariably recognized and greeted, or at least gawked at.

Usually, when children are small, they tend to resemble their parents. It's only after they're grown, and life takes over and sculpts and molds and rearranges their faces, that they often appear entirely different. Cathleen, however, still looked very much like her mother, only about twenty-five years younger. Judge Hartigan's hair was just as blond, but streaked with gray, cut shorter, and styled in a more mature fashion, and she was perhaps an inch shorter and ten pounds heavier, and her burgundy suit wasn't of a color one usually associates with the bench. But the familial resemblance—the porcelain skin and earthy beauty tempered by Gaelic humor and pugnacity—could be easily discerned by anyone who was paying attention.

We both rose as the judge approached, but there was no phony air kissing between mother and daughter. The way Maureen Hartigan beamed at her offspring with unaffected delight and affection was more demonstrative than any kissing or hugging or cooing might have been. Cathleen started to make the introductions, but her mother stopped her.

"Mr. Jacovich and I have met before, in court," she said. "I appreciate your coming tonight."

Flattered that she'd remembered me, I held out her chair for her to sit down, and she gave me a startled but not displeased look. I know holding a woman's chair or opening a door for her is considered politically incorrect these days, but I'm just old enough that the lessons in etiquette and common courtesy my mother drummed into my skull are hard to break. The judge didn't seem to mind, and actually thanked me. I guess she was old enough to remember courtesy, too.

She ordered one of Melanie's specialties—an honest, old-style gin martini straight up with an olive—endearing herself to me forever. To a purist, those designer concoctions with vodka and chocolate or mint or curaçao aren't really martinis at all, no matter what they're called.

When her drink came, she got right down to business. "What I want to speak to you about is obviously confidential," she said. "I know your reputation, and of course Cathleen vouches for you, too, so I assume that won't be any problem."

"No, ma'am," I said, again mindful of the manners I'd learned at my mother's knee.

Her smile was crooked, playful. "I wore this wine-colored suit with the daring neckline instead of my judicial robes for the express purpose of not being called ma'am," she said. "Maureen will do, if you're comfortable with that."

"Great, Maureen. And if you're comfortable with calling me Milan, I think we have a deal."

She nodded, and then looked around cautiously to see if anyone was paying attention. "Good." She lowered her voice to a commanding whisper. "The fact is, Milan—and this is very embarrassing to me—I have been royally scammed, and so has my family."

I tried not to look surprised. Maureen didn't fit the profile of con-game victim. "Do you mind if I take notes?"

She hesitated for half a second. "Discretion is very important to me."

"If I'm captured by the enemy, I promise I'll eat them," I said, smiling to take the sting out of it.

She nodded, which I took for permission to pull out my notebook and a pen.

"It started with my cousin, Hugh Cochran," she said. "He's an assistant director of the Department of Public Service here in Cleveland."

I knew the name. Vaguely. "Okay."

"About seven weeks ago Hugh was having a drink in a bar on

the west side called O'Grady's." She allowed herself a small smile. "An Irish bar, naturally, not too far from his house. For some reason it's one of those places in which Irishmen who work for the city hang out. Perfectly harmless, I assure you—and you don't have to be Irish to drink there, either."

So far all I'd written down was "Hugh Cochran" and "O'Grady's." I waited.

"About five weeks ago a young man wandered in. He had a brogue as thick as Irish stew and said his name was Brian McFall, from County Mayo."

"How young?" I said. Youth was a relative thing; the judge was in her sixties, and I suppose that to her I was a young man, too.

"In his early or middle thirties," she said, looking to Cathleen for confirmation. "No older. You may or may not know it, Milan, but a lot of Cleveland's Irish population have ancestors from Mayo. It's one of those strange sociological phenomena like the one that brought most Slovenian immigrants to this area as well."

I ducked my head in acknowledgment. My own parents had emigrated from Ljubljana after World War II, arriving in Cleveland because virtually everyone they knew from Slovenia who had come to America had wound up here, too. Ethnic neighborhoods in American cities have nothing to do with racial distrust or bigotry or even clannishness. They are all about a comfort level.

"You know how it is in a tavern," she said. "Especially an ethnic tavern. People get to talking, having a few drinks, they open up and wax nostalgic, and pretty soon everyone knows everyone else's life story."

"I have the feeling you're going to tell me Brian McFall's."

"Well, sort of. In any event, after a drink or two, and a good bit of reminiscing about how much he missed Achill Island and the Moy Valley and all that, McFall told Hugh and his friends that he'd arrived at Cleveland Hopkins Airport from Castlebar by way of Shannon that very afternoon, and that the airlines had lost his luggage, including his passport, his wallet, all his credit cards, and his traveler's checks. And that he'd come to Cleveland to get to Akron to work for his cousin but couldn't locate him."

That story would have sounded pretty lame to me, but then I

hadn't been drinking in a pub all night and wouldn't have been caught up in the emotion of a fellow Irishman in need. "I suppose your cousin had to pay the drink tab?"

Maureen Hartigan rolled her eyes toward the ceiling, and Cathleen shifted uncomfortably in her chair. "I wish it had been only that."

She stopped as the waitress came back to recite the specials of the evening. The waitress didn't go away, though, until Cathleen and I ordered a second drink, too.

"Hugh actually brought McFall to my house a few days later," Judge Hartigan said when the three of us were alone again. "He said McFall couldn't check into a hotel without a credit card, and he'd bunked in with Hugh for a few days, but since Hugh lives in a one-bedroom house and I have five, he thought . . ."

"I've got the picture."

"It was only to be for a night or two," she said, "until the airlines delivered his lost baggage."

"But they never did find his luggage, did they?"

"You've figured that out already? No, they didn't." She shook her head.

I felt like shaking mine. The gullibility of otherwise very sensible people never ceases to amaze me.

"How long did he wind up staying with you?

"Almost three weeks."

"And the job with his cousin in Akron?"

"Apparently it never materialized. Brian said he wasn't ever able to locate him."

I glanced over at Cathleen, who looked every bit as somber as her mother. "I assume that you wouldn't have called me in on this if it was just a matter of unpaid lodging and a bar tab at O'Grady's . . ."

"Not by half," Judge Hartigan said. "Briney borrowed my cousin Hugh's credit card so he could rent a car, which he did. But he also used it to run up more than two thousand dollars' worth of clothing at Nordstrom, and Brooks Brothers, too. He said that because his baggage had been lost he needed new clothing—and suitcases, as well. I gave him about fifteen hundred dollars of my own, too. In cash. He said he needed some 'walking around money.' "

"For fifteen hundred dollars he could have taken taxis," Cathleen put in.

"Limousines," I agreed.

"And he stole from me, too, Milan," the judge said. It was as though she was surprised by the fact, even after all this time. "A brooch-and-earrings set my grandmother gave me is missing, along with some other jewelry and about eight hundred more in cash. And Hugh discovered that an expensive pair of leather boots, three or four silk ties, and some valuable cuff links were gone from his house as well."

"This Brian McFall just disappeared?"

She nodded. "Into thin air, it seems. Brian McFall, Hugh's credit card, the rental car, my jewelry, the clothes, and the cash, along with some important papers and photographs—all gone. I woke up one morning and looked in his room, and he just wasn't there anymore."

I wet my whistle with my drink because I was going to ask a question I thought I already knew the embarrassing answer to. "Why didn't you notify the police, Maureen? You're a judge. I'm sure they would have made finding Brian McFall a priority."

There was a pause that was at least eight months pregnant, and mother and daughter exchanged glances that could only be classified as humiliated.

"It was a little more than simple theft, I'm afraid," the judge said. "A little more personal."

I didn't say anything; my mind was too busy trying to process what I thought I knew was coming.

"Milan, I'm an elected official," she continued. "The slightest whiff of scandal, especially in a conservative district like mine . . ."

I put up a hand to stop her. "It's all right," I said. "Those things happen. Even to judges. Nobody is judging *you*."

She looked blank for a moment, and then all of a sudden she laughed, throwing her head back and guffawing loud enough to attract some attention. "Oh my God, you think I was sleeping with him? I'm sixty-three years old!"

I stared at her, thinking that she was sexy and attractive and not too old to sleep with anybody. "I apologize, Maureen. I shouldn't have jumped to conclusions. But then I'm not sure what . . ."

I saw the second embarrassed look pass between mother and daughter, and all of a sudden I did understand, and then I *was* sure. My heart sank a little. I turned toward Cathleen.

She flushed, her Irish complexion going from pale white to bright red in a matter of moments. "I haven't dated since my divorce, Milan—you know that. And Briney was quite the charmer," she murmured, her head down. "Handsome, funny, full of stories—he even sang old Irish folk songs."

I nodded knowingly. The old-Irish-folk-songs ploy.

"This is kind of humiliating," she continued. "Give me a few points for guts, at least. The hardest thing I ever had to do in my life was to call you, knowing I'd have to tell you about this."

I reached over and squeezed her hand.

"That's why confidentiality is so important, Milan," the judge said, her eyes following my hand to Cathleen's. "I know it's the twenty-first century and all that, but in some circles a woman still has her reputation to consider."

"I'll be very discreet," I promised, "as soon as you tell me what you'd like me to do."

"I want you to find Brian McFall. I want you to bring him back so he can stand in front of me and tell me why he betrayed us all." She opened her large purse and pulled out a snapshot, which she pushed across the tablecloth to me. "That will give you an idea of what he looks like; I know that will help."

"It will," I said, and looked at it. Cathleen and a lean, young man with sharp, ferretlike features and dark curly hair were seated on a sofa together, laughing, each holding a bottle of Guinness, his arm around her shoulders. It was hard to tell, but the man seemed as if he might be fairly tall when he stood up; his legs were stretched out comfortably and looked long. In the out-of-focus background were two other people, a man and a woman, whose faces were partially turned away from the camera. It was obviously a candid shot snapped at some sort of party, and both subjects seemed unaware their picture was being taken.

"As you can see," Cathleen said miserably, "he was a real cutie."

I was itching to slap the cutie around. Not just because of him and Cathleen; that was none of my business, and she wouldn't have gone to bed with him if she hadn't wanted to. But because he was a punk—and a stupid punk at that. Assuming that he hadn't dumped the rental car off at some chop shop for ten cents on the dollar and left Hugh Cochran holding the bag for it, his larceny had amounted to not much more than a few thousand dollars in cash and merchandise. Not a bad payday for three weeks' work for most people, but hardly enough to risk getting a judge riled up at him.

Only small-timers steal small things.

"He was staying with your mother," I said to Cathleen, "but spending nights at your place?"

She nodded miserably. "Mostly, yes. I invited him to bunk in with me for the time being, but he said it would be too much trouble to move again. And Mom and I only live about six blocks from each other."

"The funny thing was," the judge said, pointing to the photograph, "that he just about went postal when that flash went off. He got very angry and said he didn't like having his picture taken. So that's the only one we have of him."

"I can see why," I said. "The guy is a scam artist. It wouldn't do for a bunch of photos of him to be floating around."

"Well," Cathleen said, "at least we have the one. That should give you something to go on."

"It does," I said. "But I can't bring him back if he doesn't want to come. Not by force, anyhow. I'm sure you know that's kidnapping."

"I don't expect you to bring him back by force, necessarily," Maureen said. "I want you to convince him that it would be in his best interest."

"You mean you want me to threaten him?"

The judge patted her lips primly with her napkin, and her eyes scanned the dining room as though she was looking for somebody she knew. "I don't particularly care to know your methods," she said tightly. "All I want is results."

"I don't imagine you'll get your money back," I said.

She nodded. "I don't really expect to recover much of the cash, if any. It doesn't matter—in the long run it was a piddling amount. And Hugh has canceled his credit card, of course. But my mother's jewelry—that's irreplaceable. I want that back, no matter what. If he's still got it, fine. If he sold it, I want you to find out to whom. I'll buy it back if I have to." She cleared her throat, scoping out the room again, looking everywhere but at my face. "And the papers and photographs that he stole. I want them returned as well."

I was scribbling notes. "Okay," I said. "What kind of papers and photos?"

"Legal papers," Cathleen put in. "And family pictures."

"An album?"

The judge hesitated, but just barely. "No. Loose photographs. In a plain eight-by-ten manila envelope."

"Again, Maureen, I'm sure you know that even if I find him, I can't legally make him return the photos."

"Let me take care of that," she said heavily.

I didn't like the sound of it, and was going to tell her so when I caught a glimpse of Cathleen. She looked devastated, and was giving me an entreating glance I couldn't really say no to.

"All right, Maureen. This picture of him and Cathleen will help, but it isn't much to go on. Anything else you can tell me?"

"He told us that his father was the executive vice president of Belleek china," Cathleen said in a way that made me suppose I should have been impressed. But I'd never heard of Belleek china. I get most of my dishes at Wal-Mart. "And he swore that for our help he'd see to it that we all—Hugh, my mother, and I—would be sent full sets of Belleek Parian china. It's some of the finest in the world."

"After he'd been gone for several days without a word and without leaving a number or forwarding address," Maureen said, "I got suspicious. So I called Belleek in Ireland. I'm sure you won't be surprised to learn that they'd never heard of anybody named Brian McFall. Their executive VP's name is Haggerty. So he lied about that, too."

"He lied about everything," Cathleen put in, mournfully but with an unaccustomed bitterness giving her tone a sharp edge.

"Can you help us?" the judge said. "Quietly and discreetly?"

"I don't know," I said. "There isn't much to go on here."

"Will you try?"

I hesitated, and Cathleen turned her hand over in mine and squeezed tight, fingernails digging into my palm. Her blue eyes were shining wet. "Just try, Milan," she said. "For an old friend."

I sighed. I'm a sucker for blue eyes, I suppose. "It might run into some serious money; these things often do."

"That doesn't matter," Maureen said, and took a checkbook from her purse. "Getting my own back matters more."

"All right, then," I said. I fished the contract from my jacket pocket and passed it over to her. She scanned it quickly, professionally, and signed it with my pen. Then she took out her checkbook and wrote me out a retainer. Before I folded it and put it away, I noticed that her checks were imprinted with adorable little kittens. Cute—but not very judicial.

"I'll want to talk to your cousin Hugh," I said, and wrote down his address and phone number in my notebook. "And now you'll have to tell me where I can find O'Grady's."

CHAPTER TWO

We were finished with dinner by about nine-thirty, and I hurriedly said my good-byes to Cathleen and Judge Maureen Hartigan on the sidewalk, because the wind off Lake Erie was beginning to howl, blowing cold air ahead of it like an advance scouting party. Fall in northeast Ohio always starts out beautiful and invigorating, with a bracing crispness in the air, Greater Clevelanders buzzing about the Browns or Ohio State football, and the turning leaves with their riot of colors giving the more celebrated New England autumn a run for its money.

And then about the end of October, which we were now experiencing, one gets the idea that fall isn't screwing around anymore. The refreshing, brisk air grows ten or fifteen degrees chillier, the northerly winds that tear across the lake from Canada get serious, and the sun goes undercover behind a bank of gray socked-in clouds to remind us that for the next several months we're going to have to bundle up, winterize our homes, and pay a heating bill five times higher than we've been accustomed to.

As someone once said, to live in Cleveland you have to be tough.

While I handed both Hartigan women into their cars, it occurred to me that in strictly financial terms, Brian McFall had not really hurt them very much, and that what they might be able to recover if I tracked him down would barely cover my fee. Apparently, a sense of personal violation was driving them to find him, and I could understand that. When things get personal, people can turn quite vengeful.

It was the kind of assignment I normally would have turned down.

But Cathleen Hartigan was a friend—someone I could have loved, I suppose, if circumstances had been different—and she was hurting. You don't walk away from friends when they need you. So I really didn't have much choice.

Since it was still relatively early on a Friday evening, I decided to get right on the job, and headed over the Lorain-Carnegie Bridge. The huge pylons, statues representing the Titans of Transportation, loomed over me.

O'Grady's is a little bar in the historic near west side neighborhood of Tremont, just down the street from Lemko Hall, a landmark that is triangular in shape like Manhattan's Flatiron Building. Once an old meeting hall, gentrification has transformed it into small offices and retail shops, one of the places that give the neighborhood its unique color and texture.

Nobody had gentrified O'Grady's. Inside, it was apparent that the owners worked awfully hard at keeping it Irish—perhaps too hard. The jukebox was blaring spirited selections by the Clancy Brothers and the New Barleycorn Singers, and there were green foil shamrocks plastered all over the walls and ceilings with people's first names pasted on them, several Irish flags, and posters of Galway Bay and the Blarney Stone and similar tourist attractions. The impression was that of false gaiety, a facade, like those glittering, neon-choked theme parks that have sprung up all over America in the last twenty years—the ones that hire cheap wino labor to run the rides and concessions, employees who secretly piss beneath the tracks of the high-speed roller coasters. Cigarette smoke hung in the tavern's atmosphere like a noxious cloud, and all the customers who were not drinking Guinness Stout or Harp or Murphy's Irish Amber were sipping Bushmills or Jameson. They probably weren't all Irish, but they were all drinking Irish— except for the Murphy's drinkers, that is; Murphy's Irish Amber is made in the Netherlands.

Go figure.

I got a few guarded looks from the patrons when I walked in. Not as many or as severe as one of them would have received had they ventured into my old stomping grounds, Vuk's Tavern on St. Clair Avenue, where any stranger is viewed with watchful suspicion, but enough so that I felt like an outlander. Neighborhood taverns, especially ethnic ones like O'Grady's and Vuk's, can be warm and fuzzy if, like the fabled television saloon, everybody knows your name; otherwise, you're in terra incognita and had better act accordingly.

There weren't many stools vacant at the long, curved wooden bar. I found one next to a middle-aged man dressed in a shiny-with-age brown suit and a tie I couldn't have described fifteen seconds later, who looked as though he might have been a loyal foot soldier in the army of the longtime Irish political machine on the west side. On the other side of me sat an attractive young woman smoking a cigarette and wearing a Notre Dame sweatshirt with the familiar logo of a belligerent leprechaun. The man nodded to me, and the woman gave me a twinkly-eyed "Hi." When all I did was return it without embellishment, she looked disappointed and went back to her conversation with two other women close to her age. I noticed they had stopped talking when she turned her attention to me, only to resume their connection when she was ready; she was obviously the alpha female of the group. Their topic, I couldn't help overhearing, was "cute guys," and the one next to me kept casting covert glances at me over her shoulder. At my age, being included in this particular category was flattering, even though at six foot three and two hundred twenty pounds I was nowhere near anyone's idea of "cute."

Wearing a bright green vest and a black string tie over a white shirt with red sleeve garters and looking like a chorus boy from *Lord of the Dance*, the youngish blond bartender came over and took my order for a Guinness. My beer of choice ever since I began drinking as a youngster has been Stroh's, but I was going to ask a favor of him and wanted to be on his good side.

He brought my draft, and I pushed a twenty-dollar bill across the bar, one of those new ones with the huge portrait of Andrew Jackson, along with the snapshot of Cathleen Hartigan and Brian McFall. "Do you happen to recognize this guy?" I said. My neighbors on either side of me turned to look, interested.

"Why do you want to know?"

"I'm a private investigator," I told him, and gave him one of my business cards. "I'm trying to find him."

The bartender, whose name tag identified him as "Bert," wiped his hands on his pants and picked up the picture with one hand and the twenty with the other. I gave him a nod, and the bill disappeared.

"I think so, yeah," he said, studying the picture. "He come in a couple of times with Hugh Cochran. Hugh's a regular in here, works for the city."

"Oh?"

"As a matter of fact, they met right here at the bar, about two months ago." He pointed down to the end of the room. "Over toward the back there."

"You never saw him before that night?"

He shook his head and put the photo back down on the bar. The woman next to me wasn't being very subtle as she craned her neck for a better look.

"Nope," the bartender said. "We don't get a lot of casual walk-ins like you here, dude. These are mostly regulars—neighborhood people—and I know 'em all. So when he come in here that night, I noticed him right off. Everybody did."

"Just like they noticed me," I said.

"Well, yeah, dude. You're not a regular."

"And did he tell you he'd just gotten off the plane and his luggage was lost and he was broke with no place to stay?"

"He didn't tell *me*; he told Hugh Cochran."

"How did that go down?"

"He walked in and went down to the end of the bar where Hugh was sittin' and ordered a beer. They struck up a conversation—you know how people talk to each other in a bar. Come to find out, he only had about fifteen bucks in his pocket, so Hugh stood him the drinks and then took him home with him until he could get squared away."

"And that's it?" I said. "You never saw him again?"

"Yeah, he come in with Hugh a few days later, and maybe one more time after that. And he always drank on Hugh's tab."

"Did he tell you his name?"

"Brian something. Brian *Mc* something."

"McFall?"

He shrugged. "Could be." His eyes narrowed suspiciously. "Why all the questions, there, dude? Is he in trouble?"

"Just for grins," I said, "let's put our heads together and try real hard to think of something else to call me besides 'dude.' Okay?"

Bert flushed pink, and fiddled with his string tie. "Sorry about that. It's just an expression."

"I know," I said. "Look, McFall isn't in any trouble. I just need to talk to him, that's all."

"Well," he said, "I haven't seen him in about three weeks, so I'm afraid I couldn't help you." He fingered my card. "If he comes in, should I tell him you're looking for him?"

"No. Please don't. But if he comes in, would you call me?"

He hesitated a moment, licking his lips. I put another twenty on the bar, and it disappeared quickly into his shirt pocket. The guy had the fast hands of a magician. "Sure thing."

He moved away to serve some other customers, and I took a swallow of my stout. It was nutty and heavy and somehow warming.

The woman on the adjoining stool leaned toward me; her perfume was faint and floral. "Mind if I take a closer look at that picture?" she asked.

I pushed it toward her. "Help yourself."

She took a pair of tiny glasses out of her purse and plunked them on the end of her nose. "Don't mind these," she said. "I just wear them to see with." She studied the picture carefully. Then her shoulders slumped. "Aw, jeez."

"You know him?"

She thought about it for a minute, her brow furrowed in concentration, and then she nodded slowly. "I think I do, yeah."

"From in here?"

"No."

"Is his name Brian McFall?"

She shook her head and removed the glasses. "No. I think it was James something. I can't remember the last name; I didn't really get to know him very well. But you know what?"

"What?"

"I think my girlfriend used to date him."

It's a small world, at least in Cleveland. Big major-league city that it is, it's really a collection of small-town neighborhoods full of people who know each other well, so it didn't surprise me that

I'd lucked out sitting next to a woman whose friend had been involved with Brian McFall.

The young woman, as it turned out, wasn't Irish at all. Her name was Jinny Johnson, which explained her Nordic complexion and light blond hair, and she told me that she lived in the Tremont neighborhood and drank in O'Grady's because it was within walking distance of her apartment. She worked as a data processor in City Hall along with her best friend, one Judith Torrence, who, being the daughter of two County Deny immigrants, did most of her drinking at another Irish bar a bit farther west. Jinny whipped out her cellphone and called her friend's home for me but got no answer, and then, since it was a Friday night, she wisely tried Torrence's favorite pub and found her.

We headed over there in my car, Jinny chatting in an animated and very flirtatious way.

The tavern was called the Shebeen, which in Ireland is a place that serves whiskey illegally. Here, however, an Ohio liquor license was prominently displayed behind the bar. But there were no Irish posters or paintings, no shamrocks, and no vivid splashes of kelly green anywhere; apparently a real, authentic Irish bar needs no such embellishments. And the Shebeen was teeth-achingly authentic. The jukebox was playing real Celtic music, not the merrily familiar Hennessy-Tennessy-tootled-the-flute songs that blared out at O'Grady's. Instead it featured the doleful, wailing ballads that celebrated Irish melancholy almost as a sacrament. The mostly male drinkers who lined the bar at the Shebeen like shooting-gallery ducks looked a lot more dedicated to the refreshments, too.

They were the neighborhood Irish, who like the Slovenians and Poles and Hungarians and Italians in their own Cleveland enclaves, live and function within fifteen minutes of where they were born.

The U.S. Census in the year 2000 told us that a lot of young adults were leaving Cuyahoga County and going to greener pastures, where the city fathers had planned more wisely for the future in high-tech industries and where jobs were more plentiful and the weather less harsh. But the young ones in the Shebeen, and the older ones, too, had probably never entertained the thought of getting out and going somewhere else. This was their neighborhood, their turf, their narrow and restricted world, and it was here they would grow up and work and marry and procreate and fight and drink. And they'd probably die here, too.

Judith Torrence was not quite as pretty as her friend, but she was dark-haired, with startling blue eyes dominating a full face. My best guess was that she was about thirty years old. She was wearing dark slacks with a white blouse trimmed with ultrafeminine lace and bows. Jinny Johnson introduced us and gave my arm a proprietary squeeze, saying to her friend, "And keep your mitts off, by the way; I saw him first."

Nice, I thought. But I was not pub-crawling that night; I was on the clock for the Hartigan family.

We moved to a booth against the wall so we could talk more privately. Groups of old men hunkering around tables or seemingly holding up the bar watched us with suspicion.

I showed Judith the picture.

She didn't have to look at it for long. "That's James," she said almost immediately. "Jamie. Jamie O'Dowd."

"Jamie O'Dowd." That was a new one on me, and I tumbled the unfamiliar name around in my head for a bit. "He told the woman he's with in the photo that his name was Brian McFall."

"Brian. Hmm." She tossed her head, making her dark hair swing. "Well, I'd imagine he has a whole list of names he uses," she said, but there wasn't a lot of bitterness in her tone. It was more like tired resignation. "He kissed the Blarney Stone for sure, because he's the perfect Irish liar."

"You used to date him?"

Judith looked at Jinny. "*Date* him? Is that what you told him?"

Jinny shrugged innocently, and batted her eyes at me. She was a relentless flirt. "I didn't know what else to call it—out of delicacy."

"I didn't *date* him, Mr. Jacovich," Judith Torrence said. "Dating implies going out places together—dinner and a movie, or even just pizza and bowling. Jamie and I never went anywhere, and the two or three times we did, I always had to pay for it. He said he'd just gotten off a plane from Ireland and they'd lost his luggage and passport and credit cards; and that he'd come to America to go to work for his cousin in Akron. So I felt sorry for him. But as luck would have it, in the three weeks he was in my house, he couldn't seem to locate that particular cousin."

I nodded at the story, almost identical to the Hartigan family's except for the name change. "He didn't happen to mention this cousin's name, did he?"

"His cousin Charley, that's all he said."

"No last name?"

"Not that I can remember."

"And he told you his father was a bigwig in the Belleek china company in Ireland, and he was going to see to it you got a full set of dinnerware?"

Surprise widened her eyes. "How did you know that?"

"Shot in the dark," I said.

"Belleek, that's the good stuff," Jinny chimed in. "I wouldn't mind having a set of that myself." She nudged my leg with her foot, rubbing her toe the length of my calf. "For my hope chest."

It felt good, but I ignored her foot as politely as I could. "Where did you meet him?" I asked Judith.

She pointed a red-tipped finger. "Right on that bar stool I was sitting on when you came in."

"He just walked in and sat down next to you?"

"Yep," she admitted. "And struck up a conversation. He had a sweet little brogue, just like my grandfather's, and a true gift for blarney. And when he told me his tale of woe, I fell for it, sucker that I am." She shook her head sadly. "Men tell me their sob stories, and I melt, I'm afraid."

"Sorry I have to get personal, but did you take him home with you that same night?"

Her blue eyes opened wide and innocent, and her shrug was helpless. "He didn't have anywhere else to go."

"Judith's big problem," Jinny Johnson told me as if we were old friends sharing a confidence, "is that she's a sucker for cute losers. She wouldn't know what to do with a winner if he walked up and bit her in the ass."

I barely acknowledged Jinny's comment; to her ill-concealed annoyance, I was more interested in what Judith Torrence had to say. I took out my notebook. "He stayed with you three weeks?"

"Three weeks and one day," she said. "Look, what's this all

about? Did he do something wrong?" With a practiced flick of her wrist she knocked back a slug of Harp, a swallow so big it made her eyes water. "Not that it would surprise me or anything, but I would like to know."

"I'm not with the police," I said. "Somebody wants him found, that's all. I'm a private investigator—that's what I do."

"Wow," Jinny Johnson said, putting a hand on my biceps and squeezing. One hand and one foot were on me now—two appendages left to go. "I never met a private detective before."

"Detective is a police department rank, Jinny. I'm an investigator."

The subtlety was lost on her. "Whatever." She gave my arm another little squeeze. "You're cute anyway."

Back to Torrence. "During the time you were together, did you pay all his expenses?"

"Everything," she said. "I bought him some clothes, bought the groceries, and he ran up a four-hundred-and-some-dollar phone bill before he disappeared." And then she added, "None of which I could afford."

"When he left, did he take anything that didn't belong to him?"

"About a hundred and twenty dollars in cash that I kept in my underwear drawer, and a diamond tennis bracelet—given to me by some other guy who dumped me later, too, by the way." She gritted her teeth and then laughed through them to cover her embarrassment. "Look, I'm just a lowly office drudge, like Jinny here. I don't have many expensive things to steal."

I was thinking the same thing. Brian McFall/Jamie O'Dowd was a small-timer. "When was it exactly that you first met Jamie?"

She had to stop and think. "I ran into him in here about three months ago. So it was around the end of July."

I made some quick calculations. He had stayed with Judith Torrence for three weeks, and then disappeared somewhere for about seven days until he resurfaced at O'Grady's to hit up Hugh Cochran.

So Brian McFall/Jamie O'Dowd did indeed have somewhere to stay locally, at least for a week.

"He left without saving good-bye?"

"Yep." Her curls bounced as she nodded. "One night I came

home from work, and he was gone. Along with the bracelet and the money."

"And you never heard from him again?"

"Not a word." She sighed wistfully. "I guess I'm the type of woman men just leave."

"Don't you believe it, honey," Jinny Johnson chimed in with fervor, squeezing her friend's arm supportively. "Men always leave women eventually."

This wasn't a conversation I wanted to get sucked into—anytime a woman begins a sentence with "Men always . . . ," it means nothing but trouble. So I tried to bring the discussion back on topic. "Judith, when he was with you, did he talk about himself very much?"

"Just what I told you—that his father was a big shot with Belleek and that he had a cousin in Akron. He liked to lie around and watch TV. Every day when I came home, he'd tell me about the weirdos on the *Jerry Springer Show*. And talk on the phone, like I said, but that was mostly during the day when I wasn't home. He hardly ever left the house unless it was with me. And he was a Chinese-food freak. I think we had Chinese takeout almost every night. I got pretty sick of mu shu pork and fried rice, let me tell you."

"Watching TV and eating Chinese food—that's all he did?"

"Pretty much, yeah," Judith Torrence said.

"I know this is an imposition, Judith, but would it be possible for me to have a look at your phone bill for the three weeks he stayed with you?"

The request seemed to trouble her. "Eeeww. That's kind of creepy, isn't it? I mean, I don't have anything to hide, but. . ."

"I know," I said. "It's an invasion of privacy, and I hate to have to ask you. But if I can find out who he was calling, maybe I can figure out where he's gone to, and maybe you can get some of your money back."

Judith lifted her shoulders and then let them fall again in resignation. "I suppose it'd be all right. Well, more than all right, actually."

"How so?"

"It's not the money so much. Frankly," she said, laughing, "I'd like to see the son of a bitch get kicked in the teeth."

"Damn right," Jinny Johnson chimed in. "He broke her heart."

Torrence turned to look at her friend. "Oh, grow up, Jinny," she said. "My heart is a hell of a lot tougher than that, for the love of Jesus. He didn't come anywhere near breaking it. He just made me look and feel like a goddamn fool. And for that, I'd love to see his Irish ass swing."

CHAPTER THREE

After our business was done, I stayed at the Shebeen and had a few beers with Judith Torrence and Jinny Johnson. They were lively, outspoken, and attractive, and I found myself having fun in their company, even though the Celtic music on the jukebox was alternately doleful and angry and militant, the singers crooning of lost loves, dead loves, and the Troubles, the centuries-old strife between the Irish and the English that was still costing lives.

I made arrangements with Judith Torrence to stop by her house the next day to look at her telephone bill. I also accepted the phone number Jinny Johnson scrawled on the inside of a matchbook, but I didn't think I'd be using it anytime soon. She seemed a little too desperate. I wasn't the man of her dreams, but I was single and handy, and I'm sure she was thinking I might turn into a keeper. I like basing my relationships on a little more than that.

I took my leave of them shortly after midnight, Judith assuring me that she'd drop Jinny off at O'Grady's to get her car. Since I was in the neighborhood, I considered a nightcap at the Velvet Tango Room, one of my habitual watering holes—with its elegance and quiet understatement it was a hundred and eighty degrees from the Shebeen—but I reconsidered. After One Walnut, O'Grady's, and the Shebeen, I'd had enough to drink. I'm getting too old—spending an entire evening drinking takes too much of a toll on my body. My favorite bartenders at the Tango, Maribeth and Linda, would just have to wait for another, more propitious time.

My apartment in Cleveland Heights, on the intersection where

Cedar Road and Fairmount Boulevard triangulate, was a twenty-minute drive from the Shebeen, and I was glad to get back to it after fifteen hours away, empty though it was. I spend far too little time at home to own a dog or a cat.

My answering machine was blinking, heralding one message, and I was almost tired enough to let it blink until morning. But I'm not the kind of person who can allow a phone to ring unanswered or leave a letter unopened: I'm far too curious, which holds me in good stead considering my chosen profession.

So I rewound the tape and listened to the call.

Milan, it's Cathleen. I just got home, and I need to talk to you. Call me back, please, no matter how late you get in. Please? Thanks.

My watch said twenty minutes before one, and I wondered if she really meant the "no matter how late you get in" part. But it was a Friday night, or more accurately, Saturday morning, and although Cleveland is a notorious go-to-bed-early town, people do tend to stay up later when it's not a school night. Still, I was whipped from my long day and from the amount of alcohol I had consumed while making my evening rounds, so I went into the bedroom, stripped off everything except my shorts, and lay down under the comforter before calling Cathleen Hartigan.

"I took your message literally," I said when she answered after the third ring. "I hope I'm not waking you."

"No," she said, "I expected you to call late."

"Actually, I was out chasing Brian McFall. Do you want to hear about it?"

"You're working for my mother, not me. Maybe she wants to hear about it. I don't." She drew a ragged breath. "Milan, going through that tonight was very humiliating for me."

"You don't have to be humiliated. I'm not judging you, Cathleen."

"Oh, sure you are. You always judge people, Milan. That's your thing, isn't it?"

"Not this time," I said, and wondered whether it was true. And then I didn't say anything more because I didn't know where she was going with all this, and I step lightly when I know I'm crossing a minefield.

"I mean, having to admit I slept with Briney McFall," she said finally. "Admitting it to you. Especially to you. Because of our . . . relationship."

I rolled over on my side. "Cathleen, we don't have a relationship, remember? We've kissed about three times in the last seven years, and that's it. We never seemed to get around to the rest of it."

"*You* never got around to it, Milan."

Every male should recognize my panic at that moment; these were the kinds of subjects women love to talk about. Relationships or the lack thereof, and whose fault was what and why this happened and that did not. Men, on the other hand, would prefer being slow-cooked over a barbecue pit.

"Okay," I said, "maybe I had that coming. Nevertheless, right now we're friends. And friends cut friends some slack. So I don't think badly of you because of McFall. We've all made mistakes like that."

There was silence on the other end, save for her breathing, which sounded forced. Finally she said, "You are the most irritating man I've ever known!" and broke the connection. She probably had a cordless phone that she deactivated with her thumb; in the good old days she would have slammed the receiver into its cradle.

Advanced technology has robbed us of so much in life that was satisfying.

I hadn't meant to sound patronizing, but I suppose in hindsight I had, because I was tired and half-drunk. Or she could have perceived it that way because she was upset. I've been called a lot of things in my day—many of them I wouldn't want the nuns at St. Vitus parish to hear—but "irritating" was a new one.

What it came down to was that Cathleen still sounded interested in me, even after all that had happened. It surprised me. I've always found that there is a time between two people where things either turn romantic or they don't; if nothing happens then, chalk it up as a near miss because the moment has passed and will not come again.

I've learned through bitter experience that I don't do well in relationships. I have a busted marriage behind me, one that ended when my wife, Lila, left me for another man, and when that happens to you, something dies inside. It doesn't just go into hibernation—it dies dead away, and you're never really the same after that. You never really trust relationships again. I have had three serious romantic entanglements since then that have gone down in flames to prove it. I was tired of hurting, and not anxious to let myself become vulnerable again.

One of my problems, I suppose, is that I'm single-minded, and when I'm working on a challenging case or assignment, I find it hard to give a lot of time and thought to anything or anyone else until it's done.

This is why, after thinking about Cathleen's phone call for a few minutes and wondering why she had bothered, my mind drifted to Brian McFall or Jamie O'Dowd or whatever the hell his real name might be. That was somehow a more comfortable place for me to be, because it really had nothing to do with me personally. It was once removed, and therefore not threatening.

McFall's con games evidently had a pattern. He had targeted two Irish people in neighborhood bars, fed them the same phony story of lost baggage and a wealthy father in the Irish chinaware business and a cousin in Akron. He had used them both, milked them for what he could get, and then robbed them before pulling his disappearing act. In Judith Torrence's case, he had conned himself into her bed as well as her pocketbook; in Hugh Cochran's, he had robbed Cochran's aunt and slept with her daughter, Cathleen.

There were a few differences, however. Judith Torrence was an office worker who didn't have a lot of money, and Hugh Cochran was part of a well-to-do and well-placed political family. I found myself wondering whether they were indeed random victims or preordained targets, especially when I realized that they both worked for the City of Cleveland.

The beers I had consumed at O'Grady's and the Shebeen, and trying to figure out the reason for Cathleen Hartigan's phone call, were finally getting to me, and I rolled over and pulled the bedspread over my face and closed my eyes. I was pulling a Scarlett O'Hara; I'd think about Brian McFall tomorrow.

Hugh Cochran lived in a rehabbed house in Ohio City, which used to be a real city but isn't one anymore since it was swallowed up by the city of Cleveland in the nineteenth century. Now it's simply a neighborhood just across the river from downtown. Gentrification was the aim fifteen or twenty years ago, but as it's wound up, half the area is rebuilt and remodeled for affluent come-lately baby boomers, and the other half is home to working-class families who have lived in the same house for three and four generations and drink Rolling Rock on their front porches and stare gimlet-eyed at anyone passing by whom they don't know.

That Saturday morning Cochran was wearing a green plaid flannel shirt and tan chinos; he was a big, beefy man with a florid face, twinkling blue eyes, and the faint outline of a network of veins visible on his prominent nose. He came to the door with a Bloody Mary in his hand; if he was in the habit of drinking every morning before ten o'clock, it might go a long way toward explaining the nose.

But his handshake was hearty and his smile seemed genuine as he ushered me into his bright, open living room.

"I hear good things about you from Cathleen," he said when we were seated. "Otherwise I wouldn't be talking to you. This is pretty damned embarrassing for me, you know."

"People who are victimized by con men are almost always embarrassed, Hugh. It's almost worse than whatever money you've lost. But Brian McFall is a predator of sorts, and I'm sure you'd like to see him out of circulation just as much as Cathleen and your aunt would."

He nodded and sighed heavily. "And I suppose that means I have to come clean. It's going to be awkward."

"I'm sorry about that."

"This goes no farther than this room?"

"Discretion is part of the job description, Hugh."

He bobbed his head up and down once. "I'm relieved. Because the main thing is, I'm feeling a little silly. And guilty, of course, because I brought down a lot of grief on my family. I'm usually pretty cynical. I've been around the block a few times, Milan, and I'm just not the type to get scammed like this. And I sure as hell never dreamed it could happen to my Aunt Maureen. She's a toughie."

I prepared to take some notes. "Why don't you tell me about it from the beginning?"

He waved his glass at me. "I'll need another Bloody Mary for that, I'm afraid. Will you join me?"

I wished he'd do his drinking after we talked, but it was his house, after all. "No, thanks. I never got into the habit before noon."

The hint flew over his head like a badly aimed mortar shell. "Well, you're a wise man, then. Wiser than I."

He went into the kitchen, which was at the front of the house and separated from the living room only by a broad expanse of Formica counter. It looked like it was well used for cooking fancy meals; a row of copper cookware hung over the range. He busied himself with the fixings of his Bloody Mary, which gave me a chance to do a quick visual scan of the place. The furniture was all dark and masculine, making a nice contrast to the clean white walls and the many windows, which were now admitting bright fall sunshine in slanting bars that shimmered on the dark green carpeting. Through the back window, which stretched across the entire wall, I could see Hugh Cochran's own little sylvan glen in his backyard, silver maples and oaks and a birch or two, all ready to drop their burnished leaves. It was a pretty impressive woodland setting for being just about a mile from downtown Cleveland.

Photographs of what must have been relatives, some old and faded and printed in sepia on yellowing paper, including one of Cathleen and another of her mother, were nicely framed and adorning the walls and almost even flat surface in the living room. Hugh Cochran was, I believed, the stereotypical Irish bachelor— too strongly tied to his immediate family and his job and his community to allow a woman inside to disrupt his orderly life.

He came back with a new drink the color of dried blood. He'd even put a fresh stalk of celery in it.

His leather and chrome chair was low and overstaffed, slanted backward like the seat in a sports car, and he settled back into it with a slight groan; big men like Hugh Cochran and me shouldn't sit in low chairs like that. "Well, then. Where to begin?" He took a moment to decide on the chronology. "On that night in O'Grady's, I suppose I should start."

And then he told me virtually the same story his aunt had, only it took him twenty minutes longer and three times as many words do so; the Irish have come by their reputation as great storytellers honestly.

I shook my head. "Forgive me for saying so, Hugh, but how could you fall for a story like that? It seems like such an obvious scam."

"It was," he said. "But I'd been drinking a lot that night." He flushed slightly, or seemed to; the natural redness of his face made it hard to tell. "Look, you're Slovenian, Milan, right? You'd probably do the same thing for a fellow Slovenian if it had been you."

"I might have stood him to a motel room," I said. "Not the rest of it, though."

"Well," Hugh said, deciding whether or not to take offense, "maybe you're smarter than I am, then. But the thing was . . ."

He frowned in concentration, trying to find the right words to describe what the thing was. "Briney was such a—such a *boyo*, you know?"

I didn't know.

"He had all the right moves, all the charm, and the gift of gab. He kept me laughing that whole first evening, even when he was telling me his tale of woe. In other words, he was a fine drinking companion—and those are rare enough to come by in this life."

"Okay," I said. "So he matched you drink for drink and made you laugh, and so you let him stay here for a while."

"I did. Right there on the couch."

"For how long?"

"Three days. Three nights, rather . . . Once I'd rented him a car, I didn't see much of him in the daylight. Then he apologized, said he was inconveniencing me, and wondered if I knew anyone who had a bigger house where he wouldn't be so much trouble. A relative, he suggested."

"*He* suggested?"

Hugh ducked his head in an affirmative. "He said only a relative would do that, because it was too much to ask of a friend."

"So you picked your Aunt Maureen."

"Sure. She's got that great big empty house to rattle around in. She has rooms in there she never even uses."

"And she was okay with this? I mean, she's a judge. She can't afford to just take strangers in off the street."

"Well, but he wasn't a stranger anymore by then, don't you see?" Hugh Cochran's smile was disarming. "He was my friend, or at least that's what I thought. He'd been living in my house for three days, eating the bread off my table. And drinking up a storm, I might add. Besides . . ."

"Yes?"

"Well, he told us that he was from Mayo, and of course so are all the Cochrans and Hartigans here in Cleveland."

"That made a difference?"

"Indeed it did. Let me see if I can explain it to you. Let's say you were living abroad—in Tokyo, perhaps. And you were sitting in a bar and you ran into an American who was having the same sort of difficulty as Briney McFall was, lost luggage and passport and all."

"Didn't you stop to think that without a passport he couldn't have cleared customs? That they would have kept him in the airport?"

He looked stunned. "Jesus, Mary, and Joseph!" he said, and drank down half of his Bloody Mary. "No. No, actually I didn't. I guess I was a total fool, wasn't I?"

"Okay," I said, "it doesn't matter. Let's get back to me and the American tourist in the bar in Tokyo."

"Yes. Well, you might just say 'poor thing' and maybe stake him to a dinner and a hotel room and that would be it. But if it was a fellow Clevelander, and a fellow Slovenian at that, you might handle it differently—the same way my aunt and I did. Do y' see?"

I didn't see at all. I gravely doubted that I'd ever take a total stranger into my home under any conditions, Clevelander or not, but I didn't tell that to Hugh Cochran. Then again, the Irish are known for their generosity, and Slovenians are reputedly tight with a buck.

He went to build himself another drink while I pondered. Finally I got up and wandered over to the kitchen area to watch him across the counter. "Hugh, tell me again exactly what happened when McFall first walked into O'Grady's."

He paused in his pouring of the tomato juice. "I'm not sure what you mean, Milan."

"When he came in, did he wander around the bar some, or did he make a beeline for the stool next to you?"

"Well, it wasn't exactly a beeline, but. . . There were only three or four empty stools at the bar right then; it was a Monday night, and the football game was on. And I was at the far end, away from the TV." He grinned. "If the Browns aren't on for me to root for, or the Baltimore Ravens to root against, I don't pay football much of a mind. I imagined Briney wasn't that anxious to watch the game, either. What would an Irish lad right off the plane care about the Seahawks and the Patriots?"

"Okay. After he was here for a few days and suggested you call a relative and he moved over to Judge Hartigan's place—what happened then?"

"Aunt Maureen was as charmed by him as I was. She deals with the worst scum of this city every day in her courtroom. She sees a lot of ugliness in her job, and I think coming home to Briney McFall and his jokes and laughter was good therapy for her. And then of course there was Cathleen . . ."

His face flushed a bright red, and he stopped talking and lowered his eyes. "This is awfully uncomfortable for me, Milan. I'm not sure how much I should be telling you here."

"If it's about McFall and your cousin Cathleen, I know the whole story. And if you want me to find McFall as much as your aunt does, you'd better be telling me everything."

He put both hands around his glass and rolled it between them as if he were trying to start a fire. "I see what you mean."

"Did he make a lot of telephone calls while he was staying with you? Did he run up a big phone bill?"

His brow creased in puzzlement. "No, I don't think so. It was only three days. I didn't really check it out carefully, but that month's bill wasn't any different than normal. Why?"

"Would it surprise you to know that Brian McFall pulled the same stunt on somebody else, a young woman, a month earlier?"

His eyebrows shot up toward his hairline. "A month? But he said he'd just gotten off the plane that afternoon." His eyelids fluttered with embarrassment, and he looked away. "Oh. Of course he was lying, wasn't he?"

"It looks that way. He made a lot of calls while he was with her—long distance, most of them, or toll calls. He stayed for three weeks.

But he told the woman the same story he told you, only under a different name. He was calling himself James O'Dowd then."

Hugh ran one hand through his hair and looked up at the ceiling. "He even lied to me about his name? Dear Lord, but don't I feel like an idiot!"

"You shouldn't. He's damned good at what he does. I think it's how he makes his living."

"A poor living it is," Hugh said. "Making jerks out of people who go out of their way to show him kindness."

"He met this other woman the same way he did you, but it happened in another Irish bar a bit farther west. It was in a little place called the Shebeen. Do you know of it?"

He nodded gravely. "I do. Everybody knows the Shebeen—every Irishman on the west side, anyway. O'Grady's is an Irish pub because John O'Grady owns it, but John was born right here in Cleveland, and it isn't very authentic. Too many fake shamrocks and pictures of leprechauns and things—oh, you've been there, so you know. But the Shebeen, that's the real deal."

"How do you mean?"

"Folks who do their drinking in there are very political, for the most part. Irish politics, not Cleveland. And Irish politics usually means pissed off. They're always going on about the Troubles, about Dublin and Belfast, the Catholics versus the Protestants, and how much they hate the goddamned English. It's too dark, too serious, which is why I rarely go there. I want to party and laugh and have fun on the weekend, not get all depressed about the Potato Famine."

In the Shebeen the night before I had certainly ascertained a lack of gaiety, especially when compared to O'Grady's, but I'd been too busy with trying to talk to Judith Torrence and fending off Jinny Johnson's flirtations to take much note of it. "Why do you think McFall went into a place like that in the first place? Did he ever talk about Irish politics with you?"

"Never a word," Hugh said. "Oh, he went on and on about how beautiful Mayo is and how I should visit it someday, and he talked a lot about his father and Irish crystal and china. Of course

I didn't know then that it was all bullshit. And he made it sound pretty real—but he shied away from any really serious subjects. As I told you, he was a fun kind of guy—and a drinker of prodigious proportions. Even I couldn't keep up with him."

I thought silently that anyone who Hugh Cochran couldn't match drink for drink must have a hollow leg.

"When did you rent the car for him?"

"Let's see," he said, leaning his elbows on the kitchen counter that separated us. "I met him on a Monday night, so it must have been on Wednesday. I called Avis."

"They let him have a car without seeing a driver's license?"

"It was my credit card, so I had to give them my license. I mean, his was supposed to be lost with his luggage, remember?"

"It didn't strike you odd that someone would fly clear across the Atlantic and put his wallet in his suitcase?"

He looked sheepish. "I guess I didn't think of that at the time. I'd had a couple of beers already."

"Right. And McFall took the car with him?"

Hugh nodded.

"Have you reported it stolen?"

"My family is trying to keep this quiet, remember?"

"You happen to have a copy of the rental car agreement?"

"Sure," he said, and went upstairs to get it, and I heard him opening drawers up there. Something had been wriggling around between my ears, an idea I would have preferred not to think about, but I had to ask him.

When he came back downstairs, I checked the rental car contract. The car was a current model Ford Taurus, a white one, and the date corresponded with what he had told me. "Can I hang on to this?" I said.

"It's my only copy."

"I'll make a photocopy of it and return it to you." I folded the document and put it in the inside pocket of my jacket. "Hugh," I said, "didn't you ever get the idea, even afterward when he'd disappeared from your aunt's house with the money and the other things, that he didn't just happen to sit next to you at O'Grady's that night by accident? That he was targeting you specifically?"

The color fled from his face, and he looked positively bewildered. "My God, no. Why would he do that, for heaven's sake?"

"You're a city official. And you come from a pretty heavy-duty political family. It might not have been simply an accident."

He gave me an aggressive shake of his head. "Oh, I'd have to quarrel with that scenario, Milan. I mean, I might be a city official, but I'm sure as hell not raking in the big bucks." His sweeping hand motion encompassed the whole house. "It's a nice little house, but it's not a mansion or anything. And my Aunt Maureen isn't that rich, either. No, I think it was just a random thing. I just happened to be in the wrong place at the wrong time, that's all."

"I hope you're right," I said.

"Why?"

"Because if you weren't just a random victim, then I have to figure out what Brian McFall was really after."

CHAPTER FOUR

Judith Torrence lived on the ground floor of a six-flat apartment building on Clifton Boulevard just a few blocks from the Lakewood-Cleveland city line on the west side. A large number of mostly white, mostly young singles who work downtown have gravitated to that particular area, where the rents are still reasonable, whereas where my apartment is, in the first suburb east of the city, the residents tend to be older and more settled.

When she admitted me, her living room was in somewhat cheerful disarray: newspapers were strewn about, breakfast dishes were still on the coffee table, and there were several piles of clothes on chairs, obviously stacked and sorted for a trip to the Laundromat.

Judith was in disarray, too—barefoot and wearing worn jeans. Her breasts looked unfettered beneath a Cleveland Browns sweatshirt, and her face was devoid of any makeup except for a trace of hastily applied lipstick. Her dark hair was in a ponytail held by a red rubber band.

"Sorry, the place is a mess," she said without embarrassment. "It's Saturday, you know? I haven't had time to clean all week."

"I won't look, I promise."

She gave me a wry, self-effacing grin. "I'm a mess, too."

"Then I won't look at you, either."

"I'm not sure if I like *that*." She went to a small desk in one corner of the living room and dug through a stack of papers. "You said last night that you wanted the phone records for the time Jamie was living here. Here they are." She handed me four pages of an Ameritech phone statement. "I circled all the long-distance calls that I'm sure I didn't make."

It took me a millisecond to remember who she meant by "Jamie." I'd begun thinking of him as Brian McFall.

"Thanks." I took the four sheets of paper she had stapled together, glancing at the total before putting it in my pocket: $423.18, which seemed excessive for a monthly residential telephone bill. "I've got a few more questions, Judith. You have time to talk for a couple of minutes?"

"I always have time for talking with a good-looking man," she said, but there was no flirtation behind her smile. "But don't take that the wrong way, okay? Jinny saw you first."

I felt my ears getting warm.

"She really took a fancy to you."

I gave her my most noncommittal smile.

"You could do worse, ya know. She's a terrific gal."

"She seemed very nice."

"And pretty, too, don't you think? Or are Scandinavian blondes not your type?"

"Yes, she's very pretty," I said.

She waited, but I wasn't about to say anything else on the subject.

"You're strictly business, aren't you, Milan?"

"I have to be," I said. "This is how I make my living."

She sighed. "Jinny's going to be very disappointed. Okay then, let's talk business."

I cleared a place for myself on her sofa and sat down. She pulled a straight chair out from the desk and straddled it backward, her arms resting on the back. "Shoot," she said.

"Did you rent Jamie a car while he was staying with you?"

She shook her head. "He asked me to, but I didn't really have the money to do that. So I left him my car to drive and usually carpooled with Jinny or one of my other friends to my job and back. There were a couple of days that didn't work out, so I just took the Rapid to work." Her smile was crooked, sour. "What I did for love . . ."

"Is it a luxury car?"

"Oh God, no," she said. "It's a six-year-old Geo."

"Tell me some of the things you and Jamie talked about while he was here," I said, stumbling on the "Jamie."

"That covers a lot of ground," she said, and I preferred to think of her smile as something other than a leer. "Can you zero in a little bit?"

"I'll try. Did he ever talk about politics?"

"Talking politics with a woman you're shacked up with?" She laughed. "Mr. Jacovich, you need to get out more."

"I can't argue with that," I said, feeling my ears grow even hotter. "But I'm asking for a reason."

She had to give it some consideration. "We didn't talk much about American politics," she said. "I'm not that interested—and him being just off the plane, he wouldn't have known anything about it either. He talked about Ireland, of course. The IRA and Sinn Fein and all that."

"Sinn Fein—that's the political wing of the Irish Republican Army."

She nodded her agreement. "He seemed really knowledgeable about it. But I think I knew more than he did." She tugged at her ponytail and then flipped it back over her shoulder and shook her head. "That's what comes from hanging out at the Shebeen, I guess."

"The people who are regulars in there are very into that sort of thing, I understand."

She nodded. "Very militant, most of them."

"Are you militant, too?"

"Me? God, no."

"Then why do you go into the Shebeen so often? Certainly there are other Irish bars that are more fun."

"Well, it's a family habit, for one thing. My father was born in Ireland, and he was about as militant as you can get, God rest his soul. Every time he saw a story on the television about the British royal family, even Princess Diana or Fergie or someone, he'd turn the air blue with cursing out the goddamn English. The Shebeen was his hangout for as long as I can remember, and he started taking me with him on Saturday afternoons when I was about seven years old, so you might say I actually cut my teeth on Irish political rhetoric. I suppose I still go in there because that's where I've always gone." She gave me that dirty-flirty smile again. "Besides, men who are passionate about anything, like freeing Ireland, tend to be passionate in other ways, too. If you catch my drift."

I caught her drift.

"You probably think that's awful."

"Not at all, Judith."

"Well, that's good. Because look, I'm twenty-six years old," she went on. "I fully expect to be married by the time I'm thirty. Probably to a nice Irish Catholic boy who is still hung up on his mother and the buddies he's known since he was five, and who'll keep me pregnant all the time so he can live life just like he's always lived it. So until then I want to squeeze every drop of juice out of being young." She made a wry face. "I've learned to be pretty philosophical about it; you take the good with the bad in this life.

"You take chances, and sometimes they pay off and sometimes you get burned. So I stuck my neck out with Jamie O'Dowd, and it turned into shit. Too bad for me, I guess, but I'll be luckier the next time."

"What about local politics? Was Jamie at all interested in that?"

"Cleveland politics?"

"You work for the city; I thought perhaps he might have asked you about your job."

"I work pushing papers," she said, "and he wasn't much interested in that." She thought for a bit. "He did want to know whether the Irish were a big force in local government, yes. He said he'd always heard that the Irish were pretty powerful in Cleveland."

"Did he ask about anyone specific?"

She shook her head. "No, not at all. I don't think he would have known who to ask about."

"What did you tell him?"

Her eyes searched the ceiling, trying to remember. "Give me a minute," she said, "this wasn't exactly one of our major conversations." Her brow knitted in concentration. "I'm sure that I told him there were a couple of city council members who were Irish, and a bunch of judges."

"Nothing more specific than that? You didn't name any names?"

"I don't know if I did or not," she said. "Hell, pick an Irish name out of a hat, and there's a judge somewhere in this town who carries it. Sweeney, Kilbane, Corrigan, Hartigan . . ."

"Did you mention Judge Hartigan to him specifically?"

She turned her hands palms up. "I honestly don't remember, Mr. Jacovich. To be frank with you, we spent a hell of a lot more time in bed than we did talking about politics and judges. Does that embarrass you?"

"No," I said. "But I think you want it to. I think you keep trying to shock me about your love life. You can forget about it, Judith. It doesn't matter to me one way or the other."

"I'm not trying to shock you at all," she said, getting a little steely. "I just tell it straight."

"Well, I appreciate that."

"If you want to know the real truth, there's not much that embarrasses me," she said, "except about Jamie. Not that I went to bed with him, but that I was such a jerk to swallow his story."

"We believe what we want to believe sometimes, Judith. What we need to believe."

"Yeah, well," she said, and didn't elaborate.

"Tell me—who's the big honcho over at the Shebeen?"

"Paddy's the bartender, and I think he's part owner, too."

"I don't mean the bartender," I said. "Who's the boss man in there? The community leader? Kind of the elder, if you will. There's been one in every ethnic bar I've ever heard of."

"Oh," she said. She put her hand up to her mouth uneasily. "You must mean Con McCardle."

She pronounced the name almost reverentially, the way a devout Catholic might speak in hushed tones of the Blessed Mother—and with good reason. Everyone who ever read a newspaper in Cleveland knew of Cornelius McCardle. A builder of medium-cost tract homes by trade, he was a throwback to the era of local Democratic political machines that finally faded away with the end of the Prendergast era in Kansas City and the demise of Chicago's first Mayor Daley. He probably didn't have the power he once had, because he had grown old and arthritic and because the Irish were now forced to share their local political plums with blacks and Italians and Slavs. Still there was no gainsaying that no matter who you were or where your parents came from, if you wanted to get elected to anything in Cleveland, it was de rigueur to stop by and pay a visit to Con McCardle.

"Can I usually find Mr. McCardle at the Shebeen?" I said.

Judith Torrence turned a few shades paler, and her head gave a little involuntary jerk when she spoke. "Every night of his life except Christmas. But please don't get him involved in this, Mr. Jacovich. He and my father were really good friends. I don't want him to find out how stupid I was." She shook her head hard as if to stop her ears from ringing. "Or slutty."

"Don't worry," I assured her. "I'll keep your name out of it. Mr. McCardle won't know anything about your involvement."

Her shoulders slumped in what can only be described as abject despair, and the look she gave me was heartbreakingly pleading. "Con McCardle," Judith Torrence said miserably, "knows everything about everything."

I stopped off at a Convenient Mart and photocopied the phone bills of Judith Torrence and Hugh Cochran; one of the good things about the techno revolution is that almost every business has a copier. For small jobs, the corner groceries or drugstores are more convenient than the big commercial printing places, where the employees all have attitudes and you have to wait overnight for the simplest copying requests. They're cheaper, too.

I got home about five o'clock and warmed up some linguini from two nights before. Single people living alone tend to eat lots of leftovers; it's a lot of work to cook up a meal for one. But I was getting pretty sick of linguini.

While I ate, I studied the two phone bills. Local calls aren't listed by number, and McFall/O'Dowd had only stayed at Hugh Cochran's for three days, and he evidently hadn't used the phone too much while he was there. I made a note to get Judge Hartigan's phone records from her the next day, even though she hadn't mentioned him running up high charges. The long-distance and toll-call statement for the three weeks he'd been with Judith Torrence showed several calls to a number in Warren, Ohio, near Youngstown, each of them less than five minutes long. There were also a few to New York City, quick ones, and at least ten to the same number in Elyria, a city just west of Cuyahoga County.

All of those were of at least ten minutes' duration. None of the calls matched any numbers on Cochran's bill.

I sighed. Tomorrow was Sunday, but I knew I'd have to go into the office to play around on my computer. So much for my plans to kick back in front of the television set in my den and watch the Browns battle the Bengals.

I washed up the dinner dishes, glad that I'd finished the last of the linguini, and read for a while before heading back out to the west side for the third time in two days. That's a big deal for most Clevelanders; east-siders rarely cross the river to the west side, and vice versa. I've never learned why there is such animosity between the two sides of town.

Maybe it was the sharply drawn ethnic lines. For some reason the east side is largely Hungarian, Slovenian, Croatian, Jewish, and African American. The west side is more Irish, Lithuanian, Serbian, Puerto Rican, and German. And the west side population tends to skew a bit younger. But the rivalry between the two sides of the Cuyahoga goes beyond ethnic and generational lines.

I got to the Shebeen at about nine-thirty. It was even more crowded than it had been the night before, but I had little difficulty in spotting my quarry. I hadn't noticed him the previous evening, but that was because I hadn't been looking for him. I'd seen his picture in the papers enough to recognize him almost at once.

I approached his table. "Mr. McCardle," I said, "my name is Milan Jacovich. I'm a private investigator." I handed him a business card. "I wonder if I might have the honor of buying you a drink?"

Cornelius McCardle was a skinny, defiant-looking little bantam rooster of a man, well into his seventies, with a face right out of a John Ford movie. He had a slightly pugged nose and brilliant blue eyes that drilled right through me beneath flyaway eyebrows that looked like little white birds perched on either side of his red face. He wore a tweed jacket, a beige dress shirt, and a knit tie of the most violent shade of green, even though St. Patrick's Day was almost five months away. His fingers, now wrapped around a pint of Guinness Stout, were gnarled and arthritic, and a few of them looked as though they might have once been broken. He was sitting at the farthest booth from the door in the gloom of the Shebeen, surrounded by four other men close to his own age.

He scanned my card carefully and then turned his fierce gaze back at me. "A drink, is it? Well now, that's very polite of you, Mister, ah . . . Very friendly. And seeing as how my companions here will probably have to get up and move to another table because I'm sure you're wanting to speak with me privately, would our friendship perhaps extend to treating each of them as well?"

He smiled triumphantly at me, and I smiled right back, acknowledging that he'd won the first round, even though up until that moment I hadn't known anyone would be keeping score. He signaled the bartender, who I assumed was Paddy, and the other four men mumbled their thanks and got up to shuffle off to another table to consume my largesse.

McCardle waited until they were out of earshot before turning back to me. His black eyes seemed to burn into my soul. "You were here last night, if I'm not mistaken. With young Judith Torrence and another woman."

"I was."

"I thought I recognized you, but I didn't know who you were then." He waved my business card. "You might be surprised to know that I've heard of you," he said. "You get your name in the papers a lot."

"So do you, Mr. McCardle."

That seemed to please him. "For some unknown reason, the press in this town finds me fascinatingly newsworthy." Paddy presented him with a fresh pint, and brought one for me, too, even though I hadn't requested it, and made a point of putting the bill down next to my elbow. McCardle gently put his new drink aside until he could finish the one he was working on. "But surely this isn't a newspaper interview, is it?"

"No, sir," I said. "I was hoping you could give me some information about a case I'm working on."

"Ah-huh," he said. "And you think you can buy this information for the price of a beer?"

"Five beers," I reminded him.

"Oh, yes, that's right. Still, it's a mean price, isn't it?"

"Does everything cost money, Mr. McCardle?"

"No. Everything doesn't cost *money*." The way he put his shoulder into the last word left no doubt that there were other ways to pay for information in his world that did not involve writing a check. "But let's never mind that for now," he said amiably. "Let's just see what you need, and we can proceed from there."

"Fair enough," I agreed, although I had misgivings. "I'm wondering if you might happen to know—or know of—a young fellow named James O'Dowd." I decided to begin with the name McFall had used the night he'd visited the Shebeen and swept Judith Torrence off her feet.

Con McCardle gave it some thought before he answered. "I know a James O'Dowd from the old Back-of-the-Yards neighborhood in Chicago, but I'd hardly call him a young fellow, since he's somewhat older than me. And the Lord saw fit to bless him with only daughters. Five of 'em, I believe." He went to work on his new pint. "Why would you come to me about this O'Dowd fellow?"

"Because you know just about every Irishman in Cleveland," I said.

He beamed, taking it as a compliment. "You know, I think I do at that." He leaned back in his chair and looked heavenward. "There was a time in this town when half the local politicians were sons of Erin, and each morning we'd all meet for breakfast over at Tony's restaurant on West One Hundred and Seventeenth Street. The mayor at that time, young Dennis Kucinich, he was no Irishman, but he'd make it his business to drop in nearly every morning as well. We'd have our corned beef and eggs and talk about the events of the day, the problems and the victories in each of the wards, problems that were before council—things like that, things you'd expect public servants to be discussing. And then we'd all grab for the morning newspapers—the *Plain Dealer* and the late lamented *Cleveland Press*. And do you know what section we'd all turn to the first thing every morning? Even before we checked the local news and the sports and the goings-on in Washington?"

I shook my head.

"The obituaries, the death notices. And do you know why?"

"I have no idea."

He took a deep breath in the way some older people do when they're about to launch into an oft-told and beloved story. "Because," he said, "back in those days when the city was smaller and more manageable—and frankly, when it was a lot whiter—we all knew our constituents on a personal, first name basis. They were our neighbors and our friends. And if we were to read that one of them had died, we would always be sure to make a condolence call on the grieving family that very afternoon, and take along some cakes or a pie or a bag of fruit, and sometimes even some whiskey for the wake. It was how we all scheduled our days." He took a deep swallow and wiped his lips with the sleeve of his Irish tweed jacket. "That's why we called the obituaries the Irish sports pages."

We shared a chuckle.

"It's not just the politicians, though. It's an Irish thing. Maybe we Irish are a little too preoccupied with death; maybe it's something in our genes. You know the banshee legend, do you?"

"I guess I don't," I said. "I know the expression about screaming like a banshee, but I have no idea why banshees scream."

McCardle leaned toward me. "Well, a banshee, you see, is a spirit, usually in the form of a wailing woman, who appears to a family when there's about to be a death. And she moans up quite a ruckus, too." He leaned forward, putting a hand up to his mouth as if to prevent someone across the room from reading his lips. "I've never heard one, but my mother always swore she did on the night her grandfather died."

"That's spooky," I said.

"It is indeed. But there are other reasons to read the obituaries each morning. My father, for instance. When my family came over here from Mayo," he continued, "my father was a bartender, in a little tavern not far from here that's gone, now. After a few years he bought the place. And many a morning when he'd read the Irish sports pages, he'd suddenly burst out cursing. The son of a bitch! Ah, the dirty bastard!' My mother and I knew without asking that one of his customers had died leaving an unpaid tab."

He chuckled, his eyes growing dreamy, giving himself up to memory for a moment, in that particular way of an old man who had lived a long time and had a lot of memories. Then he sighed.

"It's not so easy now as it used to be," he went on. "The city has changed, the old families have moved out to the suburbs, and new people we don't know have moved in. That special little personal touch just isn't possible anymore. But I'll tell you those were fine days, Mister . . ." He shook his head and shrugged me an apology for once more not remembering my name.

"What about Brian McFall?"

He raised his bushy brows in a show of innocence. "Who's that, now?"

"Do you know him?"

"I know a Patrick McFall," he said. "A printer, with a shop on Madison at around West Seventy-first Street or thereabouts. He lost his wife about seven or eight years ago to the cancer, I believe. He has a son, Michael, who's a doctor at the Cleveland Clinic, and a fine lovely girl—her name escapes me at the moment—who's a journalist of some sort in New York City. Public relations." He pronounced the last two words as if they were part of another language. "But no Brian McFall, even though, sad to say, my memory isn't what it used to be." He gave me a crafty, sidelong look. "These two fellers, this McFall and this O'Dowd, now—have they been doing something they shouldn't?"

"I don't know," I said. "I was hoping you could tell me."

"Hope is a thing with feathers," he said, "and I hate to dash yours, but the names are not familiar to me."

I took out the picture and pushed it across the table to him. "Then do you recognize this man?"

He fumbled around in his inside jacket pocket and extracted a pair of spectacles in a battered leather sleeve. It turned out they were half-glasses, gold-rimmed, and he perched them on the end of his nose like Barry Fitzgerald used to. Then he picked up the photograph. When he looked at it, his breath quickened and his face paled. He smacked his lips involuntarily.

"You do know him," I said.

"No." He wagged his head from side to side. "I don't."

"Your reaction says differently, Mr. McCardle."

He took his time removing his glasses and slipping them back into their case, which he then replaced in his pocket before answering me. "Not at all. My 'reaction,' as you call it, was because I was startled to see Judge Maureen Hartigan's daughter in the picture, that's all. Cathleen, I think her name is. Isn't it?"

"It is." And he damn well knew it.

"I remember well the day she was born. I was at her christening.

A fine affair, over at St. Colman's on West Sixty-fifth. A beautiful child she was, and she's grown into a beautiful woman, don't you agree?"

I did.

"So tell me, what does young Cathleen Hartigan have to do with this James McFall of yours, or this James O'Dowd?"

"*Brian* McFall."

He waited, crossing his arms across his chest. Then he said, "You're evading my question, Mister, ah . . ."

"Jacovich," I said, finally deciding to help him out. "That's strange, because I thought it was you who were evading mine. This photo was taken at a party. I guess he and Cathleen Hartigan are friends."

"Very close friends, from the look of them."

"And you've never seen him before?"

"I've said not."

"He was in this very bar about seven or eight weeks ago."

"I don't know everyone who comes in this bar," he said. "Most, I grant you, but not all. It's a public place."

"You noticed me when I came in last night."

"You're a fine big specimen of a man. It'd be hard to miss you."

"But you missed this fellow," I said, tapping the photograph.

"Maybe I wasn't here that night."

"You come in here every night of your life except Christmas, is what I've been told."

His neck stiffened, and he uncrossed his arms and put his fists on the table, elbows akimbo. He leaned back and took a deep breath. "*Mis*-ter Jacovich!" he said, projecting his voice into a roar, and not only suddenly remembering my name but pronouncing it properly. "Are you calling me a liar?"

The Shebeen went silent as a tomb save for the music on the jukebox, a dirge about guns and drums and drums and guns from which the tune of "When Johnny" Comes Marching Home" was lifted.

"Let's just say that I question your memory, Mr. McCardle."

His complexion had gone from waxy pale to bright red, and

his eyes glittered with rage. He leaned so far forward in his chair to get in my face that I'm sure his butt left the seat. "And in turn I question your manners, young fellow. And your common sense as well."

He picked up his pint of Guinness—the one I'd bought him, which was still full. Holding it at shoulder level, he ceremoniously poured the contents onto the floor. "I'm not such a hypocrite as to be drinking on the nickel of a man who insults me," he said, slamming the empty glass on the tabletop. "It would stick in my throat like the keenest of poisons. And now I'll thank you to leave my presence before I really get angry."

I rescued the snapshot of Cathleen and Brian McFall and slipped it into my pocket. "I'm sorry you feel insulted, Mr. Mc-Cardle. It wasn't my intention. I thank you for your time, nevertheless."

I took out two twenty-dollar bills and put them on the table to pay my tab, but he seized them and, in a show of the utmost contempt, ripped them into tiny pieces and then let them flutter down onto the floor into the spilled beer.

"Don't come back here, Mr. Jacovich," Con McCardle said. "I'll die a happy man if I never see your face again."

CHAPTER FIVE

My office is in the industrial section of the Flats, on the west side of a hairpin curve of the riverbank called Collision Bend, so named because in the old days when traffic on the Cuyahoga River was a lot heavier and two six-hundred-foot ore boats going in opposite directions would attempt to take the curve at the same time, aquatic fender benders were the norm. Even though there hasn't been such a waterborne crash on the bend for more years than I can remember, the name, like so many other colorful names in Cleveland, has stuck.

My building—in my more wistfully narcissistic moments I like to think of it as the Jacovich Building, but it doesn't really have a name—is just across the water from Tower City and boasts a fine view of the light towers of the home of the Cleveland Indians, Jacobs Field. The building's not in the high rent district, but you can see it from here, which is almost as good.

The Flats really has two faces. One, on the west side of the river, has remained pretty much as it was since the early twentieth century. Crisscrossed by railroad tracks, it's largely industrial, although the old electric powerhouse and the area surrounding it just before the Cuyahoga empties into Lake Erie has been transformed into an entertainment complex; waterside warehouses and small manufacturing outfits eventually give way to the giant steel companies and oil smelters and ore processors that make up the belly of the Flats. A little bit upriver from there is where I bought an old brick warehouse several years ago with an inheritance from my Aunt Branka, who had managed to stash away a tidy sum over the course of her long widowhood in the east-side suburb of Euclid. I don't know whether she squirreled away her social security checks, invested my uncle's insurance money brilliantly, or was running a horsebook and skimming off a ten percent vigorish. In any event, she'd left her children about a hundred and seventy-five thousand bucks each, and given me eighty thousand; instead of blowing it all on a fancy car, whiskey, and women, I opted to become a landlord on the financial advice of most of my friends.

I chose this particular building because of the view, and because it was within walking distance of Jim's Steak House, featuring an intimate, male-bonding kind of bar where businessmen, *Plain Dealer* reporters, and dockworkers rubbed elbows at lunchtime shooting the breeze with a cheery daytime bartender named Ray and eating good, honest steak sandwiches and home fried potatoes that could clog your arteries from across the room. Alas, two years after I moved in, Jim's closed its doors forever, and Ray went somewhere else. Just my luck.

I rent out the first floor of the old brick building on Collision Bend to a wrought-iron company that has been there for twenty-five years; they don't have any windows on the river though, so I can't charge them for the view. Half of the top floor, the landward side, is leased to a medical-supply house. The other half, the half with the floor-to-ceiling windows and the million-dollar vista, I keep for myself—for Milan Security. It actually makes me want to get to work in the morning. Despite the cacophony of the gulls swooping low over the river for breakfast, almost close enough for me to reach out the window and touch them, it's great in the summer, when the breeze coming through my windows from nearby Lake Erie makes air-conditioning largely unnecessary. Still, I think I like it best in the wintertime when the river is ice-covered, gray, and dangerous looking. Cleveland, for me, is a wintertime town. Perhaps I love the cold weather best because winter clothing is much more forgiving of middle-aged bodies than is skimpy, hot-weather wear.

The east bank of the Flats is something else again. Old River Road, once dusty and faceless and the last place anyone would want to spend their leisure time, for the last fifteen or so years has been home to a score of saloons and dance clubs that draw the under-twenty-five crowd, who flirt and fight and imbibe heavily, and who occasionally wind up going out onto the deck to pee or puke and pitch drunkenly off the bar-side docks to perish in the deep and dirty waters of the Cuyahoga. A few years ago they beefed up security down there after a particularly hazardous summer, and put in safety ladders and life preservers, but nothing's really going to stop a dumb kid from hurting himself after he's consumed more than a gallon of beer.

The Watermark is the stately exception to the east-bank rule. An excellent seafood restaurant whose outside deck is lapped by the gently flowing waters of the river, it's been around for seventeen years—quite an accomplishment in a city whose trends change with the tides and whose restaurants have a frightening attrition rate. It has managed to maintain its dignity when all around it has gone tacky.

It was here that I met with my pal Ed Stahl for an early Sunday brunch.

Ed is a columnist for the *Plain Dealer*, a man so modest that he keeps his Pulitzer Prize in the bottom drawer of his desk along with a cigar box full of buttons, keys that don't unlock anything, a few wrapped-up mints he once scored on his way out of a restaurant, and other mementos he doesn't consider significant. He is one of the world's last living authentic curmudgeons.

It was a bit early in the day—eleven-thirty in the morning, to be exact—for Ed's drink of choice, Jim Beam on the rocks, which he enjoys regularly despite his doctor's warning that one day it will set his stomach ulcer on fire. So we drank some coffee, which wasn't much better for him than bourbon, went through the brunch buffet line surrounded by hyperactive, sticky-fingered children and the parents who shush them—or not—and, food-laden, headed back to our table to drink some more coffee and watch the stately procession of huge ore boats and tankers heading out to Lake Erie under the Conrail Bridge.

"So you got Con McCardle angry, did you?" Ed said after I'd told him, without revealing the reason, about my previous evening's activities at the Shebeen. "I thought you were smarter than that, Milan. Con's a real force in this community, and a bad enemy to have."

Ed should know. For thirty years he has churned out five acerbic columns per week. What he doesn't know about the goings-on in our city isn't worth knowing. During his career he has made plenty of enemies, powerful and otherwise, and one of them might have done something about it if they weren't so terrified of him. We've been friends for longer than I can remember, dating back to my rookie days with the police department.

"I only know a little about McCardle, Ed—mostly what I read in the papers. What's his deal?"

Ed munched on a custom-made omelet. "His deal, as you put it, is that he came over here from Mayo when he was no more than a kid, and he's been the west-side political boss ever since Christ was a corporal. He knows every Irishman in town, if not in a three-state area. Nobody's sure exactly how he makes his money—he sure as hell doesn't earn a lot from that low-rent little building company he runs—but the rumor is that he does favors for people and they give him little gifts."

"Gifts?"

"Yes, they support his hobby. He's an art collector. Collects engravings of dead presidents."

"Very nice."

"I mean that literally. He only accepts cash or services for his favors. No checks, I hear, and no paperwork. So Uncle Sam doesn't hear about much of it."

I grinned. "Well, it's none of Uncle Sam's business, is it? What kind of favors are we talking about here, Ed?"

"The kind that most people won't do for you," he said. "Even your best friends. I really can't be more specific because I don't know. But I've heard things over the years. You know."

I knew.

"There are also some fairly persistent rumblings that McCardle is connected with Sinn Fein."

"The Irish Republican Army?"

Ed gulped coffee with one hand and shot back ice water with the other to cool down the always smoldering burn in his belly. "Sinn Fein is their political wing, yes. The Shebeen is crawling with them. That's why nobody who isn't Irish ever ventures in there. It's not exactly a fun place to drink if you're not one of the boyos."

I grimaced. "You're right. That place is about as much fun as passing a kidney stone."

"There are more reasons to drink than having a good time, Milan—although I'm hard pressed to think of any. But everyone at that bar is so goddamned militant—and they have only one subject—that most people in the know do their drinking someplace more felicitous."

"I didn't know there was any IRA in Cleveland."

"There's a little bit of everything in Cleveland. The IRA here isn't quite so vocal as some of your Eastern European groups, because they're smaller in number. But they're here, all right."

"And Con McCardle is their leader?"

Ed spread his hand flat out in front of him and tipped it from side to side. "'Leader' is a strong word, especially for someone as old as Con. He's certainly in on the top level of things here in town, probably in whatever it is they call their inner council. Whether or not he's the exalted grand pooh-bah is another story."

"Who is, then?"

"You've got me there," he said, the first question I'd asked him in years that he hadn't been able to answer. "It's kind of a secret organization, you know. They don't advertise."

"What's your best guess?"

He frowned at me over his food. "What is this, anyway? What have you gotten yourself into, Milan?"

I shook my head. "These are just background questions, Ed."

"You'd better keep them that way," he said. "Far in the background. These people are very intense, and they don't fuck around."

We stopped and watched a great black leviathan of a freighter glide by the window, its keel low in the water, weighted down with iron ore. It seemed almost close enough to reach out and touch, and even through the glass I could feel the vibrations of its huge engines clear down into my stomach.

"How well do you know Judge Maureen Hartigan?" I asked.

His Clark Kent horn-rimmed glasses had slipped down over his nose, and he looked balefully over them at me. "Pretty well, given the caveat that she's a politician and I'm a journalist. What does Maureen Hartigan have to do with the IRA or Con McCardle?"

"Nothing, as far as I know."

He scowled. "Don't play me for a sap, Milan. You ask about two

different local Irishmen in one conversation, it gets me to wondering. Is there a connection there that I ought to know about?"

I toyed with my food uneasily, fearing I'd been indiscreet. Ed
and I are close friends, but he is first and foremost a reporter. "I'm
doing some work for the judge, that's all."

"And how is McCardle involved?"

"He's not."

"Then why are you asking me about him?"

"I told you, background. They certainly know each other, but I
don't see any direct involvement."

"Not yet," he said.

I nodded. "Not yet, and probably not ever. But you know that
everyone in this town is only three degrees away from anyone
else. So there is no direct connection, but I thought he might help
me find someone I'm looking for, and I went into the Shebeen
last night to ask him."

"And he made you buy him a drink."

I grinned. "You must've asked him a question or two yourself."

"Yes, indeed," Ed said. "And I'll bet he made you buy all his
friends a drink, too."

I laughed.

"Yeah, the old farts who hang on Con's coattails at the Shebeen love it when someone wants to talk to him. And did he help
you?"

I laughed. "Not only did he not help me, he just about threw
my Slovenian ass out in the cold."

"You're lucky at that. A few years ago he would have done it
literally. And he could have—don't let the small stature fool you.
Con was a pretty tough guy. Is he at odds with the good judge
these days?"

"Not to my knowledge. As I said, it was a tenuous connection
that didn't seem to pan out."

"Well, Maureen is good people. And a good judge. A little
on the conservative side for a Democrat, but the party guys like
her."

"Why?"

"Because she knows how to get herself elected. And she's
damned good at party fund-raising."

"Where does she raise those funds, Ed? From Con McCardle?"

"Partly, I'd say. McCardle supports most Irish Democrats in the county, mostly just because they're Irish."

"Gelt by association," I said.

"Maybe so, but the last time I looked, that was perfectly legal. So don't go making a big thing out of it."

"I'm not. To get elected president costs about two hundred million bucks these days. What's the going rate on Cuyahoga County judges?"

"That pretty much depends on the judge—and the opposition," he said. "But unless I have it wrong, Hartigan was reelected last November and isn't running for anything for the next three years. So you're barking up the wrong tree, whatever it is you're trying to find out, because I'd bet my old Aunt Edna's family farm that Mo Hartigan is clean." He put down his fork and leaned forward, his journalistic afterburners kicking in. "Unless you've heard anything different."

"The judge is my client, Ed. I'm looking to help her, not hurt her."

"Well," he said, resuming his breakfast with what I thought was a suspect amount of relief, "that's good, then."

I said good-bye to Ed Stahl in the parking lot next to the Watermark and drove across the Carter Avenue Bridge to my office. There was no clanking and banging coming from the wrought-iron company the way there was on weekdays. As hard as the owner, Tony Radek, drove his employees, several of whom were his brothers, they always took Sunday off. I should have done the same.

There's something particularly lousy about having to come in to the office on Sunday, so I try to avoid it whenever I can. It only serves as an uncomfortable reminder that outside of my work I don't have much of a life.

But the office is where my computer lives, so I cracked open a Stroh's beer from the den-sized refrigerator disguised to look like a Wells Fargo safe that I keep in the corner, settled down behind my desk, and went into the software program that contains the reverse directory.

Handy-dandy little gadget, that reverse directory. If you know a telephone number, the directory tells you under what name and address it's listed. I used to have to buy them, big heavy books from the telephone company, and they were only for the local calling area. Now that software can find out who belongs to any listed phone number in the United States within seconds.

Hey, they don't call it the information age for nothing.

I spread Judith Torrence's phone bill out in front of me, all four pages of it. The charge for local calls was ninety-three dollars and change, which seemed to represent an inordinate amount of time spent on the telephone, but local calls weren't itemized, so they were of no help. Then I set to work on the long-distance ones.

I first tried checking out the calls to Warren, Ohio, a medium-sized city about seventy-some miles east of Cleveland near the Pennsylvania border, but that proved to be a dead end. There were seven of them, but according to the reverse directory, the number was unlisted.

There were three calls to one New York City number that Torrence had circled as not belonging to her. When I checked it out, I discovered the phone was listed under the name Dennis McShane, who lived on West Twenty-fourth Street in Manhattan—an old neighborhood, as I remembered. Chelsea, they used to call it—maybe they still do. I wrote down McShane's name and address and then looked for the phone number in Elyria that had been called eleven times.

It proved to belong to a William Poduska, not exactly an Irish-sounding name.

I turned off the computer and dialed the New York City number. It rang four times before someone picked up.

"Yeah?" a male voice said. It was breathy and guttural, and sounded a little guarded.

"Is this Dennis McShane?"

"Who's this?"

"I'm trying to reach a Brian McFall."

There was no hesitation. "Never heard of him."

"He called your number several times about two months ago."

"Well, how the hell should I know who it was? Either a wrong number or more probably some son of a bitch tryin' to sell me something I didn't want. Maybe that's who you are, too. What's your business?" When he began speaking in full sentences, I could detect a thick Irish accent.

"I'm calling you from Cleveland, Ohio," I said. "I'm a private investigator."

"I don't know nothing about no private investigators. And I don't know nothing about no Cleveland."

"How about a James O'Dowd? Do you know him?"

"No, I don't know him, neither. Say, who the hell is this? Is this some sort of a fookin' joke?"

"Sorry to have troubled you," I said. "I must have made a mistake." I put down the receiver gently.

Dennis McShane was Irish, all right, at least from the sound of him. And Brian McFall had indeed called him three times from Judith Torrence's phone. But over the years I've learned to read voices pretty well, and it was my considered opinion that McShane was dealing straight and not trying to pull a fast one; I didn't think he'd ever heard of Brian McFall or Jamie O'Dowd.

I scribbled some notes and put them into a file folder I neatly labeled HARTIGAN, along with Judith Torrence's address and phone number and those of Hugh Cochran and my client, and Cochran's and Torrence's phone bills. I'd transfer the notes to my hard drive later.

I picked up the phone again and tapped out the Elyria phone number. After letting it ring twelve times, I discerned that no one was going to answer. William Poduska was evidently not at home.

I hung up and sat there for a while, smoking a cigarette and finishing my beer. I checked my watch. It was two P.M., still the fat part of a fall Sunday, and I didn't have a damn thing to do. I thought about driving over to Shooters on the Water to watch the rest of the Browns game, but only for a moment. I'd already missed the first quarter, I wouldn't know anybody there, and they'd all be twenty years my junior anyway. I'd be happier watching the game in my own den.

And then I looked at the address in Elyria again and thought that even though it was in the next county, it was still only about a half hour's drive. I could listen to the game on the radio.

Besides, I really wanted to talk to William Poduska.

CHAPTER SIX

'm sorry, but my husband isn't here right now."

The woman was in her early thirties, rail-thin and plain, the kind of person you could be introduced to on Wednesday night and completely forget by the weekend. She spoke pleasantly enough, but she was peering at me suspiciously through the thick lenses of a pair of tiny steel-rimmed glasses. Her head looked larger than it really was because she had her reddish-brown hair in a big, old-fashioned pageant bun; from the size of it, I imagined that when she let it loose, it hung down almost to her waist.

"You're Mrs. Poduska?" I asked.

"That's right."

I was talking to her through the screen door while standing on the front porch of her house in Elyria, a small city just over the border to the west in Lorain County. The Poduska dwelling was a compact, neatly kept white clapboard bungalow on a street where all the houses were built fairly close together, leaving only a narrow space for a driveway, and looked pretty much alike, having been constructed by the same builder sometime just after World War II.

I showed her one of my business cards through the mesh, and then she unhooked the door and opened it just far enough to take the card from between my fingers before closing and hooking it again. Door hooks aren't much protection, especially from an intruder as big as I am; I could have easily kicked in the door. But I had no reason to, so I just waited. When she read my card, she seemed startled, as are most people who meet a private investigator for the first time.

"Oh, my goodness," she said. "A policeman! I hope Bill isn't in any trouble."

I thought that a curious first reaction from a woman about her husband, and made a mental note of it. "Not at all. I just want to talk with him for a few minutes. I'm not with any police department, Mrs. Poduska. I'm a private investigator, and I've been hired to try and find someone. I have reason to think perhaps you or your husband might know him."

"Why?"

"Well, let's just say I followed a few leads and wound up here. I'm looking for a fellow called Brian McFall. Does that name mean anything to you?"

She gave the question the proper amount of thought and then shook her head gravely. "I don't think so."

"What about James O'Dowd? Jamie?"

Over a pair of polyester black pants she was wearing a white sweater fastened almost to the neck with toggle buttons, and now one hand moved to her throat to finger the top button. Her nervous little laugh was pitched high like a flute. "I'm sorry, but I'm not familiar with either of those people."

"Have you ever heard your husband mention them in passing?"

"No, I haven't," she said. "But then my husband knows so many people. From his business, y'know." She leaned closer to the screen door, her nose almost touching it. "But should I have heard of them? I mean, why are you asking me?"

"Because this Brian McFall made quite a few calls to your home about a month and a half ago."

"Oh, no," she said, and shook her head again; maybe the gesture was a habit of hers. "I don't think so."

"Probably your husband would remember, then. When will he be back?"

"Not for several days. He's in sales; he travels a lot. That's why I don't think this whatever-his-name-is person called here that many times. I probably would have answered the phone." She took her hand away from her sweater button and touched her puffy bun with it, patting at the back of her head. "I'm sorry; it's rude to keep you standing out there on the porch, but I don't like having men I don't know in the house while Bill isn't home."

"I'm strictly legitimate, I assure you," I said. "And harmless." I took the photostat of my license out of my wallet and showed it to her through the screen. "I won't take up too much of your time, I promise. And you can leave the door open, if it'll make you feel more comfortable."

"Well . . . ," she whined. She thought it over, cocking her head like a frightened sparrow listening for the whir of the falcon's wings. Finally, she decided. "I guess it'd be all right."

"Thank you," I said.

She unhooked the screen door and swung it open. The architecture of the house was strictly functional. There was no foyer or entry hall; the front door led directly into the square living room. Inside, it was neat, clean, and unimaginative, furnished with a mismatched hodgepodge of furniture that probably came from Value City. A nineteen-inch TV set was against one wall, an inexpensive VCR balanced on top of it.

"You can sit anywhere," she said, all the while pointing to a flowered sofa. I sat down and sank into it. The sofa was pretty-, but extra soft and not very comfortable for someone like me who weighed more than two hundred pounds.

"It's funny, those names you mentioned," she said.

"Why?"

"Well, because they're both Irish." She jerked a thumb toward herself. "And I'm Irish, too—my maiden name was Mullen. Bill isn't, of course—Poduska's a Bohemian name. Czech, I mean. It used to be called Bohemia."

"I know. I'm Slovenian myself."

"Yuh. Well, it's funny, because you'd think Irish people would be calling to talk to me, not Bill."

"McFall or O'Dowd, they didn't call to talk to you?"

She giggled breathlessly. "Hardly anyone ever calls to talk to me."

I was guessing that Mrs. Poduska was one of those women who had few friends of her own, but devoted herself exclusively to the care and feeding of her husband. The feminist revolution had blown by her in a rush without even ruffling her hair.

"Does your husband ever get phone calls and you don't know who he's talking to?"

A shadow flickered over her face like a cloud scudding across the face of the sun. "Yes, sometimes," she admitted.

"You said he doesn't go to an office nine-to-five. That means he works out of the house here."

"Well, yes," she said. "When he's not out on the road, that is."

"He must get business calls sometimes."

"Oh," she said. "Yuh. Sure he gets business calls."

"Do you think he might have been doing some sort of business with McFall or O'Dowd?"

"Maybe." She made it two words. "I don't pay much attention to his business." She gave me a small, self-deprecating smile. Everything about her was self-deprecating, as a matter of fact. She seemed mouselike, timid, and she never really raised her chin up off her chest. "Business confuses me."

"And you can't remember talking to either of those people I mentioned, Mrs. Poduska?"

"Call me Donalene," she said. "Everybody does. It's kind of an unusual name. I was named after my father. Donald, of course."

"What does your husband sell, Donalene?"

"Um," she said. "Different things. I mean, he doesn't work for just one company. He represents a bunch of different wholesalers and sells to retail stores. To tell you the truth, I'm not really sure about all the stuff he does. All I know is, it keeps him on the road a lot." She allowed herself a tiny smile. "Mostly he drives, like now. But sometimes he has to fly all over the country. We're saving up frequent-flier miles to take a really special trip somewhere next summer. Maybe to Europe."

"Hmm. Eclectic."

"Pardon?"

"I meant that he sells a wide variety of things."

"Yuh. Well, Bill isn't one to be tied down to a desk and an office, you know? He's kind of a free spirit. I am, too. I guess that's why I married him. You never know what to expect with him. There are always surprises." A certain bitter edge crept into her tone on that last sentence.

"Donalene, do you have a phone number for where he is now? I really want to talk with him."

She looked away briefly, and then back at me. "Sorry, but I don't. Like I said, he moves around a lot, so I never really know where he is.

"What would happen if there was some sort of emergency?"

A vertical line appeared between her eyebrows, as if that idea had never occurred to her. "He generally calls in here every few days." She swallowed hard. "Is there? An emergency?"

"Not that I know of."

She shivered, and ran her hands up her arms. "That's good. Well. It's a relief, anyway."

"When's the last time you heard from him?"

"Well, that's the funny thing," she said. "Almost a week ago. Monday, I think it was, or maybe Tuesday. And this is Sunday already. He generally calls more often than that."

"When he does call, I'd appreciate it if you'd ask him to get in touch with me. You have my card there."

Her shoulders rose and fell jerkily. "Yuh, whatever."

I figured that for the moment I'd heard everything interesting that she had to say, but I was planning a return trip to talk to her further, and perhaps meet with her husband, too. I thanked her for her time, stood up, and started to leave.

That's when I noticed a framed picture on a little table next to the front door that brought me up short. It was William and Donalene Poduska's wedding portrait. She was in a simple white dress and had her hair done up in a more fancy arrangement, with white baby roses intertwined in her auburn locks. She wasn't wearing glasses in the photograph, and she looked almost pretty, favoring the camera with her best and brightest bride-happy smile. The groom was wearing a tacky-looking light blue tuxedo, had sideburns that were too long, and needed a haircut.

"You and your husband?"

"Yes," she said, "the day we got married."

"How long ago was that, Donalene?"

"We got married three years ago last June," she said, beaming, her hand on the doorknob.

"You were a lovely bride," I said, and she fluttered prettily.

I didn't tell her that her husband was a handsome groom, though, even though he hadn't changed a bit in three years. I recognized immediately the sharp ferret features and the dark curly hair. They were just the same as in the snapshot I was carrying in my jacket pocket, the one with Cathleen Hartigan.

William Poduska was Brian McFall.

And Jamie O'Dowd.

And God only knew who else.

Judge Maureen Hartigan never heard of any William Poduska. She told me so when I called her at home that Sunday evening after getting back from Elyria. Then I called her daughter Cathleen and her nephew Hugh Cochran; neither of them knew anyone named Bill Poduska, either.

Nor, for that matter, had Judith Torrence, who from the sharp edge to her voice was beginning to get a trifle annoyed that I suddenly seemed to be in her life on a daily basis.

And Mrs. Poduska had never heard of Brian McFall or James O'Dowd. Which made it all even.

At least I was ahead of the game now; I was looking for a person who actually existed—someone who had a real name and a social security number. At least I hoped he did.

But I had to be careful. If I let Donalene Poduska know that her husband had been assuming secret identities and sleeping with pretty young Irishwomen and stealing from them instead of making his appointed sales rounds, she'd never give me the information I needed to track him down. Besides, I didn't want to interfere in anyone's marriage; it's a tough enough institution without meddling strangers and whistle-blowers whispering gossip.

Of course, I could just hang around outside the Poduskas' house until he returned home from his business trip, but that would wind up costing Judge Hartigan a lot of money in addition to boring me silly. And it would undoubtedly get ugly.

It had been a long Sunday, and I decided not to think about it again until Monday morning. At least that was a workday.

But Monday got started earlier than I'd expected when I got a wake-up call from Florence McHargue.

Florence McHargue doesn't like me, and that troubles me.

It's not that I have this burning need to be loved by everyone. Plenty of people don't like me, and I can cheerfully live with it, because the chances are that I don't like them, either.

But Lieutenant Florence McHargue is the head of the homicide unit of the Cleveland P.D., and because of my business our paths seem to cross more often than either of us would like. So her animosity toward me sometimes makes my life difficult at worst.

And unpleasant at best.

There was a time when my relations with the department were more cordial. First of all, I used to be a Cleveland cop, and after I left the force my best friend, Marko Meglich, whom I had known since we were both ten years old, ran the homicide store, and although we'd occasionally butt heads, he was usually cooperative, and that made my job a little easier.

But a few years back Marko was killed, and it was indirectly because of me. I live with the grief and the guilt every day of my life, and it seems to be compounded every time I have to go to police headquarters and sit in Marko's old office and face McHargue's snarls and threats and snide comments across what used to be his desk.

So when I answered the phone at fifteen minutes before eight on that Monday morning—there has never been such a thing as a good Monday—and heard her curt, hard voice announce, "This is Lieutenant McHargue," it was with no joy. I was already awake, but I hadn't had my eye-opening pot of coffee yet. Dealing with McHargue early in the day without coffee was a bear.

"Good morning, Lieutenant," I said, trying to sound as cheery as possible under the circumstances. "How are you?"

"Harried and cranky," she answered.

I bit my tongue to keep from asking her what else was new. The day Florence McHargue is *not* harried and cranky, somebody had better start shipping antifreeze to hell.

"I always get this way when the first thing in the morning I get hit with a report of a new homicide," she went on. "So I want you in my office in exactly one hour. And don't keep me waiting."

"You're cranky and you want me to hold your hand?" It was stupid, but I couldn't resist it.

"No, I want you to talk to me," she snapped. "And I damn well better like what I hear."

I looked at my watch. "What am I going to talk to you about, Lieutenant? Don't I get any hints?"

"Now you only have fifty-nine minutes," she said, and hung up.

And so it was that I began my workweek driving through the

pearly dawn to the Third District police headquarters, the old Federal-style rock pile on Payne Avenue at East Twenty-first Street where once I had reported for work in a blue uniform every day. I knew the lieutenant had a penchant for herbal tea instead of the murky coffee Marko had brewed on the top of a filing cabinet, so I stopped off at Starbucks on Cedar Hill a block from my apartment and brought coffee in a super-sized cardboard cup that I took great pains not to spill as I maneuvered the staircase up to her office on the second floor, the one that used to be Marko's.

I had no idea what she wanted to talk to me about, whether it had to do with the new homicide she'd mentioned. But it didn't matter; whenever Florence McHargue summoned, I showed up scrubbed and smiling. It was the easiest way I knew to keep my license.

On this particularly chilly morning she was wearing a medium-blue wool suit, which almost matched the tinted lenses of her glasses. Her black hair, showing more than a few strands of gray, was more severe than I'd ever seen her wear it, pulled back tight into a kind of tucked-under ponytail that stretched the milk-chocolate brown skin of her cheeks.

She pointed to the chair opposite her desk, which was as close to a "good morning" as I supposed would be forthcoming. I sat down and took the cardboard cup of coffee from a brown paper bag.

The lieutenant wasn't going to waste any time on niceties. "The body of a white male, between thirty-five and forty years old, was discovered late last night in a motel near the airport." She flipped open a file, ruffled through until she found what she was seeking.

Even looking at it upside down, I could recognize the autopsy protocol used by the county coroner.

"He also looked like he'd been in a fight, because he'd been beaten up some—the coroner says it was maybe twenty-four hours or more before his death. His little finger was newly broken, and he had a homemade splint on it—a couple of emery boards. He'd been shot twice at close range with a small-caliber pistol—a twenty-two. Once in the head and once in the groin area."

"The groin area?"

"The balls, Jacovich."

I winced. "Symbolic. A Bobbitt job."

"Maybe. Or maybe just a bad aim."

"Either way, my condolences to his family," I said. "But why did you invite me down here like this to tell me in person? Did you just need a sympathetic ear this morning, or do you routinely haul me in every time you find a body?"

Her eyes narrowed behind the blue-tinted lenses. "Don't flatter yourself that you could brighten my morning on your best day. You're here because the deceased had your name written down on a pad next to the telephone in his room."

My heartbeat quickened uncomfortably as my mind raced to figure out why someone who'd been murdered in a west-side motel might have written down my name. To give myself time to think, I twisted the lid off my cardboard container of coffee and took a sip. It was French roast, strong the way I like it and still very hot, even after the fifteen-minute trip from Cleveland Heights. And even though caffeine is a stimulant, it seemed to calm down the fluttering in my chest. "Does this deceased have a name?" I asked.

"His driver's license says he was William Poduska of Elyria, Ohio."

All of a sudden a golf ball-sized lump was blocking my throat. I dosed it with more hot coffee to no avail; it didn't even begin to go away.

"Does that name mean anything to you?"

I closed my eyes for a minute, possible horror-story scenarios whipping through my consciousness like a Rolodex being spun rapidly. Then I said, "Yes, it does, I'm afraid."

"What?"

"I was looking for him. He stole something from my client."

"And who's your client?"

"Lieutenant, you know that's privileged information."

The skin on her face pulled even tighter, giving her an almost Mongolian look. "What I know is that I've got a dead body with your name on it," she said, "and I don't give a shit about privileged information or client confidentiality. This is a capital crime. A homicide. A guy got shot in the balls, and that changes all the rules."

If I told McHargue I was working at the behest of Judge Maureen Hartigan, all the things the judge wanted kept quiet, the reason she'd hired me in the first place, would spread all over the department like news from jungle drums, and the whole business would be on the front page of the paper the next morning, including Cathleen's affair with the deceased. The judge just might turn out to be a murder suspect, and even if she was innocent, of which I was sure, the notoriety would probably stick a fork into her political career for good.

"I'll have to consult with my client," I said.

She looked at her watch. "You have until two o'clock," she said. "Then I want you and your client in here."

"Thanks."

"The stiff checked into the motel driving a rental car. Rented from Avis out at the airport in the name of Hugh Cochran. Am I to assume that's the same Hugh Cochran who's at the Department of Public Service?"

I didn't say anything, but dipped into my coffee again.

She didn't say anything either. She just glared.

"Hugh Cochran is not my client," I said finally.

"You wouldn't kid me now, would you, Jacovich?"

"Me kid you? Come on, Lieutenant, we're like family now."

"Yes," she said. "And you're the white sheep." It was the first time I'd ever heard her make a racial joke. "Any idea why this Poduska guy would have your name on a pad by his telephone?"

"No. I didn't think he knew I was looking for him."

"Apparently he did, though."

"Seems that way."

"Who told him?"

"I have no clue," I said. "I talked to his wife yesterday and left her my card. She said she didn't know where he was, but she might not have been completely truthful with me. Maybe she did know, and called him and told him I was looking for him. Or maybe he called her—husbands have been known to call their wives—and she just happened to mention it to him."

"What time yesterday did you see her?"

"Late in the afternoon."

She made a sour face and took off her glasses. "Shit! That doesn't do me a damn bit of good, then. They haven't done the autopsy yet—they've scheduled it for tomorrow morning—but the coroner estimates that he's been dead since at least early yesterday morning—more probably the night before that."

"Then I don't know what to tell you."

"Maybe you'll know what to tell me by two o'clock," McHargue said. "Maybe your client will, too. That's why I want both of your asses in here. No postponing, no calling me to say you can't make it, and no other kind of bullshit, either. Do I make myself clear?"

"You always do, Lieutenant. Is that it?"

She nodded curtly, and I started to get out of the chair, juggling to replace the lid on my coffee. "Just remember something," she said.

"What's that?"

"Until I talk to the wife, and to Hugh Cochran, and to your client, at the moment I have exactly one suspect." She pointed a red-nailed finger at me like a bazooka. "And that's you."

I started to say something, but she held up her hand.

"I know, I know; you didn't do it. Isn't that what you were going to say? Well, if it makes you feel any better, I don't think you did, either. But right now, you're what I've got. If I were you, I'd make a concerted effort either to get my name off that list, or to get a bunch of other folks *on* it."

That's how we left it.

I headed directly from McHargue's office to the courthouse to break the bad news to Judge Hartigan. I knew she wasn't going to be happy.

Mrs. Poduska probably wasn't going to be very happy, either.

Whether Donalene knew it or not, her husband, William Poduska, had lived a secret life that went far beyond that of a simple salesman. He had been an adulterer and a confidence man, for some strange reason preying on the Irish of Cleveland, even pretending to be Irish himself.

Now somebody had murdered him. And I was smack-dab in the middle of it.

CHAPTER SEVEN

I don't understand," Maureen Hartigan fumed. "The whole purpose of hiring you to track down Brian McFall was to keep this out of the public domain—away from the police and the press."

We were in her chambers at the Court of Common Pleas on Ontario Street. She was wearing a dark gray business suit over a white blouse, and sensible shoes. Her judicial robes were hung neatly on a hanger behind the door, and they swished a little as she paced by them furiously. The smell of brimstone was in the air.

"The media doesn't know anything about it. Yet," I said. "It's up to Lieutenant McHargue whether they get wind of it."

"I thought I could trust you, Milan." She was almost snarling. "Because of Cathleen, if for no other reason."

"Judge Hartigan," I said, reverting to the formality of her title rather than her first name, "the parameters have changed. Brian McFall—or William Poduska—has been murdered. That puts everything into a different perspective."

She stopped pacing, turned, and faced me squarely, her eyes as cold as river ice in January. "You certainly don't think I killed him?"

"Of course not. And the police probably won't either. But your position isn't going to help you out, here. You have to talk to them."

"I'm goddamned if I will!" she said.

"I don't think you have a choice."

"There are always choices," she said dangerously.

"Not this time."

"Why not? You said you hadn't told them my name."

"I didn't, because Lieutenant McHargue was generous enough—uncharacteristically so, I might add—to give me a chance to talk to you first. That's the easy way. If you don't come in and meet with her, she'll do it the hard way. She's going to make me tell her your name, and she can do it, too. Then she's going to come barging in here with a subpoena and a lot of questions. I don't think you want that. I promised her I'd bring you to her at two o'clock."

"You had no right to promise that without consulting me."

"I didn't have any other option."

Her face was an unreadable stone mask. "I'm busy at two o'clock."

I shook my head. "Come with me, Judge Hartigan. It's the best way. You know it is."

She was still breathing heavily, as if she'd just run up a flight of steep stairs, and her look was poisonous. "Do you know if they recovered the things he stole from me?"

"Some of them," I said.

"What about the photographs?"

"Lieutenant McHargue didn't mention any photographs. You'll have to ask her about them."

She hugged herself as if a chill wind had blown through her chambers. "You know that I'm watching my career and my reputation go down in flames here, don't you? Cathleen's, too."

"That doesn't have to happen," I said. "I think that because you're a judge, McHargue won't be going public with this if it isn't necessary."

"And what if it is necessary?"

"In that case," I said, "all bets are off."

That was not what she wanted to hear.

We went back to the Third District in separate cars. The judge had called both her daughter and Hugh Cochran before we left the office, and the four of us met in the downstairs lobby at five minutes before two.

Cathleen carried her briefcase and was dressed for her law office in a gray pinstriped power suit with an above-the-knee skirt, and a light blue silk blouse with a built-in foulard tie. She was looking daggers at me, too, except there was sorrow in her glare, and probably a little fear as well. "This is going to be so humiliating, Milan," she said, obviously feeling betrayed by a man for the second time in a month. "You promised you'd be discreet."

"I have been discreet," I said. "But I'm going to have to give up your name eventually. You know that."

Promises are always problematic. Twenty-some years ago my wife, Lila, and I had promised each other "till death do us part," and neither one of us had kept that one, either. Some promises turn out to be unkeepable.

And as for Cathleen Hartigan's public humiliation, I felt badly about it, but my uncharitable opinion right then was, Who asked her to sleep with Brian McFall/Bill Poduska in the first place?

I kept quiet, though, and as we went upstairs, I fully intended to stay that way throughout the entire interview with McHargue. This was the Hartigans' party, after all; I was just the hired help.

I introduced the two Hartigan women and Hugh Cochran to Florence McHargue. The lieutenant took one look at a well-known judge of the Court of Common Pleas, an assistant director of a large city department, and a partner in a high-end downtown law firm, and for the first time since I've known her, she was rendered speechless, except for a breathy "Oh, wow!"

Her office—Marko's old one—was too small for the meeting, so she led us down the hall to an interrogation room along with her second in command, Detective Bob Matusen. I was glad he was there. Matusen used to be Meglich's number two, and they worked well together, but now he was scared to death of his new boss, as was practically everyone else who got in the way of her biting sarcasm and caustic wit. Nevertheless, he was often the voice of calm and reason when McHargue let her temper get the better of her good judgment and went off like a Roman candle on the Fourth of July, and I hoped he'd provide some sort of balance.

After we were seated, with the cops on one side of the table and the rest of us on the other, Judge Maureen Hartigan looked around nervously. "Is this being recorded?" she asked, and glanced at the large mirror, which everyone who's ever seen a cop show on television knows is made of two-way glass. "Do we have an audience?"

"Under the circumstances, I didn't think that would be necessary," McHargue said. "I'm just using this room because it's bigger than my office. We're just talking privately—for the moment."

The judge nodded stiffly. Her arms were crossed over her chest, and she sat ramrod-straight. Cathleen had her hands folded on the table, fingers interlaced, and I could see her knuckles were turning white. Only Hugh Cochran seemed relaxed and comfortable, a vague smile on his lips, and one arm hooked over the back of his chair with an insouciance that wasn't quite appropriate to the occasion. His face was flushed, and even though it was a weekday afternoon, I had to wonder whether he'd been drinking.

McHargue went into her "hard cop" routine. She had all the moves down pat, leaning forward, her palms flat on the battered and scarred wooden table, her bulldog chin aimed at Maureen Hartigan's face. "As Jacovich probably told you, William Poduska was found shot to death in a motel room. The coroner says he died about seven o'clock Sunday morning. On Friday night you hired Jacovich to find him for you. Let's hear about that, Your Honor."

Maureen rocked in her chair but didn't uncross her arms. "I don't know any William Poduska. The man I was looking for was Brian McFall—at least that's what he told me his name was."

"Brian McFall," McHargue said.

"Then who was Jamie O'Dowd?" Matusen asked.

"I never heard that name." The judge shook her head.

"So Poduska was using not one but two aliases?"

"I don't know about that," the judge snapped. "He told all of us that he was Brian McFall, and we had no reason to doubt him."

Cathleen tried to take some heat off her mother. "It isn't customary when you meet someone to ask to see their ID."

"I always do," McHargue said. "But then I'm a police officer. So tell me how you came to know this Brian McFall."

Maureen Hartigan told McHargue the story pretty much the same way she'd explained it to me at One Walnut, with Hugh chiming in with some fill-in details. When she got to the part about Cathleen's affair with McFall/Poduska, she used the word "dating" as a euphemism. I glanced up at Matusen, who was blushing. He's a deeply old-fashioned man, Matusen.

The affair part of it raised McHargue's eyebrows, too. I was surprised at that; before taking over at homicide, she'd been head of the sex crimes unit, and she's probably seen and heard more than any of us want to know. "Ms. Hartigan," she said to Cathleen, "are you here serving as your mother's legal counsel in this matter, or as a witness?"

"I wasn't aware that Judge Hartigan needed legal counsel," Cathleen replied, "but if so, I guess I am. And yes, I'm here to add whatever I can to the story. You can call me whatever you like."

McHargue made a sour face. "I can call all three of you the same thing, Counselor—suckers."

"I don't have to take insults like that from you, Lieutenant McHargue," Maureen huffed.

"Not in your courtroom you don't," McHargue said, swiveling her intimidating gaze around to the older woman. "But in this building it's my ball game, and this is a murder investigation, so you'll have to excuse me if I forget my good manners. Now, explain to me again, someone, why you hired a private investigator to find this guy?" Here she jerked a rude thumb at me. "What were you going to do with him when you found him?"

"Convince him to make amends, I guess," Cathleen answered. "And to change his evil ways."

"He stole from us," the judge said. "Money and other things. We wanted him to make restitution."

"You'll have to forgive me, Judge, but that sounds a little weak. From what you described as missing, it wasn't worth what you were paying Mr. Jacovich here."

Hugh Cochran finally cleared his throat and spoke. "It was a matter of pride, Lieutenant." He grinned almost boyishly. "Family pride. You know how we Irish are about that."

McHargue turned her laser-gun stare on him full force. "Your matter of pride seems to have gotten a man killed, Mr. Cochran," she said. "Does it make you feel any prouder now?"

"Wait a minute; that's not fair," I cut in, forgetting my vow to keep a low profile. "We don't know why Poduska was killed. It might not have anything to do with the Hartigans."

"Right," Florence McHargue said. "And pigs have wings."

She brought her attention back to the judge. I don't know why, but she seemed more intently focused on Maureen Hartigan than on the other two. "Judge, do you have any idea why Mr. Poduska would have Mr. Jacovich's name written on a memo pad by his phone?"

"I can't think of a single reason," Maureen said.

McHargue shook her head angrily. "It seems like nobody can. I hate it when nobody has answers. It just makes us cops work harder, and we've got enough to do already."

"We're terribly sorry to inconvenience you." The judge's words were hoary with frost.

There was a twenty-second silence while the two women tried to stare each other down. Maureen Hartigan was the first one to blink.

"All right," the lieutenant said, satisfied with having won the contest. "Here's what we're going to do. You three are going to write out and sign separate statements, basically covering everything that you've already told me. Detective Matusen will stay here and help you."

Matusen nodded and shifted his weight from one buttock to the other. He was favoring the outdated "Regis" look today, a dark blue dress shirt with a lighter plain blue tie, but it didn't really work because the shirt was wrinkled, his jacket was off, his sleeves were rolled up, and the tie was pulled down about two inches from his nineteen-inch bull neck. If there really were such an entity as the "fashion police," Bob Matusen would be on death row.

McHargue rose abruptly, the scrape of her chair on the linoleum floor like fingernails on a blackboard. "Jacovich! In my office, now!"

I followed her meekly down the hall. She wasn't a tall woman, perhaps five foot seven, but she had a stride like John Wayne's.

When we were seated across her desk from one another, she slammed a palm down on a case folder. "Okay, Jacovich, what kind of happy horseshit is this? A common pleas judge hires you to track down a guy who nicked her for a couple of thousand bucks? That smells so bad I've got a good notion to open the window and get some fresh air in here."

I shrugged. "As you say, she's a respected judge. What reason would I have to doubt her?"

McHargue opened the file, which was marginally thicker than it had been at nine o'clock that morning. "They took an inventory of the deceased's possessions. He had about nine hundred and change in cash on him, and most of the items Hartigan and Cochran said he'd taken from them." She flipped through some pages in the file. "A pair of expensive men's boots, an antique silver brooch and earrings, some other assorted women's jewelry, gold cuff links, and some brand-new never-been-worn suits from Brooks Brothers that were purchased with Hugh Cochran's Visa card."

"No photographs?"

"Photographs?"

"Judge Hartigan told me he'd taken an envelope full of photographs."

"What kind of photographs?"

"I don't know."

"They send *you* out to find some photographs, and you don't even know what they are?" She gave me a scornful look. "You're even a bigger sucker than they are, Jacovich." She perused the list some more. "Nope, no photographs, not counting a picture of a lady in his wallet."

"Maybe it's his wife."

"I think it is," she said. "Matusen was out visiting her this morning."

"Did she seem broken up about Poduska's death?"

"'Shattered' is the word he used, yes. So what about these other pictures he swiped? Are you sure the judge didn't tell you what they were?"

"Yes," I said.

"And you didn't ask."

"No."

She scribbled something on the inside of the file folder. "Okay, then. Besides those three little leprechauns in the other room, who else knew you were looking for Poduska?"

"I never heard the name William Poduska until yesterday. I was looking for Brian McFall, and I found Mrs. Poduska when I traced her phone number from some telephone bills of another woman her husband had scammed."

"According to the coroner, though, you didn't see the wife until after he was already dead."

"Yes."

"So what about this other woman Mr. Poduska ran his little game on? Who's that?"

I sighed. I was going to have to roll over on a lot more people before I was through. "Her name is Judith Torrence," I said. "Only she knew Poduska as James O'Dowd."

"James O'Dowd, huh?"

"He went by Jamie."

"Jamie. How cuddly. And he told Cochran and the Hartigans his name was Brian McFall?"

"That's right."

"Curiouser and curiouser." McHargue drummed her fingers on her desk. "So Torrence knew you were trying to find him?"

"She knew I was trying to find somebody named Brian McFall. Or Jamie O'Dowd. I think the name William Poduska is just as foreign to her as it is to the Hartigans."

"I'll find that out. Did Mr. Poduska charm her into the sack, too?"

I hesitated, and McHargue treated me to her nastiest laugh. "A real old-school gentleman, aren't you? Not wanting to tarnish a lady's reputation."

"Something like that."

"Tough shitsky. Did he fuck her?"

"I'm afraid so."

"And where do I find this damaged damsel?" she said. "In the mists of Brigadoon?"

"Brigadoon was in Scotland, Lieutenant. Judith Torrence is Irish."

"Pardon me, but I'm not as up on Broadway musicals as you. Do you have Torrence's address and phone number?"

"I do."

"Good," she said. "Let's have it."

I scribbled the requested information on the yellow pad she pushed across the desk at me.

"Who else knew you were bird-dogging this guy?"

"Another woman named Jinny Johnson. She's the one who put me in touch with Torrence in the first place. But she had nothing to do with Poduska—she's just Torrence's friend."

"You got her number, too?"

"She gave it to me, but I threw it away."

"Why?"

"Because I wasn't interested in calling her for the reason she gave it to me."

"You stud, you!" she said, and it wasn't meant as a compliment.

"But Judith Torrence will have it. If not, she works for the city, although I don't know what department. Jinny Johnson. But you can usually find her in the evening at O'Grady's bar in Tremont."

"O'Grady's bar again," she sighed, shaking her head. "Everyone in this case is a barfly. Okay, then. Anybody else?"

I was fidgeting for a cigarette, but McHargue enforced the ban on smoking in public buildings, especially in her office. Back in the days before the use of tobacco was viewed with the same disgust formerly reserved for public flashing, when Marko Meglich sat behind that desk, the two of us would turn the air blue with the smoke of burning Winstons. "Well, there's Cornelius McCardle."

McHargue closed her eyes as if a sudden, sharp pain had exploded behind them. "Oh, crap!" she said.

I waited for amplification, but all she said was, "I assume you know who he is?"

"Sure I do. He's Cleveland's Irish godfather."

She nodded brusquely. "An oversimplification, but I guess that's close enough. And you think I want to wrangle with him and his people?"

I suppressed a grin—not very well, I'm afraid. "Why not, Lieutenant? After all, McHargue is a good old Irish name. Maybe he'll think you're a long-lost relative from County Mayo."

"Put a sock in the racial jokes," she said, giving me a look that could wilt gardenias. "How'd you get him involved in this?"

"As I told you, Hugh Cochran first ran into Bill Poduska in O'Grady's. But Judith Torrence met him in the Shebeen. And that's unofficial McCardle headquarters. I just went in there and asked him if he knew Poduska. Or rather, Brian McFall or Jamie O'Dowd."

"All these Irish names are giving me a headache," she said. "And? What happened when you asked him?"

"He blew me off."

"Crap," she said again. "That means I have to talk to him."

"Yes, but you have a badge," I pointed out. "At least he won't throw you out of the bar."

She put her elbow on the table and rested her forehead in her hand, tapping the file folder with the eraser-end of a pencil. "Yes, I do have a badge—and you don't anymore, which you seem to conveniently forget from time to time."

"Hey, my job was to find the guy who had fleeced Judge Hartigan. Apparently, somebody else beat me to it. I'm out of it now."

"If you're smart, you'll keep it that way. You're still on the suspect list, you know."

"You're kidding!"

"Relax," she said, and I could tell she was secretly pleased at having rattled me. "I don't think you killed him. But officially you're on the list."

"Now it's my turn to say crap."

She took off the blue-tinted glasses and gave me one of her patented piercing stares. "Want to get off it?"

I just looked at her.

"Two things," she said. "First, ask Maureen Hartigan about those photographs. What they were. My guess is that the good judge didn't hire a private ticket at a hundred bucks an hour to bring back a bunch of snapshots from the Hartigan family picnic."

"I don't get a hundred bucks an hour," I said, "but I see your point."

"Like I care. Secondly, I want you to think about something. William Poduska lived in Elyria, right?"

"You know that."

"Then think about why he was staying at a hotel near Hopkins Airport, not forty-five minutes away from his home."

"And when I've thought about it?" I said.

She didn't smile. "You'll tell me."

CHAPTER EIGHT

'**ve** never been so fucking mortified in my life," Cathleen Hartigan said through clenched teeth, and with her knee she slammed shut the drawer of a filing cabinet to make sure I got the point.

It was five forty-five in the afternoon, and while the offices of her blue-chip law firm were not exactly deserted, the corridor that was partners' row was quiet, all the other important lawyers having gone home. On the far side of the building were the associates, a big law firm's version of the drone bees, all of whom would probably be there sifting through law books and protocols until well after most people had eaten their dinner and settled in front of their TV sets to drop off to sleep.

"Do you have any idea what it was like to sit there in front of that awful woman and discuss the most intimate details of my sex life?" Her lips were pressed so tightly together they were turning white. "To admit how stupid I was? She probably thinks I'm a bimbo."

"I'm sure she doesn't. She's a grown woman and lives in the twenty-first century just like the rest of us. You're not the first person in the world to sleep with someone you shouldn't have," I said. "And nobody blames you for it, so forget about it."

"I can't forget about it," she said. "Look at what it's gotten my whole family into."

"I think there's a good case to be made that it was Hugh who got the ball rolling on that one, Cathleen. And your mother after him. You were just third in line on the sucker list."

"That's an honor I'd just as soon have skipped altogether, frankly." She paused in clearing off her desk and shuddered. "I've never made love to anyone who died two weeks later. Or died at all. It makes me feel creepy."

I had to stop and think about that one for a few moments. It had never happened to me either, and I imagine that if it ever does, I'll feel pretty creepy, too. "Did McFall ever mention the name Dennis McShane to you?"

"No," she said. "Why are you asking?"

"Because we happen to know that he made several calls to a Dennis McShane in New York City."

She shook her head impatiently. "No, I mean, what do you want to know for? It's over now."

"It's nowhere near over," I told her. "Somebody's been shot to death. Homicide cops like Florence McHargue go strictly by the book. They work with what they've got in front of them, and right now that's a list of names that includes you and your family, along with a couple of other people, including me. I'm nobody, but your family is news, especially the judge, and eventually somebody from the press is going to catch a whiff of it, and then it will go public, which your mother specifically doesn't want to happen. So I figure if I can give them a few more names to play with, the rest of us with be off the hook."

"Is that what these questions are all about?"

"Yes. And I'm sorry I have to be asking them."

She stopped what she was doing and looked at me hard. "You're a good guy," she said. Her smile was no less genuine for being forced.

"No, I'm not, Cathleen. Remember, I'm a suspect, too, although probably not a very serious one. But you're my friend, and if it means anything, I certainly don't think either you or your mother are killers. But I doubt that the kind of negative publicity this thing will engender if it gets into the media is going to do either of you any good. Or your cousin Hugh, for that matter."

She shuddered again. She was stuffing enough material from the top of her desk into her briefcase to take on an extended trip to Europe.

"Besides," I added. "I don't like leaving loose ends dangling. They make me feel incomplete."

She regarded me for a too-long moment and then sat down behind her desk with a sigh, all at once seeming tired and older. "You and I—we're still loose ends, aren't we, Milan?"

I didn't say anything. The nonrelationship I have with Cathleen is something I didn't want to talk about.

"We've been loose ends for years."

"I guess so."

"Does that leave you feeling incomplete, too?"

"In a way," I said, and my collar seemed to be getting tight. I unbuttoned it and pulled down the fat knot of my tie. Most of my female friends over the years have told me that all my ties are out of date and too wide. "It's been my fault, not yours. The timing was always wrong."

She chewed thoughtfully on her bottom lip, removing what was left of her lipstick. "You know what they say about when you toss a pebble into a pond, the ripples can be felt clear around the world?"

"Uh-huh. What's that got to do with . . . ?"

"I was just thinking," she said. "What might have been."

I cleared my throat because I had to. "I've never seen any profit in wondering that."

Apparently she did, though, because she kept right on. "If you and I had gotten together seven years ago, or even two years ago, we might have stayed together, even gotten married."

"To be honest with you, we probably wouldn't have. I don't do very well at relationships."

"You just think you don't, because you've always picked the wrong women. Inappropriate women, I guess."

"No," I said. "It's me. After you get to be a certain age—somewhere around forty—you chalk up a lot of experiences of all kinds and start realizing some truths about yourself. When it comes to relationships—the kind that last, anyway—I'm one hundred percent klutz."

She shook her head dismissively and smiled. "I know you better than you know yourself."

I sighed. "Cathleen, the side of the highway is littered with the broken bodies of women who thought they knew me better than I know myself. Trust me, after one failed marriage I'm headed for perennial bachelorhood."

"You're a family man to your core, Milan."

"Well, sure—I mean, my sons . . ."

"And if you and I were together," she went on, off on her own little trip to Fantasy Island, "then there would have been no Brian McFall, or William Poduska, or whatever his name was, in my life."

A chill ran through her body, and she hunched her shoulders and hugged herself. "And then he might still be alive. Jesus."

"Don't even think like that," I said. "What happened to Bill Poduska had nothing to do with the two of you."

"How can you be so sure?"

I patted my stomach. "Gut instinct."

"Is your gut ever wrong?"

"Only after I've eaten klobasa and fried onions. And I haven't done that for a week or so."

She laughed, perhaps a little too loudly. Then she closed her eyes. "Ah, Jesus, Milan. The things people get themselves into."

"I know. We write scripts for our lives, and we try to learn all the lines and all the moves, but other people have their own scripts, their own agendas, and sometimes they get in the way."

"Brian McFall's agenda sure as hell got in mine." She rocked back in her big executive chair and put her hands over her face, and for almost a minute she stayed that way. I didn't think she was crying; it occurred to me that she might actually be hiding. Then, still not moving, she said through her fingers, "There's one thing I don't understand about him, though."

"What's that?"

"If he was a con man, why didn't he just con? I mean, why didn't he just milk us for all the money he could and then go the hell away?" She uncovered her eyes. "Why'd he have to make love to me, too?"

"I can't blame him for that. I would have, too. I guess we'll never know, but that seems to have been his MO."

"He'd done it before?"

I nodded.

She rocked forward almost violently in her chair and slammed her fists onto the desk, her face coloring a flaming red. "Goddamn it! Now I *really* feel like a fucking idiot!"

I realized that nothing I could say would make her feel less like one, so I didn't say anything for a while. Finally, she pushed her chair back and stood up.

"I might as well go home and lick my wounds," she said. "And make myself a strong drink in the biggest glass I can find. I've done enough damage here." She cocked a provocative eyebrow. "I suppose it would be futile to ask if you'd like to come home with me."

"Cathleen . . ."

"Okay, okay, okay!" She put both hands up as if to ward off an attack. "Just forget it. Bad idea. I apologize." She let her gaze flick around the office, stopping to take in the view of the turquoise-colored sky over the lake in the fading late fall light. "The end of a perfect day."

She turned around and challenged me with her eyes, her chin jutting out stubbornly. "Do you think I'm a bimbo now, too?"

"Of course not. There aren't many people left who haven't had a one-night stand of some sort or another. Or a three-week stand, or six weeks. It's the twenty-first century."

"Buck Rogers time."

"I think that was the twenty-fifth century."

"Here's a quarter—go call somebody who gives a shit."

"Cathleen," I said.

She picked up her purse. "What?"

"Those photographs Poduska stole from your mother."

"What about them?"

"That's what I want to know."

Our eyes locked for a moment; hers were very blue, and shining wetly.

"You'll have to ask her," she said. "Because I honestly don't know."

Judge Maureen Hartigan lived in a sprawling old white frame house with black trim on the near west side of Cleveland. It probably wasn't so sprawling when she and her late husband, former state senator Doyle Hartigan, bought it forty years earlier. But over the years it had been remodeled and added onto when children arrived, and the expensive landscaping in the front and back yards, as well as the sunporch that had been tacked onto the side, made the Hartigan house a shimmering showplace in what was otherwise a modest, somewhat dusty working-class neighborhood.

Prior to this, I had only seen the judge in her judicial robes or the conservative business suits she wore under them. Still it shouldn't have surprised me, at eight o'clock in the evening, that she answered the door wearing faded blue jeans, sneakers, and a Cleveland State University sweatshirt, and was carrying a half-drunk bottle of Guinness Stout in her hand.

The light on her wide, roomy front porch clicked on before she opened the door to find me standing there, and she didn't seem particularly pleased to see me. She bent her head back to look up at me, swaying a little from side to side and almost losing her balance and stumbling backward. "Well, Milan! Are you here to drag me off to some police station again?" The sarcasm made her voice seem whiny, and aggression radiated from her like light and heat from the sun. "Or do you just want to tell me somebody else got himself murdered and I'm the chief suspect?"

I didn't bother answering; I think rhetorical questions are a waste of breath. "May I come in, Maureen?"

"Invite the fox into the henhouse? Why not? Come on in." She habitually spoke precisely and clearly, and the way she was now slurring her words led me to believe the Guinness was not her first of the evening. The whole Hartigan family seemed inordinately fond of alcohol.

She stepped aside and waved me past her. The furniture in the big living room was made of dark walnuts and mahoganies to match the paneling and the trim around the doors and windows. It was all expensive, but gently aged and weathered, making it more beautiful. On the mantel was a framed black-and-white formal photo portrait of the late state senator Doyle Hartigan, and there were more candid photos of him, his wife, Cathleen, her congressman-brother Kevin, and the rest of the family on nearly every flat surface. It was a warm, welcoming living room, the kind you might glimpse through a lighted window driving by on a snowy evening that made you wish you were the one who lived there.

Its occupant, however, was neither warm nor welcoming.

"You let me down big-time," she said accusingly. I had sat

down in a flowered chintz chair, and she was standing over me, but if her intent was to intimidate me it failed badly, as she was listing a little to starboard. "You promised me you'd be discreet about Briney McFall."

"That was before somebody shot him."

She ignored the comment. "Do you suppose that when I hired you, I knew I'd wind up down at Third District headquarters, sitting in an interrogation room like a crack dealer and spilling my guts to a cop?"

"You have nothing to hide, Maureen; what's the big deal?"

Her eyes flared angrily. "The big deal is that now the whole world knows a Common Pleas Court judge was scammed like a silly old lady when the gypsies come around to sell her aluminum siding." She tilted the beer bottle to her lips and finished it off in one prodigious gulp.

"The whole world doesn't know," I said. "And Lieutenant McHargue has no reason to let them know, either."

She looked down at me, making a herculean effort to focus her eyes on me. "You simple man," she said. "You simple, naive man. You have no idea. When you're an elected official like me, there are predators behind every tree. You never know when anything you might do, even something innocent, might someday rise up and bite you in the ass."

"Is that why you wanted the photographs back?" I said.

Her look went blank, eyelids hooded, and her entire face seemed to close up, to change its shape and configuration to that of a death mask. "They're just photographs," she said, her voice as dead as her eyes.

"Of what?"

"They're just pictures. Of my husband." She waved a hand at all the other photographs of him. "Sentimental value, that's all." She turned abruptly and tottered over to another chair, plopping into it with relief, as though it were where she'd wanted to be all her life.

"The son of a bitch," she said, her voice coming from far away. "Briney. Little Briney McFall. What was his real name? Poduska? That's—what? Slovak? Where does a bohunk come up with an alias like Brian McFall? What a sleazeball! He got what was coming to him, if you ask me. Of course, nobody did." She held the side of the beer bottle to her temple as if to soothe a pounding headache. "Ask me, I mean. Using people. Fucking them over." She sighed. "No need to tell anyone I said that."

"Why would I?" I said. "I'm on your side, remember?"

She snorted as if she didn't believe it.

"Did the police ask you about your telephone bill for the time he was staying here?"

"Oh, yeah. I sent them over a copy this afternoon—per Lieutenant McHargue's request."

"You still have the original?"

"Sure," she said. "So what?"

"May I see it?"

"No, you can't see it! What the hell's the difference? You're not working for me anymore."

"I can be," I said, hoping it didn't sound self-serving. I really didn't care about making any more money from her troubles—even though that's how I earn my living. But because Poduska had written my name down on his bedside pad, I had to push it further. For my own satisfaction. And I'd be standing on more solid legal ground poking around in an open murder case if I had a legitimate client, especially one as legitimate as a Common Pleas judge.

"Doing what?" she said.

"Finding those photographs."

She frowned for a moment, thinking about that, and then her face took on a foxy, crafty look I didn't like very much. "Hmm," she said.

"Maybe you shouldn't make your mind up about that now. Why don't we talk about it again tomorrow when you're feeling better?"

"Feeling better?" She threw back her head and laughed, and lusty as it was, there was a tinge of self-pity to it. "You're so fucking polite and proper, it makes my teeth ache. Feeling better!" She waved the bottle of Guinness at me. "You really mean when I'm sober, don't you?"

"Have it your way, Maureen."

Her eyes narrowed to slits, and her face got serious and, I thought, a little dangerous. "I usually do," she said.

Maureen Hartigan was a tough woman. I should have remembered, should have thought about her reputation on the bench. Socially, she was affable and gracious in a no-nonsense way, but she hadn't reached the pinnacle of her profession by being soft and wishy-washy.

She stared at the portrait of her husband on the mantel for a long time. "Okay, then," she said finally. "You're still on the clock. Find those photographs, and bring them directly to me." She pointed her finger at me. "No police, no press, no nothing. Just to me."

"I can only promise that if they don't have anything to do with Poduska getting killed. If they do, I've got to give them to the police. I don't have any other option. Legally. And if they ask you for them, neither do you."

"Don't give me a lecture on what's legal, okay, Milan? That's *my* ball game."

"It would be a lot easier if I knew what I was looking for."

"You don't need to know."

"Then how will I know if they're the right pictures?" I asked. "You have to tell me what they're pictures *of.*"

She leaned her head against the back of the chair; the hand holding the empty beer bottle simply dangled close to the floor. In a tired voice she said, "You'll recognize them, all right. I told you, they're pictures of my husband."

CHAPTER NINE

'd been in Third District almost a thousand times, but whenever I walked through the door, the odor there always brought me up short. Big-city police headquarters have their own unique stink, like hospitals or pre-school day care centers or taxidermy shops. Stale cigarette smoke, even though in most public buildings on-premises smoking has been declared a hanging offense. The stink of forty years of tobacco had permeated the walls and the ceilings and the furniture, and no amount of repainting could banish it. Bad, burnt coffee that's been sitting on the hotplate too long. The stinging ammonia scent of disinfectant. Old sweat. The odor of fear—the fear of the power and majesty of the law, the fear of God, the fear of doing serious time in a prison cell with a three-hundred-pound guy with tattoos and body piercings who insists on calling you Rosemary. And the rank, fetid stench of old, sometimes terrible crimes.

Cop shops smell especially bad in the morning. After the night has cleansed the rest of the city of its pollution stink, the smell inside a police station is startling. This was my second early morning in a row at the Third District, and I didn't much like it.

But at least this time I didn't have to deal with Florence McHargue.

I've known Lieutenant Herbert Bialosky for the better part of my adult life. He had gained probably seventy pounds since we worked together in uniform out of the Roaring Third District, and he'd been no lightweight to begin with. As he rose from behind his desk to greet me, the expanse of white shirt across his broad belly looked like a meadow in the snow, bisected by a skinny blue river of necktie. Herb had never been the kind of cop who enjoyed the adrenaline rush of working the hard, dangerous streets, and early on he had aimed his career in the direction of administration. Now at his fairly advanced age, riding a desk put little physical strain on his considerable bulk. At present, he headed up the financial crimes unit, which in many other police departments around the country was simply known as the bunco squad.

He greeted me warmly when I walked into his office, probably remembering the good times we'd shared when we were both young and eager and full of piss and vinegar, and as he settled back into his chair with a wheeze, I realized that by now most of the police chums of my youth had either risen in rank to a supervisory level or put in their papers after twenty years.

Or, like Marko Meglich, were dead.

We caught up on the news for a while, asking about one another's families the way old friends do who haven't connected with each other in far too long. Like me, he had a son in college. Unlike me, he was still married.

"So, Milan," he finally said. "I read about you in the papers every once in a while. Since you turned in your badge and weapon you seem to have carved out an . . . an interesting life for yourself."

"I could do without the publicity, Herb," I said. "As for the rest of it, it pays the bills."

He chuckled. "You must really be raking it in."

"Hardly. I'm a PI, not a lawyer."

"Maybe I should have become a PI, too, and said good-bye to all the regulations and the rules and the paper shuffling," he said almost wistfully. Then he grinned. "But then I'd have actually had to *work*. Nah, this is better."

"Sometimes I think you're right."

"For me, maybe, but not for you. To be a good cop, you gotta have it in your bones." He patted his chest over his heart. "In here. Like painters and writers and ballet dancers—they've just *gotta* do what they do or they'd shrivel up and die. You weren't like that. You were a good enough cop, but you didn't love it enough to put up with the saluting and the shoe shining and the paperwork and the politics—you weren't really comfortable in the department."

He was right about that.

"And me?" He heaved his big shoulders. "Now that Barry is grown up and in school, Lois is always after me to put in my papers so we can move to Florida and I can take up golf and learn to play gin rummy. There's a certain appeal to that, I gotta admit. But God help me, Milan, I still can't *wait* to get up in the morning and pin on my badge and *do* it."

"You're a happy man, Herb."

"What's happy? I don't know. I just know that I bleed police blue. I'm too old and fat to go out and chase skels through back alleys, but I like being here. I like putting the puzzle pieces together. And every once in a while, I actually make a difference." He fiddled with the points of his shirt collar. "So what brings you to the sanctum sanctorum of a fat, aging Jewish cop? Are you here in a professional capacity, or just catching up with old friends?"

"A little of both," I said. "A con man named William Poduska got shot to death Sunday morning."

"Right," he said. "Lieutenant McHargue has already been over here to talk about it." He rolled his eyes toward the stamped-tin ceiling. "Boy, howdy, isn't *she* a piece of work?"

I smiled without committing myself. Flo McHargue might be a righteous pain in the ass, but she's also a cop like Herb, and I'm not one anymore. So it was all right for him to criticize her, but I didn't feel I had that right. There *are* drawbacks to leaving the department, I thought.

"Did Poduska have a record?" I said. "He was running a few small-time scams when he bought it."

"He had no sheet, but let's just say that his name was familiar in this unit," Herb said. "Or the various names he used, anyway. We were never able to nail him with anything we could put him away for, but he had an active imagination and used it to screw people."

"Irish people?"

Bialosky pulled a file across the desk and opened it. "Not always," he said. "But they were almost all women."

I nodded. "That fits what I know about him."

"But it was penny-ante stuff, all of it. I don't even know how he managed to pay his bills. From what I have here, and what

McHargue told me, two or three grand a pop was a major score for him. Who the hell would want to ice a guy over two thousand dollars?"

"You ought to get out from behind that desk and back onto the streets where the violent crimes are, Herb," I said. "People get killed these days for pocket change, or a clean pair of Nikes."

"I suppose. But still, most people would shrug it off, or at the very worst maybe smack him around a little. Not shoot him in the head."

"Somebody did smack him around," I said. "Except according to the M.E. the beating took place at least twenty-four hours before his death. That says to me there were two different perps— one hitter and one shooter. I mean, why would somebody beat him up one day and then come back and kill him the next?"

He turned his hands palms upward. "You're asking the wrong cop. I'm way out of my depth here, Milan—with a guy getting himself shot in the balls. I get involved when somebody swindles a sweet old lady out of her life savings, or sells phony stocks in a Brazilian tin mine that doesn't exist." He tapped the file on his desk. "Or runs a bunco scheme on a sitting judge, which in itself is major-league dumb. But I don't do homicides. That's why we have Flo McHargue."

"Maybe one of those sweet little old ladies in your file decided to get even with him."

He shook his head. "I don't think so. Besides, the last papers I have on Poduska are two and a half years old."

"Yes, but he doesn't even live in Cuyahoga County. Maybe he's got a sheet in Elyria. Or several other jurisdictions."

"I'm sure McHargue is having her people in homicide follow that up," Bialosky said. "At least locally. But a guy like Poduska might have been running his games anywhere—Chicago, Detroit, Pittsburgh."

"That's why police departments have computers, Herb."

"Yeah, I know. But even so, I'm glad it's McHargue's paperwork and not mine." He sighed, his bulk heaving. "In fact, since he was so well known to us here in the Cleveland area, it would only make sense for him to have expanded his operations elsewhere in the last few years. I'm frankly surprised he surfaced again around here, and especially so because he targeted somebody as high up and well connected as Mo Hartigan."

"When the returns come in, is there any chance of your letting me know?"

Bialosky frowned. "Letting you know what?"

"Who some of the other complainants against Poduska were. Like, from out of town?"

"Whoa, Milan," he said. "It's McHargue's case. I probably won't even see those names. And if I did and I gave them to you, you know she'd have my ass hanging on the door."

"Come on, Herb, you're both lieutenants. And you have seniority."

"That doesn't matter with her. She'd make a big deal out of it. Everybody walks softly around McHargue, even captains. She got that reputation when she was working sex crimes a couple of years ago. She is, to quote Ernest Hemingway, a barbarous woman." He sat back in his chair, which was almost too small for him, and wheezed slightly. "I wish Marko Meglich was still sitting in her chair. Damn it, Milan, I really miss him."

"*You* miss him?" I said sadly. "Tell me about it."

It was no trick at all to discover that Shamrock Homes, on Brookpark Road, was where Cornelius McCardle maintained his daytime headquarters. I simply called Ed Stahl at the *Plain Dealer* and asked him. Ed is a walking encyclopedia of Cleveland; what he doesn't have stored away in his fertile brain about the city—its history, its movers and shakers, its warts and wens and scandals, and the first name of every bartender in town—isn't worth knowing.

I got to Shamrock at about ten-thirty. It was housed in one of those nondescript, low-slung, yellow-brick and cinderblock buildings that were hastily thrown up in every major city in the country right after World War Two, and the sign on the window was, not surprisingly, rendered in emerald green, complete with three-leaf clovers. The spaces in the small parking lot beside the building were all labeled with little tin signs, and the one that said "Mr. McCardle" was unoccupied. I supposed that a man

McCardle's age who spent every night drinking in an Irish bar couldn't be expected to show up for work very early.

Then again, according to Ed, Shamrock Homes wasn't really the main source of McCardle's income.

Preparing for what might be a long wait, I parked my car across the street and rolled down the driver's-side window to let the fresh October breeze air out the car. In the spring, when I'd traded in my vintage Pontiac Sunbird for a new one, I had vowed not to smoke in the car anymore, so the air inside was not as sour as in the old one. In fact, it still had that pungent, satisfying new-car smell. But the soft wind refreshed anyway. It was chilly, perhaps in the low sixties, but in a very short time icy winter would descend like Thor's hammer, and there would be no more open windows in northeast Ohio until May.

I had left home too early that morning to read the newspaper, but I had brought it with me, and opened it up now, briefly scanning the national and international news, giving a quick look at the sports pages and the offensive problems of the Browns, and dutifully reading Ed Stahl's column. Then I turned to what really interested me—the Metro section, with its tales of politics and zoning and municipal hanky-panky, as well as the local gossip and a smattering of syndicated columns from other newspapers. I especially enjoy the columns of Maureen Dowd of the *New York Times*, who is often even more acerbic than Ed. Every so often I would glance across the street to see if my quarry had finally managed to drag his poor old Irish ass out of bed.

Finally, at a few minutes past eleven, a new, dark green Lincoln badly in need of a trip through the car wash entered the Shamrock parking lot and eased into the space reserved for the chief honcho. I opened my door and walked across the street just as the driver was getting out of his car.

"Mr. McCardle," I said.

His legs were swung halfway out, a position momentarily vulnerable to attack, and when he saw my bulk looming suddenly up in front of him, he was startled and frightened, and he began scrabbling in his pocket, which made me worry that he might shoot me first and ask questions later. And then he recognized me, and the mask of fear his face had become turned to one of anger.

"Didn't I tell you to never let me see your face again?" he said, the unmistakable threat in his tone transforming him from bantam rooster to bird of prey.

"Yes, sir," I said. "But the rules have changed."

I moved toward him to help him out of the car, but he shook his fist at me and I backed off. He extricated himself, slammed the door, and stood up straight and proud and defiant.

"Around here *I* make the rules, Mr. Jacovich. As you'll soon find out."

He pulled a silver whistle out of his pocket; it was like a police whistle, the same kind that women are sometimes given in case of an attack, and I realized that was what he'd been searching for seconds earlier. He raised it to his lips, and I wondered what kind of help would come pouring out of the Shamrock Homes offices to help him. I imagined that his security was more than adequate.

But I never got the chance to find out. Just as he was taking a big, deep breath preparatory to blowing the whistle on me, I said, "Mr. McCardle, William Poduska has been murdered."

The usual ruddiness of his complexion drained away as if a color TV set had all at once faded to black-and-white, and he put a hand to his face, fingertips stroking his whiskered and sagging cheek. For a moment it seemed he couldn't speak. Then finally he managed to stammer Poduska's name—only he pronounced it "Pazuska" with a question mark at the end. It wasn't very convincing.

"The man in the photograph I showed you," I said, even though I knew he didn't need further amplification.

Finally, he got himself under control. He pointed his nose in the air and said, "I'm not acquainted with anyone by that name."

I lost patience. "Mr. McCardle, why don't we stop bullshitting each other? You knew William Poduska—I don't know *how* you knew him, but I saw it in your face when you looked at the picture. And I can tell from your reaction just now, when I told you he was dead. So you can have a little chat with me now, or you can tell it to the police later, but either way, you're going to have to talk to somebody eventually. Why can't we make this easy?"

The old man's shoulders drooped, and he seemed to age twenty years right in front of me. The wind ruffled his gray hair, and he put a hand up to smooth it. He wiped at the corner of his mouth with the sleeve of an alpaca coat, then hawked up a lunger and spat it on the ground at his feet.

"Come inside, then," he said, defeated, "if there's no deterring you from deviling me."

We crossed the parking lot and went inside the building, the interior of which was every bit as drab and uninspiring as the outside. In the front room a young man sat beneath a large color photomural of a thatched cottage somewhere in Ireland. He was large and beefy and flame-haired, his thick neck ballooning out over the collar of his white dress shirt, his cherubic, pink-cheeked face marred by a broken and badly set nose that made him look better suited to wrestling beer kegs on the back of a Budweiser truck than manning a reception desk in a real estate office. His face had one of those mean and sulky looks I was willing to bet was perpetual. There was another young man, almost as big and twice as mean-looking, standing beside him with a clipboard— and then I knew who would have responded to Con McCardle's whistle. Receptionist-slash-bodyguard. And who knew what else.

The kid leaped to his feet when we walked in and, practically tugging on his forelock, said good morning to his employer. But McCardle didn't even break stride, simply rasping out, "I'm not to be disturbed, Francis," and walked past him into an inner room.

The office wall looked like a photo gallery. There were nearly a hundred framed black-and-white eight-by-tens of McCardle grinning beside Bill Clinton, Lyndon Johnson, Al Gore, Hubert Humphrey, Jimmy Carter, and Walter Mondale; former Ohio senators John Glenn and Howard Metzenbaum; the mayor; former congressmen Louis Stokes and his late brother, former Cleveland mayor Carl Stokes; and almost all of the local incumbent Democrats, including Judge Maureen Hartigan and her late husband.

In the center of the wall, in a place of honor and almost shimmering like an illuminated medieval manuscript under a ceiling-mounted pin-spot all its own, was a gold-framed enlargement of what seemed to be a candid snapshot of a much younger Con McCardle and John Fitzgerald Kennedy, the nation's only Irish Catholic president. In the picture McCardle appeared proudly and blissfully drunk, and JFK, looking at someone or something off-camera, seemed amused.

Cornelius McCardle obviously had been around a long time and was on intimate terms with a lot of pretty heavy people, and the gallery was more than a testament to that fact. It was a none-too-subtle and intimidating declaration of power. McCardle knew the heavy hitters who could swing the bat for the fences, and wanted to make sure everyone realized it.

He dropped into the chair behind his desk and sat there for almost a minute, chin on his chest and looking quite sad. After a while he seemed to regain a little of the starch in his spine and lifted his head to confront me. "I have exactly five minutes to spend with you, young man," he said, pointing his jaw at me like the prow of a clipper ship. "*Some* of us have to do an honest day's work."

"I like that 'young man' part, Mr. McCardle."

"Don't flatter yourself. At my age, everybody seems young. What do you want with me?"

"I'm here to find out about Bill Poduska."

He put his head down like a bull getting ready to charge. "All right, so I knew him. I know a lot of people."

"Why did you tell me you didn't?"

"Because it was none of your damn business!"

"Did you know he was dead?"

"Now, how in the hell would I know that until you come up to me out there and blurted it out so brutally?" His eyes were hollow and dark with pain. "It was a shock to me. I'm still in shock."

I believed him. "How did you happen to know him?"

He didn't reply right away, but his rapid eye movement hinted that he might be quickly reviewing his options. "I know a lot of people," he said again. I suppose he realized that was a nonanswer, so he added, "He did some work for me from time to time."

"What kind of work?"

"Whatever I asked him to. He wasn't on the payroll here—it was strictly on an as-needed basis." His bristly brows lowered into a frown. "You know, a lotta these young fellas today, they don't have a real trade or a real job, and they have a certain aversion to anything they have to put their backs into or dirty their hands on. They make money wherever they can, from all different sorts of people. And for a lot of—employers—it's cheaper to use them when they're needed instead of putting them on the books, with all the insurance and the withholding and the paperwork and the bullshit from the Department of Human Resources in Washington. Well, that's the way it was with Pazuska."

I wondered if his mangling of Poduska's name was deliberate, trying to make me think he hardly knew him at all, or whether he was just one of those people who as a matter of course mispronounce anything with more than two syllables. I decided to believe the latter; he'd been far too stunned when I told him Poduska was dead to have resorted to any calculated subterfuge.

Or maybe he was even craftier than I thought he was.

"When's the last time you talked to him?"

He shrugged. "Last week—I don't remember which day exactly. He called in, wanted to know if there was anything going on, but I didn't have anything for him. He needed money, I suppose." His upper lip curled. "A man like that, he always needs money."

Last week. That meant that when Poduska called Con McCardle, he had already left Maureen Hartigan's home and Cathleen's bed and checked into the motel where he'd eventually been found.

"What do you mean by 'a man like that'?"

"A man with no real profession. He was a pieceworker. God rest his troubled soul."

"Who's Dennis McShane?" I said.

McCardle gasped audibly and his head snapped up, instantly on the alert. His stare was fierce. "Dennis McShane," he repeated. "What does Dennis McShane have to do with Bill Pazuska?"

"Bill Poduska," I said, giving the dead man's last name special emphasis, "called a Dennis McShane in New York City several times. I wondered, McShane being an Irish name and all, whether you might know him."

"You think I know everyone in the world with an Irish name?"

"No, sir. But you knew William Poduska. And Poduska somehow knew and was calling Dennis McShane. It's only logical to wonder, isn't it, that there might be a connection?"

"How do you know he called McShane?"

"Telephone records," I said. "From Judge Hartigan's house and from—somebody else's, too."

"Somebody else's? Who else's?"

I shrugged.

"It was the Torrence girl, wasn't it?" He ran a hand over his eyes. "Ah, for the love of Jesus! I warned him not to fool around with her. Too close to home. But he wasn't in the vein of listening to his elders. He didn't even show me that much respect. I don't mean to speak ill of the dead, you understand, but young Billy never was the sharpest knife in the drawer. He thought too much with his weenie. I usually make it a point to never completely trust a man who thinks with his weenie. He's too easily distracted from business."

"What business?"

He rapped his fist softly but firmly on his desk. "The poor, dumb son of a bitch," he said, talking as much to himself as to me. "Making long-distance calls from other people's houses like that so the phone records could be traced. To save a pitiful couple of dollars." His head wagged from side to side. "At the end of the day, he was nothing but a small-timer and a womanizer, damn his eyes—that disgusts me, a married man like him. And he was a conniver, too—I should have known that from the beginning and said good-bye to him."

"What do you mean?"

He shook his head. "It doesn't matter, now. None of it matters. He's gone now. Let's let the dead rest."

"We can't do that, Mr. McCardle. He didn't just pass away in his sleep. He was shot to death. And somebody beat him up a day before that, maybe even a different somebody. The police are involved now, and it's a homicide case so they're not going to let it slide."

"I certainly don't know anything about a homicide. The boy was my . . . my friend. I didn't kill him—I had no reason to. If anything, I'd like to find out who did this terrible thing to him even more than you would."

"I believe that, Mr. McCardle. But the police might not, and before long they're going to come around asking you all sorts of questions. Given your position in the Irish community and the

Democratic party in this city, they might be pretty embarrassing ones. So maybe if you lay all your cards on the table and tell me exactly what's going on here, what 'business' you're referring to, I can help you."

He drew himself up haughtily—again, the bantam rooster puffing out his chest. "It'll be a black day when Cornelius McCardle needs the help of some Polack private dick."

"Slovenian, not Polish. And maybe this is a black day, because from where I sit, you're in a corner."

One side of his mouth curled into a sneer. "Looking to fatten your wallet here, Jacovich?"

"Not at all. Everything isn't about money."

"*You* say."

"Yes, I do say. So, like the drinks the other night, Mr. McCardle, this one's on me. And by the way, if you want my help, you can call me Milan. Or Mr. Jacovich, if you prefer. But not just Jacovich. You say you want and expect to be treated with respect—well, so do I. That's just the way it is."

"Oh it is, is it?"

"Yes, it is."

"You fancy yourself a tough guy, do you?"

"How bad do you want to find out?"

He looked at me for a long time, taking my measure. For a moment I thought he might blow his little whistle to summon Francis and his ugly buddy. Instead, he inhaled deeply, and the air seemed to make him grow and expand. "All right, then, *Mister* Jacovich. Have yourself a seat there." He pointed to the desk opposite his chair. "And let's see if we can both put our cards on the table."

CHAPTER TEN

I don't know you from Adam's off ox, *Mister* Jacovich," Cornelius McCardle said. "Except by reputation, of course. And to be perfectly frank with you, I'm loath to tell you all my personal business. If I'm going to have to deal with the law anyway, I don't see where it profits me to talk to you at all. So it's incumbent upon you to convince me of that, first. You start laying your own cards face up where I can see them, and after that we'll just have to see."

He was good, McCardle—a tough negotiator who didn't scare easily. It was no wonder he'd risen to the position of power and respect that he now enjoyed in the Cleveland Irish community. I admired him even as he frustrated me. "What is it you want to know?"

"I should think that'd be obvious," he said. "Where do you fit in all this? You were looking for Pazuska. Why?"

"For a client."

"And that client would be . . . ?"

"Confidential," I said. "You know that."

"Ah, confidential. So you tell me nothing, and I spill my guts to you—is that how it works?"

"You said William Poduska was one of those people with no regular job. You were right. He was an active penny-ante confidence man, whatever else he did for you. My client was a victim of one of his scams, and engaged me to find him and perhaps recoup some of the financial losses."

"You still haven't named your client, though, have you? Look,

Mr. Jacovich, you're asking me for a lot, and I'm damned if I'll give it to you if I don't know who I'm dealing with."

I wet my lips; the air in the office was dry and stuffy. Maureen Hartigan wanted my discretion—but someone had been murdered, and the old rules had been tossed in the trash can. Her name was bound to come out somewhere. And from all I could glean, especially from the photo on the wall, Cornelius McCardle was her friend and supporter. I finally decided that giving up her name was a risk I had to take.

"I'm working for Judge Hartigan," I said, and the saying of it was hard and bitter for me. "And that goes no further than this room."

The shaggy, flyaway brows that had been overshadowing his eyes took a leap upward on his forehead. "Maureen Hartigan," he breathed. "Holy Mary, mother of God."

"I know she's your friend," I said, "so I'm hoping you'll find it in your heart to help me out here."

He didn't answer me. He was deep in thought.

"I trusted you, Mr. McCardle. Those are my cards—face up on the table. Now I'd like to see some of yours."

He nodded. "I'm sure you would, but I'm calculating things here. My business is private, so I'm calculating what it is you need to know."

"That's fair."

He rubbed his right eye, blinked both of them, and shifted his weight in his chair, obviously having come to some sort of decision.

"It's no secret that I have many interests outside the business of Shamrock Homes," he said. "Political interests, some of them. And not all of them having to do with Cleveland or Cuyahoga County or even the United States of America. You follow me?"

"I do."

"Not that I'm not as good and loyal an American as anyone could find," he said, and actually put his right hand over his heart as if he were pledging allegiance. "I'll stack my patriotism up against anyone's, yours included. But I'm an Irishman, too. My parents came from there, from Mayo, and Irish home rule, the freedom from oppression, the well-being of Ireland are of utmost concern to me."

"I've heard that," I said.

He put his head back and looked at me down his nose. "Oh you have, have you?"

"Yep."

"What else have you heard?"

"Sinn Fein," I said.

He seemed impressed with my knowledge. "And where, pray tell, did you hear that?"

"I get around."

He smiled unpleasantly. "And *I've* heard *that*. Well, it's no matter—you don't have to tell me. Suffice it to say that I have my causes, and being as I'm not as young as I once was, I sometimes employ people who assist me. One of those people was William Pazuska."

"Po-dus-ka," I said, finally getting irritated over his resolute mispronunciation of the dead man's name. "But he wasn't an Irishman."

"Sadly, no," Con McCardle said. "But he was married to a nice Irish girl, so he had a smattering of understanding and empathy. Also—and don't you underestimate the power of this for a single minute—he was money-hungry, willing to do almost anything to turn a dollar, and it suited my purposes from time to time to engage him as a messenger. A courier."

"Of what?"

He waved a hand at me as if swatting at a mildly annoying fly. "Let's just say they were things too sensitive or important to trust to the U.S. Postal Service. Otherwise, it's of no importance to our discussion."

"It might be, Mr. McCardle," I said. "Especially if he took it into his head to keep something valuable you'd entrusted him to deliver and perhaps sell it to a higher-bidding third party."

He bristled, shaking his head. "That never happened. Mainly because he wouldn't have had the guts."

"Are you sure?"

"I'd be the first to know. And it never happened."

"Of course, you'd say that even if it had, knowing that you or someone close to you had taken revenge on him."

He screwed up his face as though he'd just smelled something foul. "You have a very bad habit of suggesting that I'm a liar, Mr.

Jacovich," he said. "This makes twice. I don't take kindly to that at all."

"When I showed you Poduska's picture Saturday night, you did lie to me about not knowing him."

He drew himself up haughtily. "That's because I didn't owe you the courtesy of the truth. I still don't, for that matter. Truths and trust have to be earned, and you've not quite done that yet." He scowled at me. "But for what it's worth, I'm giving it to you now anyway. Because someone killed the boy."

"That makes a difference?"

"It does," he said. "He was married to Donalene Mullen, whose father John Mullen was one of my dearest friends, God rest his soul. A stonecutter, by trade. A fine and gifted craftsman. You can still see many of his headstones in St. Joseph's Cemetery, in Holy Cross, even a few out on the east side in Lake View where all the rich folks are buried."

"Is Dennis McShane one of the people Poduska sometimes made deliveries to? In New York City?"

He folded his hands on the desk in front of him the way most of us over forty were taught to do in first grade. "All right then, since we've come along this far. Dennis McShane is my good friend."

"You seem to have a lot of good friends."

"I do," he said almost defensively. "And Mr. McShane is one of them who shares some of my commitments and passions. So yes, he knew . . ." He stopped, labored manfully to get his tongue around the Bohemian mouthful, like a toddler learning to talk. "Dennis knew Poduska."

"When I first met you in the Shebeen, I asked you about some aliases that Poduska had been using. Irish names. James O'Dowd and Brian McFall."

McCardle shook his large head from side to side. "I told you then and I'll tell you now again. I never heard of those names." He pointed a thick, crooked finger at me, and I could see that the top joint was arthritically swollen and bent. "You'd do well to remember that I wasn't the boy's principal employer. If he did two jobs in a month for me, that was a busy month, and he didn't support himself off me. You say he was running con games on the side—perhaps that's the area in which you should be looking, although I doubt too many of his victims would readily come forward and admit their stupidity. Wasn't it W. C. Fields who once observed that you can't cheat an honest man? People who get conned usually do so because of their own culpability or greed. Plus I'm hardly the only one who used him as an errand boy."

My stomach fluttered. I leaned forward in my chair and gripped the edge of his desk. "Who else?"

"Well now, how in the hell should I know?" he said with some irritation. "He didn't tell me his business."

"Yet you admit you trusted him with some pretty sensitive assignments."

"I did trust him, fool that I was. Because of Donalene."

"That's how you met him in the first place? Because he married Donalene Mullen?"

"I was at their wedding," he said, nodding. "Shortly after they were married, Donalene called me and asked if I might not have something for the boy to do that could bring in a dollar or two. Believe me, it wasn't for him I took him on—it was for her."

"Yet you didn't know who else he was running errands for?"

"There are some things about your friends or acquaintances that you're happier not knowing. Let's just say that anyone in Cleveland who dabbles in things they might not want to see written up in the *Plain Dealer* on Monday morning, they probably knew and perhaps had occasion to employ Bill Pazuska. Poduska," he corrected himself hurriedly.

And then he stood up abruptly, pushing off the desk with both hands, elbows splayed. "There it is, *Mister* Jacovich. We've seen one another's cards, although I'm quite sure I haven't gotten to see all of yours, any more than you've seen all of mine. And I hope that convinces you that I had no motive to harm the Poduska boy. On the contrary, as he was someone who occasionally was valuable to me, I had good reasons for keeping him healthy. My associates knew that, and they didn't kill him, either, or they'd be answering to me personally." He swiped a hand across his eyes. "And now I'll repeat what I said to you in the Shebeen. It's my fondest wish to see the back of you for good and all."

I stood up.

"If you come around this office any time in the future," he

warned, "I'll ask young Francis out there at the desk to show you the door. And he'll bring a few of his friends, too."

"He'll have to," I said.

He seemed amused. "Ah, yes, that's right. A tough guy."

"When I'm squeezed."

"You'll do well to remember that I don't like being squeezed either," he said, his face turning a darker red. "And so I'll say to you that if there are any legal repercussions from our little conversation this morning, there will be consequences. Do you follow me? *Mister* Jacovich?"

I got the idea, all right. Whatever help and support I had received from Cornelius McCardle thus far was all that would be forthcoming. And although I wasn't too worried about young musclebound Francis or anyone else he might bring along with him to do McCardle's strong-arm bidding, I figured that any further attempts to extract information from the old Irish warhorse would be futile.

But he had given me something that might be useful. I'm not sure whether it was by accident or obliquely by design, but he had told me that anyone in Greater Cleveland who might dabble in things they wouldn't necessarily want to be made public knew Bill Poduska.

And that pointed me squarely toward the number two "dabbler" on the depth chart of northeast Ohio's biggest and best-organized mob family—my old pal and Cathleen's former lover, Victor Gaimari.

I sighed. Everything shady in Cleveland seems to wind up pointing to Victor Gaimari. He had become my bane, my bugbear, like a distant relative you'd love to disavow because he exposes himself in public places and who somehow seems to pop up at inopportune moments to bedevil you. If Victor or his uncle, Don Giancarlo D'Allessandro, don't have their fingers sticking into something, chances are it isn't worth poking in the first place.

I crossed the street and got back into my car. My vow to eschew cigarette smoking while I drive was wavering; I usually needed some sort of pacifier to soothe my soul before tackling Victor. But

I was still enjoying the new-car smell of my Sunbird, and decided to stick to my vow. Before I started the engine, I pulled out my cellphone, flipped it open, and dialed his number. By now I knew it by heart; sometimes I think I ought to include it on my speed dialer.

There was genuine warmth in Victor's voice when the operator at his stock brokerage finally put me through to him. For reasons I have yet to figure out, Victor likes me very much, and Don Giancarlo truly believes I hung the moon. I'm an ex-cop, a law-and-order guy right down to my toes, and they're organized crime. Yet I know they count me as a friend.

I don't understand it.

Nor do I completely understand why I like Victor, too.

"It's so good to hear from you, Milan," he said, that peculiar, high-pitched voice of his strong through the receiver. "It's been far too long. I miss your company." Victor is a big man with a deep, broad chest, and I have no idea where that little girl voice comes from. Don't think, though, that just because he's Italian and the de facto boss of what might charitably be described as the Cleveland mob he talks like a bit player from a Martin Scorsese movie. Victor is highly educated and has culture to spare.

And class. I always have to cede him that.

He's a very classy guy, Victor.

"Victor, I've got a problem," I said.

There was amusement in his tone. "You usually do when you call me. What's up?"

"Can we get together sometime today?"

"How about lunch? It's nearly lunchtime."

"I don't feel like sitting in a public place discussing this, okay?"

"That works out perfectly," he said. "Come on up to the brokerage. You haven't been here for a long while, so you couldn't know that we've remodeled the offices and put in a restaurant-style kitchen. Every day one of the people in the office cooks. It saves time and money for everyone, and it's kind of a bonding experience for the staff. Would you like to join us today? We usually start serving at noon."

Only Victor would think of installing an industrial kitchen

in a brokerage firm. He never does anything you'd expect him to—that's why he's as successful in his legitimate business as he is in the illegitimate one.

And socially successful, too. Good-looking, charming, and cultured, and very rich, Victor Gaimari is one of Cleveland's social lions, and has cut a wide swath through the ladies of the city.

"I'll be there," I said. I folded up the phone and put it in my pocket, then started the car and headed for downtown and Victor's office in Terminal Tower on Public Square.

Bigger buildings have risen in Cleveland since the fifty-two-story Terminal Tower was built in 1930, but the Tower still remains the most familiar Cleveland landmark, and in my opinion the most beautiful, the finger of its tall spire pointing toward the sun. Victor Gaimari's stock brokerage was on the eleventh floor.

His receptionist didn't like me. An efficient, grandmotherly woman, she'd never gotten over the fact that I had once punched her employer in the nose and he'd bled all over the office carpet. She has never quite trusted me since then. Whenever I walk in the door now, she doesn't look at me or greet me, but simply turns her head away to show me her disdain and picks up the phone to let Victor know I've arrived.

I've seen her many times over the years, but I don't even know her name. Funny, isn't it, how people can become semiregular fixtures in our lives and yet we know virtually nothing about them?

Victor came out into the reception area to greet me, simultaneously shaking my hand, hugging me, and kissing my cheek. The older he gets, the more he resembles the Latin-lover movie star of the forties, Cesar Romero, with his deep tan and his neatly trimmed mustache. Victor was perhaps an inch shorter and a lot slimmer than I, and the expensive suit he wore—today black with a discreet blue windowpane thread—wouldn't have been found hanging on any retail rack. I don't think I've ever seen Victor wear the same suit twice.

"You're looking well, Milan," he said. "Staying out of trouble?"

"If I stayed out of trouble, I'd be out of business."

"Ha ha," he said. I've never actually seen Victor laugh. "Ha ha" was as close as he ever comes.

"Follow me," he said. "I want to show you the kitchen. We installed it about four months ago, and it's the best money we've ever spent."

He led me down a long corridor that was aromatic with cooking smells—onions and spices and garlic. Although a strange thing to find in a brokerage house, the smells were somehow welcoming and intriguing. The kitchen had been installed in what used to be a storage room, complete with a large butcher's-block table; and a six-burner range, two ovens, a large sink, a dishwasher, and a refrigerator in which a good-sized man could have stood up easily, all in gleaming stainless steel.

Standing at the range was a young fellow with curly black hair. His glasses had small lenses and wire rims, and he was dressed like a rainmaker of the nineties in a French blue shirt with the sleeves neatly turned up, red power tie, and wildly patterned suspenders. The white chef's apron he wore didn't quite go with the rest of the ensemble.

"Milan Jacovich, this is Rich DiRosso," Victor said. "One of our best producers and our chef for today."

I shook hands with the young man. "This kitchen is amazing, Victor."

"Our clients seem to think so," he said, smiling. "Now, whenever they want an appointment, they always angle for sometime around midday so they can eat." He went over to the range and deeply inhaled the aroma coming from a large pot of sauce, fanning the air toward his nose with a neatly manicured hand. "Mmm," he said, "if this tastes as good as it smells, Rich, I can hardly wait."

"I hope you'll like it, Victor," the kid said. "You too, Mr. Jacovich. It's my mom's recipe."

"Every Italian dish in the world started out as somebody's mom's recipe," Victor said. "I'll be sure to send her some flowers." He took my elbow and guided me back out into the hallway.

"We usually all eat in the conference room in shifts," he said. "But I have an idea that what you want to talk to me about isn't for general knowledge, so I've arranged to have lunch served in my office. If that's okay."

"Perfect," I said.

Victor's office was sparely but exquisitely furnished. Near

the big picture window, which faced north, overlooking Public Square with a view of the lake beyond, was a small table which had been laid for two—linen cloth and napkins, sterling silver, fine delft. A bottle of good Chianti, already opened to give it time to breathe, complemented the two crystal wineglasses.

A setting fit for a seduction.

That was apt, I thought wryly, because in the long and sometimes stormy history of our relationship, Victor always manages to seduce me—with his friendship and cooperation and charm, even while I loathed the things he stood for.

Hate the sin but love the sinner, I suppose.

"And your uncle?" I said as we sat down opposite each other at the table. "He's well, I hope?"

"He's eighty-three years old, and he's not as well as he would be if he took better care of himself. Of course, Mrs. Sordetto rides herd on him, making sure he eats properly and doesn't drink too much dago red, but he cheats whenever he can."

Mrs. Sordetto was Don Giancarlo D'Allessandro's longtime companion, Regina, the widow of one of the don's old associates, who had perished in a car bombing on the east side more than twenty-five years earlier. Whether that assassination had borne the fingerprints of D'Allessandro's fine Italian hand had been a matter of conjecture for years, but nonetheless some six months later the widow Sordetto had moved into his home and has been there ever since.

"Please give him my best," I said.

"I will. He'll be sorry he missed you." Victor picked up a telephone from the corner of the table, pressed a button, and spoke into it briefly but kindly. "Angela, we're ready for lunch as soon as you are."

He hung up the phone and settled back in his big leather executive chair. "So, Milan, what stroke of good fortune brings you to break bread at my table this afternoon? Nothing serious, I hope."

"It's serious to somebody. A man was murdered in a motel room out by the airport a few days ago. His name was William Poduska."

He didn't even frown. "I'd heard that, yes."

"You knew him?"

"No, not really. I may have met him sometime in the past, but I frankly don't remember it. I know *of* him, though."

"How?"

He gave me a smile that dripped canary feathers. "How do I know *anything* that goes on in Cleveland, Milan? I just know."

"Point taken," I said.

"Poduska is a small-time punk. Was, I suppose I should say. He ran a few small-time con games around town—all penny-ante crap, nothing major. With a little hard work and elbow grease he could have made more money at a regular day job. But working legitimate just wasn't his style. He preferred being a chump who worked for chump change. He was also for hire to anyone who needed him to run errands. He was a bagman."

"For whom?"

"As I said, anyone who'd pay him. To pick up and deliver slightly tainted cash—bribes or kickbacks, even drug money on occasion, as I think I heard somewhere." He leaned forward. "That's just a rumor, as far as I'm concerned. You know how antidrug we are around here."

And that was the truth. It was Don Giancarlo's hatred of narcotics and the illegal trade's effect on children that kept the Cleveland area relatively drug-free until well into the nineteen-eighties, long past the time when the cores of other cities had deteriorated into shooting galleries.

"Poduska was a drug mule?"

Victor shook his head. "I don't think so. As far as I ever heard, he never touched the actual drugs, neither to use them nor to deliver them. I don't think anyone thought he was smart enough to handle drugs without getting himself caught."

"Do you know that he sometimes worked for Con McCardle?"

"Old Con's name is in the mix, yes. But McCardle doesn't fool around with drugs, if that's what you're suggesting. Never has. What he does get involved in is putting the arm on his friends and associates to raise operating capital locally for the IRA—specifically Sinn Fein. I believe he sometimes used Poduska to deliver that money to the big IRA mavens in New York. My guess is that the funds were used to purchase weapons."

"A guy named Dennis McShane, perhaps?"

"We don't pay much attention to international politics. At least not Irish politics, so I couldn't tell you for sure. The name Dennis McShane does ring a bell, but it's a distant one."

"You said no one thought Poduska was smart enough to handle drugs. Do you suppose he was stupid enough to take some of the money he was supposed to deliver to Sinn Fein in New York and put it in his own pocket, and maybe that's why somebody took him out?"

"Nobody is *that* dumb, Milan."

"I'd hope not," I said. "But somebody iced him."

"Sadly, yes."

"And somebody knocked him around pretty badly, too. At least twenty-four hours before he died."

Victor looked surprised, and I'm ashamed at how much pleasure it gave me. He always knows everything, and it pleased me to spring something on him he hadn't heard before.

"Interesting," is all he said. Maybe he would have expanded on that, but a pretty young woman wearing the skirt to a tailored blue suit and a crisp white blouse came in rolling a bar cart with our food spread across it.

"Ah, Angela," Victor said. "Right on time. This is Milan Jacovich. A good friend of ours."

"Hello, Mr. Jacovich," she said, dimpling prettily. "I hope you're hungry."

"The aroma alone would give anyone an appetite," I said.

As Angela proceeded to serve us, Victor said, "Angela's interning here. She goes to your alma mater, Milan. Kent State. She's a grad student in economics."

Lunch was chicken breast with a honey-mustard glaze, and angel-hair pasta with squid ink in an aromatic pesto sauce, accompanied by the familiar football-shaped rolls that were unmistakably the work of Cleveland's own Orlando Baking Company. Victor poured the wine, and we clinked glasses. "To old friends," he said.

The wine was full-bodied and assertive, a perfect balance with the food, and I dug in with gusto.

"Speaking of old friends," he said, "I assume you're asking about Bill Poduska because of Maureen Hartigan."

I stopped eating and put down my fork.

"Cathleen called me last week, way before Poduska was killed, and filled me in on what was going on, although the bad-boy name she told me was Brian McFall. I was the one who suggested her mother call you."

I didn't say anything for a moment. Then I reached for my wineglass. "I'm a little stunned," I said.

"That I know about Poduska and the Hartigans?"

I nodded.

"I can't imagine why. You know that Cathleen and I are close. It's only natural that when something like this comes up to trouble her family, I'd be the first one she'd call."

"I know. But I feel like a damn fool walking in here and telling you something you already knew."

"I didn't know Poduska was McFall until I heard he got killed. Then I did some checking around. I actually put it together only last night."

"So I'm a day late and a dollar short. Literally."

"A day late, maybe," he said, smiling broadly. "Only short about thirty-five cents. But now Poduska's dead—he doesn't need to be found anymore. So as delighted as I am to see you, why are you here today? Except to sample Mama DiRosso's amazing pesto sauce, that is."

"Poduska stole some things from Judge Hartigan and from Hugh Cochran. They'd like to get them back."

"That's understandable. Maybe the grieving widow is someone you should talk to."

"I've already done that, Victor. Only neither of us knew she was a widow at the time."

"I'm impressed. You do good work."

"According to the police, Poduska had written my name on a telephone pad by his motel bed," I said, "which means that somebody contacted him and told him I was looking for him. And that gives me a nagging suspicion that in some way I haven't figured out yet, I was the one who got him killed."

He frowned, thinking about it for a little while, staring into his food. "Possible, but doubtful."

"Why?"

"Poduska was a pretty sorry excuse for a human being. A scrounger. A bottom feeder. He was also a scam artist, and I don't like that. He preyed on innocent people, sometimes people who couldn't afford it. That stinks." He patted his lips with the linen napkin. "And he preyed on women, too. He was an incorrigible womanizer."

"Victor, no offense intended, but so are you."

"Ha ha," he said again. "Yes, I do enjoy the company of beautiful women. As do you, so don't get moralistic on me. But with a difference. Number one, I never lied to anyone just to get them into bed. And number two, I'm a bachelor; Poduska was a married man. Not only did he screw around, but he didn't really work for a living to support his wife, and that's the first responsibility for a man, wouldn't you say? But he just hung around sucking the asses of important people, hoping they'd throw him a crumb. Fortunately for him and his wife, quite a few of them did."

"Anybody in Warren?"

He blinked. "Excuse me?"

"Warren, Ohio. Do you know of him doing any bottom-feeding with any of your associates in Warren?"

All of a sudden Victor's face seemed to close up; the smile remained, but there was no longer very much warmth behind it. "My associates in Warren?" He pronounced the words carefully.

"Victor, don't insult my intelligence," I said. "I know, and practically everyone else knows, too, that twenty or so years ago a lot of the old mob guys from Cleveland, guys who were very highly placed in your uncle's extended 'family,' retired and moved east to Mahoning and Trumbull counties—Warren and Youngstown and Niles, places like that."

"You're right. That's no secret," Victor said. "But why would Poduska have anything to do with them?"

"I don't know that he did; that's why I'm asking. But I know he made several calls to Warren a few weeks before he died. The number showed up on a telephone bill. I'd like to find out who he was calling."

"Why don't you just call the number and find out, then?"

"I'm going to," I said. "But I don't like surprises. If I'm going to be stepping on the toes of some heavy-duty people, I want to know about it."

"And you want me to clear the way for you," Victor said, making it a flat statement. "You're going to ask me to make a few phone calls and tell them it's all right to cooperate with you."

I started getting a fluttery feeling in the pit of my stomach. "Was Poduska's involvement with them so serious that you'd need to do that?"

"Frankly, I don't know what he did for them. It was none of my business." He put some weight behind the last sentence.

"Meaning it's none of mine, either."

He chuckled. "The key word is 'retired,' Milan. Those gentlemen are all elderly, in their eighties or more. Playing bocce is about as strenuous as they get. If they were dealing with Poduska, I doubt it was anything terribly illegal."

"Then why the secrecy?"

"Because of the nature of their business when they were younger, they lived their whole lives in secrecy, and I suppose it's become a habit with them."

"Does that mean nobody will talk to me?"

"Let me make a few phone calls," Victor said. "I'm making no guarantees, of course."

"Understood."

"If you do get a chance to sit down with anyone, you'll do well to treat them with the same kind of respect and kindness you show my uncle." He took another sip of wine. "Remember who they are."

"I'd be unlikely to forget, Victor."

CHAPTER ELEVEN

The widow Poduska's face was a study in grief, like that of the Virgin Mary of Michelangelo's *Pieta*. Her dark auburn hair was down and loose now, reaching well below her waist, and she was wearing a black long-sleeved blouse and greenish corduroy pants. She chain-smoked Camels relentlessly and was gulping hot black coffee as if she were suffering from either severe windchill or a terrible thirst.

She wasn't looking at me; she really hadn't done so since inviting me to sit down. Her gaze was off in the distance somewhere, a place far beyond the walls of her living room. Memories and regrets flickered across her face like images on a silent movie screen, jerky and blurred and indistinct.

"I feel like I don't know what hit me, Mr. Jacovich," she said, rhythmically rocking back and forth in a chair that was not designed to be rocked in, hugging her breasts and hunching her shoulders as if expecting a blow. "I'm still in shock. I don't know what to do or where to turn."

"I'm sorry for your troubles," I said in the traditional Irish way. It was the third time I'd said it, or something close to it, since I'd walked into her house five minutes earlier.

"It was just so unexpected," she went on, as though I'd not spoken. "You just aren't prepared for something like this. Murder and shooting." She looked wildly about, as if murder and shooting, like the Furies, were flying around her head, dive-bombing her. "It's something you read about in the newspaper, but you never really believe it could happen to you. Who would want to kill my husband? He didn't have an enemy in the world."

Except perhaps the Hartigan females and Hugh Cochran and Judith Torrence and all the other people he'd scammed and victimized, all the women into whose beds he'd fibbed and charmed his way, whoever they were.

"The police—that Detective Matusen? He told me Bill had done all sorts of terrible things." She put her palms together in front of her as though she were praying. "I don't believe it, Mr. Jacovich. I can't allow myself to believe it. He was a *salesman*. I know he was a salesman . . ."

"You thought he was on the road for the past several weeks?" I said. "You had no idea he was right down the road in Cleveland?"

She shook her head almost violently. "No. He told me he was on an extended trip through Illinois and Michigan and Wisconsin. I had no reason to doubt him." Her mouth turned into a tight straight line, something the artist had quickly added almost as an afterthought when the portrait was already finished. "He'd never lied to me before. At least, not that I knew of."

That was some qualifier. I couldn't help wondering how many other dalliances there had been in the late William Poduska's resume besides Judith Torrence and Cathleen Hartigan. I doubted they were the only ones, and so he had probably lied to his wife many times.

"All the years you were married, didn't you ever see any of his paychecks or pay stubs?"

"No. Bill was the man of the house. He took care of all the finances; he filed the income tax return. I didn't know anything about it—I just signed it. He used to give me an allowance every month." She filled her lungs with smoke and then let it out with a shudder. "In cash."

The telephone rang. It was on the end table near the sofa and had a very loud ringer, a high-pitched birdcall that cut through the air like a policeman's whistle, and so the sound was an almost shocking interruption. Donalene Poduska pushed herself to her feet and crossed the room, nearly staggering. She put her hand on the receiver and then looked at the caller identification box. Her brow furrowed, she shrugged, and came back to her chair. After five total rings, I heard an answering machine click on.

"That was the *Plain Dealer*," she explained, sinking into the cushions wearily. "For the fifth time today. That's another thing—the press. They've been bothering me all day. There was even a camera crew out on the lawn this morning from Channel 12, but I wouldn't talk to them, or even come to the door, so finally they went away. I haven't talked to any of them." She looked at me plaintively, needing validation. "I don't think I should have to talk to the reporters, do you?"

"Not if you don't want to."

"Why can't they just let me alone to grieve in peace? Damned vultures!" She put her face in her hands, her fingers muffling several racking sobs.

I fidgeted, finally pulling out a Winston and lighting it. I figured if she was smoking in her living room, she'd have no objection to my following suit. The last thing I wanted to do was grill a woman with difficult questions when she was so obviously grief-stricken. But I had a job to do.

Sometimes I don't like my job very much.

"Mrs. Poduska," I said.

"Donalene," she corrected me through her fingers. "Last time, I asked you to call me Donalene. Remember?"

"Sorry. Donalene. My client believes that your husband took something valuable from her home while he was staying there."

"Bill was no thief!" she proclaimed vigorously, taking her hands away from her face and raising her chin to its highest and most defiant level since we began the conversation.

"I don't know if she thinks he's a thief. But maybe he took something by accident when he was packing up." That sounded lame, even to me.

"What was it?"

"A large manila envelope—full of photographs."

She didn't say anything.

"Have you seen anything like that around here?"

"No, how could I? I told you, Bill hasn't been home for five weeks or so. How could he have left them here?"

"Are you sure he didn't slip into the house while you were out and you didn't even know he'd been here?"

"Why would he have to sneak into his own home?" She lit another cigarette from the glowing end of the one she'd smoked down to a butt. "If he'd come back for a few minutes and I wasn't here, he would have left me a note." Her chin quivered. "He was always leaving me little notes around the house—when he was going to be gone, he'd hide them, so I'd find them one at a time, and that way I wouldn't miss him so much. Sweet notes."

He was a real cuddle-bunny, Poduska.

"Those pictures," she said, "weren't they with him in that. . . that motel?"

"No, they weren't. Didn't he have a room here in the house he used for an office?"

"Yes, the spare bedroom."

"Would you mind if I took a quick glance around in there?"

She looked stricken.

"I won't disturb anything," I said. "I promise."

She used up about thirty seconds of my life making up her mind. Then she said, "I suppose. I don't see what difference it'll make—now." She got out of the chair with effort, as though she'd weighed at least a hundred pounds more than she actually did, and led me down a small hallway. There were three doors: one to the master bedroom, one to the bath, and one to what turned out to be William Poduska's office. That one was the only door that was closed.

Donalene opened it, reached around to turn on the overhead light from a wall switch, and stood aside so I could go in. It was a small room, as spartan as a monk's cell. There was a fiberboard card table set up in the corner, atop which was a beige-colored IBM Selectric that must have been twenty years old, a plastic goosenecked reading lamp, and half a ream of typing paper. A small, cheap bookcase held several telephone directories, a two-volume zip code directory, and a set of AAA travel guides and road maps. A lone, off-white phone sat atop it. In the corner was a two-drawer cardboard filing cabinet, and over that hung a wall calendar—not the kind you'd purchase in a bookstore, with art scenes or cuddly kittens or even swimsuit models, but the strictly utilitarian variety that you might buy at Office Max, with the daily squares big enough to write in your appointments. The calendar displayed the month of August—and this was October.

Otherwise the little room's resemblance to an office was faint. It looked more like a temporary campaign headquarters for a very minor local election, except that there was no computer in evidence, no fax machine, no copier. There was not even a desk. It hardly seemed like the kind of set-up that would be used by a salesman who worked freelance out of his home.

That got me to wondering. Donalene Poduska really had no idea how her husband earned his money. She thought he was a salesman. In addition to being a con man and a messenger boy for people like Cornelius McCardle, maybe he *was* selling something—some contraband commodity that would make it extremely unwise for him to keep written records.

Drugs, maybe? I turned away so Donalene couldn't see what I was doing, and wrote the word down in my notebook followed by a big, fat question mark.

There was a small, square closet, the door open. It seemed to be where William Poduska had stored his winter clothing—there were two parkas, a brown overcoat, four or five wool shirts, and an equal number of plain gray sweatshirts on hangers; several scarves draped over the rod; and on the floor work boots, high-top Nikes, and a pair of old rubber Totes. There was a shelf above, but standing on tiptoes, all I could see on it was a battered Scrabble game, an out-of-date Cleveland Yellow Pages, and a dusty, clip-on sunlamp.

And that was all.

No manila envelope of eight-by-ten glossies of Doyle Hartigan—none that were in plain sight, anyway.

"May I look through the file drawers?" I asked.

Donalene Poduska put an uneasy hand up to her mouth. "I'd really rather you didn't. I'll look through them when I can, and if there is any envelope of photographs in there, I'll let you know, okay?"

The police might come back with a search warrant and look at whatever they wanted to, but as a private investigator, I had no legal right to open the file cabinet drawers and search them without her permission. For all I knew, the envelope of pictures I was looking for was no more than five feet away, but there was no way I could get to it.

"Okay, thanks anyway," I said, frustrated at having come up empty. She crossed her arms on her chest and waited politely for me to step back out into the hallway before she turned the light off and closed the office door.

We went back into the living room and resumed our places. The way she dropped back into her chair, making the cushion go *whumpf,* was like a great tree falling to the woodsman's ax.

I said, "Is there anyplace else in the house those photographs might be, Donalene?"

"I don't know anything about any photographs." Self-pity seemed to shrink her right in front of me, the big overstuffed chair suddenly dwarfing her. "I don't know anything about anything."

"Did Bill have a safe-deposit box?"

She rubbed her eyes with her knuckles, like a toddler who's getting sleepy. "If he did, he never told me about it. I guess there were a lot of things he never bothered sharing with me."

I took the opportunity to observe her closely while she wasn't looking at me. Was it possible that she was so completely ignorant of the man she'd lived with? I suppose there are many marriages like that, full of secrets and hidden agendas, where the two participants live virtually separate lives even while sharing a bed and a bathroom. Everyone has his or her own private life, and there were certainly things I did not tell my ex-wife, Lila, during our marriage—nothing that was really a secret, I suppose, but just things she didn't need to know, like how much I spent for lunch every day or who I'd hoisted a few beers with at Vuk's Tavern on St. Clair Avenue. And there were many things she didn't share with me—especially not her two-year-long affair with Joe Bradac, a kind of annoying wimp we'd both known in high school, who owned a small machine shop in Collinwood and for whom she eventually left me.

But I never kept my business or my financial affairs from her. If something had happened to me, she certainly would have been aware of the existence of insurance policies or a hidden stash of money and valuables in a safe-deposit box. I always took care of my family.

"I'm sorry to be bothering you with these questions at a time like this," I said. "I'm just trying to do what I was paid for."

"Who *is* paying you, anyway? Someone that Bill—one of the people Bill is supposed to have cheated?"

"I'm afraid so," I said.

"Who is it?"

"I can't tell you that."

"Why not?"

"Client confidentiality," I explained. "It doesn't matter, really. My client isn't the one who killed him."

Her head snapped up and she looked at me sharply. "Are you trying to find out who shot my husband?"

"That's police business. Lieutenant McHargue is very good at what she does. They'll find him," I assured her, all at once wondering if the killer was a "him" at all. There might have been several women, seduced and abandoned like Torrence and Cathleen, who didn't wish Bill Poduska well.

"No, they won't," she said, her mouth twisting into a sneer. "He was a criminal, they said. They don't give a damn about him, or who killed him."

"Of course, they do, Donalene. If everyone who's ever done anything they're ashamed of got killed and the police didn't do anything about it, the streets would be deserted."

She shook her head stubbornly. "Justice is for rich people, not poor ones like us." She ground out her cigarette—it was an angry, deliberate gesture, and I wondered whose face she was seeing in the ashtray. "Look, I wish I could help you, but I don't know anything. I'm finding out I didn't even know who my husband was, for God's sake. I'm just very confused right now."

"I understand."

"I don't mean to be impolite, but I think it would be better if you left," she said. "This is all too much for me to handle."

I was strangely touched by her graciousness. We both stood up, and she saw me to the door, both of us looking for a moment too long at the wedding photo, and when she said good-bye it seemed that her jaw was a little firmer and her eyes were hard and glittering. I thought perhaps she was reaching way down inside herself to find some extra strength to get through her bereavement. At least I hoped so.

That evening I found a couple of pork chops hiding in the back of the freezer. I thawed them in the microwave and then baked them for dinner while I boiled a handful of pasta bowties. My apartment used to be my office, and after I moved my business down to the Flats, I hadn't bothered to get myself a dining-room set to go where my desk used to be. So I ate quietly in the kitchen, washing down the chops, and pasta with oil and garlic and cheese, with my habitual Stroh's, and playing an old Stan Kenton big band album which had been digitally remastered to a CD on the boom box in the living room, cranked up loud enough so I could hear it from the kitchen table. I guess I'm a hypocrite; I always get annoyed when teenagers play their rap and hip-hop at full volume, but the fact is, if you're going to listen to Stan Kenton at all, it has to be loud. That incredible brass section with Shorty Rogers on lead trumpet really gets you in the middle of your chest.

I had just finished washing up the dinner dishes and was standing at the kitchen sink drying my hands when Victor Gaimari phoned. He always did have impeccable timing.

"I hope I'm not interrupting anything, Milan."

"Not at all. I've just finished eating."

"How can you have dinner so early, for God's sake?" he said, his tone amused. "It's barbaric."

"I was hungry."

"Even after that lunch?"

"Hey, I'm a big guy."

"I can't imagine eating before it gets dark out."

"It is dark out, Victor—it's almost November."

"You're missing my point, Milan."

"I apologize. But surely you didn't call me just to discuss your disapproval of my proletarian dining habits?"

"Well, no," he said. "But don't think the subject is closed." He cleared his throat. "I did some calling around out in Warren. I want you to know that I really had to tiptoe. Those old guys value their privacy."

"But you came up with a name."

"I did. It wasn't easy. He didn't want to talk to you. I had to put my uncle on the phone to convince him."

Great, I thought. Now I was beholden again not only to Victor, but to the old man, to Don Giancarlo D'Allessandro. It had happened once before, some years back, and when I had returned his favor, I'd nearly gotten myself killed.

"Who is he?"

"I don't know how much good it's going to do you, but here's the name. It's one you'll probably recognize."

I waited while he milked the moment for all it was worth. Victor has a flair for the dramatic.

"It's Dante Ruggiero," he finally said.

Oh boy.

It was a name I recognized, all right. Dante Ruggiero—formerly *Don* Dante Ruggiero—was a contemporary of D'Allessandro's, somewhere in his eighties now. Nearly thirty years earlier there had been quite a power struggle between the two of them for dominance in the "family," one that D'Allessandro had eventually won.

The coup had been bloodless; Ruggiero's people had agreed to quietly fade from sight, and the don himself had moved to Warren, some ninety miles east of Cleveland near the Pennsylvania state line, where he spent his forced semiretirement running a wholesale Italian food importing business and overseeing the operation of several massage parlors on the side. Warren, otherwise a nice small city in a pretty part of the state, is probably the massage-parlor capital of Ohio—there are even billboards advertising them on the sides of the freeway.

"That's a pretty heavy name, Victor," I said. "What does Dante Ruggiero have to do with Bill Poduska?"

"Milan, you and I both know that Poduska used to do . . . uh, odd jobs for a lot of people. I managed to discover Mr. Ruggiero has used his services on more than one occasion."

"Whom did you discover that from?"

"Not really important, is it?" His tone was sunny, but the meaning was clear—don't ask unnecessary questions. Victor is always a man who plays his cards very close to his vest. Whatever information I'd ever gotten from him in the past had been strictly on a "need-to-know" basis.

"I suppose it isn't," I said. "Exactly what did Dante Ruggiero use Poduska's services for?"

"I didn't ask. As I said, he's pretty closemouthed. All the old-timers are—even my uncle. They haven't quite figured out that life is different now and we operate in very different ways."

"Progress," I said.

"Yes," he said, "but most of the older ones don't see it that way. At any rate, we were finally able to persuade Don Ruggiero to sit down and talk with you. I don't guarantee how open he's going to be about his private affairs, but at least you've got a foot in the door."

"Yes."

"And that's a whole lot better than nothing at all, isn't it?"

"I appreciate the favor, Victor," I said. "And please be sure to thank your uncle for me as well."

"You can thank him yourself one of these days. He expressed the desire to have dinner with you, to share a bottle of wine. You know how much he cares for you. It's been too long, Milan."

"I'd like that very much." Victor and I both knew that "sharing a bottle of wine" was a euphemism. In his younger days the don drank only homemade dago red, even though Victor was a wine connoisseur with his own temperature-controlled cellar at home. Now, because of failing health, his doctors had forbidden the old man even that small pleasure, so he only drank it on the sneak when Mrs. Sordetto wasn't watching him.

"Excellent. He'll be very pleased. Now—I told Mr. Ruggiero you'd be contacting him soon. If I were you, I'd call for an appointment the first thing tomorrow morning—before he changes his mind." He read off the phone number for me, and I scribbled it on a napkin.

Great, I thought, wondering how early I dared call. "Thank you, Victor. I know you went out of your way for me."

"What the hell, we're friends," he reminded me. "That's what good friends do for each other, isn't it? Help out when the other one needs something. Isn't that right, Milan?"

There it was, I thought, just as I'd expected—the promissory note. Now I was obligated. "Right, Victor," I said, verbally signing it.

CHAPTER TWELVE

'd showered and shaved, dressed, eaten a breakfast of bagels and cream cheese, and read the entire morning paper by the time I figured it was late enough to call Dante Ruggiero's office in Warren. But I didn't get to speak to the man himself. Instead I made arrangements with a briskly efficient woman I assumed was his secretary, even though her voice sounded as if she were about fourteen years old. The appointment she made for me was for two-thirty that afternoon.

I went to my office. I somehow preferred killing time there than in my apartment. At least I had a river view to ponder.

At about eleven o'clock Bob Matusen called from his car phone, said he was five minutes away, and wanted to know if he could come up for a while. I invited him with a certain amount of relief, reasoning that if I was still a serious suspect in William Poduska's murder investigation, no police officer would have called in advance to ask permission.

I heard his heavy tread on the stairs. Bob Matusen is not a particularly big guy, but he's a wide one, and very little of his endomorphic breadth is fat. He'd been a Cleveland police officer for a long time, and while he wasn't the type to spend half his life at the gym pumping iron and buffing up, he knew the value of staying in relatively good shape. A tough man, to be sure, but in past dealings, I always found him to be reasonable and decent.

And he was incorruptibly honest, too. Marko Meglich would not have had it any other way.

A few years ago Bob Matusen was Marko's good right hand,

which is how I'd met him in the first place, and when he was temporarily assigned the top job in the homicide division after Marko got killed, I think Matusen cut me a little slack because he knew Marko and I had been best friends since grammar school. When Florence McHargue later moved into the lieutenant's chair and bumped him back to number two, though, he had modified our relationship a little. It quickly became obvious that McHargue doesn't like me a dime's worth, and Matusen works under her, so now he takes careful pains to appear completely professional in his dealings with me, especially when she's in the vicinity. Like everyone else down at the old rock pile on Payne Avenue, Bob Matusen was a little bit frightened of her.

But he was a good cop for all that. He'd had the best teacher—Marko—and he did his job with dogged determination and a smattering of street smarts. Under other circumstances we might even have been friends.

"Hey, Milan," he said when he came in the door.

I stood up and we shook hands, and then I poured him a cup of coffee, and he sat down across the desk from me and took a moment to enjoy the scenery. This morning the seagulls were doing aerobatics outside the window, flying high above the river and then swooping down on any fish unwise enough to have made its way into the Flats. We were easy with each other.

But he had to get around to it, and eventually he did. "I spoke to Mrs. Poduska this morning," he said.

"How's she doing?"

"She said you were out there to see her again yesterday."

"I was. I'm not trying to step on your case, Bob. I was there on a related but totally different matter. I think even McHargue would approve."

He waved his hand at me to let me know he wasn't mad. "You've always been a pretty good judge of people—I mean, you studied psychology in college. How do you read her?"

"McHargue?"

He grinned ruefully. 'Well, yeah, her too, but that's a subject for another time. I was talking about Mrs. Poduska."

"What do you mean?"

"I just wanted to get your impression of her. To see whether it coincides with mine."

"You can't take my impressions to court, Bob. Or yours, either."

"Yeah, but you know damn well that sometimes the best part of police work comes from the gut. You've still got your cop instincts. So I just wondered what you thought of her."

My personal opinion of Donalene Poduska had nothing to do with the task I'd been assigned—namely, finding those mysterious photographs for Maureen Hartigan, so I hadn't really given it much thought before now.

"Well," I said, "even taking into consideration that she's just lost her husband unexpectedly and in a *very* brutal way, she still seems like a pretty timid person. If she were a guy, I might even call her a wuss. She's not anyone who has her own opinions or stands up for herself."

"What makes you say that?"

"The way her marriage was, for one thing. I know that a lot of men of Eastern European descent insist on wearing the pants in the family, but even taking that into account, she was apparently under her husband's thumb quite a bit. She let him run everything. She's completely in the dark about the family's finances or what Poduska did to earn his money or even if he had insurance—and any wife with even a tiny bit of independence would know that. And she's pretty shaken up about what she's learned about him; evidently, she had no idea he made a practice of jumping on any female who walked, even though from what we've found out about him he was pretty much a charmer. Whatever question I asked her, she generally told me she didn't know."

"Maybe she's just stupid," he suggested.

"There is that possibility. But I somehow don't think so. My guess is that she's just very passive, which could make her seem dumb."

"You think she's telling the truth about all that?"

"She'd have no reason to lie—unless, of course, she killed him herself. My so-called cop instincts tell me that isn't the case. But I doubt if there's a soul in the world who's incapable of taking a human life when their back is to the wall. Through Mrs. Poduska's timidity I could see a little steel in the spine, too, although I figured she was just beefing herself up to get through her bereavement. She'll be okay eventually. I think."

"But she *is* timid," Matusen said. "That's not the standard perp profile. Killing someone in cold blood requires a certain amount of guts."

"Anything's possible, Bob. Including the fact that Poduska was a con man, and there must be a lot of people out there bearing him a grudge."

He nodded.

"But that's your department, not mine. I'm just out to recover some stolen property."

"Let me run another possibility by you, then," he said.

"Sure, why not? Want some more coffee?"

"No thanks, I'm good." He put his empty cup on top of the desk. Then he said, "Judge Maureen Hartigan."

"For murder one?" I shook my head.

"Why not? Just because she's a judge? That doesn't automatically confer sainthood on her. Remember the Judge Steel case about twenty years back? He sure as hell didn't flinch about putting a hit out on his wife."

"Judges aren't any more holy or incapable of committing a criminal act than the next guy," I admitted. "But if Maureen Hartigan was going to kill Poduska, why would she have hired me to find him two days before she did it?"

"Maybe she wasn't planning to do it—maybe it just happened," he said. "Maybe she found him somehow before you did and she wanted her property back, and when he wouldn't give it to her, she iced him on the spot. Or maybe she brought you on board because she *was* planning it, and hiring you would make her look innocent."

"As I said, anything is possible."

Something in his face changed slightly. Not much—just enough to let me know that his next question was a serious one. "Including the judge's daughter or the Torrence woman getting highly pissed off because they were fucked and forsaken and were getting their revenge the hard way? You know Irish women have tempers."

"Bob, you asked me for a psychological evaluation of Donalene Poduska," I said, "who by the way happens to be Irish, too. That's all I can address. I'm certainly not about to incriminate my client with an unfounded opinion. But I don't see any of these women as killers."

"Just because they're female?"

"You and I both know gender has nothing to do with the capacity to kill. Especially when the victim is a rat with women like Bill Poduska. I just don't happen to think we've met a female killer on this case yet."

"And what if you're wrong?"

"Then I owe you a lunch."

"Johnny's Downtown?"

"You have excellent taste in restaurants, Bob. Sure."

He laughed, and got to his feet and buttoned his suit jacket. "Is it really that simple with you?"

"I'm only being pragmatic," I told him.

That just about ended our discussion, and we shook hands. He was halfway down the stairs when I thought of something. I went quickly to the office door and called down to him. "Bob, I've got a question for you."

He turned and looked up the stairwell at me.

"The autopsy results on Poduska . . ."

"Cause of death, a twenty-two caliber bullet in the skull. The one in his balls must have hurt, and it certainly would have slowed down his womanizing. But it wouldn't have killed him if he could have gotten some quick medical attention."

"I know that," I said. "But Lieutenant McHargue told me that Poduska was punched around some at least one day before he died."

"Right. So?"

"Were his knuckles bruised or abraded, too?"

He came back up the stairs, stopping so that his left foot was on the top step and his right on the one just beneath. "His knuckles? No. His pinkie was broken, but otherwise I don't remember anything about his hands. Why?"

"Because if there was no trauma to his knuckles, that means he wasn't in a fight. It means he was beaten up by somebody and he didn't resist."

"So?"

"So why would anyone just sit still for a beating?"

"You tell me, Milan."

"Because the beating was administered by someone Poduska

was scared of," I said, "and he didn't resist because he was afraid if he did, it would be worse than a beating."

Matusen shoved his hands into his pockets, thought about it for a while, and then nodded. "That's not a bad theory, you know, Milan? You should've stayed in the department."

"Don't you start that," I said. "That was an ongoing battle between Marko and me."

"Your staying a cop?"

"Yes. He was really pissed off at me when I put in my papers."

"He was right."

I nodded sadly. "Marko was usually right. But as your friend and mine, Lieutenant McHargue, points out almost every time she talks to me, I'm not a cop anymore. I'm just a private citizen working as a snoop for hire. It's not my job to figure out who killed whom."

"For a private citizen, you sure manage to show up an awful lot whenever somebody gets offed in this town. Now, why the hell is that?"

"I've wondered myself," I said.

He waved and continued down the stairs. I closed the door behind him and went over and sat on the windowsill, looking out at the towers and turrets and light standards of Jacobs Field and at the great humped back of the Gund Arena across the river, and for a moment considered where I stood regarding the silly games that were performed in both venues. I'd played varsity football at Kent State—nose tackle—and had been a sports fan all my life, but in the last few years I'd sort of drifted away from it. Maybe sports, even watching them, are a young man's fancy, and I was just getting old. Perhaps the bumbling Browns who'd returned to town in were not as inspiring as the Kardiac Kids of Brian Sipe or the later, well-oiled machine of Bernie Kosar. And the Indians just weren't my Indians anymore after the Alomar brothers left and Manny Ramirez went to Boston. More likely, it had simply come to me that paying a man almost forty thousand dollars every time he picks up a baseball bat or dunks a basketball into a hoop is really obscene, and I didn't want to support it anymore.

I thought about what Matusen had said about Irish women and their tempers. It was a stereotype, of course, but it got me connecting some dots, and after a few minutes I went back over to my desk and fished the Maureen Hartigan file out of the drawer and looked up the number of Dennis McShane in New York City.

"Yeah?" It was the same voice I'd heard the last time.

"Hello, Mr. McShane. I'm the person who called you a few days ago looking for a Brian McFall, and you said you didn't know him."

There was a long pause. Then, "Is this Jacovich?"

I tried to remember whether I'd told him my name during our last conversation. It was my recollection that I had not, that our phone time was too short for me to have done anything more than simply identify myself as a private investigator from Cleveland. I wondered to whom he'd been talking about me. It was probably Cornelius McCardle, but possibly Donalene Poduska as well. It surely must have been McCardle who'd mentioned to Poduska that a certain Milan Jacovich was hunting him, causing Poduska to write down my name on the memo pad near his bed sometime before someone came and put two bullets into him.

"Yes," I said, recovering quickly, "this is Milan Jacovich."

"Well, listen up, Jacovich. I didn't know no Brian McFall the first time you called, and I still don't know him now, and I got no time to waste passing pleasantries with you on the telephone."

"But you knew Bill Poduska." I heard him suck in some air, and I rushed on. "Don't bother denying it, because Con McCardle here in Cleveland has already told me you knew him."

"That don't mean I want to talk about him," McShane said. "And I don't have to, either, 'cause you ain't no cop."

"No, I'm not. But I'm sure you're well aware by now that William Poduska was shot to death in a motel room in Cleveland. If you don't talk to me right now, the local police would be very interested in knowing that the two of you were acquainted, that he called you several times within a few weeks of his death. So, I'm sure, would the Justice Department. And I'm sure you don't want them looking into your . . . political activities, do you?"

His voice got very quiet all of a sudden, bruised and seething. "Jesus Christ, what kind of man are you, Jacovich?"

"A determined one, Mr. McShane," I said, "with lots of friends in high places. So are we going to talk or not?"

I could almost hear the wheels and cogs in his brain grinding. Then he said, "Give me your number, and I'll call you back in fifteen minutes."

"What's the matter with right now?"

"I'll call you back, or it's no deal," he said vehemently.

I gave him my number. "Fifteen minutes, Mr. McShane. After that my phone's going to be busy because *I'll* be making a few calls."

"Don't you be threatening me now, ya fookin' bastard," he snarled, and slammed down the phone.

I hung up, got myself another cup of coffee, and smoked a cigarette to pass the time. I didn't have to wait fifteen minutes—he called me back in twelve. I could hear background noises this time, muted music, and conversation and laughter, as if he was in a restaurant or bar.

"Jacovich?"

"I'm here. Where are you?"

"At a pay phone in the saloon down the block. My home phone might be tapped; the bastards have done it before."

"What bastards?"

"It don't matter."

"Don't you have a cellphone?"

"Using one of them things is like broadcasting your conversations on the fookin' radio. Listen here, now—I don't want my name getting around. I'm not in a position where I appreciate publicity."

"What position is that?"

"None of your business."

"Sinn Fein?"

He gasped, then swallowed hard. Finally, he said, "Goddamn you to everlasting hell, Jacovich."

"I don't give a damn one way or the other, Mr. McShane. Your secret is safe with me."

He took a while to consider it. "So then what I tell you remains between the two of us. Agreed?"

"If I can," I said.

"What the hell does that mean?"

"It means that a murder has been committed, and if you tell me anything I think will shed light on that, I have to tell the police."

"I don't know nothing about no murder. And I haven't even been off of Manhattan Island in the last year and a half, and I can prove it."

"Then you have nothing to worry about."

He made a sound that could have been either a laugh or a scoff. I couldn't tell. The music in the background became Celine Dion singing that inescapable song from *Titanic*. I guessed that the bar he was calling from was not an Irish pub like the Shebeen.

"What do you want from me, Jacovich?"

"Just some general information about William Poduska," I said. "How did you know him?"

"I hardly knew him at all. And I sure didn't know him under those names you threw at me the other day. He was just a messenger."

The old story about killing the messenger popped unbidden into my head. "A messenger from whom?"

"Friends of mine in the Cleveland area."

"Con McCardle?"

"Sometimes."

"And what did he bring you from Cleveland?"

"Not your business. Not important."

The resolute way that he said it told me I would have to accept that for now. I was fairly certain I knew what Poduska had been carrying to McShane anyway—cash, under-the-table IRA money that Con McCardle had raised in Cleveland and wasn't anxious to run through a checking account. "Was there ever any evidence that he didn't bring you . . . uh . . . everything he was supposed to? That he was keeping part of it for himself?"

"If he had, I would have cut the little poove's heart out," McShane blurted. "And if I didn't, Con McCardle surely would." He made a gurgling sound as if he'd gotten a kernel of popcorn stuck in the back of his throat. "Ah, Jesus, that didn't sound so good, did it?"

"I'm not a policeman," I reminded him, "so it doesn't matter how it sounded. Okay?

"I don't want to speak ill of the dead."

"He'll never know. You didn't like Poduska very much?"

"He was all right. A little cocky, fancied himself a Romeo, I think. But I never completely trusted him with our . . . business . . . because he wasn't Irish."

"Apparently Con McCardle trusted him, though."

"Ah, but that's because he was married to Con's niece."

"What?" I said.

"You didn't know?" He seemed pleased that he knew something I didn't. "That's right, Con's sister's daughter. So if Con trusted him, it wasn't my business to interfere, don't you see?"

I saw, all right, but I wanted to back up a bit and rehash that nugget about Cornelius McCardle being Donalene Poduska's uncle. McCardle had told me the late John Mullen was his "friend," but he'd neglected to mention that Mullen was married to his sister. I didn't imagine, though, that Dennis McShane knew anything that would further illuminate that little twig from the Poduska family tree.

And I doubted whether McCardle would talk to me about it, either.

It was beginning to fall together for me, though. The Irish, like many other immigrant cultures in America, are fiercely protective and supportive of their families. So it made sense that Con McCardle would not only have hired Bill Poduska to be his errand boy because of his ties to him by marriage—even trusting him to hand-deliver whatever was too sensitive to send through the mails to Dennis McShane and Sinn Fein—but that he would also have seen to it that his associates around the city, even the non-Irish ones who might have owed him a few favors, would keep Poduska in mind when there was an odd job to be done.

"One more question, Mr. McShane," I said, "and I think I can get out of your hair."

"Praise Jesus for that!"

"Do you know anything about an envelope full of photographs that might have come into Poduska's possession in the last few weeks?"

"Photographs? Of what?"

"I'm not sure," I said.

"That's helpful."

"I'm sorry, it's the best I can do. I know that there's a prominent Cleveland politician involved somehow. An Irish politician."

"Ah," he breathed. "And what's his name?"

"It doesn't matter," I said. "He's been dead for several years. His family wants the photos back for sentimental reasons."

He laughed right into the phone. "Do you take me for a fookin' child, Jacovich? Sentimental reasons, my arse!" I heard him breathing. "Well, no matter, because Poduska never showed me any photographs," he said at last. "What would I do with 'em? Why the hell should I care about some Cleveland politician anyway? Besides, I haven't seen Poduska in about eight weeks or so."

"You haven't?"

"There was no reason to," he said. "Con McCardle didn't need him to come see me."

"Did you ever give Poduska anything to message back to Cleveland from New York?"

"No," McShane said. "Although he was always callin' me up and begging for work—and I'll wager Con knew nothing of that, either, or he'd have skinned the boy alive."

That could have explained the calls to McShane on Judith Torrence's telephone bill. I scribbled some quick notes on a scratch pad.

"You've been very helpful, Mr. McShane," I said. "I appreciate your talking with me."

"And well you should appreciate it, when you fairly blackmailed me into it, didn't you?" he said. 'Well, thanks be to God, I'm quit of you now, Jacovich. You can call the Justice Department or the police or fookin' George Dubya Bush for all I care—but we'll talk no more after today."

And he hung up.

CHAPTER THIRTEEN

Ohio Route 422 East is the quickest way to get to Warren from Cleveland. After the freeway sort of peters out into a two-lane highway as soon as it crosses the sprawling Mosquito Creek Reservoir, it's a rustic, almost lazy road, passing through several municipalities so small that if you blink when you go by the gas station, you'll miss them altogether. It was about ten days past what the TV weather mavens always refer to as "the peak leaf-peeping weekend," but the leaves on the trees—oak and sumac and birch and catalpa—were still wearing their red and gold autumn colors, although now they were a trifle faded, as if they'd grown bored with hanging around for people to gawk at and couldn't wait to take that kamikaze dive off a branch and into a pile to be raked away or burned.

I had to admit it felt good to get out of the city for at least one bright afternoon. A lot of North Coasters can't wait to escape the metropolitan area for a vacation each year; favored getaway spots for well-off Clevelanders are Hilton Head, the mountains of North Carolina, and Naples, Florida. Not me. I don't like vacationing out of town very much, except perhaps for a weekend here and there. I love my city, and can have more fun there than I can basking on some far-off beach drinking effete rum concoctions with paper umbrellas in them and worrying about my nose getting sunburned.

So the ninety-mile road trip to Warren, in Trumbull County, was like a minivacation for me. Or it would have been, had I not remained so focused on business while I drove.

I had to keep telling myself that my only job was the retrieval of Maureen Hartigan's photographs, about which she maddeningly continued to be secretive; the matter of who had put two bullets into William Poduska was none of my affair. It was perplexing, however, especially since I couldn't really eliminate my own clients from the list of suspects.

That's what I get, I thought, for having friends as clients.

I was wondering why Poduska had been beaten up one day and then shot the next. It seemed likely that the two incidents were the work of the same hand. But if so, why didn't they just kill him the first time?

I put those thoughts into a compartment at the back of my mind when I pulled into the parking area outside Dante Ruggiero's import company, which operated out of an ugly warehouse just off Route 422. It had the look of those dreary, boxy cinder-block-and-steel structures that had sprung up just after World War II—strictly utilitarian with no thought toward aesthetics.

The door opened right onto the warehouse floor. It seemed that Ruggiero's office was on the second level, a glass-enclosed cubicle with a clear view of what was going on downstairs; it was accessed only by a metal staircase. There was no receptionist or any other sort of greeter, although off in one corner a very young woman, no more than twenty, sat at a desk with a telephone glued to her ear. I guessed she was the one with whom I'd scheduled the appointment. She noticed me when I walked in, gave a slight nod of acknowledgment, and indicated with a roll of her eyes and a point of her chin that I should go upstairs. The warehousemen, busy at their work stacking crates of olive oil and pasta, gave me only cursory glances as I climbed to the second level and knocked on the door.

Back when he still lived in Cleveland, I'd seen Dante Ruggiero many times in newspaper photographs, but this was the first time we'd ever been face-to-face. I was surprised to find that he was just a little man, no more than five foot four now, although I imagined that his eighty-odd years had whittled an inch or two from his height. As opposed to Don Giancarlo D'Allessandro, who always seemed comfortably rumpled in aged tweeds or shiny blue serge, Ruggiero was something of a fashion plate in a natty blue pinstriped suit; he wore the jacket, maybe because the warehouse was refrigerated and the chill seeped into his office, but more probably because he looked more imposing and elegant that way, especially with a white carnation for a boutonniere. His shirt was starched and gleaming white with a muted blue tie. On his left pinkie finger was a big, heavy diamond ring set in rough gold. It was a pretty fancy getup for coming to work in a food warehouse, even for the boss. He was almost completely bald, and what remained of his hair was a mere fringe of white just over his ears, circling around to the back of his head and cut very close to the scalp, and his pale pink cheeks were smooth and lightly powdered with talc.

I knew that among the families of organized crime, Ruggiero was considered a fossil, a dusty relic of a past era. Giancarlo D'Allessandro may have been around the same age, but he'd been wise enough to keep up with the times, more or less, with Victor's help and guidance. Dante Ruggiero had always operated as though he thought Prohibition was still the law of the land.

"You're Jacovich," he rumbled from behind his desk, telling me something I already knew. It didn't seem as if he was going to rise or offer a handshake, so I kept my own hands at my sides.

"I'm grateful that you agreed to talk to me, Mr. Ruggiero," I said. My first instinct was to address him as "Don," but since he'd been eased out of the organization so many years before, I wasn't sure if it would be appropriate.

"I see you only because D'Allessandro asked me to, okay?" he said. "I don't get involved in the crap anymore, all the shit in the city. I'm a businessman. I import food from Italy and Greece, okay? Some guy gets himself shot over in Cleveland, I don't know nothing about it. But D'Allessandro says talk to you, so I'm talking to you, okay?" He spoke in the hoarse half-whisper of an old man, and his speech bore only the barest trace of an Italian accent. I knew that he'd been in America for more than sixty years.

"I'll try not to take too long."

"That's good, because I'm running a business here," he said, and waved me into an uncomfortable office chair.

He leaned back in his own chair, high-backed and leather, on the other side of the desk, and interlaced his fingers over his little pot-belly as if he were about to take a short nap. "You know me, right?" he said. "You know who I am?"

"Yes, sir."

"Then you got to know I don't like talking about my business."
He raised one hand, finger pointed to the heavens. "Not that I got
anything to hide, okay'? But it's just—whatchamacallit—instinct
with me. Regular cop, private cop, don't make a difference. People from my era, from my, uh, background, it's not easy to talk
about our business with outsiders, okay?"

"I understand."

"That's good, because I want you should accept what I tell
you and you don't push me about other stuff. I don't like being
pushed. If you push, this meeting is over. Okay?"

"Okay."

"All right. Now about this Poduska kid," he said. Victor had
obviously briefed him. "I feel bad that someone took him out,
okay? He was a pretty good kid, all things considered. Kind of an
asshole sometimes, especially with women, but that's because he
was a kid."

"He was in his late thirties."

"Kids, they don't use their heads; they think with their zippers.
They act like they rule the world these days, but if you ask me,
anybody who's under forty, they wouldn't know where their own
ass is if they searched for it with both hands in the dark. But all in
all, this Poduska was a good kid. So I feel bad he's gone, okay?" He
unclasped his hands and pointed a finger at me. "I tell you this so
you don't think I had anything to do with his death."

"I never thought you did, Don Dante," I said, deciding that if
I were to err in his title, it would be on the side of politeness and
diplomacy.

"Well, that's good," he said, and seemed pleased with how I
addressed him. "Lotsa people, they seen too many gangster movies; they think anybody with an Italian name goes around killing
people for looking at them the wrong way." He put up a hand. "It's
all right, I know you're not like that—because Victor Gaimari says
you're his friend. But that ain't the Italians. The blacks, they'll do
that—kill you for a pair of tennis shoes. Black kids, I mean. Italians got more sense than that."

"How did you meet Poduska?"

His shoulders lifted slightly under the smartly tailored suit
jacket and then fell again. "Who remembers where you meet this

one or that one? You know, guys like him, they hang around with certain people long enough, if they keep their noses clean, they get a reputation for being reliable and discreet, and a friend tells another friend. Like that, okay?"

"What friend told you about him?"

His eyes narrowed. "I don't remember."

"Was it Cornelius McCardle in Cleveland?"

He frowned. "I said I don't remember. Don't push, okay?"

"Sorry. What did you have Poduska do for you?"

"Whaddaya think, he was my accountant who cooked my books for me?" His wave was dismissive, almost contemptuous. "He was an errand boy, that's all. Stuff I maybe didn't want to send through the mails and I didn't have an extra man to spare here, so then maybe I give it to Poduska and he delivers it for me. No place too far away—Cleveland, Pittsburgh, Detroit, Toledo. Places you could drive to. Maybe Chicago once in a while. Shit errands, like that. It was convenient for me, and he needed the money. Also, sometimes I'd fix it up for him to get a free, you know, massage at one of my places before he went home."

"That's all he did. Errands?"

"That's all he was smart enough to do."

"Just for you?"

"For me, for my friends if they need it. Just as a favor to Mc-Cardle, so's maybe the kid could see a couple a bucks once in a while."

"Nothing else? No rough stuff?"

He leaned forward in his chair without undue haste or agitation. "You're pushing again," he said quietly, not raising his voice. "And you're insulting me. I told you I don't do no rough stuff anymore. I'm a legitimate businessman. Whatsamatter with you, don't you fucking listen?"

"I don't mean to insult you," I said quickly. To an Italian of his vintage and walk of life, an insult was tantamount to stepping on Elvis's blue suede shoes. "I'm just trying to figure out if you ever had him lean hard on somebody and they might have gotten mad enough to kill him."

"Never happen. First of all," Ruggiero said, ticking off the points on his fingers, "it's pretty obvious somebody was mad enough to ice him—but it wasn't nobody that had to do with me.

Second of all, the kid was a scrawny little bohunk, and I wouldn't send him out to push around an eight-year-old girl, much less anybody else. Thirdly of all, I already told you I'm not involved in any of that shit anymore. And fourthly of all, even if I was, you really think I'd just spill it to some low-rent Polack shamus like you just because you're a friend of Victor Gaimari's?"

I tried not to smile at "low-rent shamus." Ruggiero really *was* a dinosaur, with side-of-the-mouth patter out of a nineteen-forties Bogart movie.

"I'm Slovenian, not Polish, Don Dante," I said.

"Right, like I care."

"And I didn't mean to offend you."

He crinkled up his nose—his way, I suppose, of letting me know I hadn't really offended him. "What do you give a shit about who killed him anyway? You're no cop, even though you look like one and smell like one."

"I used to be one," I admitted. "But I'm sure you knew that already."

He nodded an affirmation.

"And you're right. Whoever killed Poduska is none of my concern."

"What *is*, then?" Ruggiero asked, relaxing back against the high back of his chair. "What exactly is your concern? That you should have to come all the way out here to sit down with me?"

"Actually, Poduska stole something that belongs to my client, and I'm trying to get it back."

"Stole what?"

"Photographs."

"You mean porno, shit like that?" he said, his mouth turning downward at the corners with distaste. "Something disgusting that somebody took through a keyhole?"

"No."

"Not kids, is it?" he said, looking dangerous and turning a little bit more pink. "Little kids? Jesus, I *hate* that filthy shit. It makes me want to cut somebody's balls off."

I made a mental note of the imagery, considering Poduska had been shot in the testicles. "Nothing like that," I said, uncomfortable because I wasn't really sure I was telling him the truth. "But

I thought Poduska might have mentioned them to you. Or shown you."

"He didn't show me no pictures," Ruggiero said. "Why would he? I don't look at pictures. Listen, the kid was nothing to me, okay? He wasn't my best friend, he wasn't part of any organization of mine, and he wasn't even an employee here. He was just contract labor."

The telephone at Ruggiero's elbow rang. He leaned forward and pushed a button and snapped, "What?"

Through the crackling and popping of the speakerphone came the impossibly young voice of the woman downstairs, echoing as if she were speaking from inside a cave. "I'm sorry to interrupt, Mr. Ruggiero, but Mr. Michael Marks is here for his appointment."

"Tell him two minutes and then send him up," he said into the speaker and then shut it off. He chuckled. "Little twist down there sounds like jailbait over the phone, don't she? She's twenty-two. Legal." He preened a little bit. "Listen, I gotta say good-bye now; I got business."

"One more question before I go, Don Dante," I said. "If you don't mind."

He ran a hand over his smooth, bald head. "What's the difference if I mind? You're gonna ask it anyway, am I right?"

I smiled. "Only with your permission, sir. How active are you in Cleveland politics?"

"Cleveland? I hardly even know who the mayor is no more. Let me 'splain something to you," he said, pronouncing it the way Ricky Ricardo used to. "The people in Cleveland think that Warren here is just part of their big happy family of suburbs. But Warren people think they're part of Pittsburgh. There's more Steelers fans here than Browns fans. I don't read the Cleveland papers, I don't pay attention to Cleveland politics, okay? And I don't give a shit whether the city slides into fuckin' Lake Erie and disappears like, whatcha-macallit it, Atlanta."

"Okay," I said. "Just asking." It would not have been advisable for me to point out the difference between Atlanta and Atlantis—not to the don.

I stood up to leave, uncertain whether to shake his hand or not. Since he made no effort to rise, I elected to skip it.

As I headed for the office door, Ruggiero said, 'Wait a second. Now *I* got a question for *you*."

"Yes, sir?"

His small eyes were shiny—crafty. "I been giving you a lot of answers; now how about you give me one? Exactly who is this client of yours who's looking for the missing pictures?"

"Don't push, Don Dante," I said, trying to make my tone playful. I was hoping he'd laugh.

He stared at me for a full half a minute before he finally did. I laughed, too, but it was more from relief.

On my way down the metal stairs I came face-to-face with another man on his way up. He was about sixty years old, with an olive complexion and dark hair shot through with silver, and dressed as expensively as Ruggiero, in a gray suit and plain gray silk tie over a buttery gray shirt. He was a big guy, hard-looking, but not in the way of a thug. He appeared to be a self-made man who had attained a certain measure of success in life and who would cheerfully tear out the lungs of anyone who threatened to take it away from him.

He looked up and continued toward me in a most determined fashion, and for a moment I thought it was going to be a Robin Hood and Little John impasse resulting in a duel with stout staffs on the bridge. But I deferred to his age and turned my body aside so he could get by me.

"Sorry," I said as we brushed so close together on the narrow stairway that the scent he was wearing—Ralph Lauren's Polo—stuck to my clothes. I assumed he was the Michael Marks who had an appointment.

Just like I'd had.

CHAPTER FOURTEEN

When I got home to my apartment, I used what little advanced twenty-first-century technology I've been able to master to check the phone messages at my office. There were several calls I didn't particularly want to return, and a few, like Cathleen Hartigan's, that I did. The only imperative one, however—the one I felt I had to answer right away—was from the police department.

McHargue. Call me.

A woman of few words, Lieutenant McHargue. But then when I finally got through to her, she didn't want to talk at all. She wanted to listen.

"What have you got for me?" she said.

I didn't have much, because I certainly couldn't give her Dante Ruggiero. I'd made no promises about it, not to him and not to Victor. But it was a tacit understanding, and as binding as a three-hundred-page contract hammered out between high-priced attorneys, and I knew it. Ruggiero had done me a favor, and in return I was to keep the Italians out of it unless I couldn't help myself.

"I have one interesting little family-tree item," I told McHargue. "Did you know that Donalene Poduska is Cornelius McCardle's niece?"

I could hear her breathing over the otherwise silent connection. Then she said, "Oh, goody. That's all I need."

"Sorry," I said.

"Where'd you hear that?"

"Does it matter?"

"I suppose not. Not right this minute, anyway. If things should change and it does start to matter, you're going to tell me whether you like it or not."

I nodded, but of course she couldn't see me.

"Are we clear on that?"

"Yes," I said. "Clear as crystal."

"Damn!" she said, and I could hear her exasperation. "I don't relish going one-on-one with McCardle. He's a mean old buzzard, and he's got connections in this city that would make your hair turn gray. Including some heavy-duty ones right here in this department."

"Are they good enough to save him from an indictment?"

"If it comes to that—if I get enough on him to make an arrest—I wouldn't care if he was the mayor's long-lost father."

I relaxed in my chair a little. "That's good to know, anyway."

"What else have you got to tell me about, Jacovich? Have you been able to track down those photographs?"

"I'm working on it," I said.

"Work harder."

"It'd help," I said, "if I knew what they were."

"If I were you, I'd start holding my client's feet to the fire pretty hard."

"You don't lean on a judge."

"No, *you* don't lean on a judge! As for me, I don't give a damn if she's the reincarnation of the Blessed Mother. You're walking around looking for those photographs like a blind man with a paper sack over his head. I haven't pushed on this *because* she's a judge, and because I was counting on you to clear up this end of it. But I'm a woman of very little patience, as I'm sure you've discovered in our long and unhappy relationship. And she's only a judge in her courtroom, wearing her black robes. When she's out of it and in civilian clothes, as far as I'm concerned, she's no better than the Roto-Rooter man. So make her talk to you. Or you better believe that I'll make her talk to me."

"I suppose you're right."

"Of course, I'm right," she said. "I'm always right. I've got the badge." Her tone took on a razor edge. "Remember that, Jaco-vich."

And then she abruptly broke the connection.

"Cathleen," I said, "I need to see you and your mother as soon as possible. Tonight."

Her sigh came through the receiver like a lonesome wind wailing through a pine barren. "Is this absolutely necessary?"

"I think it is," I said. "If she wants me to go on working for her."

"I suppose we could meet at her place . . ."

"Not this time," I said. I didn't want to go back to the judge's home, nor to Cathleen's, and I was quite sure that neither of them would want to risk having our discussion overheard in a restaurant. My respect for Maureen Hartigan's political vulnerability and my relationship with Cathleen had made me turn soft in the matter of William Poduska. Now, out of necessity, I had to take charge of things, and that meant meeting on my home turf where I was in control and where I couldn't be summarily asked to leave. "I want you both in my office. Seven o'clock?"

"I'll have to check with mother . . ."

"You do that," I said, "and call me right back."

"She may be hard to reach this late in the afternoon . . ."

"*Right* back, Cathleen," I said, and depressed the OFF button on the telephone handset.

She called me back within ten minutes with a confirmation. Then I set about straightening up the place a little bit, emptying the ashtrays and washing out the coffeepot, dusting the computer and Lemon Pledging the desk. It wasn't often I had as illustrious a visitor as a judge of the Court of Common Pleas.

They arrived at seven o'clock, the appointed time. They both wore business suits, Maureen Hartigan's slightly rumpled, probably from wearing it under her judicial robes all day. Cathleen seemed tense and nervous; the judge looked grim and more than slightly annoyed. She wasn't used to being summoned; in her position she usually did the summoning.

They marched through the door like an invading horde of Visigoths. "Have you located the photos?" Maureen asked.

No hello.

"Not yet."

"Then what is so important that we had to drop everything and come rushing over here?"

"Please, sit down, both of you. It's those photographs I want to talk to you about."

"I don't see the necessity . . ."

"I do!" It came out rougher than I'd intended, and I lowered my voice. "Maureen, I'm working in the dark here. I don't even know what I'm looking for, and that's not a good way to operate."

"Well, you'll just have to," she snapped.

"I'm afraid that's not an option anymore," I said.

"Why not?"

"You claim that Bill Poduska stole those pictures from your home."

"I *claim*?" she bristled. "Are you questioning my truthfulness?"

"Not at all, Judge. Hear me out, all right?"

She puckered her lips as if she'd bitten into something sour.

"Even though he was spending most of his nights at Cathleen's place, he insisted on living at yours, which means that he was probably hunting for those photographs in the first place." Cathleen was looking more and more uncomfortable. "He found them, he disappeared with them, and then he turned up dead."

"Well?"

"He may have been killed because of them," I said. "And that makes it imperative that I know what they were if I'm going to find them at all."

"I don't see it's imperative at all."

"Of course you do. This has gone beyond a sting—beyond a simple theft. It's a murder case, now. Lieutenant McHargue thinks it is imperative. Out of respect for your office she's allowing me to ask you the question first. But if you don't come clean with me about the pictures, I'll have to report that to her, and then *she'll* ask you. And not so nicely, either."

The judge was sitting bolt upright, her knees pressed tightly together, staring at a point somewhere over my head, her jaw as rigid as if she were trying not to cry out in pain.

"That was the whole point of hiring me in the first place, wasn't it? To get the pictures back?"

"What do you mean?"

"All the other stuff Poduska screwed your family out of— Hugh's cuff links, your grandmother's jewelry, a few dollars—you didn't really care about any of that. It was all a smoke screen, wasn't it?"

Anger was darkening Maureen Hartigan's brow like a thundercloud.

"So you wouldn't have to tell me about the photographs." I shook my head. "I can't work for a client who doesn't level with me. I can't do it anymore that way, Maureen. It's getting too complicated."

"Are you quitting?"

"No, not at all," I said. "But I have to insist that you be completely honest with me from here on out. Tell me exactly what I'm looking for. So I can help you. So I can keep my license."

She swallowed hard and managed to look at me. "What if I just fire you? What if I tell you to stop looking?"

Cathleen gently put her hand on her mother's arm. "It's too late for that now, Mother."

I nodded. "It *is* too late, Judge. I'll have to answer to Lieutenant McHargue either way."

Judge Hartigan took a deep breath. When she finally let it out, she seemed to shrink in the process, like a blowup doll slowly deflating. She pinched at the bridge of her nose with two fingers and shuddered. Then she turned to her daughter.

"Cathleen, I want you to wait downstairs."

Cathleen gasped, turning in her chair to face the older woman directly. "You've got to be kidding!"

"I rarely kid, Cathleen, as you know. Please go."

"Not a chance! You think anything you can say is going to shock me? I'm a big girl now."

"Nevertheless . . ."

"I'm involved in this as much as you. Even more," she added bitterly. "I have a right to know what's going on."

"Yes, but there are things you don't *need* to know."

"The hell I don't!" Cathleen's chin was set as implacably as her mother's, and the two women were glaring daggers at each other.

"This is a fight that needs to be taken home, ladies," I said more gruffly than I'd intended. "At the moment, you're on my time, and I want to talk about those photographs."

"Milan's right," Cathleen said.

"I know he is," her mother shot back. "So go downstairs."

"Judge Hartigan!" I said, as exasperated as both my visitors.

"Oh, all right, damn it!" The judge looked from me to her daughter, and there was a hollow hopelessness in her eyes that I didn't like to see. "You asked for this, Cathleen; I hope to hell you can live with it afterward."

Cathleen's smug, triumphant smile wasn't pretty. Not pretty at all.

"What is it you want, Milan?" Maureen asked.

I sighed, leaning forward and putting both elbows on my desk. "Honesty, that's all. Straight answers, no evasions, no vagaries. I want to know about the photographs. Specifically."

She regarded me with interest, as if seeing me for the first time. Then she folded her hands in her lap. "You're very good—as good as your reputation. You're right, I only came to you because of the photos, although it would be nice to get the jewelry back, too, and the money."

"Go on."

"I told you the truth before. The pictures are of my late husband," she said, adding unnecessarily, "Senator Doyle Hartigan."

"Yes, but that was only a half-truth," I said. "Pictures of Senator Hartigan doing what?"

She scanned the ceiling in vain for the right words. "Doing something that might be considered . . . incriminating."

"Are they pictures of Senator Hartigan with another. . . ?" Now it was my turn to fumble for words—genteel words, discreet ones. But they came hard. "Was he in some sort of sexual situation?"

Cathleen Hartigan put a fearful hand to her mouth. Her mother looked startled at first. Then blank. Then she threw back her head and laughed. *Really* laughed from the gut, lustily, and the way in which she did it suggested it had been some time since she'd let it all out like that.

Finally, she sniffled, took a tissue from her purse, and dabbed at her eyes. "Sexual situation? Doyle Hartigan? Oh, you're cute, Sparky. You're just adorable."

I sneaked a look at Cathleen, who seemed just as puzzled as I. Then we both waited.

"No," the judge said in a tone more befitting the serious occasion. "Senator Hartigan was not caught on camera in a 'sexual situation.' He didn't *have* sexual situations, at least not with other people. He and I were both virgins when we met, do you believe that? Of course, that was more than forty years ago, and people—nice people, good Catholics like we were—didn't take sex as casually as a handshake the way they do these days."

Cathleen stiffened at the implied rebuke, and Maureen directed the next remark to her. "Unlike you, Cathleen, neither of us had anything to do with another person in all the years we were married." She forced a smile. "As far as I know, anyway. And if your father ever did, I sure as hell don't want to know about it now."

"Then in what way are the pictures incriminating?" I said.

She kept staring at Cathleen, hard. Then she looked away quickly, all traces of mirth vanished. 'They show the senator in conversation with . . . a well-known underworld figure."

Cathleen's whole body jerked as though from an electric shock.

"What underworld figure?"

Maureen shook her head firmly.

"Judge, if I do manage to locate the photographs, I'm going to have to take them out of the envelope and look at them to make sure they're the ones you want and not somebody's wedding pictures. So you might as well tell me—I'm going to find out anyway."

She chewed off the color on her bottom lip. "This is very upsetting."

"I know."

She let her emotions war with each other for a few moments. Then she took a deep breath and told me. "It's Giancarlo D'Allessandro."

Now we were *both* upset.

"Oh, shit," I said.

"Shit is right." It was nice having Cathleen agreeing with me.

"But there's no crime in knowing a mobster, even for a lawyer or politician. And I know from the past that your family and the don's family were friends." I looked at Cathleen. "You even used to *date* Victor Gaimari."

"Dating is one thing," Maureen said. "But this . . ."

"Your husband didn't know his picture was being snapped?"

She shook her head. "I'm sure he didn't. They were taken on the street—in front of the old Hollenden Hotel on Superior Avenue—from a hidden vantage point. Probably a parked car."

"When was this?"

"Almost twenty years ago, I'd say. From the clothes they were wearing and the way Doyle's hair was cut."

"And they were just having a conversation?"

She lifted her chin and turned her head, looking out the window at the gulls, showing me a profile like that on an antique cameo. "It's a little more than that, I'm afraid."

"How much more?"

She looked at me beseechingly. She didn't want to tell me, and she certainly didn't want her daughter hearing it. But I couldn't let her off the hook anymore; it had gone too far.

She squared her shoulders and spit it out. "The senator is very clearly seen . . . accepting an envelope."

"An envelope."

"Yes. A thick one, wrapped in a rubber band."

All at once I realized my neck and shoulders were tight with tension, and I rotated my head around a bit, hearing little gravelly clicks inside. It didn't help. "I'm very sorry, Maureen."

She pressed her lips together to control her emotions, and nodded. I looked from her to her daughter; Cathleen's face was beginning to crumple, and her eyes brimmed with tears.

"The pictures are twenty years old. I don't see the problem."

Her nostrils flared like those of a spirited horse. "The tearing down of a man's good reputation doesn't seem like a problem to you?"

Not enough to go through all this trouble, not ten years after his death. But I didn't offer that opinion aloud. "How did you happen to have these pictures in your possession?"

"I found them by accident, several months after my husband died," she said. "When I was cleaning out his study, you know, the way people do when someone they love passes on. I'd never seen them before. Naturally, I was horrified."

"I don't understand. Why in hell would you keep something like that in the first place?"

"I don't even know why I kept them." Her chuckle was brittle and had a sharp, sardonic bite. "Maybe because I always thought my husband was a saint. Too much of a saint, actually. It's very hard to live with someone who has no flaws and no vices, Milan. It makes one feel woefully inadequate. So I guess I hung onto them as some sort of talisman, a reminder that Doyle Hartigan actually had a few human frailties, just like the rest of us."

"Why would somebody like William Poduska want to steal them after all this time?"

She lifted her shoulders helplessly, then let them droop again.

"Blackmail," Cathleen said through clenched teeth.

"About what?" I said. "The senator has been dead for more than ten years—the pictures can't hurt him now."

"But they can hurt mother. They could even jeopardize her re-election if they became public. And my brother is a *congressman*, for God's sake! It would ruin his career, too."

Maureen seemed to have gotten herself under control. "It would put a stain on everyone in my family who holds public office. And it wouldn't do Cathleen's law career any good either."

"Oh, mother," Cathleen said, her voice low and unbearably sad.

"But beyond that—Doyle Hartigan had a legacy in this state, in this town. A reputation for integrity and decency matched by very few people in public life. These photographs would shoot the hell out of that, and that's really what I couldn't possibly endure."

"Who knew about the photographs?" I said. "About their existence?"

The judge shrugged. "The one who took them, I suppose. I don't know who else."

"I don't see how a small-timer like Bill Poduska would have known about them. Unless someone sent him to you—or to your cousin Hugh, rather—specifically so he could hunt for them."

"I can't imagine who that might be," she said.

"Has anyone approached you in the last few weeks? Tried to get money from you for the pictures?"

"I don't have any money, to speak of," she said. "I've been a public servant all my life."

Yeah, right, I thought. There's no such thing as a rich public servant, is there? Nevertheless, I started sniffing down another trail. "What if it wasn't money that they were after? What if they wanted something else from you?"

"Like what?"

"Something less . . . less tangible."

Maureen closed her eyes. "Please don't be mysterious. I'm simply not up to it today."

"You're a judge," I said. "You have influence in many areas." And then I couldn't help myself—I added, "Just like Senator Hartigan did."

Her jaw got hard, and her eyes turned to slits. "I suppose I deserved that, or rather my late husband did. But it was really shitty of you to say anyway."

"Sorry," I said. "But if those pictures aren't going to be used to blackmail or coerce you, there's no reason for anyone to want to steal them. No one has contacted you about them?"

"If they had, I wouldn't be sending you all over creation trying to locate them, would I?"

"Nothing on your upcoming court docket that might suggest someone wanting to get to you?"

"Nothing," she said firmly. "It's the usual collection of criminal cases, the kind I've been hearing for the last fifteen years. There's nothing particularly unusual about any of them."

I swiveled my gaze to Cathleen. "What about you? The release of those pictures of your father would be almost as damaging to your reputation as to your mother's. Are you involved in any legal matter right now that someone might want to put pressure on you to throw?"

She flapped her hands ineffectually. "I doubt that very much. My specialty is antitrust cases. Those guys play rough in the courtroom, but they don't usually pull low dirty tricks like this outside of it. I don't think there's anyplace to look on my side of the fence."

"Do you have any idea how mortifying this is for both of us?" Judge Hartigan said, opening her purse and fishing for a tissue. "Spilling our family secrets all over the table like crumbs?"

"Every family has secrets, Maureen," I told her. "For the lucky ones, the secrets stay secrets."

CHAPTER FIFTEEN

The judge left shortly after that, her head down and her shoulders slumping, dragging the heavy baggage of humiliation and guilt behind her. Having admitted to me about Senator Hartigan and Giancarlo D'Allessandro had taken the guts right out of her. She'd obviously known about it a long time, but the saying of it out loud, the actual words being released into the ozone, had made it impossible for her to stuff it away and ignore it anymore, and now she was permanently damaged. I wasn't sure she'd ever again completely get her chin off her chest.

Cathleen didn't leave with her; instead she hung around, obviously needing to talk. I asked if she'd like to go somewhere for a drink, but she said that even though she could certainly use one, she couldn't face being in a crowd right now. So I offered her a beer from the little office refrigerator, and she accepted, turning up her nose when she saw it was my brand, Stroh's, but being too polite to say anything about it.

We drank straight from the bottle. An honest, working-class beer like Stroh's should be consumed no other way.

"That must have been rough for both of you," I said. "I'm sorry it had to come down like that."

"Like what?"

"Hearing about your father that way."

She tilted the bottle almost upside down, her lips wrapped around the mouth, the beer gurgling down her throat. Then she gasped a little, and coughed; she'd polished off about a third of it in one gulp. "It looks like the personal and political honor of the entire Hartigan family is going down in flames because of that little shit-heel, Brian McFall. Or Bill Poduska, or whatever the hell he was calling himself."

"This might not be so bad," I said. "It could be the pictures have nothing to do with Poduska's death. Maybe he took them by mistake."

She tilted her head, interested.

"Maybe he simply grabbed whatever he could find, and later he didn't know what they were so he just threw them away. If that's the case, nobody will have to know about them."

"That doesn't sound very realistic to me."

"Probably not. We won't know until I find them."

"If you find them."

"I'll find them," I said with more confidence than I was feeling. "Now that I know what I'm looking for."

She stood up and walked over to the window, beer in hand. It was after six-thirty, deep dusk now, and the lights of Jacobs Field glowed brightly against the purplish turquoise sky; sometimes they keep them on even when there's no ball game—even when the season is over.

"It's very important to me that you don't think too badly of my father, Milan," she said.

I didn't answer her.

"There could be all sorts of explanations for those pictures."

Sure there could. "Look, I know that your family and the D'Allessandros have been friends for a long time."

"Yes, but . . ." Her shoulders quivered. "I can't believe my father would actually take money from him."

"It happens all the time," I said softly. "In politics, and everywhere else. Unfortunately, that's the way business is done."

"Well, it stinks."

I nodded.

"You probably think everyone in my family is corrupt, now."

"I don't think anything of the kind," I assured her, getting out of my chair and going over to the window where she stood. "You and I are good friends, aren't we? And whatever is going on in those pictures has nothing to do with you." I put my hands on the tops of her shoulders and massaged gently. Her muscles were tight and knotted with tension. "Or with our relationship."

"Our relationship," she murmured, moving away from my hands. "Such as it is." She took another hefty pull on her Stroh's, emptying the bottle, and then put it down on the windowsill and turned to face me head-on. "I have a long and depressing history of relationships with inappropriate men, don't I? Victor Gaimari. Brian McFall." Her smile was self-deprecating and wormwood-bitter. "And let's not forget my ex-husband, the Weasel."

"Come on, now. Neither one of us has such a great track record in that department."

"I know," she said. "I thought my mother was the only person I'd ever met who was happily married, but it turns out that she was living with a crooked politician for thirty-five years." Her eyes were filling up again. "Why does it have to be this way? Is everybody rotten? Corrupt?"

"Everybody has the seeds of corruption in them," I said. "Some people just don't allow them to germinate, that's all."

"Like you," she said, and I don't think she meant it as a compliment. "Mister Straight Arrow. Mister Integrity. Mister Incorruptible."

I shook my head. "I have my moments."

"No you don't. You're the only person I've ever met who never has moments. That's why we never got together, isn't it, Milan? Because I used to go with Victor Gaimari, a mob figure, and that made me an untouchable as far as you were concerned, even though he's your friend."

"It was *because* of the friendship," I said. "A gentleman doesn't sleep with the ex-girlfriend of a friend. That's the rule, I think. Who Victor happens to be had nothing to do with it."

But she knew I was lying. And told me so.

And then she went back to the desk and picked up her purse, heading for the door, her heels loud on the hardwood floor. "Why do people have to be so corrupt? Even Brian—or Bill, I should say. Goddamn him anyway!" She stopped, turned around, and looked at me. A tear ran down her left cheek, leaving a trail through her makeup, and she didn't even bother wiping at it. "Why couldn't he have just stolen the money and the credit cards and stuff— even the pictures of my father—and let it go at that?" She rolled her eyes toward the ceiling, awash in self-pity. "Why did the son of a bitch have to fuck me, too?"

The son of a bitch had to fuck her, I thought after she'd gone, after I'd heard the sound of her car downstairs in the lot receding into the fast-falling night, because there are some men like that—married or not—men who, because of whatever demons live within the deepest shadows of their souls, have to score with every woman who crosses their path. They don't have to love her, or like her, or even be particularly attracted to her. They just have to have her. For the challenge of it—the thrill of the hunt. For the heady rush of conquest. For the variety, for bragging rights, for another notch on their bedpost.

For fun.

And because in some way it validates them.

I didn't know about all of William Poduska's activities in the bedroom, of course. I didn't want to. But I knew about Cathleen Hartigan, and Judith Torrence, and the women who worked in Dante Ruggiero's string of massage parlors in Warren. I knew enough to realize that, with all of Poduska's many other faults and failings, he was also a sex addict, or pretty close to being one, anyway.

It was a damn shame, considering how he made part of his living—running that just-off-the-plane-from-Ireland scam on good-natured people. In the cases of Cathleen and Judith, at least, the sexual victimization was merely adding insult to injury.

But why did he swipe the damned pictures? That's what I couldn't figure out. He had no use for them himself, and couldn't have known of their existence unless someone told him about them. And hired him to secure them.

For blackmail, without question. But I doubted that the blackmailer was after money. Maureen Hartigan was certainly comfortably fixed but, as she had pointed out, far from wealthy. And the whole process seemed so roundabout and complicated that it wouldn't have been worth any blackmailer's time and effort to hold her up for a few thousand dollars.

Then I started thinking about Cathleen. Being a partner in a downtown blue-chip law firm, she was certainly better off financially than her mother. Perhaps she was meant to be the extortionist's mark.

Still, there had to be some foreknowledge of those pictures, or Poduska would never have taken them. And that led me to thinking about who might have had intimate access to the Hartigan family.

I did a quick search through the telephone directory, found what I was looking for, and locked up the office. I was hungry, but I figured dinner could wait awhile. I locked up the office, went downstairs to my car, and headed west.

David Gowan lived just over the Cleveland border in the suburb of Lakewood, in one of the elegant high-rise condos that were strung along Lake Avenue on the shoreline of Lake Erie, an area known as the Gold Coast. I'd never met him, but of course I knew who he was—not only had his disbarment been top news a few years back, but he was also Cathleen Hartigan's former husband.

Lawyers weren't supposed to do what he did; they couldn't deliberately ask their witnesses to lie, knowing it was a lie. It is called suborning perjury, and he was lucky he got off with only a disbarment and no jail time. He should have known better, I thought, just like he should have known what a wonderful, special wife he had in Cathleen. But he didn't know, because he was a jerk.

And a sleaze.

Since he was no longer allowed to practice law in the state of Ohio, he'd set himself up as a legal consultant of some sort; at least that's what I'd heard. He must have been making pretty good money at it, whatever it was, to be able to afford a Gold Coast condo like this one.

They had a security set-up in the vestibule of Gowan's building, naturally. You can't nick somebody for three hundred and fifty thousand dollars and a-grand-a-month condo fee for what was basically a very nice, roomy two-bedroom apartment and not give them all the trimmings. I looked at the simple lock on the double glass doors; it wouldn't have taken the greenest journeyman burglar sixty seconds to open it. But I wasn't a burglar, and even if I had been, it was eight o'clock on a weekday evening, and there were lots of people around.

So I found Gowan's name on the directory, picked up the telephone that was mounted on the wall, and punched in the required code.

The receiver crackled and came alive. "Yes?"

"Mr. Gowan?" I said, probably too loud.

"Yes?" He was matching my volume, an aggressive, slightly throaty voice I didn't care for.

"My name is Milan Jacovich. I'm a private investigator. I wonder if I could have a few minutes of your time."

"You're who?"

"Milan Jacovich. I'm a private investigator."

He was silent for about five seconds. Then he said, "I can't talk to you now."

He broke the connection.

I depressed the cradle, then went through the routine again, listening to the rings. There were three of them.

"What?"

"Mr. Gowan, it would really be in your best interest to talk to me."

"Fuck you. Beat it."

And he was gone again.

Now he was beginning to get on my nerves. I dialed a third time.

No greeting at all this time. "Listen, if you don't get the hell away from here and stop bugging me, I'm going to call the police."

"If you don't let me come up for a minute, you'll be talking to the police all right, but they'll be calling *you*."

"Are you threatening me?" he said, but this time his voice betrayed the tiniest quaver of doubt.

"I don't have to. Release the door down here, Mr. Gowan, and save yourself a lot of trouble. Trust me."

I guess that got to him, co-opting some of his lawyer-speak. Every attorney in the world knows what it means when one says, "Trust me." In any event, after a moment he said, "Fourteen B, and you'd better make it fast," a discreet buzzing sound filled the vestibule, and I pushed the glass doors open and headed across the inner lobby toward the elevator. I didn't pay much attention to the furnishings in the lobby—the silver-and-white-flocked wallpaper, the never-used chairs and sofas, and the equally useless urns and bowls—but if I'd been asked to testify in court later,

I would have said my impression was that the lobby was all silver and mirrors.

The inside of the elevator was similarly mirrored, and on my trip up to the fourteenth floor I had a chance to regard myself in its reflection. I looked too beat-up for such an elegant setting. My craggy, high-cheekboned Slavic features bore the ravages of a collegiate football career and too much knocking around since then. And I had medium brown hair that was receding faster than I would have liked and which I liberally dosed with pH-balanced shampoo. A lot of things are pH-balanced these days—shampoo, toothpaste, mouthwash, cosmetics. I don't know what pH is or why it needs to be balanced, and I'll bet no one else does either. There's probably no such thing as pH, anyway.

I noticed that I was probably a few pounds heavier than I should have been, too, although my six-foot-three frame was able to handle it all right. I was wearing a gray corduroy jacket with elbow patches, navy slacks, a dark blue dress shirt, and a lighter blue tie. Most of the men who stepped into this elevator were probably wearing Armani or Brooks Brothers suits.

But I supposed I was dressed appropriately for my mission, which was nothing more than a fishing expedition. I certainly didn't expect David Gowan to admit that he'd ordered those photographs stolen in order to blackmail his former wife and mother-in-law. The best I could do was to observe him carefully, looking for an unusual or suspicious reaction. I hoped I'd find one, frankly. I was all prepared not to like Gowan. For several reasons.

Fourteen B was one of four units on the floor, each one occupying a corner of the building, which guaranteed each a lake view. Gowan's place was on the northeast corner, allowing a spectacular vista of downtown as well. Its towers were lighted up at night and seemed to rise magically out of the water like the Emerald City of Oz. Don't tell me Cleveland isn't a beautiful city.

David Gowan was not beautiful. He was about forty, and like me, his hairline was receding. He made up for it by wearing a short-cropped beard at the end of swooping sideburns, and a mustache that drooped at the corners of his mouth like Marlon Brando's in *Viva Zapata!* About two inches shorter than I, he was wearing a cream-colored silk shirt, black tassel loafers on sock-less feet, and an astonishing pair of extra-tight doeskin leather pants. Either he'd stuffed a gym sock into his underwear, or one of his distant forebears was an elephant.

"Jacovich," he said when he opened the door to my ring. "You're a friend of Cathleen's, right?"

"That's right, Mr. Gowan. And my first name is Milan, if you're comfortable with that. Otherwise it's *Mister* Jacovich. Okay?"

"Well, excuse *me*," he said, and reluctantly moved aside so I could come in.

His sprawling living room had all the coziness of an insurance-company high-rise office. There were no carpets; instead, there was black compound flooring with a pebbled texture. His obvi-ously expensive furniture, complete with velvet throw pillows, was all medium red, as was the wallpaper. Two of the walls were glass, to take advantage of the view, and opened onto a wrap-around balcony.

"I'd ask you to sit down, but I'm expecting company," he said, looking at the gold Rolex on his left wrist. "So make it snappy. What's this about?"

"I'm investigating a robbery."

"I look like a bank robber to you?"

"I didn't say it was a bank."

He shrugged. "Nothing else worth robbing."

"And I'm not accusing you of anything."

"A damn good thing you're not," he said. "There are slander laws that protect people from accusations like that."

"Judge Maureen Hartigan's house was robbed recently."

"Maureen," he snorted, as if remembering something unpleas-ant. "Well, that just breaks my heart."

He tried to put his hands in his pockets, then realized his pants were too tight to hold a credit card, much less a fist, and he let his arms dangle awkwardly. Nervous energy seemed to radiate from him like the blast of a space heater, his eyes darting around the room as if he'd never seen it before. My guess was that he was rid-ing the crest of a crack high, but I'm no expert.

"I haven't seen Maureen in two or three years," he said. "And that's not long enough. So I don't know what I can tell you about any robbery."

"Do you know anyone named Brian McFall?"

"No. Am I supposed to?" His expression never changed, not even his eyes.

"How about James O'Dowd?"

"What is this," he demanded, "a list of the Irish Rovers? I never heard of either of them."

"How about William Poduska?"

"No, not him, either," he said, and then thought about it. "Wait a minute, that name sounds familiar." He chewed on it for a while, his gaze wandering to the window and his fantastic view. "Yeah, wasn't he the guy who got shot in a motel a few days ago?"

"That's right," I said. "You knew him?"

"How the hell would I have known him? I read about it in the newspaper like everybody else in town." He raised his chin proudly. "I've got one of those photographic memories. That's how I happened to remember *your* name. Cathleen mentioned you once or twice. In passing. And I've read about you in the newspapers, too."

"Just like I've read about you," I said.

He didn't like that, which was fine with me because I hadn't meant him to. His cheeks took on an angry flush. "So what's the deal, here? I don't know any of these people. And if they have anything to do with the Hartigan family, I don't want to know them."

"You're mad at the whole family?"

"Mad at them? No. I just hate their guts."

"The divorce wasn't amicable?"

"You can sing that in G," he said. "You ever been married?" He didn't wait for an answer. "In the vows it says, 'for better or worse,' right? Well, Cathleen doesn't understand that. When it was 'for better,' oh sure, when we were rockin' and rollin' and getting invited to all the best parties, everything was fine. But the minute things got 'for worse,' the bitch bailed out"

I didn't much care for his choice of words. "Kind of like a ship leaving a sinking rat."

"Hey, you have no call to talk that way to me," he said resentfully, his smallish brown eyes getting even tinier as he squinted at me in what he hoped, I'm sure, was a glare. "You don't know anything about me. So watch your mouth."

"You'd better watch yours, too, Mr. Gowan," I told him. "Cathleen is a friend of mine."

He let that register. Then he looked at his watch again, growing more hyper with every tick of the second hand. It was little more than a minute later than the last time he checked. "Okay, come on, come on, let's get our asses in gear here," he said, pacing back and forth impatiently.

"When you were married, did you spend much time at your mother-in-law's house?"

He shrugged. "Some. As little as possible, frankly. I was never Maureen's favorite person, even before my . . . difficulties."

That didn't surprise me. "Did you ever hear anything about Senator Hartigan having similar difficulties?"

"I never knew him. He was dead before I ever met Cathleen. But from what I heard, he was some sort of a fucking plaster saint." His eyes glittered, growing crafty. "Are you saying Doyle Hartigan was dirty?"

"I'm not saying anything," I said. "I'm asking."

He nodded. "I wouldn't be surprised, though. The Hartigans are a nasty bunch once you get to know them."

"Oh?"

"The Clan of the Cave Bear. And holier-than-thou, too. You know the type. You can't even say 'Jesus Christ' in front of Maureen without her glaring at you and saying 'Blessed be His holy name.'"

"So it wouldn't upset you if something bad happened to them?"

He wet his lips, all at once on guard. "Well, I wouldn't want any of them to *die* or anything. But if you want to know whether I'd like to see them all fall on their fat, white Irish asses? Be humiliated in this town? Get voted out of office, or lose their cushy jobs? Bet on it."

"Kind of bitter, aren't you?"

"You know it. The brother, the congressman, is a pious, mackerel-snapping son of a bitch. The judge is . . . well, the mother-in-law from hell. And Cathleen?" His mouth twisted with hatred. "Cathleen is a cunt."

I reached out my left hand and gathered the front of his silk shirt into my fist, taking some petty satisfaction when two of the buttons popped off and clattered onto the floor, and drew him close to me so that we were almost nose-to-nose. "I told you to watch your mouth about my friends, Mr. Gowan."

For a moment his eyes widened in real terror. Then he said in a scared voice that almost squeaked, "Hey! I could press charges on you. This is assault!" And he pointed with a trembling finger to his shirt wrapped in my hand. His years of experience as a high-priced lawyer had not gone to waste.

"You're absolutely right; it is assault," I said, raising my other fist. "And if I punch your fucking lights out, it's battery. Now that we've got the legal definitions out of the way . . ."

He wrenched away from me. "This little bull session is over," he said, smoothing the wrinkles in his shirt, even though two of the buttons were now gone. "Get the hell out of my home."

He opened the door for me, motivated by his anxiousness to get me out of his sight rather than by politeness. I walked out into the hallway, and he slammed it shut.

I pushed the DOWN button and waited, hoping deep inside me that he was behind the theft of the photographs. But I didn't think so. He'd showed no reaction when I'd mentioned Poduska's name, or either of his aliases, either. Of course, there was always the chance that Poduska had more phony names than the guest register of a cheap motel, but mentally I was crossing David Gowan off my suspect roster, even as I was installing him on my own personal shit list.

I heard a discreet little *bong*, and the elevator door slid open. I had to stand aside to let its passenger out—a tall young African American with shiny processed hair, wearing a floor-length, black leather trench coat, hanging open. Around his neck was a thick braided gold chain, heavy enough to keep the Prisoner of Zenda attached to the wall of the dungeon forever. Under his arm he carried a small package the size of a couple of pork chops, neatly wrapped in white paper.

He grinned at me. "Whazzuuuup?" he said, his tongue lolling obscenely out of his mouth.

Those Budweiser Super Bowl commercials have a lot to answer for.

He brushed past me and turned to his right, heading directly for David Gowan's apartment. I got into the elevator and pushed the button for the lobby, the door whispered shut, and the car moved downward.

It must be nice to have as much money as Gowan, I mused. Your crack dealer makes house calls.

CHAPTER SIXTEEN

I f the general public ever discovers how easy it is to find out just about anything they might want to know, there will be little need for private investigators like me. We have none of the special privileges accorded to law enforcement officers, but instead are forced to pore through public records.

Except for bank accounts and medical histories, most records are open to public scrutiny. Marriages and divorces, births and deaths, wills, property, real estate holdings and purchase prices, court trial transcripts—they're all right there, available for perusal by anyone who's interested and knows where to look. And there's a frightening amount of even more personal information that can be found on the Internet with the click of a mouse.

The difference is, private investigators know where to look.

So first thing the next morning I found myself downtown on Ontario Street at the Cuyahoga County Courthouse, armed with a brand-new yellow legal pad and several pens, poring through Common Pleas court records—specifically, the cases that had been heard in Judge Maureen Hartigan's courtroom over the past six months, and those she was scheduled to adjudicate in the next six.

The place smelled stale and dusty. It seems as though almost all government offices and buildings, new and old, bear that particular odor—city halls, the IRS and FBI headquarters, and all the other city, state, and federal departments that collect mountains of paper and perform arcane and mysterious functions no one ever understands. I wondered how long it would take for the brand-new, state-of-the-art, high-rise federal courthouse downtown on the edge of the Cuyahoga River to start smelling that way. Or maybe there was some sort of old and obscure law, and the contractors had been instructed to build in the musty smell from the beginning.

The problem was, I didn't know specifically what I was looking for.

When I had located Judge Maureen Hartigan's upcoming court calendar, I sat down at a long table and dutifully copied down all the pending trials on a pad of yellow paper. The names meant nothing to me; the newspapers hadn't reported most of the crimes, and if they had, I hadn't registered them because there had been no necessity to do so:

Henry Pinkard, who was to stand trial for possession of crack cocaine with intent to sell.

Angelo Marcantonio, accused of aggravated rape, assault, and gross sexual imposition.

Juanita Morley, arrested for solicitation and prostitution.

Robert Tufts, grand theft auto.

The list went on; it took me more than an hour to fill up seven and a half pages with the crimes and misdemeanors and sins and extralegal transgressions of my fellow Clevelanders.

If the poor bastards on the list were found guilty, Maureen Hartigan would probably come down on them like a wrathful Jehovah. By reputation, she was hell on criminals of all stamps and varieties.

But none of the names sounded familiar. None of the cases or crimes seemed to jump out and bite me to point me in the direction of the missing candid photographs of Senator Doyle Hartigan. Nevertheless, I tore the sheets from the pad, folded them, and put them in my pocket, to be transferred to a disk later. I've learned after long experience never to throw anything away. Like a Native American carving up a buffalo, I make sure nothing ever goes to waste.

I went back to the office and painstakingly typed the court calendar onto my computer in the HARTIGAN folder. It was probably an exercise in futility, and it took me a while to finish it, too. I hadn't worked very hard in typing class back at St. Clair High; in those days, guys didn't really want to learn how to type. Typing was for girls, we thought. And then the computer age came along, and we all wished we hadn't been so arrogantly macho.

Then I made the phone call I had been dreading.

"Victor," I said when he came on the line, "it's become very important that I talk to the don as soon as I can. Is that possible?"

He was silent for a moment. When he did speak, it was with exquisite care. "Is there a problem?"

"I don't know," I said. "That's what I'd like to find out."

Another pause. Then: "Well, you know my uncle always enjoys your company, Milan. Would you like to have dinner tonight?"

Dinner again. Victor always insisted on making everything social. But I knew that to refuse him was to insult him, and to insult the don as well. "Dinner would be fine. But it's on me this time."

"That would make my uncle very unhappy, Milan. And me, too. We'd be very pleased if you would be our guest for dinner. Would Giovanni's be all right? At seven-thirty?"

Giovanni's, in Beachwood, was one of the finest restaurants in town. Victor was piling up the favors I owed him, and I think he knew it. I shook a cigarette out of the pack on my desk and stuck it in my mouth. "Giovanni's is always all right. Thanks."

"Good," he said, and his tone of voice made me think he was actually rubbing his hands together in anticipation. "We'll both look forward to seeing you."

"Victor?"

"Hmm?"

"Just the three of us this time."

"Oh? What's that all about?"

"I'd prefer it if you didn't invite Cathleen Hartigan. All right?"

I could hear him breathing. "Did you two have a falling-out?"

"Not exactly."

"I thought you were friends."

"We are," I said. "But I don't want her at this particular dinner. It's strictly business."

"Ah," he said.

"You'll understand when I tell your uncle what I need."

"Is this about the Poduska thing again?"

"That's right."

"It doesn't have anything to do with Dante Ruggiero, does it?

I think you realize that neither my uncle nor I will have anything more to say about him one way or the other."

"It has nothing to do with Ruggiero."

Once more he was quiet, but I knew his wheels were turning. "All right then, Milan," he said finally, making his tone chillingly noncommittal. "Have it your way. It'll just be the three of us."

At five minutes to seven, I found them seated at the bar in Giovanni's Ristorante on Chagrin Boulevard. The lounge is a small, tasteful space, recently remodeled, with several roomy booths over which are displayed some of the playful restaurant and cafe paintings of Guy Buffet. Behind the bar, even the TV set is elegantly framed in gold.

Victor blended in with the rest of the well-dressed crowd in an expensive dark blue suit and a discreet tie, if it could ever be said that he blended in anywhere. He was nursing his usual martini and checking out the beautiful women in the room. There were quite a few of them to look at. I wondered how many of them he had dated.

Don Giancarlo D'Allessandro was sipping at a glass of designer water. He had on a faded tweed jacket he'd probably owned for thirty years, because it hung on his frail shoulders like a hand-me-down from a much larger relative, but under it he wore a spiffy beige mock-turtleneck that looked is if it were silk. He was in dire need of a haircut; gray wisps hung down over his substantial ears and spilled over the back of his collar. For most of the time I'd known him, he had been ill with some unspecified malady that just might have been no more than the attrition of his years. He no longer went every day to the social club he'd always used as his headquarters, a dusty room over a restaurant on Murray Hill in Little Italy, which is where I had first met him under less than optimum circumstances. And while he left the nuts and bolts of running the interests of his "family" these days to his nephew Victor, there was no doubt in anyone's mind that he still was consulted on all the major decisions.

The don was a survivor in the truest sense of the word. And in this town, something of a legend.

The don's father had perished during Cleveland's "Sugar Wars" of the Prohibition era, so-called because two of our city's mob families—one from Little Italy and another from farther east

on Woodland Avenue—were in a battle to control shipments of
sugar in and out of the region. They sold the sugar to bootleg-
gers for profits that rival those of today's cocaine trade, and gave
the nickname "Bloody Corners" to the intersection of East 110th
Street and Woodland Avenue because of all the drive-by mob
hits that had occurred there. It's often been said that there was
a still in virtually every house in the neighborhood back then. A
gruesome mass shooting in a card room behind a storefront, in
a building that still stands on that corner, left young Giancarlo
fatherless. The resultant funeral of Carmen D'Allessandro, the
cortege of which led from his house on Murray Hill to Calvary
Cemetery, was one of the biggest events of the Italian-American
social season.

When Giancarlo claimed his heritage and began building
his own crime family just before World War II, he managed to
weather the reign of famed crime-buster Eliot Ness, who became
Cleveland's safety director after his adventures with the Capone
mob in Chicago. He had cracked down on the gambling interests
of the North Coast when he wasn't searching—with ultimate lack
of success—for a local serial killer known as the Mad Butcher of
Kingsbury Run. There was talk of a contract being put out on the
life of the former Untouchable, but it was Don Giancarlo who
urged the other local families to back off the idea; Ness was a ce-
lebrity, and his death would have brought unwanted media attention and, as a result, more heat. As it was, D'Allessandro escaped
relatively unscathed from the glaring spotlight of Senator Estes
Kefauver and his congressional hearings on organized crime in
the fifties. During the Bobby Kennedy frontal assault on Jimmy
Hoffa in the early sixties, D'Allessandro's name was mentioned,
but he was somehow never subpoenaed. After that he managed
to live quietly in the house on Murray Hill where he'd been born
and rule his fiefdom efficiently without getting his name in the
papers.

The don saw me and pulled his lips back into a skeletal smile
that illustrated where the expression "long in the tooth" had come
from.

"Milan Jacovich," he said; it was his standard greeting to me.
He offered me his ancient-parchment cheek, and I bent down to
give it a respectful kiss.

"You're looking well, Don Giancarlo."

"Nah, I'm looking old. Feeling old, too. Don't even have the energy to go take a haircut anymore; look at me, it's like I'm growing a ponytail back there. Come, sit next to me," he said, patting the barstool beside him. "I haven't seen you for a long while. We got lots of catching up to do, no?" Despite there being several people standing up at the bar, there was a vacant stool next to Victor as well, and I imagined that the D'Allessandros were pretty well known in Giovanni's and not many people would presume to sit next to them without an invitation.

I sat down and told the bartender to bring me whatever Victor was having. Then I scooped up a handful of mixed nuts from the generous dish on the bar, trying unobtrusively to make sure I got at least one pecan. They're my favorite nuts.

"How are the kids?" the old man asked. "Your boys? They're okay?"

"They're just fine, thank you. My older son is playing varsity football at Kent State."

He nodded his approval. "It's good to get an education. Me, I quit school in the tenth grade." He gave me a kindly nudge in the arm with his elbow. "But then I guess I learned whatever I had to know the hard way, eh?"

"Milan," Victor said, leaning forward to see around his uncle. "Have you spoken to Mr. Ruggiero yet?"

"I did," I said, "and thank you for making that possible, Don Giancarlo."

The don chuckled. "Dante, he's a funny old son of a bitch. Dresses like he's going to a christening. Powders his face like an old faggot, even at his age." He pointed his gnarled finger at me, the joints swollen from arthritis. "But he don't lie, that's one thing. Whatever he tells you, you can take it to the bank."

"He didn't tell me much," I said.

"Then that means he don't know much. I ask him to be straight with you, and he does it. He would of said 'I won't tell you,' straight out. He wouldn't of said 'I don't know.' That's how he is."

I nodded. The bartender set my Bombay Sapphire gin martini in front of me, and I picked it up and raised it in D'Allessandro's direction. "Your health, Don Giancarlo," I said.

He waved a dismissive hand at me. "My health is nothing

to drink to, because it's shit. They won't even let me have wine no more." He pointed to his bottled water. "They got me on this health diet so bad I don't even wanna eat anything. I'm eighty-four. What's the point?"

"The point is," I said, "we all want to have you around a while longer. So I drink to your health whether you want me to or not."

"In that case, I thank you," he said, and touched his glass to mine. It was very good crystal, and the *ping* resonated.

After taking a reluctant sip of his water, he said, "So this Poduska kid that got shot in the motel room . . ."

"Yes, sir?"

"He did some work for some people from time to time, but I never met him. Victor says he was a punk."

"Some people would call him that, I suppose."

"So, yeah, then," the old man said, "what's the big fuss? Punks like that, they get killed all the time. It's too bad, but that's the chance they take when they decide to be punks instead of players."

"The trouble is, this punk took something from my client, and I'm trying to find it and get it back."

"Why don't we move to a table and have some dinner before we get down to the serious stuff?" Victor said quickly. "I always find I'm more comfortable talking after I've enjoyed a great meal."

He signaled the host, who ushered us to a smaller oak-paneled alcove to the rear of the main dining room, with only a few other tables and none of them occupied. Again, the paintings on the wall were impeccable, only in this room they were Picassos. I knew that everyone in the place watched our passage through the dining room to our table, but none did so openly. One simply does not gawk at Giancarlo D'Allessandro.

I imagined Victor had called ahead and booked that particular table. It was against the back wall of the restaurant, and afforded the don a view of the front door and whoever might be walking in. Now, there had not been a mob hit in Cleveland for twenty-five years, no one had made a threatening move toward Giancarlo D'Allessandro since long before that, and no one was likely to do so anytime soon. But old habits die hard, and he wasn't about to have a meal in a public place, even one so elegant and eminently respectable as Giovanni's, with his back to the door.

Call it the Wild Bill Hickok syndrome. That particular American legend was shot in the back because he made the mistake of not facing the door when he sat in on a poker game. And Giancarlo D'Allessandro had once told me that he learned from other people's mistakes because it was a lot easier than learning from his own.

The meals were spectacular. There was an appetizer of beef-and-veal ravioli called *panzotti* that will dance forever in my head like visions of sugarplums. The don had special-ordered a salad very sparsely dressed and plain pasta with olive oil and garlic and a light sprinkling of cheese. After the entrees were cleared away, the waiter came over with coffee and after-dinner cognac for Victor and me, and for the old man a small dish of plain vanilla ice cream and a cup of decaffeinated coffee, compliments of Carl Quagliata, the boss man at Giovanni's.

"Decaf," the don said with disgust, tapping the cup with a horny fingernail. "All my life I take seven, eight cups espresso every day, and now they make me drink this crap." He took a tentative sip and wrinkled up his nose. "I think people wash their socks in this before they bring it out. Decaf . . ."

Victor leaned back in his chair, swirling the brandy around in the snifter and holding it up to the light. "Milan, I think there was something you wanted to ask my uncle, wasn't there?"

I took a quick hit of my own cognac. "Yes, Victor, thank you." I turned to his uncle. "Don Giancarlo, this is awkward."

The wrinkled brow became even more furrowed. "Awkward? We're friends, yes?" he said.

"I hope so."

"So there should be no awkwardness between friends. You wanna ask me a question, you just ask me it, and I'll understand you're asking out of respect and friendship. Now Victor tells me you're doing a job for Judge Maureen Hartigan, is that right?"

I nodded.

"I been friends with Maureen and her family for thirty years or more, and that's no secret. So if I can help her out in any way by helping you, it would be my honor to do so. You mentioned earlier that this Poduska who got killed the other day stole something from her."

"Yes, sir. An envelope full of old photographs."

He didn't say anything, but one grizzled eyebrow lifted.

"They're of the judge's husband."

"Doyle."

"They were taken in secret, without his knowledge."

He made a disapproving clucking sound with his tongue and shook his head sadly. "That stinks. It's an invasion of privacy. Just because a man is a public figure, like a state senator, the vultures, the punks, they think they can take advantage." He scooped up some ice cream and brought it to his mouth. "What was he doing in the pictures anyway?" he said, smacking his lips. "Something bad?"

There was no way out now, and no turning back, either. So I just took a deep breath, and said it. "He was accepting an envelope from you."

The don froze for a moment, looking hard at me. Then he put the spoon back into the dish very carefully and dabbed at his mouth with his napkin. "Is that so?"

"Yes, sir."

"When was this?"

"Judge Hartigan thinks the pictures are about twenty years old. They were taken in front of the Hollenden Hotel."

He sat back and folded his hands on the edge of the table like a kid in third grade trying to impress the teacher. "Okay, so maybe I used to go to the Hollenden Hotel a lot. So did Senator Hartigan. It was a beautiful hotel—I hated it when they tore it down. So what's the big fuss about? The pictures are twenty years old, and he's been dead for, what, ten?"

"Why would anyone want to steal those photos now?"

He considered. "To embarrass the Hartigan family."

"Or to embarrass you, Don Giancarlo?"

"What are they gonna embarrass *me* with?" he said. "Even Eliot Ness couldn't embarrass me, that *strunz*. The Kefauver commission couldn't embarrass me. Bobby *Kennedy* couldn't embarrass me. Now? Who gives a damn whether I'm embarrassed or not? I'm yesterday's newspapers."

"Not exactly," I said. "But I think you're right anyway. Someone wants to embarrass the Hartigans."

"Or to blackmail them," Victor said. "Has anyone tried to contact them about that?"

"Not that I know of."

The don rubbed his face with his hand, and I could hear the rasp of his whiskers against his palm. "I know I ain't exactly respectable company for a senator. At least back then I wasn't. But nevertheless I was friends with him. I was good friends with a lot of the local politicians. I still am. I think that was what you would call common knowledge."

"Yes, Don Giancarlo," I said as gently as I could. "But the envelope . . ."

He sighed, massaging his temples. "It was a long time ago, Milan Jacovich. I'm not so young anymore; sometimes I don't recall things."

Victor gave his uncle a concerned glance and then shot me a dark, warning look.

"Okay, hold on awhile," the old man finally said. "I think I do remember. Senator Hartigan did me a favor back then. Never mind what, it's not important twenty years later. It was a favor, that's all. And we met at the Hollenden for a drink, so I could thank him."

"The envelope was your way of thanking him?"

"Milan . . . ," Victor rumbled.

D'Allessandro held up his hand. "That's okay. Yeah, that was my way of thanking him. You're surprised?"

"No," I said.

"You're shocked?"

I smiled to take some of the sting out of it. "Well, maybe a little bit."

"Don't be a child!" he scolded. "What have you, been living at the bottom of a coal mine all your life? You don't know how things work? I thought you were a smart fella."

"It doesn't matter to me one way or the other," I said, even as I realized uncomfortably how much it *did* matter. "All I care about is why William Poduska stole those photographs."

"I knew the guy, Milan," Victor reminded me. "He wasn't smart enough, and he didn't have the stones to do it on his own."

"Which means he stole them on commission for somebody else."

"That'd be my guess."

"And maybe once he had them, perhaps he realized how valuable they were and decided why should he give them away when he could make some real money on them himself? So maybe he cut out the middleman and didn't hand them over where he was supposed to."

"Which probably pissed somebody off," the don put in.

"And they took them away from him and killed him."

"That's a pretty long stretch," Victor said. "Even for blackmail. Judge Hartigan doesn't have enough money to make it worth anyone's while to shoot Bill Poduska to get those pictures."

"Well now, wait a second," D'Allessandro said.

Both Victor and I stopped and looked at him, waiting while he took another sip of his decaf and made a face. "I'd give my left ball for an espresso."

"Uncle Gianni, you know that's not going to happen," Victor said, smiling easily. "Not on my watch, anyway. Aunt Regina would skin me alive."

The don was disappointed enough to actually pout.

"But you were about to say something," Victor reminded him.

"Yeah." He leaned his elbows on the table, speaking directly at me. "Maybe the amount of money wasn't enough to ice somebody, no. But there's a principle involved here. In the old days if you hire somebody to do something for you and he crosses you, that's reason enough. Because if he does it and gets away with it, then the next guy is gonna try you, too. And pretty soon you're out on your behind selling pencils on the corner. Or you're at the bottom of the lake. You understand what I'm saying to you? Everything is, how do you call it, negotiable." His face darkened. "Except a cross. Somebody crosses you—somebody you like and trust—then that's not negotiable anymore."

"There are other reasons for blackmail besides money changing hands directly," I said.

"Like what?" The don's eagle glare was challenging.

"Maybe you want somebody to do something for you he doesn't want to do, and you can't pay him for it and you can't muscle him, so you get yourself some leverage," I suggested.

D'Allessandro cocked his head quizzically, the ropy tendons of his neck stretching. "Leverage?"

"You find some other way to make him do it."

The old man's eyes grew crafty. "Or her," he said. "Some other way to make *her* do it. Like maybe a judge."

"And it would have to be something really important to kill somebody like the Poduska kid," Victor said. "It's not like the old days anymore."

"So if I find the reason," I said, "I find out who stole the photographs."

He gave me a small, chilly smile. "I wouldn't be at all surprised."

"As I told Victor," I said to the don, "Poduska made several phone calls to a number in Warren. An unlisted number. That's why I wanted to talk to Don Dante Ruggiero."

"Lots of people live in Warren," the old man said.

"People from the old days. From on Murray Hill."

He nodded. "Warren, Niles, Youngstown. A lot of the old guys, when they retired, you might say, they left town, but not too far. They all moved east a ways. Don't ask me why—I'd go nuts if I ever left Cleveland."

"Could you give me some names?"

His eyes suddenly focused on me, boring in. "Names?" He rolled the word around on his tongue gingerly, like someone who'd taken a canape that was too hot.

"Of some of the guys who retired from Cleveland and moved to Warren."

D'Allessandro frowned, tapping his cup with his fingernail again.

"That might be problematic," Victor said.

"We don't talk about our people," the don said severely. "You should know that by now."

"What could it hurt, Don Giancarlo? They're retired."

"Doesn't matter. It's the principle of the thing."

I took a big chance. "Maybe it should matter," I said, "since those photos are of you."

The old man pursed his lips, thinking about it.

"Don't you want to know if one of your old pals is using you to get at Maureen Hartigan?"

"I told you, nobody can do nothing to me anymore."

"Yes," I said, realizing that I was pressing. "Pushing," as Dante

Ruggiero had called it. "But it's kind of a betrayal of trust, isn't it? Somebody's got their own agenda going, and they use you to get what they want without your knowing it. You said yourself, everything is negotiable except a cross."

"Nevertheless," Victor said, "I don't think we can . . ."

"Wait, Victor." The don put both hands palms down, as if he were manipulating the strings of a marionette. "Milan Jacovich has got a point there."

Victor compressed his lips. Then he said, "If you think so, Uncle Gianni."

"Yeah, I do think so. Maybe he's right. Now if I can only remember." He looked at me and shrugged apologetically. "When you get as old as me, sometimes you can remember stuff from fifty years ago like it was last Tuesday, but you can't remember what you had for breakfast."

He tapped his temple. "Warren. Who's in Warren?" He played a piano solo on the edge of the table with his other hand. "Lou Lucarelli, for one. He moved there maybe fifteen years ago. Tommy Brancato, he left town after his wife passed away." He strained to remember. "Benny the Hat—Benny Simonetti. Nah, I'm wrong there. Benny went to Youngstown."

I whipped out my notebook and wrote down the names, which Victor regarded balefully.

"Help me out, Victor. Who else is in Warren?"

"Nunzio Valentino," Victor put in, but I could sense his reluctance. "But he's almost ninety."

"Yeah," the don agreed. "Who else? There were some other guys . . ."

Victor shrugged. "How about Mickey Marcantonio?"

I sat up straighter. I had heard that name somewhere before—recently. I wished I could remember where.

D'Allessandro shook his head sadly. "Yeah, Mickey. He's living in Warren. When he left town, he even changed his name. That made me very sad. Like he's ashamed of being Italian."

The name echoed inside my head, and I felt my pulse quickening. "What did he change it to, Don Giancarlo?"

"Urn, let me remember . . . Marks, for God's sake. Imagine an Italian guy picking a Jewish name? Mickey Marks, he calls himself now."

Michael Marks, I thought. The man I'd met on Dante Ruggiero's stairway. I wiped perspiration off my upper lip. "That name sounds familiar. Tell me a little about him, if you can."

"He was a goddamn cowboy, Mickey. A rebel. He thought he was some kind of tough guy. A hothead—always going off doing his own thing, making his own deals. It was disrespectful to the families. Finally, they kicked his ass out about ten years ago. He went out there to Warren after that, went into business of some kind—I can't remember what."

I thought I remembered why the name was familiar. "Did he have a family?" I asked. "Mr. Marcantonio? Does he have kids?"

"All Italians got kids, except me," he said a little sadly. "My Carmela, she could never have kids." He brightened then, and smiled at his nephew. "So Victor, here, he was like my own kid. Still is." Victor sipped at his espresso. "Milan. Why are you so interested in Mickey Marcantonio in particular?"

I put my notebook away. "I was just curious," I said, but I knew he didn't believe me. Giancarlo D'Allessandro grimaced as he finished the last of his decaf, and coughed. "Milan Jacovich," he said. "Curiosity killed the cat."

CHAPTER SEVENTEEN

After dinner, for which Victor simply signed a tab, we walked outside to the parking lot. D'Allessandro's driver, John Terranova, waited patiently in the Lincoln Town Car as he always does. He and I had past dealings, too—not pleasant ones. But it was a long time ago that Victor sent him and two other goons to my apartment to tune me up, and since then Terranova and I have found it expedient to consider the matter ancient history.

As soon as he saw us, he jumped out of the driver's seat of the old man's Lincoln and ran around to open the rear passenger door. That having been accomplished, he nodded at me and half-smiled.

"Hey, John," I said, nodding back.

The old don paused before getting into the car. "I told you some shit back in there I probably shouldn't of."

"I thank you for that, Don Giancarlo."

"Use it wisely, then," he counseled.

"I will," I said. "I promise to be very discreet."

"I know you will. That's why I like you. You're a stand-up man, and you know it's stupid to hold grudges. You know what it is to be a friend."

"It's my honor to be your friend, sir."

He ducked his head in acquiescence. "And you know what to say to people and what not to. Anything comes of what went on in there at the supper table, you know that you didn't hear it from here."

"That goes without saying."

"Nah, nothing goes without saying. It's way better to say it. That way there won't be any misunderstandings later. And I don't like having no misunderstandings with my good friends."

He opened his frail arms wide. "Come kiss me good night, Milan Jacovich. Would you believe it's getting past my bedtime?"

I wrapped my arms around him and kissed his cheek again. He was an old, tired tiger, and he'd fought and killed like one in his day, a day I suppose is best forgotten. And even though who he was and what he'd done ran contrary to everything I believed in and stood for, I couldn't help liking and respecting him.

He stepped out of my embrace and bundled himself into the back seat. "Johnny, put in the record—ah shit, what do you guys call it now? The CD. The Puccini. And turn it up loud so I can stay awake until we get home. I hate falling asleep in the car like some fucking old man."

"Sure, Mr. D'Allessandro," John said. He closed the rear door and started around to the driver's side. "Anything else, Mr. Gaimari?"

"No, that's good for tonight, John," Victor said. "Drive carefully."

Terranova grinned. "I always do."

The two of us stood there watching until the Lincoln had pulled out onto Chagrin Boulevard and headed west, its destination Little Italy and the old man's house. The October night brought with it a chill wind, and I put my hands in my pockets. Victor turned to me.

"Quite a guy, my uncle."

"A legend, that's for sure."

He flicked a microscopic speck of lint off his lapel. "That's all bullshit now, the legend stuff. As he said, it's yesterday's newspapers—what we teach the new puppy to pee on. He's just a lovely old man. And he really cares about you, Milan. And trusts you. He wouldn't have given up those names to you if he didn't. He thinks of you as almost part of the family."

I guess I blinked hard at that one, because Victor laughed at me. "Not *that* family," said. "His real family."

"For the past few years he *has* been kind of like an uncle to me. I don't know how that happened, exactly, but I admit it feels good."

"You love him, don't you, Milan?" he said simply.

I had to think about that for a while. My own father and my uncles had been dead many years. Ed Stahl was only eight or ten years my senior, and although he gave me help and advice whenever I asked for it, he was hardly a paternal figure to me. It came as a start to realize that Giancarlo D'Allessandro—the *capo di tutti capi*, the godfather of the Cleveland mob—was the closest things to an older male role model that I had.

"Yeah, Victor, in my own way I do."

"In spite of yourself."

I couldn't help the laugh, even though it was at my own expense. "It's not that hard," I admitted.

"Then make sure you take good care of him," he warned. "Those people in Warren, the old guys—even though they aren't as active as they used to be, they can still be dangerous. Mickey Marcantonio, especially. If he hadn't gotten out of Cleveland when he did, there would have been bad trouble. Like the old days. Nobody wants that again, do they? So whatever you're doing out in Warren, don't put my uncle in harm's way."

"You know I won't."

He nodded. "I do know that. And be careful yourself, too, Milan."

"Thanks," I said. "And for dinner, too."

We shook hands rather formally, and then he threw his arms around me and pounded me manfully on the back. He let go and turned away abruptly, almost as if hugging me had embarrassed him. He crossed the parking lot to where he'd left the shiny black Mercedes sedan that was as sleek and powerful as he was, moving with the grace of a leopard. The door closed with very little sound; the engine coughed, turned over, and purred like a kitten, and Victor guided it to the driveway and out onto the street.

I climbed into my own car, switched on the ignition, and just sat there listening to Dan Poletta's all-night jazz show on the public radio station, WCPN, for a while, wondering at the way life twists and turns like the crooked Cuyahoga River even while you're trying your damnedest to keep it on course. Wondering how things had come to such a pass that the Italian godfather of Cleveland had come to recognize a Slovenian ex-cop like me as a surrogate son.

But I didn't dwell on that too long; it was more important to digest what I had just learned from him. The digital clock on the dash told me it was almost eleven o'clock, but I was too excited to go home; a name was pulsating inside my brain like a relentless headache. Instead I headed west, taking Fairhill Road down the hill to University Circle and then continuing downtown to my office.

Unlike the gaudier sections of the Flats—the dance clubs and shot-and-a-beer bars of Old River Road on the east bank and the flashier and slightly more respectable Nautica Entertainment Complex across the Cuyahoga on the west—Collision Bend is a dark and lonely place in the middle of the night, so much so that I always feel perfectly safe there. I'm not one of those urban paranoiacs who refuse to come downtown after the sun has set and who drive the streets at night fully expecting to be mugged. There are certainly neighborhoods of Cleveland that are less safe than others after dark, just like anywhere else, but I haven't had any trouble yet. Maybe it's my size and heft; the predators of the night can spot a born victim a block away—and they're also canny enough to know who *not* to mess with.

I looked around for some wood to knock on, but I was out of luck.

I parked my car in the lot, unlocked the steel security door, and went upstairs. I had left the windows open—being on a high second floor, they were no invitation to burglars—but the night was too cool to keep them that way, so I closed them. It was very quiet outside, the hum of traffic from downtown barely noticeable, and the shrieking gulls that patrolled the river during the day evidently asleep. Across the water, Tower City seemed close enough to touch.

I put on my reading glasses, booted up the computer and opened the HARTIGAN file, and scrolled down the list of forthcoming cases on Maureen Hartigan's court calendar. The name I was looking for fairly glowed in the dark.

Angelo Marcantonio. Age twenty-four, with a home address in Warren, Ohio, with a trial date set for the second week in December, a week before Christmas. He had been charged with two counts of rape and gross sexual imposition, and another count of assault and battery in Cleveland.

I sat back and lit a Winston, putting the pieces together in my head. Mickey Marcantonio, aka Michael Marks, was a former made guy, and a friend and perhaps a business associate of Don Dante Ruggiero. Ruggiero was the sometime employer of William Poduska, who ran errands for Irish and Italian mob guys and their pals—and who had stolen photographs that would very much embarrass the family of the judge who would preside at the rape trial of the young man I was almost certain was Mickey Marcantonio's son.

I didn't want to ask Victor or his uncle anything more about their friends and associates in Warren—they had told me all they'd wanted me to know. And I seriously doubted whether Don Dante Ruggiero would be any more forthcoming. If I pushed them any further, it might rupture the delicate membrane of our relationship.

I wanted to reach Michael Marks. I knew that the Warren phone number Bill Poduska had called before he died was unlisted, but I was fairly certain that Marks's business was not. However, I had no idea what he called it, so there was no way of looking it up, save under MARKS. I tried doing that, accessing the white pages of my computer program. I also gave MARCANTONIO a shot, but I came up empty-handed both times.

I picked up the phone to tap out the numbers that Poduska had so frequently called in Warren, but thought better of it. If it was indeed Michael Marks's home phone, I wasn't ready to talk to him; I preferred seeing him in person, and I didn't want to alert him to my participation in the Poduska story just yet. I have found it's always better to have the element of surprise on one's side.

It was getting late—about ten-thirty—but I was still too wired for sleep, and a nightcap or two seemed to be in order. The Velvet Tango Room was just moments away, up the hill from my office, but its sophistication and élan were not what I was looking for. I decided to drive east on St. Clair Avenue to the neighborhood where I was born and raised, to an old hangout I hadn't visited in a long time—Vuk's Tavern, just off East Fifty-fifth Street.

Vuk's is a neighborhood shot-and-a-beer bar, patronized mostly by the Slovenians who live on the surrounding side streets between St. Clair and the lake and within walking distance of

St. Vitus's Church. The area was once called "Chicken Village" because when the first wave of Slovenian immigration from Ljubljana hit Cleveland just before World War II, most of the householders built chicken coops in their backyards. The horrendous East Ohio Gas explosion in destroyed many of the homes and the chicken coops as well, but the neighborhood was all rebuilt now, in much the same style as the old one.

I'd taken my first legal drink of alcohol at Vuk's Tavern, where my father had held up a corner of the bar before me, and I had courted my ex-wife, Lila, at one of the tables. Louis Vukovich, known almost universally as "Vuk" except to his nonagenarian mother, had been behind the bar then, and he's still there—older, more cantankerous, sporting the walrus mustache he's worn for forty years, his enormous Popeye forearms crossed over his chest as they always are when he's not cranking open a beer bottle.

The corners of his mouth twitched upward slightly when he saw me walk in. I don't think I've ever seen him smile completely except when the Indians made it to the World Series in 1995, and the smile quickly vanished when they lost to Atlanta. His greeting was the same as it's always been, even though he hadn't seen me for about nine months: "Whaddaya say, Milan?"

He dipped into the cooler for a frosty bottle of Stroh's, jacked off the cap with the old-fashioned opener fastened to the inside of the bar, and placed it before me. No glass. I don't believe anyone has ever thought to ask for a glass for his bottled beer in Vuk's. Glasses are for straight shots, highballs, and boilermakers, and that's about as esoteric as the drinks get. If you want a martini or a Manhattan or, God forbid, a grasshopper—go somewhere else.

I climbed onto a stool and leaned my elbows on the scarred wood that Vuk polished every morning of his life, relishing the feel and the familiarity of it. Vuk's Tavern is just a low-key and low-rent neighborhood beer joint, but I'm sure the long walnut bar is worth a fortune.

"How've you been, Vuk?" I said, picking up the bottle and enjoying its stinging chill.

He heaved his massive shoulders. "Just tryin' to make ends meet when my regulars like you stop coming in."

"Sorry about that. Life gets complicated sometimes."

"I know," he said, nodding. "You get into an OK Corral gun-fight downtown, and I gotta read it in the papers." He sniffed disdainfully.

"I was gonna call you up about it, but then I figured you didn't give enough of a shit to come in here to let me know you were okay, so I passed."

I winced. The previous winter I had indeed been in a shootout in the Fountain Court at Tower City, which couldn't help making the papers and the television news shows. I hadn't called anyone to report my survival, though; if they'd heard the news, they'd know. But that was Vuk for you—a loyal and loving friend, but gruff and quick to take offense.

"Well, I'm okay," I said. "As you can see. And I just haven't been getting out very much lately; that's why I haven't been in."

"New girlfriend?"

"I wish."

He studied me. "You wanna know the trouble with you, Milan?"

I looked away and took a pull on my beer, loving the bite in the back of my throat. The last thing I wanted to know was the trouble with me, but I figured I was going to hear it anyway.

"You got too far away from your roots. You moved out of the neighborhood, you hang out with fancy downtown people, you go out with women who think they're better than you, and it always gets screwed. Right?"

I shifted on the stool, suddenly uncomfortable. Of course, he was right. Vuk had acquired a lot of wisdom from spending forty years behind the stick.

"I married a girl from the neighborhood," I reminded him. "And look how that turned out."

He stroked his mustache. I've often noticed that men who sport mustaches can rarely keep their hands off them. "Yeah, well, Lila, you know, she's a Serbian, and that's a different kind of cat altogether. But there's lots of nice girls, Milan—nice Slovenian girls. You just don't get a chance to meet them living where you do in Cleveland Heights." He spoke the name of the inner-ring suburb where my apartment was as if he'd been talking about Siberia.

I fished in my pocket for my Winstons and fired one up; Vuk's was one of the last remaining public places where someone could light a cigarette and not be glared at as if he were a child molester.

"Could we forget about my love life, please?" I said, choking a little bit on the smoke.

"Sure we can. You forget about it all the time, anyway." With a towel he wiped at an imaginary spot on the bar. "How 'bout the Browns, huh? New coach making a difference, you think?"

He drifted off to serve another customer before I could answer. It was a rhetorical question anyway—Vuk was a baseball fan through and through, and the wall behind the bar was festooned with Indians memorabilia—team photos and pennants and a World Series program from 1948, and his treasured autographed photos of Bob Feller and Rocky Colavito and Early Wynn, framed in gold like holy pictures. The Tribe was where Vuk's heart was. He knew only enough about football and basketball to make small talk with the patrons who cared about them.

I looked around at the mostly familiar faces and tried to calculate how many hours of my life had been spent sitting at that bar. Vuk's isn't that much different than O'Grady's or the Shebeen, when you get right down to it. A different ethnicity—craggy Slavic faces instead of round Irish ones. A Slovenian flag was framed above the bar in place of shamrocks. Stroh's and Rolling Rock were served instead of Guinness and Harp. And the jukebox was stocked with Frankie Yankovic polka records instead of gloomy Irish ballads. But it was the same kind of cozy, friendly neighborhood comfort zone, where pretensions are left at the door and a lone female can drink without the pressures of lounge lizards and married guys who slip their wedding rings into their pockets.

Victor Gaimari and his uncle would not fit in. Nor, for that matter, would the imperious Irish godfather, Cornelius McCardle, because nobody holds court in Vuk's except Vuk.

I found myself wondering whether I fit in here anymore, either. Even though I've done a lot of drinking in Vuk's since moving out of the neighborhood, only a few of the faces at the bar were still familiar to me. I had changed a lot over ten years, as we all do, but I don't think I really belong at places like Giovanni's and One Walnut and Johnny's Bar and the Velvet Tango Room, either, where I am always uncomfortably aware that most of the other patrons have more money in their pockets than I have in the bank.

Not many nice Slovenian girls from the neighborhood frequent those places. And even if they did, how many of them would put up with me and my old-fashioned ways? Or with the job I love dearly but that is frequently sleazy and occasionally downright dangerous?

Well, what the hell, I thought—maybe I was getting too old to drink in saloons anyway.

Nevertheless, I sat propped up at Vuk's bar for three beers more, brooding, and thinking about how I was going to find Michael Marks in the morning and what I would say to him when I did without stepping on some dangerous toes, including those of my good friend Giancarlo D'Allessandro.

That friendship had always been a two-edged sword, and I knew it. But now I was really in a tight spot. Suppose Michael Marks/Mickey Marcantonio had indeed been planning to blackmail Maureen Hartigan in order to save his son from doing some hard time for rape, and suppose he had killed William Poduska for those photographs—and probably for being the stupidest crook in the history of stupid crooks. How was the old don going to feel about my pumping him for information about Marks only to have me turn him over to Florence McHargue?

Sure, Victor said D'Allessandro's legendary crime days were yesterday's newspapers. But the old man had been around too long to change his feelings about the police, and I was fairly certain that if I sent Mickey Marcantonio over, my dinner invitations from Victor and the don were going to be history.

Maybe I'd be history, too.

I drained my current bottle dry, aware that my head was getting a little fuzzy. For some reason it's never easy for me. I suppose when you're in the business of messing in other people's lives, moral dilemmas come with the license and the territory, but that didn't make me any less sick of it.

Vuk was down at the far end of the bar; I waved at him to bring me another beer. But he approached me with empty hands, wearing his most stern and disapproving expression.

"You haven't been in here in nearly a year, and now you're trying to make up for it all in one night? Forget it, Milan—you're cut off."

"I'm not drunk," I said.

"I know. But you're morose, and that's worse. Go home."

And he turned his back on me and walked away.

So I went home. I didn't have any other choice.

CHAPTER EIGHTEEN

The hangover of the following morning wasn't much to complain about, even after a martini and two cognacs at Giovanni's and too many beers at Vuk's—just a mouth that tasted like the Iraqi army had marched through it, and the barest essence of a headache. Upon arising, I swallowed three Tylenols to muffle the drums.

Despite my overindulgence, I'd had enough presence of mind to set the alarm for seven o'clock before I conked out the previous night. After I showered and brushed my teeth, I toasted a bagel, chugged down almost a quart of orange juice and four generous mugs of coffee, and set off for Warren just after nine.

The morning was an industrial gray one, and in the grassy front yards at the side of the road on Route 422, squirrels played tag with the swirling orange, red, and yellow leaves as the brisk northwestern wind ripped them from the branches. When I was halfway to my destination, the rain started—not a downpour, but enough to soak the ground and make the streets shiny slick.

I had traded in my old thirty-eight-caliber police special a few years back for a nine-millimeter Glock, which I kept on the top shelf of the guest closet in my apartment. It was now tucked comfortably under my left arm. I wasn't really expecting to have to use it, but then one can't ever be too careful. I hadn't been a Boy Scout when I was a kid, but being prepared is never a bad idea, and I knew enough of Mickey Marcantonio's reputation to plan for any contingency.

Finally reaching the courthouse in Warren, I left the Glock in the glove compartment so it wouldn't set off the metal detector at the door. It took me more than two and a half hours to find what I was looking for, checking real estate records and business licenses and sneezing at the dust. A lot of the information was computerized, but there were still old plat books and paper files to pore through as well.

What I eventually came up with was a business license for Michael Marks—I guess he'd changed his name legally—taken out in 1993, doing business as Naples Construction Company. Checking the firm's address, I consulted a street map of Warren and discovered the company headquarters were just inside the westernmost city limits.

It was not quite one o'clock, a time when most people are at lunch; Michael Marks might have been eating at that very moment, and the growling of my stomach told me I should be, too. I doubled back to Route 422, where I had noticed a "family" restaurant, and had a delicious bowl of lentil soup and a burger and fries, washing it down with a Diet Pepsi.

Finally, a few minutes before two, I consulted the map again and made my way to Naples Construction. It had stopped raining by then, but the trees and lawns and sidewalks were damp and cold.

Like Dante Ruggiero's food warehouse, Marks's building was of unlovely cinderblock. To one side of it, a Cyclone fence surrounded a large yard full of heavy earthmoving equipment, small cranes, and concrete-mixing trucks, all glistening wet from the rain. I parallel-parked on the street half a block away, took the Glock out of the glove compartment, put it in the shoulder harness I was wearing beneath my jacket, and walked back to the building.

The woman at the desk in the front room was in her late forties, with puffed-up hair dyed the color of black shoe polish. When I explained that I didn't have an appointment but I wanted to see Mr. Marks, she looked me up and down dubiously, then picked up her telephone handset and punched some buttons on the console.

"Could you come out here a minute?" she said into the receiver, making no effort to keep me from hearing her. "Some guy here wants to see Michael."

Some guy. Right out of the Miss Manners office etiquette manual. She replaced the handset and sat back in her chair, giving me a self-satisfied sneer that I didn't really think I deserved; she'd apparently made a snap judgment about me—a habit of which I am myself often guilty. It didn't bother me, though; I knew where I was and with whom I was dealing.

After a few minutes a man entered from an inner door. He was about forty-five, short and wide and solid, wearing a white-on-white shirt through which he'd sweated at the armpits, and a navy-and-black silk tie. His skin was bad, and he obviously got his hair dye at the same store as the receptionist. Eyes the color of Tootsie Rolls examined and judged me as carefully as if I were a piece of defective equipment that had just been delivered in error.

"Yeah, what can I do for you?"

"I'd like to see Mr. Marks," I told him.

"What about?"

"It's a personal matter."

"A personal matter?"

"That's right."

He licked his lips, and put his fists on his hips the way Errol Flynn did in *Robin Hood*. The effect was not the same. "Are you a cop?"

"No."

"You look like one."

"I can't help it—it's in my genes. My grandmother looked like a cop."

He took his hands off his hips and held them loosely at his sides as though he were getting ready to throw a roundhouse at me.

"Now can I see Mr. Marks?"

"I'm Eddie Vietri, the senior vice president around here," the guy said, inflating his barrel chest. "He has no secrets from me."

"Even personal ones?"

He hitched up his pants, which had slipped down below his round belly. "That's right."

"Let's let him decide, okay?" I handed him one of my cards.

He read it carefully, black brows knotted into a frown. "You're a private investigator?"

"That's what it says."

The receptionist pushed her chair back noisily, got up, and went through the door to the back of the building.

"I knew you were some kind of cop. Regular or private, it's no difference," Eddie Vietri said. "I could smell it all over you, even before I read the card." He looked at me again. "What's this all about?"

"It's personal between Michael Marks and me, Mr. Vietri. I thought we went through that already."

"What are you, a smart guy?"

"Yes," I said, "it beats hell out of the alternative."

He frowned, puzzled.

"Being a dumb guy," I elaborated. I was only trying to clarify, but he took it personally.

He puffed out his chest, with the unfortunate side effect of puffing out his gut, too, and drew himself up to his full height. "Hey, I think you'd better take a fucking walk, okay?" he suggested. "While you're still able to."

"Are you always this warm and welcoming to visitors?"

He pointed at the bulge under my jacket. "Yeah. Especially to visitors who come in here carrying hardware." He wiggled his fingers at me. "Give it."

I laughed. I couldn't help myself.

"Give it, I said." He lowered his voice to a growl so I'd know he was being serious.

I lowered my own—and mine was a hell of a lot deeper than his. "Dare to dream, Sunshine."

His pasty cheeks flushed. "You can have it back when you leave."

"I can have it right now," I said. "This is a pointless discussion, isn't it? Especially because I'm carrying, and you're not. And I'm not about to reverse the situation just because you want me to."

He considered his options. "I could call for backup," he said.

"I don't doubt it. Wouldn't it just be easier, though, to ask Mr. Marks if he'd talk to me? It concerns his son."

The man's face changed, closed up like a fist. "What about his son?"

I sighed. "You need to develop your listening skills, Mr. Vietri. It's *personal*," I said again.

The inner door opened, and Michael Marks came out. He was wearing a yellow hard hat and a water-repellent jacket beaded with drops of rain. The receptionist peered anxiously over his shoulder from inside, but she didn't follow him out; the door closed behind him.

He looked at me hard, and I could see he was straining to remember where he'd seen me. "Who the hell are you?" he said.

I was going to present one of my cards, but Eddie Vietri handed him the one I'd given him. Marks fingered it curiously. "So?"

"I'd like a few minutes of your time," I said.

"Time is money." His voice was low and precise.

"Okay, how much do you charge an hour? We can prorate it."

"Funny. He's funny, Eddie."

"He's not so funny, Mickey." It was probably the first time in his life Eddie Vietri had ever contradicted his boss.

"Sorry, my gag writer is out with the flu today," I said. "Look, we can stand around here all day and trade clever quips, or you can talk to me for ten minutes. It's in your best interest if you do."

"In my best interest, huh?"

"Yes. I'm a friend of Victor Gaimari's."

Marks blinked. "I don't know anybody by that name."

"Don't insult my intelligence, okay, Mr. Marcantonio?"

He flinched at the name. "It's Mister Marks to you."

"He said it was about Angelo," Eddie said.

Marks snapped his head around to look at me so abruptly that the hard hat didn't move fast enough to keep up with it and wound up slightly askew, making him look unintentionally comical. But the bright hardness of his gaze could have pierced the thickest fog. "What about Angelo?" he rumbled, a Rottweiler growling low before he snapped.

I looked at Eddie, then back at Marcantonio. "I'd rather discuss it with you privately."

Marks took off his hard hat and hefted it in his hand as if he were weighing it. "Eddie, stick around in your office."

Eddie nodded, then stepped aside as his employer led me through the rear door, down an uncarpeted corridor, and into a spare office cubicle with a window looking out on the equipment yard. He tossed the hard hat onto the top of a metal filing cabinet and turned around to face me, his fists clenched. Apparently, neither of us was going to sit down.

"You be fucking careful what you say about my son." He pointed a finger at me like kids will do when pretending they have a pistol—or like they *used* to do before that became grounds for expulsion from school. "He's a stupid asshole who thinks with his dick, but I'm the only one who can say that about him. Not you, and not anybody else. Understand?"

"Actually, this is only peripherally about Angelo," I said. The way his brow creased made me think he'd never come across the word before. "It's really about William Poduska."

His expression changed again, his features morphing themselves into those of the bad guy in a video game. "I don't know who that is."

"I think you do, Mr. Marcantonio. Because he was also a friend of Dante Ruggiero's."

A light went on behind his dark eyes. "That's where I seen you before, isn't it? At Dante's place."

I nodded.

"Well, just because I know Dante doesn't mean I know everybody he knows, for Christ's sake."

"Bill Poduska was murdered in a Cleveland motel room last week."

He didn't seem startled, didn't even try to fake surprise. "My condolences to his family."

"Poduska sometimes did work for Ruggiero. Never anything heavy. Mostly small-time stuff—errands."

He shook his head adamantly. "You're telling me a lot of shit about people I don't know or care about."

"I think you do know them."

His jaw set like the granite his construction company poured into the driveways of new tract homes in Trumbull County. "You have a lot of balls walking into my office uninvited and calling me a liar."

I forced a smile. "I'm not calling you a liar."

"Then you're calling me a murderer."

"This might surprise you, but frankly I don't give a brown rat's ass whether you're a serial killer."

"Then what are you bothering me for?"

"I'm working on behalf of a client who lost something. I thought maybe you might have it."

"You always talk in circles like this?" he said, and I could tell he was growing impatient with me. "I don't know what you're babbling about."

"Okay, let me be more direct. You're an ex-mob guy from Cleveland—don't bother denying it."

He lifted his chin defiantly. "I'm not denying it. But the key word is ex. I've been cut off from all that shit for the last ten years or so."

"If you say so."

"I do."

"You're also acquainted with Dante Ruggiero, another *ex*-mob guy, who sometimes employed Bill Poduska to do things that were . . . well, let's call them extralegal."

"That's Don—that's Mr. Ruggiero's business. I don't know nothing about who he hires or don't hire."

"Work with me here, all right? One night several weeks ago, in an Irish bar on the west side of Cleveland, Bill Poduska approaches a city employee by the name of Hugh Cochran with a pretty crude scam, and eventually winds up living in the home of Cochran's cousin under an assumed Irish name. Now as luck would have it, that cousin is Judge Maureen Hartigan, whom he not only fleeces out of some money but robs as well, taking something that might be embarrassing or incriminating to her. And that judge just happens to be presiding at your son Angelo's rape trial in six weeks."

Marcantonio looked at me with flat, dead, dangerous eyes, but I was on a roll now and not about to stop.

"Poduska splits from her house in the middle of the night without even a good-bye, and a few days later he's found shot to death in a cheap motel not forty-five minutes from his own house. Not only that, but he'd been roughed up a little too, probably the day before he died. And that incriminating item he took from the Hartigan house? It's missing."

Marks/Marcantonio didn't answer for quite a while, but his face had gone slack. He looked stricken. He spent some time staring out the window at an idle cement truck, shiny from the recent rain. Then he turned back around to face me. "And so just like that you jump to the conclusion."

"It's not a very big jump. It's one the police would make, too."

"The cops don't know if I ever met this Poduska guy, or whether he met Mr. Ruggiero either."

"Not yet, they don't."

"The only one who could tell them, who could put all the pieces together for them, is you."

I didn't say anything.

The look he was giving me was chilling. "That puts you in a hard place, doesn't it, Jacovich?"

"How do you figure?"

"Because," he growled, "I can have you killed in the fucking parking lot for a buck and a quarter."

"That would be a bad idea."

"Yeah—for *you*."

"For you, too. I told you I was a friend of Victor Gaimari's. He doesn't like you much anyway, Mr. Marcantonio, and never has, which I'm sure you know. He's certainly not going to like the idea of your involving his uncle with stolen photographs to blackmail a Common Pleas judge."

"Blackmail? What pictures? I don't know nothing . . ."

"Let's not waste each other's time with bullshit, all right? You know exactly what pictures I'm talking about."

He leaned over the table and pushed a button on the phone console. "Eddie!" he called.

"You're making a big mistake, Mr. Marcantonio. I'm under the protection of Don Giancarlo D'Allessandro. And if anything happens to me, he's going to be one very angry old man." I fumbled inside my pants pockets, finally pulling out a dollar bill and a shiny new quarter, and tossed them onto his desk. "Here's the buck and a quarter—give it to Eddie."

He stared at the money, and then closed his eyes.

His senior vice president came bursting through the door, fists clenched, ready for action even though he was slightly out of breath. "I'm here, Mickey!" he said. I was amazed he could move that quickly.

Marcantonio all at once seemed older and wearier. "That's all right, Eddie," he said. "False alarm."

"You sure?" Eddie said. "You want me to stay here?"

His boss shook his head.

"I'll stay here, Mickey."

"Eddie," I said.

Eddie looked at me, like the big bad wolf huffing and puffing and preparing to blow my house down.

"You know I'm packing a piece, right? You saw it under my coat." I patted the Glock through my jacket, more to reassure myself that it was still there than to impress Eddie Vietri.

He frowned.

"But still you come running in here to help your boss with nothing but your fists?" I took his fat face in my hand and squeezed it the way I had once lovingly squeezed my son Stephen's round baby cheeks. "Get it together, Eddie, and stop being such a doofus, okay? I wouldn't want to see either you or Mr. Marcantonio get hurt." I squeezed a little more, making his lips purse comically, and then I let go.

He was too enraged and humiliated to say anything; he just looked at his employer for a sign.

"Go on out, Eddie."

For a moment Eddie was like a tennis spectator, his head swiveling back and forth from Marcantonio to me. Finally, he realized it was my advantage. Hiking his pants up over his belly with both hands, he spun around and walked out, leaving us alone.

"You're kind of a mean fucker, aren't you, Jacovich?" Mickey Marcantonio said.

"I try extra hard not to be. But I'm going to be as mean as a snake until I get what I came for, because you're all out of options. You have me whacked, and you've got the D'Allessandros to worry about. If you don't come clean with me, you're going to wind up talking to the cops—and with your past and your reputation they'll take you down like the Browns' defensive line and laugh all the way to the lockup. But if you make nice with me, there's a chance everybody can walk out of this clean. Do we understand each other, Mr. Marcantonio?"

He was chastened, almost pouting—obviously, he was a man who wasn't used to losing. He took in a lung full of air and blew it out noisily between his lips. "Sit down, Jacovich," he said with a little less of a snarl in his voice than previously, indicating a metal chair opposite his desk. When I did as he asked, he plopped into his own chair.

I was aware that I had crossed over a line, one from which I'd always been careful to keep my distance. Despite the good relationship I'd had with the D'Allessandro family, this was the first time I'd ever used Don Giancarlo's name as a threat. Doing so now made me no better than the young punks who strutted Murray Hill with cubic zirconium rings on their pinkies and gleaming gold crucifixes nestled in their chest hair, intimidating people into thinking they were mafiosi because once, a quarter of a century ago, the old man had patted them on the head while having his shoes reheeled at their father's repair shop. I wasn't proud of myself. I wiped my mouth with the back of my hand.

But Mickey Marcantonio hadn't noticed; he was too busy thinking about his own predicament and how to get out of it. He swiveled his chair around to give me his back, staring out the window once more, and for a long while he was quiet. I did nothing to interrupt his reverie.

"I worked my butt off to build up this fucking business," he said at last, almost to himself. It was hard to hear him with his back to me. "I was kind of a hothead in the old days; I suppose you know that. Around Cleveland, people knew my name, and I was respected. It wasn't easy walking away from that kind of respect and starting over again when I was past fifty. But you do what you gotta do to survive, to exist. So I started this business. What I knew about construction back then you could stick in your ass, but I learned everything I could about it. I'd socked away enough money so I didn't have to worry about my next meal, but still I made Naples Construction *work*—so I could have something solid to leave to my son."

He turned his chair back around. His eyes had gone hollow, and his face was creased with lines of pain. "Are you a family man, Jacovich? You married? Have you got kids?"

I nodded. "I'm divorced, but I have two boys."

He nodded. "Then you know the deal. Anything threatens them, you'd kill to make them safe, right?"

I just looked at him.

He flushed. "Jesus. Okay, that was a lousy choice of words. But

I didn't kill anybody, see? Let's get that understood between us from the jump."

I wasn't sure whether I believed him, but I nodded anyway. He obviously wanted to talk, and I wasn't going to do anything to stop the flow.

"From before, from when I was connected, I learned it's always better if you have an edge. I got me a kid. He's a dumb kid, I admit, and a hothead, but he's my kid, and he's looking at doing some serious time. He's not very tough, either, and he's pretty—you know, how some Italian boys are pretty? So he'd do real *hard* time in the joint. You understand me?"

"Yeah," I said.

"So I went looking for an edge—something that'd pull his nuts out of the fire. Don't tell me you wouldn't do the same thing."

"If it was my kid who'd raped a woman, I'm not sure that I would," I said. "I'd get him some help, I'd try to make it easier for him—but I've taught my boys to take responsibility for their actions. Where you come from you call that being a stand-up guy, don't you, Mr. Marcantonio?"

He seemed incredulous. "You'd let your kid do a stretch in the joint? Let some big nigger turn him into his bitch?"

"If he were a rapist? I don't know what else I could do," I said.

He waved his hands in front of him. "Come on, Angelo didn't rape nobody. He was out on a date trying to get a little nookie, just like any other guy his age. And that little bitch was a cock-teaser, leading him on. She was asking for it, and he gave it to her. That's what he told me, and I believe him. It's what they call consensual sex, okay? End of story."

"Was she also asking for the beating he gave her?" I asked. "I think I remember reading that he broke her nose and two ribs."

He looked as if he was going to cry. "It's my *kid*, Jacovich," he pleaded, and his naked helplessness was making me uncomfortable. On the one hand, I could relate to his concern for his son. On the other hand, there was murder and blackmail and rape. The scales were tipped too far for me to just walk away now.

"Why don't you start at the beginning, Mr. Marcantonio? Tell me about the pictures. Who took them in the first place, and why?"

"They were taken twenty years ago. What's it got to do with anything now?" he whined.

"Humor me."

He ran a hand through his hair. "It was back when I was pretty young. Not that many of the big important guys were taking me into their confidence, you know? So I'll just tell you what I remember."

I didn't want to spook him by pulling out a pen and notebook, so I just nodded. "I couldn't ask for more," I said.

CHAPTER NINETEEN

Mickey Marcantonio sat back in his chair like a kindly uncle about to tell the children a bedtime story.

"Let me put this in perspective for you," he said. "In context. It was a different time; things weren't like they are now, okay?"

"Okay."

"Even back then, Mr. D'Allessandro was getting old already. Some of the guys—you know, some people who were high up in the organization—they thought he was getting a little soft, too."

I tried not to laugh. Even as an octogenarian the old man was about as soft as the white cliffs of Dover.

"I mean, it was because of him that the families didn't get into the drug business in Ohio back in the sixties. He didn't like it and didn't want it. Some of the people from Detroit had to come in and start things up. That cost our local guys some money. Some of 'em were pissed off."

"I could get all this stuff from the library," I said.

"I know, but wait a minute. So there's this one guy, fairly high up in the . . . you know, the pecking order."

"What guy?"

He shook his head. "I'm not naming names, all right, because it's got nothing to do with anything. Besides which, the guy's dead now. Okay, so he decides he wants to squeeze Mr. D a little bit, maybe get him to rethink a few things and give him a little bigger taste of the pie. The money from the heroin. He'd heard something about a deal going down between him and Senator Hartigan."

"Where did he hear it?"

"How the fuck should I know?"

"What kind of deal?"

Marcantonio frowned. "Are you gonna let me tell the fucking story or not?" He shrugged, turning both hands up. "I don't know what kind of a deal, it doesn't *matter*!"

I nodded, because he was right. "Okay, sorry. Go on."

His storytelling skills vindicated, he huffed through his nose. "So he hires some guy—I don't know who it was—sends him out with a camera to follow Mr. D around to his meeting with Hartigan, and has him snap a bunch of pictures. He figures he's getting something on Mr. D that he can use later, you understand?"

"I should think it'd take more than that," I said.

"You're right there. The way I heard it, Mr. D just laughed at it."

"That doesn't sound like Mr. D."

"Yeah, well pretty soon he stopped laughing. And the guy, the one who paid for getting the pictures, all of a sudden he's not around anymore."

My stomach did a flip, and all of a sudden I was tasting my lunch again, my throat burning. It wasn't the first time that my fondness for Giancarlo D'Allessandro had made me forget who and what he was, or had been, and the things of which I knew he was capable.

"What happened to the photographs?"

"They wound up with Mr. D."

"How did Judge Hartigan get hold of them?"

"The way I heard it," Mickey Marcantonio said, "Mr. D sent them to Senator Hartigan, to let him know they existed and to reassure him they weren't ever going to be used."

In the strange world of the mob, with its grand gestures and its strict code of honor, that seemed to make some weird kind of sense. "All right. That's the history. Now tell me about Poduska."

His cheeks sagged and turned gray. "How do I know I can trust you not to go to the cops?"

"If you killed Poduska, you can't," I said.

He raised his voice. "I already told you I didn't kill him."

"Did you have it done?"

He shook his head resolutely.

"If that's the truth, you can trust me. If you tell me what I want to know, you can trust me, too. But if you jack me around even a little bit, I'm walking out of here and making a phone call to Cleveland."

He took a deep breath, his chest expanding. "You've got my nuts in a wringer here."

"You put them there yourself, Mr. Marcantonio. Now tell me a story, or let's stop wasting each other's time."

He leaned his forearms on the desk, clasping his hands in front of him, his chin down so far that his ears were on the same level as his shoulders, and sat there growing older.

"The Poduska kid was a suck-ass," he finally said. Then he stopped talking as if that were the entire story.

I decided to wait him out, and after a few moments he figured out that I was still waiting.

"He was a small-time grifter who made his pitiful little chump money running little cons on little people. Old ladies, young broads, whoever was . . . vulnerable. I didn't have much use for him, to tell you the truth. But he's related in some way to old Cornelius McCardle from the west-side Irish. He must be related by marriage, because Poduska isn't no Irish name. You know McCardle?"

I nodded.

"The old man—McCardle—he used to keep Poduska around to do odd jobs and shit, like a delivery boy. He was a bagman for whatever ball games Con was running out there."

"The west side of Cleveland is a hell of a long way from Warren," I said.

"Yeah, but McCardle and Dante Ruggiero were old friends from way back. Well, not friends. More like acquaintances, both of them being in kind of the same business. I suppose that's how Poduska came to Don Dante."

"Probably," I said.

"So Dante uses him the same way McCardle does—for errands, as like a go-between. I get to know Poduska through him, and as a favor to Don Dante, I threw him a couple of things to do now and then, give him a couple hundred bucks for his trouble. It wasn't like he really worked for me, you know?" He unclasped his fingers and pointed one at my face. "I run a legitimate construction business here, and that's it. I'm out of all the rest of the shit."

"So you used Poduska to mix cement?"

He scowled. "I couldn't of done that even if I'd wanted to. This here is strictly a union shop."

"Then what kind of work did he do for you?"

Marcantonio's eyes glittered, then almost disappeared. "I'm not saying I don't have a few things going for me out here on the side."

"Okay, fine."

"So Poduska used to call me up—usually whenever he needed money—begging for something to do. And he used to brag on the little one- or two-grand scores he used to make scamming people. One time he calls and tells me he's screwing some Irish girl he met in a tavern out of a couple of thousand bucks by telling her he was just off the plane from Ireland, a real greenhorn here in America, and didn't have a place to stay."

That dovetailed nicely with the calls to Warren from Judith Torrence's phone and from the judge's house.

"I guess he learned how to do a pretty good Irish accent from spending so much time with Con McCardle."

I took out my notebook and read the phone number off to him. "Is that your number?"

He turned slightly pale. "It's my home phone. Shit, where'd you get that from? It's supposed to be unlisted."

"Your little errand boy wasn't much brighter than the village idiot," I said. "He called you from Maureen Hartigan's house. It showed up on the bill. It took me a while to find you because you're not in the directory, but the Cleveland police would have run you down sooner or later."

He glowered at me, his face purpling rapidly. "You mean I'm spilling my guts to you, and the cops were gonna come calling anyway? You fuck!"

"Take it easy, Mr. Marcantonio," I said. "If your story hangs together for me, maybe I can put in a good word for you with the head of the Cleveland P.D. homicide unit."

I crossed my toes when I said it; Mickey Marcantonio had no way of knowing that the only word I could possibly put in to Florence McHargue that she'd listen to was "good-bye."

"So come on," I prompted him. "I want to hear how you got Poduska into the Hartigan house."

He ran the edge of his thumb over one corner of his mouth; I was willing to bet he'd learned that one from watching too many Bogart movies. "Well, after I heard about him and the Irish broad—you know, saying he was just off the boat and all and getting away with it, I thought to myself that there just might be an opportunity knocking on my door here."

"How so?"

He gave me the kind of withering look one usually saves for a slightly dotty uncle. "Because, shit-for-brains," he said, "Judge Hartigan is going to try my kid for rape."

"How did you know she still had the pictures?"

"I didn't know she had them. I was hoping she did. And I figured that if I could get Poduska into that house, even if he couldn't find the pictures he might be able to come up with something else. Some leverage I could use."

I shifted uncomfortably in my chair, taking no joy in having been right. That must have been why, with all the Irishmen in Cleveland, Bill Poduska had sat down next to Hugh Cochran in O'Grady's bar on that fateful night. It was a set-up from the very beginning.

It also explained why, even though he'd been having sex with Cathleen almost every night at her place, Poduska had insisted on maintaining his home base in the judge's house.

"So it took him three weeks," I said, "but Poduska finally found the photographs. And when he did, he just picked up and left Judge Hartigan's?"

"Sure," Marcantonio said. "Once he got what he wanted, there was no reason to hang around."

"Is that when he checked into the motel near the airport?"

"Right. He didn't like doing that business at his house. I don't blame him. With his wife there and all, she would of found out he was banging the Hartigan broad, and from what I hear about her, she would have done a Bobbitt on him for sure." He scratched his head. "Married guys that chippy around on their wives—I don't know, sometimes I don't understand them."

"You're not married?"

"Not anymore. My wife, she passed away about twelve years

ago, God rest her soul. Cancer. And after that I said to myself that once was enough."

I've walked that road.

"But that meant I had to raise Angelo on my own, without a mother," he continued. "He grew up kind of wild. I couldn't help it. I was too busy trying to get my head above water after the D'Allessandro family . . . uh . . . invited me to go live someplace else besides Cleveland."

"Growing up without a mother doesn't excuse rape."

"It wasn't rape!" he exploded. "These fucking date-rape things, they're all a matter of who you believe."

"Are these fucking breaking-two-ribs-and-a-woman's-nose things a matter of who you believe, too?"

"Look," he said, his face turning mean and ugly again, "do you want to hear this or don't you?"

"You're right," I said. "I want to hear it. So Bill Poduska was really working for you."

"Yeah. But just to get the pictures. The rest of the shit he took, he did that on his own."

He seduced Cathleen Hartigan on his own as well, I thought.

"So that's when he called you and said he had the photos?"

Marcantonio nodded.

"Called you at home?" I asked, thinking of the unlisted number.

"Yeah."

"And?"

"I told him to bring them to me. But he goes no, he doesn't want to. He said he'd prefer it if I came and got them. At the motel." He gritted his teeth, a man unused to the word "no." "The fucking nerve of the guy. He'd *prefer*."

"Yeah, some people have a lot of nerve. Did you go to the motel?"

"Yeah, I did. He had them, all right."

I waited.

"The pictures."

"Uh-huh."

"He told me he'd looked at them and realized they were worth a hell of a lot more than I was paying him."

"What *were* you paying him?"

"The deal was for five grand."

"And he wanted more?"

Marcantonio leaned forward in his chair, his lower jaw protruding like a bulldog's. "The little cocksucker knew about Angelo, about the trial. And he tried to hold me up for fifty large!"

I shook my head. I've always believed that deep down where it counts, most criminals are stupid; otherwise they wouldn't be criminals. More and more, it was appearing that the late William Poduska had been a walking poster boy for stupidity.

"So you took them away from him?" I said.

"You're damn right I did! I had to make him tell me where they were first, though."

"That's why you beat the crap out of him."

A brusque nod.

"Broke his finger."

"I don't like being crossed," he said. "We had a deal. A handshake deal. I trusted him. He crossed me. So?"

That certainly jibed with Mickey Marcantonio's earlier reputation as a hothead. "And where were the pictures?"

He snickered; it was a nasty sound. "The dumb son of a bitch had them hidden under the mattress!"

"How long did it take you to convince him to be a smarter son of a bitch?"

Marcantonio preened a little bit. "About three minutes."

"And then what?"

"I left him whimpering like a pussy on the floor and went home. Whaddaya think I did?"

"You didn't go back the next day and shoot him?"

He looked offended. "Naw. Why the hell would I do that?"

"Like you said, he crossed you."

Marcantonio shrugged. "He only crossed me a little. That's why I slapped him around and busted his finger. But I got what I came for, and I didn't pay him the original five grand, so I was money ahead. After that we were quits."

"Seems like he's quits with everybody now," I said. "Now that somebody blew him away."

He stood up and stretched. "Look, Jacovich, it isn't like the old days. Not like in some goddamn godfather movie. Nobody gets whacked like that anymore. When's the last time you remember a mob hit in Cleveland?"

"Nineteen seventy-eight or so," I said, remembering the car bombing of gangster Danny Green in the parking lot of a medical building in Beachwood, and another car bombing on West Twenty-fifth Street and Detroit Road that took out tough guy Shondor Birns.

"That's right, a hell of a long time ago," Marcantonio said. "Rough stuff like that, it's bad for business. For everybody. Besides, I'm out of the loop now. I live out here, I work out here, and I mind my own business."

"Like blackmailing a judge?"

His face turned mean again. "Judge Hartigan *is* my business, okay, Jacovich? It's about my kid."

"Okay."

"Other than that, I don't even know about any mob stuff in Cleveland anymore. Or anyplace else, for that matter."

"You think the police will believe that?"

"I thought you said no cops."

"I did. But that will depend on whether or not you hand over those pictures of Senator Hartigan and Don Giancarlo."

His laugh was a single bark. "You're just flat-out nuts," he said. He leaned back against the window and stuffed his hands into his pockets. "You must be some kind of wacko."

"Why?"

"You think I'm just going to hand over those pictures and kiss you good-bye? Get real, Jacovich—they're my kid's insurance policy."

"I'm afraid the policy has just lapsed, Mickey," I said. He flinched at my use of his first name, his old mob name. "My job is to get the pictures back to the judge. If I do, nobody will know where I got them, and I'm out of it for good. If I don't, I'll have to use other methods."

His look was incredulous. "You'd actually go to the cops?"

"In a second."

He sneered then. "Victor Gaimari might not like that."

"He probably wouldn't," I said, "but I'd talk to him, and he'd understand. But if anything bad happened to me because of you, some phony-looking accident, he might get downright pissy about it." I stood up, too. "If we do it my way, everybody's happy.

If we don't, everybody's unhappy—you more than anyone. Easy or hard, it's your call. But from where I sit, it's a slam dunk."

He looked as if he'd bitten into something foul and sour. He was squirming like a butterfly on a pin. "I'm gonna remember this, Jacovich."

"Don't threaten me, Mickey. You've got nothing to back it up with besides Eddie out there, and I could clean his clock on my worst day. So why don't we cut out the macho posturing and get down to business?"

"Business," he said bitterly.

"*My* business. The photographs."

His face was gray; his eyes deep-set, dark smudges. "What about Angelo?" he said. "Am I just supposed to write him off? My own son? Am I supposed to just leave him twist in the fucking wind?"

"He has a good lawyer, doesn't he?"

Marcantonio rubbed his eyes. "His lawyer is a lurp, you ask me."

"Get him a better one, then."

"Who?"

"What about Tom Vangelis? He's the best criminal lawyer in the state."

He snorted, the corners of his mouth heading ever downward. "Vangelis is Gaimari's lawyer," he said. "And Mr. D's. He wouldn't touch me."

"He might if I asked him to," I said. "I did a little work for him last year, and he might feel he owes me a favor."

"Victor wouldn't let him."

"I can talk to Victor, too, if it comes to that."

He looked amazed. "You'd do that for me?"

"If I get the photographs I want, sure."

The muscles at the sides of his jaw were jumping; he must have been gritting his teeth pretty hard. "It looks like I don't have any choice."

"You have two choices, Mickey. One smart one and one stupid one. You don't look like a stupid man."

He raised his eyes to me; his face was a sad clown's. "They're in the safe," he said.

He moved to a closet door and opened it. I could see there was a small safe on the floor of the closet. He knelt down in front of it and began twirling the dials; I could hear the tumblers clicking into place.

"Do you have a gun in there, Mickey?"

His fingers stopped moving. "As a matter of fact, I do."

"You'd do well to remember that I have one, too. So if I were you, I'd move very slowly."

"What? You think I'm gonna cap you right here in my office?" he said with disgust.

"A guy can't be too careful."

I moved my hand to my jacket, my fingers an inch away from my own weapon, and watched as he swung open the door to the safe. Sure enough, there was a nine-millimeter automatic resting on the top shelf. There was also a good bit of money inside, in neat little bundles.

He glanced up at me. "Why don't you take a picture?"

I laughed. "I left my camera in the car, or I probably would."

He reached to the back of the lower shelf and pulled out a large manila envelope like the one Maureen Hartigan had described. Then he pushed himself upright, came out of the closet, and passed it to me with both hands, gingerly, as if it were the Lost Ark of the Covenant.

I took it from him. I almost expected it to feel warm.

"Check it out if you want to," he said. "Make sure I'm giving you the real goods."

"I trust you."

He brushed off the knees of his pants legs. "Thanks."

"Besides, I know where to find you."

I started for the door.

"You won't forget about Tom Vangelis, will you?" It was naked pleading, a worried father trying to save his son.

"I'll call him tomorrow. Word of honor." I gave him a jaunty-wave. "Nice meeting you, Mickey."

When my hand was on the doorknob, he said, "Jacovich."

I turned around and locked gazes with him, half expecting to see the gun in his hand. But his arms dangled empty at his sides. He looked about as lost and forlorn as any man I'd ever seen.

"If you found me through my number on that telephone bill, chances are the cops will find me too, right?"

"I wouldn't be surprised," I said. "But I'm sure as hell not going to tell them. Besides, if you're as innocent as you say you are, you've got nothing to worry about, do you?"

"Yeah," he said. "But you knew they could make me out from the phone number. You knew it all along."

I shrugged.

He smiled with only one corner of his mouth, but his dark eyes were as cold and dead as those of a basking shark. "You're a real son of a bitch, you know that?"

"I know," I said.

CHAPTER TWENTY

I was never one of those kids who can't wait until Christmas, kids who shake and sniff and squeeze the packages trying to discern what's beneath the gaudy wrappings and then, at the crack of Christmas dawn, go tearing into the living room and pillage the pile of gifts, leaving torn colored tissue paper and ribbon and empty boxes strewn all over the place.

I was more patient than that. I could wait.

I still can.

So it was that I didn't even open the envelope I'd managed to bribe and wheedle and cajole and threaten out of Mickey Marcantonio until I got back to my office. It was late in the afternoon of an already dark gray fall day, so I switched on my desk lamp and spread the photos out in front of me.

There were twelve of them.

I didn't really remember Doyle Hartigan all that well. I had never met him, although I suppose I'd seen him on television often enough. The handsome Irish features and the shock of white curly hair seemed familiar to me, though, even behind the dark glasses he was wearing in the photos.

Both men in the pictures were wearing topcoats, and the day had been gray and overcast. Nobody wears sunglasses in Cleveland on a day like that—unless they are pretentious assholes.

As if the dark glasses would disguise them from anyone who knew them. As if they were movie stars.

Giancarlo D'Allessandro didn't look much different in the

twenty-year-old photographs than he does today. His hair was a little darker, but not much—and he had a little more of it, especially at the temples. He was a bit heavier then, and the skin of his face didn't hang as pendulously low from his jawline. And he seemed taller; I guess it's true that when people get older, the pressure of standing up straight for so many years compresses their spine and makes them shrink.

He had been an old man when I first met him; he was even older now and much more frail. But to me he'd always been a constant, almost like a Cleveland landmark—a man comfortable in his own skin and easy with his own considerable power. Here he was in black-and-white twenty years ago, already in his sixties, no longer young but already showing the ravages of age and of a life lived out loud. The photos made me wonder about him and how he had looked, what he'd been like even earlier than that. It was hard for me to visualize.

Maybe if I'd known him then, he wouldn't have been imprinted on my brain as the old man he now was. In my mind his whole life spooled out like a movie. I tried to picture him in his twenties, the testosterone rising like maple sap in the spring, but smarter and cooler than the other young punks in Little Italy, biding his time, waiting to claim his birthright as the leader, the big man, Mr. D. I imagined him in his forties, when he was at the height of his power and influence, when the people who would bow their heads to kiss his hand really meant it.

In the photos there was no question that he was putting a fat envelope into the hands of State Senator Doyle Hartigan, and the expressions both men exhibited left little doubt as to the legality of the exchange. The senator looked like he'd just chewed up an aspirin tablet without water, and D'Allessandro wore the look of a medieval baron rewarding a serf.

Like he had it coming to him.

In a way the photos were more innocent-looking than I had imagined. No prosecutor would take them to trial without having something more. But were they ever to be made public, the very juxtaposition of a state senator, a mob kingpin, and a thick sealed packet would surely do some serious damage to reputations.

In a smaller, white envelope inside the larger manila one were the negatives, all in a strip. They hadn't been developed commercially; my guess was that they'd originally been souped in someone's private darkroom.

I called Judge Hartigan at the courthouse to give her the joyous tidings that the photographs had been found, but her bored-sounding law clerk told me she had already gone home.

I sighed. I didn't want to deal with a half-drunken Maureen again so soon. But I dutifully tapped out her home number.

"That's good, Milan," she said in a dry voice when I told her of my success. "I'm glad. It's a real relief to me."

"The negatives are there, too, Maureen—so you won't have to worry about the pictures coming back to bite you in the future."

"Wonderful," she murmured.

Not exactly the reaction I had been counting on. Maybe she had grown numb because of the death of Bill Poduska. Or maybe the photos weren't really that important to her after all. But I wasn't making any snap judgments; nothing in this whole case had proceeded according to expectations.

"Shall I drop them off now?"

"That won't be necessary," she said almost too quickly. "You can bring them down to me at the courthouse tomorrow if it's convenient. That would be much easier, I think."

I hung up, puzzled and irritated and very much bent out of shape. All of a sudden, the panic and urgency in Judge Hartigan had disappeared into the ozone like steam vapors.

And there was not so much as a thank-you, either.

I suppose that I did what I was paid for and she felt no gratitude was necessary, but I was annoyed anyway. I had taken on this case only because of my friendship with Cathleen, and I'd spent a good deal of my political and emotional capital with Victor and his uncle to crack it. I guess I had expected more of a reaction from Maureen than behaving as though she'd just been sent a seven-dollar refund for overpayment of her income tax.

My next phone call was to Victor Gaimari; I caught him just as he was leaving his office.

"You'll be happy to know I have the photographs," I said.

"I am. Did Marcantonio have them?"

I didn't answer him for a moment. Then I said, "He's not going to get hurt if I tell you that, is he?"

"Don't be an idiot," Victor said impatiently.

"In that case, yes—he had them. His son Angelo is going on trial for rape in December. Maureen Hartigan is the presiding judge."

"That son of a bitch." He sounded more amused than angry.

"I guess when it's your own child at risk you tend to do crazy things."

"Stupid things," he said. "Really stupid. Did Marcantonio have to kill Bill Poduska to get them?"

"He swears he didn't."

"You believe him?"

"I think I do, yes."

"Why?"

"Because," I said, "he admitted that he went to that motel room and worked Poduska over to get him to cough up the pictures. Whoever killed him did it the next day. Marcantonio would have no reason to take him out, once he got what he wanted."

"Poduska double-crossed him, Milan. For a guy like Marcantonio that would be reason enough."

"That's between him and the police."

"Police?" The word crackled through the receiver, sharp and hard.

"I didn't rat him out, and I won't. But eventually they'll track him through the phone calls Poduska made to him in Warren from Judge Hartigan's phone—just the way I did."

Victor sighed. "Poduska was so damned stupid that if someone hadn't shot him, he would've cut his own throat trying to shave. What's Marcantonio going to tell them when they find him?"

"He hasn't had time to think that one out yet."

"You're delivering the pictures to the judge?"

"Tomorrow," I said. "And the negatives, too."

"How bad are they?"

"Didn't you see them twenty years ago when your uncle first got hold of them?"

"Twenty years ago I was in grad school in Columbus," he said. "Nobody showed me anything back then."

"Well, they're bad enough that anyone with half a brain would know what they were, and not bad enough to get anybody put in jail."

"I suppose that's all that's important."

"Victor, I told Mickey Marcantonio that I'd talk to Tom Vangelis about representing his kid."

There was a slight change in the pattern of his breathing, and I listened to it for a while.

"I don't like that," he said.

"I didn't think you would, but . . ."

"But you did it anyway."

"Well—yes."

He breathed for about twenty seconds more. "Why are you telling me, then? It isn't like you to ask permission."

I gritted my teeth. "I'm not asking permission, Victor; I'm telling you as a courtesy."

"Because we're friends," he said.

"Yes."

"And . . ."

"And to ask you not to do anything to screw it up. He's your lawyer, not mine, so I'm running it past you. Tom owes me a favor, anyway."

"It must be very hard for you trying to keep track of all these favors, Milan. Favors you owe, favors you're owed . . ."

I got his message. "Sometimes it is."

"Marcantonio's son is a rapist," he reminded me. "Since when do you go to bat for rapists?"

That stung—badly.

When I'd offered to intercede with Tom Vangelis on behalf of Mickey Marcantonio's kid, I'd realized that I was most probably aiding someone who had committed one of the most loathsome and morally indefensible crimes. What hadn't struck me until right that moment was that I had done so on behalf of a client trying to protect the reputation of a man who had committed another crime more than twenty years before. A man long dead. And now my client no longer seemed even interested.

Somewhere along the line I had forgotten to balance the two on my scales—and I had made a deal with the devil.

But it *was* a deal, and now I had to play it through.

I fumbled for a cigarette. "You know damn well how I feel about rapists, Victor. Frankly, if the kid is guilty, I hope he swings."

"If he's guilty?" Victor's cynicism was overflowing his cup. "Come on, Milan, you're stroking yourself."

"Maybe," I said. "But I did what I had to do. Angelo is Marcantonio's only son, and when I took those photos from his father, I took away any leverage he might have with the judge. Mickey's desperate, and he told me he had a lousy lawyer. It took a little persuading, but eventually he was straight with me. So I told him I'd try to do whatever I could for him. Tom Vangelis is the best criminal attorney between New York and Chicago—you know that. So I said I'd ask him. That's all."

"Mickey, as you call him, was my uncle's enemy."

"That was a long time ago, Victor. In another era. Now he's just a very worried father."

"Yes, one who was going to drag the don in on a scheme to blackmail a judge," Victor said.

"It couldn't have possibly hurt the don. You told me that yourself. So did your uncle."

"What's gotten into you?" Victor said, "I've never known you to rationalize a moral point like this."

That made me angry—probably because I had to admit the truth of it. "Are you upset because a probable rapist is getting a good lawyer, Victor? Or is it grinding your ass that Mickey Marcantonio might be getting a break?"

He didn't speak for a long while, and I waited for the explosion of anger. Victor and I had not had a confrontation like this one for many years, and I suppose that our friendship and my closeness with his uncle had lulled me into forgetting who and what they were. Now, after accepting a favor from him, I was butting heads—and I didn't know what to expect.

At one time, in his younger days, Victor Gaimari might have been something of a cowboy, a hair trigger—perhaps more like Mickey Marcantonio than he would ever care to admit. But with experience and maturity had come wisdom, or at least patience, and now he had become one of the most judicious men I'd ever known. He was thinking it over.

Finally, he cleared his throat. He had a very prissy way of doing that, as if he wanted to be sure he had your attention before he spoke.

"Go ahead and talk to Tom, then," he said. "I won't lean on him about it one way or the other."

The muscles in my neck had been knotted with tension. Now I released them; the relief felt wonderful. "Thanks, Victor."

"But that's just for the rape case, Milan—for the son. Because that's what you were foolish enough to promise him. But if Mickey Marcantonio gets into any shit about the Poduska killing, he gets himself another lawyer. I won't let Vangelis represent the father. It would be a conflict of interest, anyway."

"How do you figure that?"

"The only motive Marcantonio would have for murder is those photographs—whether to get them back or to get revenge on Poduska for crossing him. Either way, it's my uncle in those pictures. Ergo, conflict of interest."

"I see."

"Good. What you *don't* seem to see is that the don is not exactly a young man anymore. He lives quietly now, with no excitement. If Marcantonio gets busted for doing Poduska, the photographs will be evidence, and that will mean a *lot* of excitement. I don't want that."

A frisson of uneasiness fluttered in my stomach. I had known Victor a long time, and I knew what was coming.

"I'm sure Judge Hartigan doesn't want it either," he went on. "I mean, wasn't the whole point of her hiring you to get those photos and suppress them?"

"I suppose so," I said.

"Then don't you think it would behoove you, for the sake of both your client and my uncle, to find out who did kill Bill Poduska?"

"Private investigators are not allowed to investigate capital crimes like homicide."

"They aren't allowed to drive over the speed limit, either—but when's the last time you went under seventy miles an hour on I-71?"

He cleared his throat again. "What if I got Tom Vangelis to hire you? He's an attorney; that would be legitimate."

"You just said you wouldn't let Tom represent Mickey Marcantonio. And if he doesn't, he can't hire me, either."

"You have a point," Victor said. "But I don't want it to get that far. I have no love for Mickey, but I don't want him arrested for this one. I don't want him indicted, and I don't want him to go to trial."

"I don't see how I can stop that, Victor."

"Why? You believe in his innocence, don't you?"

"Well—yeah."

"Then prove it," he said. "Prove it before the cops run him down and start asking about photographs."

"Jesus . . ."

"When you needed help on this one," he reminded me pointedly, "we stepped up to the plate, didn't we? My uncle got right on the phone with Dante Ruggiero and set up a meeting for you. And you just now asked me to let my own personal attorney represent Mickey's lousy rapist kid, and I agreed to it, didn't I? Well, now we're asking for your help."

I didn't say anything. The glare from the desk lamp I'd turned on earlier to study the Hartigan-D'Allessandro pictures was giving me a headache; I switched it off and put one hand over my eyes.

"So we help you; now you help us. That's how it works, remember, Milan? With *friends.*"

After we said good-bye, I sat at my desk for a while, mainly because my legs felt too heavy for me to stand. Idly, I doodled on the yellow pad in front of me. Ever since I was a kid, my doodles had always been rather grisly—an empty gallows, the noose swinging ominously. I wondered now whether this time they were really symbolic—and whether I had condemned my relationship with Victor and the don to death.

It had been a curious sort of friendship from the start—beginning in anger and violence, continuing for a while as a ridiculous flexing of muscles and showing of machismo and mutual mistrust. It had somehow morphed into a cautious acceptance, then trust, and finally genuine affection. Curious for me, because I am not one to seek out the gray areas between right and wrong, and Victor and Don Giancarlo represented everything I'd been against all my life.

Yet there had never been a time when they weren't there for me when I needed them, and that weighed heavily with me. I opened my business to handle industrial security, but somehow I kept getting into situations where it was a comfort knowing that friends as loyal and powerful as the D'Allessandros had my back.

How badly that loyalty and friendship had just been ruptured, I didn't know. Time would tell, I supposed, but in a strange and unsettling way the thought of never seeing Victor or his uncle again filled me with melancholy. I knew that Victor's request for help wasn't really a request at all, but a hard and fast assignment I couldn't turn down.

I looked at the photographs of the don and Senator Hartigan one more time, wishing that the two men would step out of the fuzzy black-and-white past and talk to me, and then I replaced them in the envelope and put them in the utility room—hid them, actually, under the lid of a scanner. I'd bought it a few years back when I'd gone high-tech, but I had never bothered to attach it to my computer. I didn't have a safe in the office—unless you count the little refrigerator over by the window that looked like a safe but contained two six-packs of Stroh's, a couple of bottles of designer water, and a few cans of Pepsi.

But the door to the utility room locked, and I had to be content with that. There were only four people in the world who cared about the photos anyway—Victor and his uncle; Judge Hartigan, who had no reason to bust in and steal them since I was giving them to her the next day; and Mickey Marcantonio, who wasn't stupid enough to do a B&E to pilfer something that could so easily be traced back to him.

I went back to my desk and called Tom Vangelis, gave him the skinny on Angelo Marcantonio. Told him I'd cleared it with Victor.

"That wasn't really necessary, Milan," he said, sounding miffed. "I'm Victor's attorney, not his employee."

Yeah, right, I thought. A real independent, Vangelis. I would have bet the farm that he'd be on the phone with Victor thirty seconds after we disconnected, making sure it was okay for him to represent Angelo Marcantonio.

I wasn't much better myself; I danced to Victor's tune as nimbly as Vangelis ever did.

I started cleaning up the office. I emptied the old grounds from the basket of the Mr. Coffee machine. Then I took everything off my desk and wiped away the cigarette ashes. Went into the little john, wiped down the basin with a paper towel and swished a toilet brush around the bowl. I had a cleaning service that came in two nights a week, but tonight wasn't one of them. And in my business I never knew when a client or a cop was going to drop in on me unexpectedly.

Or Jinny Johnson.

But all of a sudden there she was; I could hear her heels clicking on the stairs before she materialized magically in my doorway, still dressed as she had been for work in a blue shirtwaist dress—no power suits for her, she was a midlevel City Hall clerk. Her dress was covered by a gray trench coat, her medium-length hair very blond and slightly windblown. She looked a lot better than she had the night I'd met her in O'Grady's.

"Hello, Jinny. You took me by surprise," I said, speaking the truth. I still had the toilet brush in my hand.

"Cute," she said. "Is that what all the trendy private eyes are carrying these days instead of packing a rod?"

"Yeah, this is a lot scarier than a gun any day," I laughed. "Packing a rod? Where'd you come up with that? The last person I heard talking about packing a rod was Jimmy Cagney in *White Heat*."

"Huh?"

"Not important." I ducked into the bathroom and replaced the brush in its holder, then squirted some Purell on my hands before I came back out.

"So," I said, looking at my watch rather pointedly. "To what do I owe the honor of this visit?"

"I came to take you to dinner."

I just stared at her.

"I got the feeling that if I wanted to see you again, I was going to have to make the first move, because you weren't going to call me. And I'm a creature of impulse, so here I am."

"Well. . ."

"You're not one of those old-fashioned guys who think that any woman who asks a man out is either desperate or a brazen hussy, are you?"

"No, I don't think that at all," I said, not sure of the veracity of my own words. "But people do tell me I'm old-fashioned."

"I think that's what I liked about you right off." She took off her trench coat and threw it over the back of a chair. "Don't tell me you already have plans, because I won't believe you."

"Why not?"

"Because a guy rushing off to a dinner date doesn't stop to clean his office toilet first."

"You should be the private eye," I said.

"So?" She put her hands on her hips, feet slightly apart. The only other time I had seen her, she'd been wearing jeans. This time I noticed her legs. With pleasure. "Are we on or not?"

At that particular moment, mired as I was in other people's agendas—Victor's, Maureen Hartigan's, even Florence Mc-Hargue's—the prospect of spending an evening looking at Jinny Johnson seemed very agreeable indeed. "I guess so," I said. "You kind of took me unawares here."

"I took myself unawares, actually. But I was sitting around in my office today, pushing paper and crunching numbers, and it occurred to me that I find you very attractive. I was going to call you, but that would have given you too much of an opportunity to say no. So after work I just drove over here—on an impulse. It's on my way home, anyway."

"You always follow your impulses?"

"Stick around," she said. "You'll see."

CHAPTER TWENTY-ONE

J inny Johnson was confident and thorough. She had it all planned out ahead of time, and had even reserved a table at Kosta's, a quiet and elegant little restaurant in Tremont, near where she lived. Just in case.

We traveled in separate cars.

There was a lively crowd sitting at the bar, mostly under forty. The lounge itself was long and thin, the walls painted a comfortable forest green with large, bold pop-art paintings of cartoon figures like Wonder Woman and Batman adorning them. We sat and had a drink while waiting for our table; Kosta's makes as good a martini as anyplace in town. I wondered whether Victor had ever been here; Bombay Sapphire martinis were his drink of choice.

Jinny whipped out an American Express card to pay for the drinks before I could even reach for my pocket.

"Uh-uh," she said. "I invited you."

We went inside to the dining room—the color scheme was identical to the bar's, but it was darker in there, and not quite as noisy. We were given a booth right by the front window so Jinny could look out at the traffic on West Eleventh Street—what there was of it.

I scanned the menu. "This is awfully nice of you," I said.

She inclined her head gracefully. "I hope it doesn't threaten your masculinity that I'm paying for dinner."

"My masculinity isn't all that fragile."

"Then you're a rare bird," she said. "But I figured that about you when I first saw you."

"Oh?"

"The way you told Bert, the bartender at O'Grady's, not to call you 'dude.' That was way cool."

I shrugged. "I just happen not to like that expression, that's all. It's a kid's word. For a guy my age, there's something disrespectful about it."

"And when you don't like something, do you always do something about it?"

"Generally. Otherwise it makes me a victim—and that's not a role I play very well, I'm afraid."

"You're probably right," she agreed. "But what do you do when you *do* like something?"

I took a sip of my drink. "I suppose that's your subtle way of asking me why I didn't use the phone number you gave me?"

"I've been wondering, yes."

"I'm in the middle of something—business. It's pretty important, and I didn't want to get distracted. Plus my job isn't exactly nine-to-five, so I didn't want to start something I wouldn't be able to finish."

"You like big finishes?"

I laughed. "I like to finish what I start."

Her gaze was penetrating. "And what else?"

"What else what?"

"Is there another lady in the picture?"

"No, I'm a free agent. You?"

"Oh, yes. Now tell me why a big, good-looking hunk like you is running around loose? Why hasn't somebody snagged you?"

"I've been snagged a few times," I said.

"And been burned?"

"Show me a grown-up who hasn't been."

She nodded gravely. "I guess that's why I wanted to help out when I saw you flashing Jamie O'Dowd's picture around. That and because I thought you were hot-looking. Judith got burned bad that time."

"Oh?"

"She puts on a good act, tries to pretend she doesn't care. But that bastard really hurt her."

She fumbled in her purse for a cigarette, and I leaned across the table and lit it for her. The waiter came by, recited the daily specials, and we ordered.

She waited until he was out of earshot before she continued.

"You're a single guy," she said. "You've dated, right?"

"Of course. Some."

"Then you know how things go sometimes. Look, everybody in the world has gone to bed with somebody they shouldn't have. It comes with the territory of being single. And there are lots of guys who are like that, who are just out for a score, another notch on the gun. Women like to think that's not true, at least with this one particular guy, but it still happens. All the time."

"Poduska was looking for more than a quick lay," I said. "For him that was only the dessert. He was a con man."

"They're all con men. You think it's going to work out with someone, but it turns out to be a one-night stand—or one-week, even. But what O'Dowd did with Judith—damn! It was just so ... so calculated. So mean! It was bad enough he fucked her, but then he had to go and rob her, too."

"He was bad paper, all right."

She frowned and sat back in the booth. "Was?"

I toyed with the stem of my martini glass. I didn't want to get into this, but it was all going to come out anyway. "Jamie O'Dowd is dead."

She blinked, and her face lost a little of its color. "What do you mean?"

"Just that. He was killed a few nights ago."

"Killed? How?"

"He was shot."

She gulped, took a few deep breaths. "Wow."

"Yeah."

All of a sudden she seemed not to know what to do with her hands; she finally settled for putting the smoldering cigarette into an ashtray and folding them on the edge of the table like a second-grade kid. "Can you tell me what happened?"

"I can tell you what I know. His real name was William Poduska."

She lifted an eyebrow. "How did he manage to get O'Dowd out of Poduska?"

"Oh, he could be as Irish as Paddy's pig when he wanted to be. He was married to an Irishwoman."

Her look darkened. "He was *married*? My God, what a little shit he was!" She glanced away. "I'm sorry, that was pretty cold, wasn't it? Under the circumstances, I mean."

"He was a professional scam artist. Judith wasn't the first person he'd victimized—and I guess one of them got even."

She was completely stunned, I could tell. She sat there staring into the depths of her drink for a while, processing the information. Then her face changed, and she looked desperately concerned.

"You don't think Judith . . . had anything to do with . . . ?"

"I'd doubt that very much. So would the police. But they'll be contacting her anyway, if they haven't already."

She shook her head. "I don't know if they have; I didn't talk to her today. My God!"

"Poduska evidently knew I was looking for him. He had written my name on a pad in the motel room where he died." I reached out and covered her hands with one of mine. "So you can see why I'm kind of busy right now."

"Yes, sure." She forced a smile. "I didn't mean to be pushy."

"You weren't."

"When I asked you out to dinner tonight, why didn't you just tell me to go to hell?"

"Hell in October is off-season," I said. "Don't worry about it. I never do things I don't want to do." I knew it was a lie when I said it. At the moment I was steeped in doing things I didn't want to do.

The smile deepened and got a little more genuine. "You mean you wanted to see me?"

"When you walked into my office tonight, I couldn't think of anything I wanted to do more."

Relief flooded her face, and a little smug satisfaction, too. "Well, at least that's a start."

"I ought to warn you that I don't do very well in relationships."

"Show me a man who does," she smiled. "But we're not quite in a relationship yet. This is just dinner."

I took my hand away from hers as the waiter came with our food.

"I can't be romantic with my dinner in front of me."

"Oh, you're very romantic," she said. "Mysterious."

"That's not me, it's my job. Bogart and Bacall, all that stuff."

"I'll bet you even have a trench coat."

"Sure I do," I said. "So do you. This is Cleveland."

"And I knew you would order beef tonight," she said. "A meat-and-potatoes he-man. So you'll have the strength to chase down all the bad guys."

"I'm just a working stiff, that's all."

"Oh, come off it, will you? You're fascinating. You walked into O'Grady's that night like you owned the place. You walked in here the same way. You're comfortable in your own skin, which is a rarity these days. I don't think I've ever met anyone more confident."

"Don't romanticize me, Jinny."

She leaned across the table. This time her hand covered mine. "You've got a lot to learn, Milan. Of course I'm going to romanticize you. Don't you know by now that that's what women *do*?"

No, I thought. I don't know what women *do*. I've never been able to figure that out. Maybe that's been part of my problem.

Her purse chirped like a deranged cricket. "Damn!" she said, looking annoyed. She opened it and took out her cellphone, squinting in the darkened dining room to make out the number on the caller ID. Then she put it back in her purse.

"One of my other girlfriends," she said. "She's in love with a married man and can't stop talking about it. She can wait until tomorrow. Right now I'd rather talk with you."

And then she saw the look on my face and leaned forward, frowning. "Milan, what's wrong?"

I didn't answer her. Up until now I had been relaxed, enjoying the evening, the excellent meal, and the company of an attractive young woman. But now I could feel my neck and shoulder muscles bunching from tension, and my mind was racing at warp speed.

"Earth to Milan," she said.

"Jinny, I'm sorry. Can I use your phone?"

"Don't you have one?"

"It's in the car. Please? It's important."

She opened her purse again. "Well, sure. But what's . . ."

I was already dialing.

When the operator at the Third District answered, I told him I was trying to reach Lieutenant McHargue.

"She's not in," he said.

"Can you try to reach her? This is Milan Jacovich—I'm a private investigator. It's urgent."

"Lieutenant McHargue isn't going to like being bothered at home," he said. Apparently, she had him terrorized along with everybody else.

"She will this time," I said.

"Hold on. I'll try."

He was gone for more than a minute.

"Milan, what's going on?" Jinny asked.

I waved a hand at her. The cop came back on the line and said McHargue's home phone wasn't answering.

"Can you try her cellphone?"

The put-upon sigh blew through the receiver. "Hold," he said, and was gone again.

I put my hand over the mouthpiece and tried to explain to my date. "Jinny, I can't go into detail, but I just thought of something very important."

"I sure as hell hope it is," she said, put off. I couldn't blame her.

"It is, trust me."

"And you're calling the cops?"

I nodded.

"Is it about the murder?"

I started to answer, but the officer came on the line again. "Sorry, I can't raise the lieutenant."

"Would you try Detective Bob Matusen then?"

His voice through the receiver turned officious and annoyed. "Look, is this an emergency, sir?"

"There isn't a crime in progress, if that's what you mean."

"Well, this isn't a social club, sir. You'll have to call back in the morning." And he broke the connection.

"Goddamn it," I said.

"What?"

"Jinny—I've got to go."

Two red spots appeared on her cheeks as if I'd slapped her back and forth. "Right now?"

"I'm really sorry." I reached for my wallet. "Here, let me get the check."

Her eyes narrowed. "I invited you," she said. "Don't let's argue about it."

"But I'm ruining your evening."

She shook her head. "I was having a perfectly lovely evening up until two minutes ago. And I was hoping the rest of it would be even lovelier."

"I know. I feel really lousy about it." But I didn't, really; in my head I was already out of there.

"Lousy enough to call me again when you've finished with whatever it is you're doing? I figure the least you owe me is a dinner."

"I promise."

She pulled her credit card from her wallet. "You're a damned fool if you don't," she said.

I hurried out to my car, which I had parked on a side street because Kosta's had neither a parking lot nor a valet service. The night had turned chilly; it wasn't unusual for the North Coast to have snow in late October, but the air didn't feel that way right now—just dry and cold, borne on a stiff breeze coming off the nearby lake.

As I headed for the freeway, my emotions were swirling. It was funny how a seemingly meaningless incident can trigger a thought process that could clear up all confusion regarding a completely unrelated matter, but that's what had happened to me in Kosta's—and now I had to act on it.

I knew I was going to be stepping on Florence McHargue's toes, and I was justifying my actions in my own mind because I had, after all, tried to contact her.

I made my way up the on-ramp and into the flow of traffic on I-90, and as I did so, I felt a pang of regret. I hadn't wanted to leave Jinny Johnson sitting alone at that table, waiting for the server to bring a credit card slip for her signature. She was pretty and bright and bubbly and vivacious, and for the first time since

since my divorce I wasn't feeling flutterings for someone who was way out of my league, like ex-lovers Mary Soderberg, who was a high-powered TV executive, and Nicole Archer, a neonatologist. Jinny's background was blue-collar, just like mine—and for some reason she was actually interested in me. That didn't happen to me so often that I could afford to blow it off when it did.

My luck.

But I owed Victor big-time. I owed the judge. And in a peculiar way, I owed Mickey Marcantonio, too—so my decision to desert Jinny was not arbitrary.

I was doing my job. What I get paid to do. And once more it had blown a hole in my personal life.

Business.

CHAPTER TWENTY-TWO

There wasn't much traffic on the interstate, so it took me only about forty minutes to get to Elyria. On the way, I did something I almost never do: I used my cellphone while I was driving, an action for which I routinely curse other drivers. I considered this an emergency, though, because I was once again trying to reach Florence McHargue or Bob Matusen, hoping I would connect with a different and more cooperative duty officer at the Third. I was as equally unsuccessful as I had been on Jinny Johnson's phone in Kosta's.

It was well after ten o'clock when I finally arrived at Donalene Poduska's house. There was a car already parked in the small driveway, so I left mine on the street and made my way up the short walkway. The porch light was off, and evidently only a small lamp on in the living room, because the light coming through the blinds in the front window was weak and yellowish, with a blue flicker that told me the television set was on. There was another faint light shining from an upstairs window, and a shadow moving behind it.

I rang the bell and waited. For more than a minute there was no answer. I tried again.

After a few moments I heard Donalene Poduska's voice coming faintly through the closed door. "Yes?"

"Donalene, it's Milan Jacovich."

I could hear her moving around inside, but she didn't answer for a while. Then she said, "It's awfully late."

"Sorry, but we really need to talk."

Another hesitation. "You'll have to wait a minute," she said, "because I'm not dressed."

"Take your time."

She took me at my word; it was another five minutes before she finally returned. I had smoked a cigarette while I waited, and when I heard her unlocking the door, I pinched off the burning end of it and field-stripped it, rubbing it between my fingers until the paper ripped and the loose tobacco drifted off in the breeze. I put the filter in my pocket.

My army training.

She stood in the doorway, one hand resting on the jamb and the other holding a half-smoked cigarette. She was dressed in a baggy-white chenille bathrobe, buttoned to the neck, with a faded peach-colored towel wrapped around her head like a turban, completely covering her hair. On her feet were what my mother used to call "carpet slippers," but I noticed she was still wearing hose.

"Sorry to keep you waiting, Mr. Jacovich, but you caught me when I was in the shower," she explained through the screen door. I found that hard to believe; she was still wearing her makeup, and there was no trace of moisture anywhere on her that I could see.

"Can I come in?"

"This isn't exactly a convenient time. I was just going to bed. Can't whatever it is wait until morning?"

"I'm afraid it can't."

Her shoulders slumped beneath the robe, and she looked exhausted, defeated. "All right," she said reluctantly, and unlatched the screen door and stood aside so I could enter.

The living room was dim and glum looking, and had a musty odor that cut right through the scent of her cigarette. Except for the flicker of the television set, which had been muted, it was as if no one had used the room for a long time.

Donalene Poduska closed the door and leaned against it, watching me without comment as I looked around and tried to decide where to sit. I finally opted to remain standing.

"What's this all about, now?" she said impatiently, fingering the top button of her robe. "I'm not really comfortable with your being here at this hour."

"I told you before, Donalene, I'm harmless."

"Yeah, that's what they all say." She snickered unpleasantly and took a quick puff of her cigarette; the smoke jetted out of her mouth when she spoke. "But I know men, all right. Here I am, a brand-new widow, and alone. Men get funny ideas about that sometimes. And sure enough, here you come sniffing around at almost eleven o'clock at night."

Did she actually think I'd come there to make a pass at her? "Your virtue is safe with me."

"Sure." She leaned down and ground out the butt in an ashtray on the table, right next to her wedding picture. She didn't move away from the door. "All right, what's so important, then?"

"It's about your husband."

"Sure," she said again, and rolled her eyes upward to look at the pebbled ceiling. "Already the police have told me so many terrible things about him. Things that he did. Things I never even knew about." She ran a hand over her eyes. "All those years, and I was married to a man I didn't even know! Can you imagine how that feels? To hear about it after he's dead?"

"I can imagine."

She pointed an accusing finger at me. "Well, I don't want to hear any more bad things about him from you, okay? I just couldn't take it right now."

"I don't think I'm about to tell you anything you don't already know."

"Then why bother?"

"Work with me here, okay?"

She shrugged and looked away as if nothing I had to say to her could make the slightest difference in her already troubled life.

"You told me you hadn't talked to your husband for almost a week before he died, is that right?"

"That's what I said, yes."

"But he called you several times before that week?"

"Yes. I told you once before, he used to check in with me every day or two when he was on the road."

"And you didn't know where he was all that time?"

"No. He said he was traveling through Illinois and Wisconsin, moving around every day. I had no reason not to believe him."

"Are you sure?"

Her shoulders grew rigid. "What's that supposed to mean?"

I took a deep breath and let it out. Here comes the hard part, I thought. "When I was here the last time, Donalene, your telephone rang. You looked at the caller ID and decided not to answer it because it was the newspaper, bothering you again."

"I don't remember that," she said.

"I do."

"All right. What of it?"

"So your phone has caller ID. When your husband called you, you could see the name and number of the phone he was calling from. You knew he wasn't anywhere in Illinois—you could see he was right down the road in Cleveland, calling from the home of a Maureen Hartigan."

Her face turned so white that I was afraid she was having a heart attack. At that point I didn't care.

"And before that, he was calling from another Cleveland number, belonging to someone named Judith Torrence. And you knew that, too."

With her teeth she worried the skin beside her thumbnail, and then nervously put her hand into the pocket of her robe. "I don't see your point."

"The point is that you lied," I said. "I'm wondering why."

She didn't answer me, but her mouth was a razor-thin line of anger, as if by compressing her lips she could prevent words from flying out.

"Or maybe I know why."

I couldn't tell whether her left eyebrow was lifted by quizzicality or disdain.

"Your husband wasn't the brightest guy in the world, Donalene. He should have been carrying a cellphone. That's why even though he told you he was on the road, he was making those calls from numbers that could easily be traced. When he called you from the Torrence home or the Hartigan home, he never even stopped to think that your phone had caller ID and that you'd know where he was."

She opened her lips long enough to wet them with her tongue, then compressed them again.

"I guess you were suspicious of his womanizing ways for a long time, but you were in denial about it because you preferred not to believe it. It was easier to keep on with your relationship if you didn't. He'd always been very secretive in the marriage—you admitted that. You didn't know much about what he did for a living or where he was when he was out on the road. He took care of all the bills, he gave you a small allowance, and you accepted that meekly. But when he called you from the homes of two different women, you had to face the reality. You were a betrayed wife, and mad as hell about it."

She drew a sharp breath in through her nose. 'Wouldn't you be mad as hell if you were in my position?"

I felt my ears growing warm, remembering things about my ex-wife, Lila, that I usually preferred to keep stuffed way down inside where they wouldn't hurt anymore. "I've *been* in your position, Donalene. The difference is, I guess, that you did something about it."

"Did I?"

"I think you did. Your uncle Cornelius knew where Bill ended up—in that west-side motel. He had to know, because the night before Bill died, he warned him that I was looking for him; that's how my name happened to be written down on a pad of paper next to the phone in his room. And I'm guessing that your uncle told you."

For a reason I was unable to discern, the tension in her neck and shoulders seemed to ebb from her, and she leaned backward against the front door, rubbing her back against it like a bear scratching itself on the trunk of a tree.

"You'd had a few weeks to think about it, and you worked yourself up into a real rage. So you went to his motel that night— armed. He must have been really surprised to see you."

I couldn't be sure, but I thought her eyes seemed to twinkle for the barest moment, like winking lights on a Christmas tree. Nevertheless, she maintained her silence.

"You confronted him about the other women, and you probably didn't care when you saw that he was all banged up, that someone had given him a beating. Did you think some jealous husband or boyfriend had caught up with him?"

She still wasn't answering me, but her gaze was steady, drilling into me like a bright, hot light.

"That's when you lost it, Donalene, and you shot him—first in the testicles, because that's where all your hate and anger were directed. I should have figured it out from that, and so should the police—but there were so many other people with a good reason to hate your husband, we all got sidetracked. And then, to finish the job, you shot him through the head."

She pursed her mouth as if for a kiss. Then she said, "You have a pretty good imagination."

"I'm not only imaginative, but observant, too."

"Oh?"

"Yes. Like I don't believe you were in the shower when I rang the doorbell just now. Unless, for some strange reason, you put a plastic bag over your head to protect your makeup."

Perhaps she was picturing that comic scenario, because the corner of her mouth turned up in a wry half-smile.

"You're not even damp."

She sighed.

I pointed at her feet. "And with someone waiting at the door, you wouldn't have taken the time to put on stockings if you'd been showering. The truth is, you were trying to stall me before you let me in."

"Why would I want to do that?" she murmured dreamily, as if in a secret reverie of her own.

"Probably you saw me coming up your walk, and you wanted some extra time to call somebody and tell them."

She took the towel off her head and dropped it on the floor, shaking her auburn hair out to its full length. As I'd suspected, it was dry. "Why don't you be comfortable, Mr. Jacovich, and take your jacket off?"

"That's all right."

"No, it isn't," she said. "Because I'll shoot you dead if you don't."

That's when she took the gun out of the pocket of her robe and pointed it at the widest part of me. It was a small, blue-plated twenty-two, the type of weapon men often bought for their wives or girlfriends to keep under the pillow for protection—the same kind of gun that had killed Bill Poduska.

"I guess I was right," I said.

"You were close enough. You're good, Mr. Jacovich. Now how about that jacket?"

"I'm not armed, if that's what you're wondering."

"I'd like to see for myself, if that's okay."

Donalene was polite, anyway. I slowly unbuttoned my jacket and let it slip off my shoulders; I didn't want to get her nervous by making any sudden movements while she had a bead on me.

"Toss it over here, please."

I did. It didn't make a clunk when it hit the floor, and she noticed. She didn't pick it up, though, but nudged it with her foot and then kicked it off to one side.

"Turn around."

I swiveled slowly, feeling like a high-fashion model on a runway, so she could see there was no weapon tucked into the back of my waistband.

When I was facing her again, she said, "You mind showing me whether you're earning an ankle gun?"

"You're very thorough," I said, pulling up both pants legs.

"I watch a lot of television." She motioned with the pistol. "Sit down on the couch there and relax."

"Hard to relax when you're waving that thing at me."

"Try."

I eased myself down onto the flowered sofa, sinking into the cushions as I'd done before. It wasn't the type of furniture a large man like me could rise from very quickly. I was at least sixteen feet away from her, so making any sort of heroic effort to relieve her of the gun was out of the question. I'm big—but I'm not fast.

She remained where she was, leaning against the door. "Now put your hands behind you, and sit on them."

"You've got all the moves, Donalene," I said with a certain amount of grudging admiration.

"Thanks."

"You're not really going to shoot me right here in your living room, are you? The neighbors would hear the shot, there would be blood all over, and you'd have a very large body to dispose of. That would just cause more trouble. You don't want all that, do you?"

"No," she said, "I don't. But don't think I won't do what I have to do. They can only hang me once. Now sit on your hands."

I shoved my hands beneath my buttocks. It wasn't very comfortable. "Is that the same gun you used on Bill?"

She didn't answer, but I saw her mind working, and a speck of saliva was glistening at the corner of her mouth. If I wasn't mistaken, she was reliving the moment.

"Not very smart, keeping it in the house like that," I said.

I let her think about it for a while. In the end it didn't seem to bother her.

My mouth was dry and cottony—not surprising, considering I might be counting the minutes I had left to live on my fingers. "I don't suppose you'd let me have a drink of water, would you, Donalene?"

"Don't insult my intelligence, okay?"

"Okay," I said.

We sat there for a little while longer.

"What are we going to do now?" I said.

"Wait."

"For what?"

For the first time since I'd walked in, she surrendered herself to a genuine smile. "I can't tell you. It'd ruin the surprise."

"I doubt it." I figured I had been right about her making a phone call—and I knew just who she'd made it to, too.

She shrugged elaborately and shifted her position against the door, but the ugly little bore of her weapon stayed steady on me.

"Aren't *you* going to sit down?" I asked.

"That's okay; I'm good right where I am." She darted a glance toward the hallway. "The back door in the kitchen is double-locked, by the way, in case you were thinking of making a run for it. I'd shoot you dead before you got out."

"Make a run for it? You *do* watch a lot of television, Donalene."

"Not much else to do while my husband was out fucking half the women in America," she said. "God, I can't believe I was so stupid.

My nose began itching, and I crinkled it to relieve the tickle.

Funny, isn't it, how something like that always happens when your hands are too involved elsewhere to do anything about it?

"You probably think I'm a terrible person," she said accusingly, as if shooting her husband for his infidelities shouldn't necessarily put her in that category. "Well, I'm not. At the beginning I loved Bill with all my heart. Oh, I knew he was kind of irresponsible, but I was hooked on him. I gave up everything for him, and turned myself into a little brown wren who stayed home and kept his shirts ironed and the house clean because that's the way he wanted it. When I realized he was cheating on me—with God knows how many different women—I felt used. I felt like the last three years were a waste. A lie. And when my uncle told me where he was—in that crappy little motel—I just had to go down and tell the cheating little son of a bitch what I thought of him." A tremor ran through her, but it wasn't strong enough to destroy her aim. "I didn't go there to kill him, whether you believe that or not. I just wanted to tell him off."

"Then why did you take the gun with you?"

"I didn't," she said. "The gun is his—it was right there, out on the nightstand in plain sight."

It probably hadn't been there the day before when Mickey Marcantonio walked in and smacked him around and broke his finger; he'd taken it out so it would be within easy reach if Mickey came back.

"When I told him I knew he'd been screwing around, he laughed at me. He actually laughed. He told me to grow up," she went on, "and he said that I couldn't really expect a man like him to be content with one woman. And then all of a sudden my head started swimming, and I actually saw red. I know that's supposed to be just an expression, but it actually happened to me. The next thing I know, the gun was in my hand, and . . ."

She shuddered again. "You're right—I did aim for the crotch deliberately. I wasn't thinking, I suppose, but I really wanted to hurt that part of him. So he'd never be able to fuck another woman, so he'd never be able to hurt me that way again."

"He might have survived that, Donalene," I said, "if you'd called an ambulance right away."

She nodded. "I know, but like I said, I wasn't exactly clear-headed. I shot him the second time to stop the screaming."

I retasted my dinner from Kosta's, unbidden at the back of my throat. Whatever Donalene's state of mind at the time of the shooting might have been, her recounting of it now was so mat-ter-of-fact, so unemotional, so completely cold. It chilled *me*. "Didn't anyone else hear the shots?" I said. "Or the screaming? Motels have pretty thin walls."

"Whoever heard it probably wasn't any more anxious than I was to have the police around. It was that kind of motel. I saw two prostitutes walking around in the parking lot when I drove in, and a couple of men who looked like drug dealers were skulking in the shadows."

"And when you went out?"

"I guess whoever had been out there made themselves scarce as soon as they heard the first shot. So nobody saw me leave. And the ones who saw me come in weren't likely to tell the cops about it, or they might have been asked what *they* were doing there."

I looked at her closely. She was pretty in a rather bony sort of way, but the dead cold flatness of her eyes ruined the effect. She had transmogrified from house mouse into killer with hardly a ripple.

"You're remarkably cool about all this," I said.

"I wasn't at the time," she admitted. "I was a basket case. I was shaking so bad that I almost ran off the road and killed myself driving home on the freeway. But now that I've had time to think about it some more and get organized—yes, I suppose I am okay with it."

Okay with it. She took a human life, the life of a man she had once loved—and she was "okay with it."

"No regrets?"

"Except for being dumb enough to marry him in the first place? No, not really," she said. "Bill deserved what he got. Oh, I suppose if I had it to do over again, I wouldn't have killed him, because it's turning my life inside out. But am I sorry he's gone? No."

She looked down at the gun strangely, as if noticing that it had suddenly started growing out of her hand. "He's been gone for a long time. I didn't know it then, but he's been long gone from me, from this marriage." She shrugged her shoulders. "I just finalized the deal, that's all."

"You really expect to get away with murder?"

"Oh, I know I will."

"Eventually, the police will figure it out, you know, even if I'm not around to tell them."

"I suppose they will," she said. "But when they do, I won't be anywhere they can find me."

It was beginning to clarify in my brain, this muddle into which

I had found myself thrust—the puzzle pieces were beginning to fit. "Let me guess," I said. "Your uncle Con knows hundreds of people in Sinn Fein, all over the country—some of whom are using assumed names. He knows about keeping identities covert, doesn't he? So he'll just arrange for you to disappear, and then show up in another town a long way from here, with a brand-new name, and a built-in, solid Irish support group to keep you safe."

She nodded. "Like I said, you're good, Mr. Jacovich."

"Good enough to know you're not just going to skate, Donalene. The police can be slow, sometimes, because they've got rules and regulations to follow that private investigators like me don't have to worry about. But they're not stupid. They'll figure it out."

"And do what about it? I'll be off in Iowa or Arizona somewhere."

"They'll find you."

"I don't mean to be rude," she said—a curious choice of words for a woman who was pointing a gun at me and had just threatened to shoot me dead. "But I don't really want to talk anymore. It's giving me a headache."

"I'm just trying to help you."

"Then shut your mouth," she said. "That's how you'll help me."

I didn't want to shut up. I had a lot of questions to ask. But in my experience, the person holding the gun makes the rules, so I remained quiet and waited for my hands under my butt to start getting numb, watching a cable movie on the silent TV set. It was one of Boris Karloff's last films, called, as I remembered, *Targets*, and its subject matter—a young man who killed his wife and mother and then went and sat up on an oil tank adjacent to the freeway in Los Angeles and sniped at cars driving by with his long-range rifle—didn't make me feel any easier.

Where, I wondered, was *Singin' in the Rain* when you needed it?

I sat there uncomfortably, Donalene Poduska's eyes never meeting mine, for another forty minutes or so until I heard a car pull up outside at the curb and cut its engine. Three doors slammed. It figured; that was about how long it took to get from the west side of Cleveland to Elyria in light traffic.

And despite Donalene's promise of a surprise, I knew exactly who was going to walk through that door when she turned the knob, opened it, and stepped aside to allow her visitors to enter.

Cornelius McCardle appeared in the doorway, his face flushed and anxious-looking from his niece's hurriedly phoned summons for help. Behind him was his receptionist, Francis, along with the other hulking young man I had seen in the front room of Shamrock Homes, and a third man I had never seen before. He looked enough like Francis to be his brother.

It was as I had imagined. What I hadn't been able to dope out yet was how I was going to save my own life.

"*Mister* Jacovich," McCardle said, pronouncing it correctly; there was no need to play dumb or innocent anymore. No need to be cute and go for the one-upmanship. He was more than one up on me.

"Hello, Mr. McCardle."

He came all the way into the room, his minions following, and Donalene closed and locked the door behind them. It was a fairly small living room, and it was filling up fast; the two muscle guys stood shoulder-to-shoulder in front of the door like a large, wide wall.

"I think you've made the acquaintance of my great-nephew Francis here," he said. "And these other two are Ryan and James."

How polite of McCardle to introduce everyone.

"He figured it out, Uncle Con," Donalene said. "All of it."

The old man nodded sagely. "Yes, I imagined he would, eventually. Just not quite so soon."

He took the few steps across the room to stand directly in front of me. He loomed there, his fists on his hips like a principal confronting a truant, and I looked up at him, seeing the hard set of his jaw, the angry fire in his eyes, and the thick nest of gray hairs in his nostrils.

"I told you to let it go, didn't I, Jacovich?" he said, his bushy white eyebrows dancing up and down. "I begged you to back off. But you wouldn't listen to me, damn your eyes!"

"Mr. McCardle," I said, "this problem can be dealt with. Don't make it any worse than it is."

"You have a way of saving things that sound friendly and help-ful, but you really are self-serving, aren't you?"

"If you mean, am I trying to talk you out of killing me?—yes, I suppose you're right."

"Well, it isn't anything I relish," he said. "But this is about fam-ily. If a man doesn't go the whole limit to protect his family, he can't count himself much of a man, now, can he?"

"Bill Poduska didn't deserve to die, Mr. McCardle, no matter what he might have done. This is a civilized society—we can't just go around shooting the people who piss us off."

"I told you I regretted his death, even though he was a nasty little shit who caused my family a good deal of pain," McCardle said. "I still do. And I have had strong words about it with Do-nalene. But she's my niece, and I can't stand by and leave her un-protected when it's within my power to keep her safe." He hitched up his trousers. "Blood is thicker than water."

"It's not going to work."

"That remains to be seen. Right now the priority is to keep a lid on this for as long as we can. And you're the fly in the oint-ment."

"You think shutting me up is going to make it all go away?"

"For the moment," he said. "And life is lived in the moment. Sorry, but that's the way it's going to have to be. Now put on your jacket, Mr. Jacovich. We wouldn't want you catching cold."

CHAPTER TWENTY-THREE

As McCardle and his goons led me from the living room and out to their car, Donalene Poduska actually stood in the doorway and said good-bye to me, with a sad little wave thrown in for good measure. And she told me how sorry she was that I'd gotten involved in all this.

Her touching concern made me feel warm all over.

Outside it was almost completely dark, save for one street lamp down near the corner. Elyria, like Cleveland, is a go-to-bed-early kind of town, and at almost eleven-thirty at night I had no hope of anyone being around to see our little tableau and call the authorities. The three younger men were all armed with hand-guns, and once outside they roughly patted me down for non-existent hardware and relieved me of my shoes. I suppose that was so if I did somehow manage to get away from them, I'd have difficulty running. McCardle held the shoes gingerly between his fingertips as he walked over to my car, opened the door, and slung them inside.

They also took my car keys. The old man gave them to the guy I hadn't met before—the Francis clone, whose name I think was James—and I stood there helplessly and watched him drive away in my fairly new Sunbird, complete with my nine-millimeter Glock in the glove compartment.

I figured it was headed for a west-side chop shop and would be nonexistent by morning.

Then they hustled me into their car. It was a two-door Chevy Malibu, and they made me squeeze my bulk into the cramped backseat so there was no chance I could open a door and roll out to safety once we were under way. Francis was my seat companion; he sat on the driver's side, holding what looked like a thirty-eight-caliber police special pointed at my stomach. I couldn't even get funny and whack the driver on the head and cause a car crash. Besides, like Donalene, they insisted that I sit on my hands. They'd thought of everything.

Why not? They were pros. I had no illusions that Cornelius McCardle had never played out this scenario before.

The other big guy I'd seen at Shamrock Homes—whose name was Ryan, if McCardle was to be believed—slipped behind the wheel, and the old patriarch ensconced himself in the passenger seat, and we took off. After a few minutes we roared up the ramp to I-90 and were heading west.

"In a way, it's a dirty shame, Jacovich," McCardle said easily, twisting around in the seat so he could look at me. "You've been a boil on my ass from the first moment I saw you, but I was kind of beginning to like you."

"Well, you know how that is, Mr. McCardle. New friends come, and new friends go."

"Indeed. But new friends—or even old ones, for that matter—don't mean a thing when your family is being threatened. A man has got to learn to prioritize; otherwise he's not worth a damn."

"And Donalene is your priority."

He nodded his head once, bluntly. "It goes without saying. She's my blood. And that is your misfortune." His smile grew crafty and mean. "Did you by any chance hear the banshee scream last night?"

"You think I can just disappear without a trace and nobody is going to ask any questions?"

"Oh, surely there will be questions. But none that I'll have the answers to. I told you that I'd read about you in the papers. Well, after your first visit to the Shebeen, I did some further checking. You have quite an interesting career behind you. You're a tough guy."

"I get paid for it."

"Ah, yes. But there have to be a lot of folks out there who are pretty mad at you. Holding grudges. Have reason to want you dead."

"I suppose," I said. "But there are some who actually like me. Like Giancarlo D'Allessandro."

He chuckled. "Ah, don't be shakin' the mafia in my face, now. They don't scare me."

"They should."

"They won't make the connection—not enough of one to do anything about it, anyway. Neither will the police."

"You'd better hope they don't."

He turned around to face the front, watching woods and farms go by in the darkness, but kept talking. "You know, there's a big misconception afoot about Irish people. People think of us as happy-go-lucky, singing songs about our mothers and Galway Bay and leprechauns and shamrocks and shillelaghs, and getting shit-faced on green beer on Saint Patrick's Day and all. But the reality is a hell of a lot different."

I didn't say anything; I was too busy looking for a way out. But McCardle was leaning against the door, blocking the handle, and Francis still had a bead on me, so my efforts were frustrated.

"The reality is," the old man went on, "that our history is one of oppression and starvation and bad times. Ireland was under the thumb of the goddamned English for centuries. Then we starved during the Famine. A lot of fine young Irish boys died during the Troubles. And those who came to America in the early part of the twentieth century had to face the same kind of discrimination as blacks and Jews. It took nearly two hundred years for an Irishman to become president of the United States—John Fitzgerald Kennedy, God bless him. And then we had to hear bad jokes, like him changing the national motto from 'In God We Trust' to 'In the Pope We Hope.' To this day, some people think all Irishmen are ineffectual bums who spend their lives living with their mothers, or else drunkards and not to be trusted. And yet we survive, we persevere, and we flourish. So you're wasting your time trying to intimidate me by throwing around the name of your Italian gangster friends. Because we're not scared of the guineas and we're not scared of the police."

"But you're scared of me, aren't you, Mr. McCardle?"

"Don't make me laugh."

"I'm not trying to. You're afraid of me, and so you're going to kill me."

His eyebrows climbed high as he looked at me over the back of the seat. "Well, that's a fair assessment, then. But I prefer to think of it as neutralizing you before you can hurt someone who is very dear to me. Now don't embarrass yourself by begging for your life."

"Begging?" I said, putting a bite into it. "In your dreams, Mr. McCardle."

"I have to admire that, Mr. Jacovich," he said. "But sadly, it doesn't change a damned thing."

"I didn't think it would," I said. "You're a classic case of not being able to see the forest for the trees. You're so wrapped up in your own cause, in your own rhetoric and your own bile, that you can't even tell right from wrong anymore. In the name of justice for the Irish, you countenance racketeering, you justify corruption, and now you even justify and condone cold-blooded murder for your goddamned cause."

He gasped. Francis stirred a little bit, as if he was thinking about making me be quiet, but McCardle shook his head at him, and he subsided.

I took that as tacit permission to continue. "And in the name of 'family,'" I said, "you turn a blind eye to one murder and are about to commit another. You think that you're God's nobleman or something, but the fact is you're no better than any other selfish petty tyrant who wraps himself in the cloak of patriotism and idealism and makes pretty speeches and kisses babies while lining his own pockets and convincing himself that he's the savior of his people. Well, take a good look, Mr. McCardle—because you're nothing but a glorified hoodlum masquerading as a leprechaun."

While I talked, his face had been growing progressively redder. Now I feared he was about to have a stroke.

He leaned over the back of his seat and screamed in my face, spittle flying. "Nobody talks that way to me, you goddamned shit pig.'"

"What are you going to do about it? Kill me?"

We were practically nose-to-nose; I could smell Guinness on his breath, which was coming hard and labored, his anger clutching at his throat and inhibiting the airflow. And then all at once he smiled, and settled back in his seat and folded his hands over his old man's paunch.

"Yes, Mr. Jacovich," he said, apparently content now to enjoy the ride. 'That's exactly what I'm going to do about it."

About five minutes later I experienced the greatest nicotine craving of my life, all at once. For a lifelong smoker such as I, that need is never far from the surface, but in times of stress it asserts itself in the most terrible ways. "You mind if I smoke, Mr. McCardle?"

"It's Ryan's car, ask him."

The driver barely moved his neck to glance back at me. "Go ahead. I don't give a shit."

"The condemned man gets a last cigarette? Is that how it goes?"

"Something like that," McCardle said.

Francis leaned forward on full alert, raising the gun slightly as I took my hands out from beneath my thighs, shook them a little to get the circulation going, and then dug into my jacket pocket for a Winston.

McCardle shifted around again to look at me. "If you're thinking about playing games with the book of matches back there, I'd advise against it. Francis will shoot you dead before he puts out the fire."

"The thought had crossed my mind."

"I'd have been disappointed in you if it hadn't."

I lit my cigarette carefully and put the spent match in the backseat ashtray. Then I put the matchbook away. "Come to think of it, what's the difference if I get it here or wait until we get to wherever you're taking me?"

"The difference of perhaps an hour," he said. "Most men I know would forgo a foolish act of false bravado for an extra hour of life."

"You're right," I admitted.

"I've no doubt you're entertaining some false hope of a last-minute reprieve, too," he said. "Or a miracle. That's good. Keep that hope burning, Mr. Jacovich; it will make it easier for you in the long run."

McCardle opened his window just a crack so I could let the smoke jet out into the slipstream and dissipate into the darkness of the night.

Easier for me.

I remembered that many years ago, Giancarlo D'Allessandro told me the only thing worth wishing for was an easy death. But there is no such thing. Whether one dies in a plane crash, at the point of a gun, or from a lingering and painful disease, or quietly slips away while asleep, death is hard because in every living creature there's the primal and passionate desire to live, to survive, to see another morning. And at the moment, the possibility of another sunrise in my future seemed remote and almost unattainable.

I was angry. I was sad that I would never again gaze upon the faces of the sons I loved. I regretted the books I'd never get to read and the meals I'd never enjoy eating, and yes, the women I had left unkissed. I was even bitter about leaving the lovely and intriguing Jinny Johnson sitting at a restaurant table alone, waiting for the check.

Death would not be easy at all. And so I decided to take Dylan Thomas's advice and rage against the dying of the light.

What I had to figure out now was how.

CHAPTER TWENTY-FOUR

'd finished my cigarette, and McCardle told me to toss the butt out the window. I didn't worry about starting a forest fire; it had been an unusually wet autumn, and the shrubbery was still damp and as fire-resistant as it ever got. Then he ordered me to sit on my hands again.

I wasn't quite granted the hour that McCardle had promised me; I felt cheated. It was only about forty-five minutes after leaving Donalene Poduska's house that Ryan, the driver, twisted the wheel and sent the car squealing down a dark exit ramp off I-90, turned northward toward the distant lake, and headed down what could only be called a country road.

Northeast Ohio is like that. There you are in urban Cleveland, with its impressive skyline and the gray industrial hulks of the now-silent mills, and then you get in your car and hit the freeway, and in barely a few minutes you're either in the woods or on the farm.

It was woods that McCardle and his crew had in mind, evidently. There were only a few houses, all with their lights out at midnight, and they were all set well back from the road. We passed one small BP America station, but it had probably been closed since dusk.

It had been a long time since anyone in the car had spoken. McCardle had said his piece and I had said mine, but the two young roughnecks who were our traveling companions seemed disinclined to make small talk. And rightly so—it was a pretty grim occasion, especially for me.

McCardle leaned forward, both hands on the dashboard, and peered through the windshield at the headlights stabbing through inky blackness. "Turn right here," he barked.

Ryan dutifully turned down an even smaller and narrower road—two stingy lanes with no shoulder on either side. The trees, not yet bereft of their fall leaves, rose up beside and in front of us, their branches arching gracefully over the pavement. It was like driving through a tunnel.

After another two minutes, during which we passed no buildings of any kind, the old man directed Ryan to turn onto what was no more than a rutted dirt drive. We bounced along, the trees so close on either side that their branches scraped the car's flanks, and stopped at a small clearing just big enough for the car to turn around in and head back the way it had come when the patriarch announced, "Right here. This is good."

Ryan cut the engine, and he and McCardle got out; Ryan had his pistol out, too. It was too dark to be sure, but I thought it was a nine-millimeter Sig-Sauer. The old Irishman pulled the front seat forward so I could wriggle through, and Francis emerged on the driver's side; we were both big men, so getting out of the backseat of a two-door car was awkward and difficult.

After my cigarette I'd been sitting on my hands again, so now that they were free, they were tingling unpleasantly. I flexed my fingers.

I didn't know whether they had been through this routine before or whether McCardle was directing them with silent hand signals, but the two men moved to the trunk, Francis opened it, and they extracted two large shovels, which they slung over their shoulders like Snow White's dwarves, their weapons held at the ready in their free hands. Then McCardle took a small flashlight from his pocket—it fit in his palm but it had a powerful beam— and gave me a none-too-gentle nudge in the small of the back, indicating that he wanted me to precede him and walk deeper into the thicket of trees.

As Robert Frost wrote, the woods were lovely, dark, and deep— and my mind was racing feverishly to figure out a way I could stay alive to travel the miles I had to go before I slept.

The fallen leaves crunched under our feet—less so beneath

mine because I had been relieved of my shoes back at the Poduska house.

Sharp dry twigs poked painfully through my socks, and once
or twice I stumbled.

The trees were thick here, oaks and sugar maples and a few
slender birches, some of them no more than ten or twelve feet
apart, and there was virtually no light coming through the
branches from the sliver of a moon I had noticed while we were
on the road. The old man was behind me, but the beam from his
flashlight bobbed ahead of me as we walked.

We got about a hundred and fifty yards into the woods before
McCardle told me to stop.

I did, and turned around. He was standing with his back
against a tree, breathing heavily from the exertion of the hike.
He didn't look as if he worked out, and he didn't strike me as the
outdoors type, so the walk had taken something out of him.

"This will do, I suppose," he said. He turned to Francis while
keeping the flashlight beam trained on me, and held out his hand.
Francis pressed his gun into his great-uncle's palm.

"You're actually going to do it yourself?" I said.

"Donalene is my blood, so it's my responsibility." He shined the
light beam on the gun—it reflected under his chin and made him
look like a creature in a bad horror film.

McCardle looked down at the weapon in his hand as if it were
a poisonous snake and he had no idea how it had gotten there.
"I'm not used to these goddamn things," he said.

Francis moved forward and showed him how to use it, then
retreated. Ryan still had his gun trained on me.

"Anything you want to say, Jacovich?"

"Not really. Not to you, anyway."

In the reflected light I saw him frown. "Aren't you afraid, for
God's sake?"

"I'm not afraid of dying," I said, "although I have to confess
that it's my second choice."

"Every man is afraid of dying."

"No," I said. "Nobody wants to, but many people don't fear it.
I've lived the most interesting life of almost anyone I know. It
hasn't all been wonderful—as a matter of fact there have been
stretches of it that were downright shitty. But life doesn't owe

me anything, because it has never, ever, for one moment been boring—and I suppose at the end of the day that isn't such a bad epitaph."

"You're a brave man, son. I keenly regret the necessity of this."

"Then don't."

"Ah, but I have to, don't you see?" he said, almost whining. The flashlight beam, which had been aimed just below my chin, wavered a little. "My duty is to my niece, and the way I look at it, it's either you or her. So my responsibility is clear, I'm afraid."

I edged closer to him—not more than eight inches, but it was the best I could do without attracting undue attention.

"Would you kneel down, please?" he said—politely, and with a tinge of regret. His voice, usually strong and ringing with conviction, sounded shaky and uncertain. Con McCardle might be many things, but he was not an executioner, and this wasn't setting well with him.

I shook my head. "No. I won't die on my knees, Mr. McCardle."

He sighed. "Dead is dead, for the love of Jesus! You are the most stubborn bastard I've ever laid eyes on!"

"So are you," I said.

"Me?"

"Yes, you. You're so caught up in the blood-and-family thing, you don't realize that the police are eventually going to figure out it was Donalene who killed Bill. You may spirit her out of town and hide her, but that won't stop them from sniffing around. And while they do, they're going to uncover a lot of things about you—about your political activities. Questions are going to be asked. Some of your friends and associates will have their covers blown. The FBI is going to get in on the fun, and the Justice Department, too, and the organization you've been building for so long is going to come crashing to the ground. You talk about the greater good—but you're putting all your people at risk. And eventually, someone will figure out what happened to me, and then you and your boys here are going to be looking at murder raps, all three of you. It doesn't seem worth it."

"What can I do about that?" he asked almost helplessly.

"Have Donalene turn herself in. That will stop all the questions. Get her a good criminal lawyer—I can even recommend one. They can't prove premeditation, because the gun was Bill's, already there. And a good case can be made for the emotionally shattered, betrayed wife suffering a blackout, a bout of temporary insanity, and pulling the trigger without knowing what she was doing." I inched a little closer, bruising my sock-clad foot on a pebble. "If she cops a guilty plea, I wouldn't be surprised if she didn't do any time at all. A little while under a psychiatrist's care, and she'll be good as new."

The forest was silent for a while, save for the whisper of wings in the trees and the occasional murmur of a far-off owl. It was too dark for me to see McCardle's face, especially with the glare of his flash in my eyes. But I knew he was thinking about it—and agonizing over it.

I decided that for the first time that evening I had an advantage, and I decided to push it. "All your Sinn Fein friends," I went on, "who've been begging and stealing and then laundering money for the cause, who've been buying illegal arms, and doing other things that perhaps you don't even know about. They'll all go down, Con—these men who trusted you to watch out for them—and you'll go down with them. And when you do, they'll eventually poke around some more, and they'll nail you for doing me, too. Whatever they give you for it, at your age, that's a life sentence. You'll die in prison. Is that what you want?"

The flashlight beam lowered, almost to my shoes. "Jesus, Jacovich . . ." Con McCardle said.

"Don't listen to him, Uncle!" Francis shouted suddenly. His voice was shrill, almost prepubescent. "He's just trying to save his own ass!"

Another county heard from—the bloodthirsty little shit. But his shout was just the distraction I'd been looking for. As I saw McCardle's head turn toward his nephew in the darkness, I took one step forward and brought my foot up hard into the old man's crotch. It would have been more effective had I been wearing shoes, but it got the job done, because when all was said and done, Con McCardle was frail and brittle. He screamed, and I slammed him back against the tree trunk. Both his gun, which he hadn't had much of a grip on to begin with, and the flashlight dropped to the carpet of leaves from his old hands. I kicked out at the flashlight hard, bruising my toe on it, and didn't even wait to watch it sail through the air about ten feet, land hard against a tree trunk, flicker, and go out.

Now there was hardly any light at all, and nobody really knew where anybody else was—some shadows were darker than others, that's all.

Francis dropped his shovel and made a lunge for his uncle's fallen gun, but he ran into my upraised knee with his forehead and fell back with a grunt. Ryan, who had been standing off to one side, snapped off a shot at me—flames leapt from the muzzle of his gun—but it was too dark for any shooter not equipped with an infrared sight, and the bullet went by about three feet from my head. I felt the scorched breeze, smelled it. That was still too close.

I turned and ran off into the thicket of trees, ducking and dodging as I heard Ryan's gun again, until I was well away from all of them, perhaps fifty feet or so. I could still hear old Con whimpering from the kick, and part of me felt sad about it. I groped blindly with my hand and found a fairly thick tree, and moved behind it, waiting.

If McCardle's flashlight had been their only means of illumination, I might be okay—but if one of the other men had one as well, I was a dead duck.

They were crashing around in the underbrush, yelling to each other. Without a light I didn't know if they could even find McCardle's dropped weapon, but I knew Ryan was still armed, and I wasn't taking any chances. I pressed myself against that tree trunk like a caterpillar getting ready to spin a chrysalis.

If I'd had time to think about it, I would have realized that they could simply wait me out until morning light—that wouldn't be for several hours, yet. But there wasn't much I could do at this point unless someone came within arm's reach of me. I was running on hope.

I heard McCardle's throaty bark—"Spread out! Find him!"—and I had to smile, although it was a pretty tight, mirthless grin. Spreading out was the best thing they could do for me. When you're outnumbered, divide and conquer.

I stayed motionless. The fallen leaves were my friends, as they made a nice, crunchy carpet on which the three Irishmen were forced to make plenty of noise while moving around.

One of them was coming closer, moving very slowly and carefully. I could hear his shoes pulverizing the leaves and twigs, and from the heaviness of the step I knew it wasn't the old man.

Every muscle in my body tensed, and then I willfully relaxed them—all except for the doubled-up fist.

I couldn't see a damn thing, but I could sense the man's closeness in the darkness, almost feel his body heat and hear his breathing. A large, dark shadow moved around the tree—and I sucked in as much air as I could and stepped forward, putting all my weight into the punch I drove into his kidneys.

The sound he made was half scream and half groan. His knees buckled from the pain and the impact, and as he started to sink to his knees, I cracked him hard across the back of his neck with the edge of my hand. I'm not trained in martial arts, so I probably did it wrong, because the blow sent fiery pain all the way up my arm to the shoulder. It wasn't until he hit the ground like a stack of newspapers thrown from a moving truck that I could tell it was Francis.

He didn't move, and I crouched down and checked the pulse in his neck to assure myself that he was still breathing. He was, and I was relieved about that. I wasn't looking to kill anybody.

"Francis?" I hear McCardle calling from a distance through the velvety blackness. "Are you all right?"

I moved quickly, getting as far as I could from where McCardle had heard the scream. My shoeless feet made less noise than those of my pursuers on the floor of the forest, so I figured I would be all right for a while.

I found another tree and waited, listening. I couldn't hear any footsteps—maybe I had moved too far away from them.

Somewhere in the high branches an owl screeched, scaring the hell out of me.

I thought about McCardle. I wasn't sure, but I think that at the last minute he had been wavering about killing me, because what I'd said to him made sense—and because he was no killer, anyway.

Nobody is, I suppose, except maybe the crazies and looney tunes—the Jeffrey Dahmers, Timothy McVeighs, and Osama bin Ladens of the world who managed to justify killing in their own warped heads. Everybody else commits their homicides because they feel as if they've been driven into a corner and there is no other option. They're usually wrong, but that's the way they look at it. I know McCardle had been thinking that about killing me.

I'd lost most of my sense of direction by then, but I began moving toward where I thought we had all been. It was a long shot, but I was hoping I'd find McCardle's gun where he'd dropped it. It would still be two against one—three, if Francis regained consciousness anytime soon—but at least I'd have a fighting chance.

I bumped smack into Cornelius McCardle in the dark.

Instantly, I realized it was he; he was almost a foot shorter than his two companions.

"Son of a bitch!" he said, and I wrapped my arms around him, pinning his wrists to his sides. He flailed around, and stomped quite effectively on my unshod foot with the hard heel of his shoe, but I held on. Then I managed to turn him around so that my forearm was across his throat.

"Stop struggling," I said. "I don't want to hurt you."

And I was surprised to find it was true. Two minutes earlier he'd been ready to kill me—but strangely I felt no anger toward him.

Ryan had evidently heard him, because he came crashing toward us, making more noise than a charging rhino. When he was about ten feet away, I said, "Hold it, Ryan. I've got your boss in a choke hold here, and if you don't drop the weapon right now, I'm going to snap his neck like a matchstick."

I could see his hulking silhouette stiffen. "Mr. McCardle?" he said.

I loosened my hold on the old man's throat. He sucked in as much air as he could and then let it out, and in doing so he seemed to deflate against me. He was defeated—and he knew it.

"Do it, Ryan."

"Toss the gun in this direction, Ryan," I said. "Underhand."

I saw his shadow move, and there was a clunk on the ground at my feet. I let go of my death grip on Con McCardle, bent, and retrieved the gun. The butt felt warm in my hand.

"All right," I said. "It's over."

CHAPTER TWENTY-FIVE

Cornelius McCardle seemed close to collapse; he slumped back against me, and I found myself holding him up so he wouldn't fall. His breath was coming hard, and he rubbed gingerly at his bruised throat.

"What happens now, Mr. Jacovich?" he said.

I was *Mister* Jacovich again. Apparently, with Con McCardle, respect depends upon which side of the gun you happen to be on. But in the darkness his voice sounded weak and ancient, at least a hundred. The way he slumped against me was almost cuddly.

"Ryan leads the way with you right behind him and me behind you. Armed. We go back and find Francis. Then we all drive back to Donalene's house." I gave him a slight nudge away from me. I sometimes like being cuddled, but McCardle didn't pass the physical. "Let's get going."

The two of them lined up in front of me, and we began moving slowly through the trees. I kept the gun in my hand but held it at my side. There was no more threat, because there was no more fight left in Cornelius McCardle. I longed for the flashlight, but I had evidently broken it when I kicked it—and my own small flashlight was on my key ring, and was long gone in James's capable hands.

I remembered the story of "The Little Mermaid"—not the movie, but the Hans Christian Andersen story in which every step she took felt like knives going into her feet. I was experiencing the same pains; every twig and pebble and stick ground into the bottom of my feet through my socks—or what was left of them. I couldn't tell whether it was the night's dampness underfoot or whether I was bleeding, but my soles felt wet. I tried hard not to limp.

"You misunderstand me," McCardle said over his shoulder as we trudged along. "What I meant was—what happens when we get back to civilization? What are you going to do?"

I hadn't really thought about that. For the last two hours my focus had been on finding a way of staying out of the hole in the ground Ryan and Francis were prepared to dig for me. Now I had some decisions to make. I quickly riffled through my options like the pages in a picture book.

"It depends. The best way would be if Donalene turns herself in," I said. "It will go much easier on her if she does. Talk her into it. If she won't, I'll do it for her. You can try to sneak her out of the state, or even out of the country, and hide her somewhere before the cops can get to her, but if you do, I'll make sure the authorities know all about your extracurricular activities—yours and your friends', too. A lot of people will go down—trust me."

He was silent for about thirty seconds as we walked. Then he said, "Yes, but what about—all this?"

"All what?"

"I tried to kill you."

I gave that one a little more thought. "No, you didn't," I said finally. "You just thought about it. You're a tough guy, but you're no killer, Mr. McCardle. You're a foolish old man who used very bad judgment, but there's no crime in that. So—if things go the way I want them to, maybe we can all just forget about what happened here tonight."

He stumbled a little bit, and fell against Ryan's back, then quickly righted himself. "That's very generous of you—under the circumstances."

It was, I suppose. But I couldn't see any profit in putting Cornelius McCardle in jail to die. He was a proud, stubborn man, and he had acted out of a knee-jerk response that I could relate to: he was a patriarch taking care of his family. He very well might have killed me, although I knew at the end there he was wavering. But in the end no one was dead except William Poduska, and I was going to make sure Donalene would have to answer for it.

The rest of it—Mickey Marcantonio's blackmail and strong-arm tactics, Doyle Hartigan's long-ago payoff from Giancarlo

D'Allessandro, Poduska's betrayal of his wife, even the victimization of Judith Torrence and Cathleen Hartigan—was none of my business. I had to resist my unfortunate predilection for trying to cure the world's ills.

After about two minutes we got lucky and found Francis—mostly by following the sounds of his groans. He was still on the ground, rubbing the back of his neck, but at least he was conscious. Ryan pulled him to his feet—not an easy task considering the boy's bulk—and held his arms fast around him in a bear hug to keep him from lunging at me with intent to kill. He screamed curses at me. It didn't seem to bother him that I was armed. He was a real hothead, Francis.

Once he calmed down a little, I made him head up the procession, in front of Ryan. I wanted him as far away from me as possible, if for no other reason than to avoid the necessity of shooting him if he came after me again.

A strong, cold breeze kicked up, and the moon came out from behind a blanket of clouds. It was about three-quarters full, and didn't provide much illumination through the foliage, but at least we could see where we were going without walking head-on into the trunk of a tree.

We were quite a ragtag bunch. Francis, still dizzy from my karate chop, was careening around, bouncing off trees like a Pachinko ball. McCardle was obviously in physical distress and walked haltingly; he was too old to be running around in the forest at night playing commando. And I was limping badly now, my socks in shreds and my feet bleeding. Only Ryan seemed unscathed.

It seemed as if we were headed in the right direction; the topography was beginning to look familiar. But I couldn't be sure—I'm a city boy, and to me a tree is a tree.

Finally, we arrived at where they had first stopped—the spot that had been designated as the site of my execution. I figured that out because I stepped on the hard plastic flashlight on the ground and winced.

"Does anyone know how to get back to the car from here without a light?" I asked.

"I think I do," Ryan said, and pointed. "Walk a straight line that way."

"Good. Let's do it."

"Lord, couldn't we stop for just a bit?" McCardle was pale and sweating, almost gasping for breath. I was afraid he was going to have a heart attack.

"Do you want to sit down?"

"No. Just let me lean against the tree here for a minute." The old Irishman put one trembling hand on the trunk and bent over at the waist, his feet spread apart and his head down, and I could hear him greedily sucking in air.

"I gotta sit down," Francis said, and slumped down against another tree, his knees level with his eyes. He rubbed the back of his neck and grimaced.

"I don't suppose," McCardle said between breaths, "that an apology really makes it here, Mr. Jacovich. But this was a mistake on my part. A rash mistake, arrived at in haste. It was stupid."

I silently agreed with him. Everyone had been stupid, from the very beginning before Judge Hartigan hired me. Hugh Cochran had been stupid, the Hartigan women had been stupid, Judith Torrence had been stupid. The late senator had been stupid, Mickey Marcantonio had been stupid, and Bill Poduska, who apparently had been unaware of telephone records and caller ID, had been the stupidest of all.

Except for maybe me—I was stupid for even getting involved in the first place, for trying to cut the police out of the loop, and certainly for walking into Donalene Poduska's house unarmed to accuse her of murder.

The five minutes we stayed there felt more like five hours. Nobody spoke, or even made eye contact. There was no sound except for the ambient noises of the woods, Francis's moaning, and McCardle's labored breathing.

Finally, I could wait no longer. "How are you doing, Mr. McCardle?" I asked.

He straightened up, and his answer sounded dangerously shaky. "I'm fine, just fine."

"It's time to go. Are you up to it?"

"I've been walking all my life," he said, flaring.

"Okay. Shall we get started?"

He turned and looked at his great-nephew, who still sat at the base of the tree, rubbing the back of his neck where I'd hit him.

"On your feet, Francis. And stop your damned whimpering. For the love of Jesus, be a man!"

Francis looked up at the old Irishman sullenly, resentfully, and the little mewling noises coming from the back of his throat stopped. He fell over onto his side slowly. Then he rolled over onto his hands and knees so that his butt was the first portion of his anatomy to rise. He used one hand against the tree trunk to haul his huge frame to an upright position.

"Does anyone have an idea which way the car is?" I said.

"I think so," Ryan pointed. "I think if we walk straight that way, we'll come to it."

"Let's go, then," I said. "Ryan, lead the way."

The platoon resumed its forced march, this time with Ryan on point about ten yards ahead of the rest of us and just barely visible in the weak blue moonlight. He was followed by Francis, then McCardle, who was right in front of me. I still held the gun, but it was down at my side now, not needed; all the fight and resolve had drained out of Con McCardle.

Ryan's sense of direction proved to be pretty good. The car was off to the right, about fifty feet ahead of us, a hulking shadow with moonlight glinting off the windshield. I found myself relaxing for the first time since Donalene Poduska had aimed a gun at me. It felt as if it had been a month ago.

All at once Francis spun around and dropped into a semi-crouch. "Goddamn you, Jacovich!" he bellowed, and the sound ricocheted eerily off the trees. I could see in the faint light that he held a gun in both hands like some television cop.

Damn! McCardle's gun that he'd dropped when I'd kicked him. I'd forgotten about it. Francis must have found it by accident when he was crawling around at the base of that tree.

"Francis!" the old man said, standing directly in front of his towering nephew. "It's no good anymore. Put that thing down."

I raised my own weapon. "Put it down, Francis; I don't want to hurt you."

"Nobody puts his hands on me, ya fuckin' bastard!" he screamed. Even in the dark I could see the whites of his eyes.

What happened next was one of those slow-motion moments, the last terrifying seconds of a nightmare before you wake up in a sweat and are afraid to go back to sleep. McCardle jumped for-

ward toward the younger man, his arms up in protest. His timing, unfortunately, was rotten, because Francis chose that moment to pull the trigger. I don't know whether he got spooked by
his great-uncle's charge and fired reflexively or whether he was
actually aiming at me, but the bullet tore through the old man's
neck. I felt a hot spray on my face, and smelled the coppery scent
of blood.

I dropped to the ground to make myself a smaller target, and
in the near dark, I squeezed off a shot that struck Francis in the
widest part of his body, which was his bull chest. My aim was
truer than I could have hoped for, because the slug hit his heart
dead-on.

Francis twisted around from the impact and crashed to the
leaf-covered ground, dead before he landed, like a great, felled
tree. If there had been no one in the forest to hear him, he might
not have made any noise at all, but Ryan and I were there, all
right—and the sound of him falling was ugly, shocking, and terribly final.

Something deep inside my chest hurt, too, and then died as
well.

"Holy Mary, mother of Jesus," Ryan said as we both rushed to
the fallen McCardle.

I knelt down, wishing I had more light so I could see what I
was doing. The hole was clean, the bullet having gone through
the side of his neck and exited out the back. His blood was spurt-
ing copiously, like a burst water pipe, and I pinched both wounds
with my fingers to stanch the flow. I could see that he needed
medical attention immediately, or he wasn't going to make it.

"Help me get him to the car," I ordered Ryan. "What about
Francis?"

I looked down at the crumpled body. "There's no help for him.
Come on, man, be quick!"

Together we gathered McCardle into our arms, my ringers still
pinching, and staggered toward the car with him. His bones felt
small and fragile, like a bird's. We loaded him into the backseat,
and I crawled in there with him, tenderly placing his head on my
lap; it felt as if it hardly weighed anything.

Ryan started the engine and began backing up, twisting the
wheel, trying to get the car pointed in the right direction so we

could drive forward out of the woods. "Where are we going?" he said.

"Get back onto I-90. Head for Vermilion—I think that's the closest emergency hospital. You have a cellphone?"

"No," he said; he seemed embarrassed about it.

"Damn! Then just drive. Drive like hell."

The engine screamed and strained as Ryan finally got it into third gear. After bouncing down the dirt path out of the trees at about forty miles an hour, which didn't do the wounded McCardle any good, Ryan ignored the speed laws completely. We must have been doing seventy on the two-lane country road, and well over a hundred when we finally hit the freeway again. I figured that if we were stopped by the state highway patrol, they'd take one look at the old man in the backseat and give us an escort to the emergency room, complete with lights and sirens.

I could feel McCardle's blood pulsing against my fingers. He shivered, and I tried to draw him closer to take advantage of my body heat. The inside of the car was airless and stuffy, and smelled like the back room of an abattoir.

I fought my gag reflex.

Once McCardle opened his eyes and strained to focus them, his lids flickering like the wings of a dying butterfly. Then he looked at me. He was grimacing in pain, so it was hard to tell, but I think he attempted a weak smile. There was a moment of sad, quiet understanding that passed between us—a mutual forgiving—and then he closed his eyes again.

"Faster, Ryan."

"I'm flooring it now," he said. He was obviously terrified; his voice was choked and forced.

About five minutes later I heard the unmistakable rattle in the old man's throat. His body stiffened as if from an electric shock. Then the breath whooshed out of him, and his body relaxed, his head lolling to one side of my lap.

Sadly, Cornelius McCardle, one of the leaders of Cleveland's Irish community', was going to be the featured story in the Irish sports pages.

CHAPTER TWENTY-SIX

Ryan and I spent the rest of the night in the Lorain County Sheriff's Department substation. I tried to explain what had happened, but when I started telling the story it sounded stupid, even to me. With what amounted to a double homicide, the sheriff himself was awakened and summoned, which put him in a sour enough mood to call the Cleveland Police Department and insist that Lieutenant McHargue be rousted out of bed in the middle of the night.

Mud runs downhill; when McHargue arrived sleepy-eyed at the sheriff's station, Bob Matusen was with her.

I had all I could do to keep Ryan from being charged with kidnapping and attempted murder. I finally told the Lorain County authorities that I would refuse to press charges or to testify against him. It wasn't out of sentiment or altruism or to pay off any perceived debt to Con McCardle, who had after all died trying to keep his great-nephew from killing me. Ryan was too far down the food chain anyway, and I didn't see why he should get into trouble just for following orders. Since he was the only one of our little band with a sense of direction, he led them to the spot in the woods where they could recover Francis's body. Finally, they cut him loose.

They kept me around a while longer, since I'd fired the fatal shot at Francis. But the whole business was so messy, so complicated, that finally the Lorain cops were only too happy to kick it back to Cleveland. I was released in McHargue's custody, and paid for it by getting my ears blistered in the car all the way back to the Third District on Payne Avenue.

I explained to McHargue that I had tried to call her before setting off for the Poduska house, but it didn't sink in with her until we got back to headquarters and the desk sergeant's log confirmed it. I told her only what I had to.

The Elyria police, after a phone call from McHargue, picked up Donalene Poduska and kept her in jail until late the next afternoon; then they turned her over to a Cleveland homicide unit delegation led by the sleepless Bob Matusen. She was taken back to town for booking.

I never mentioned the photographs of Senator Doyle Hartigan and Giancarlo D'Allessandro. They were not germane to the investigation of William Poduska's murder, and as much as Lieutenant McHargue threatened and harangued me, I kept mum about them, explaining that I was working for Judge Hartigan's attorney, her daughter Cathleen, and therefore enjoyed the extended lawyer-client privilege. McHargue didn't like the best part of that, but couldn't do anything about it except tell me that the next time our paths crossed on one of her murder investigations, my ass would belong to her.

I didn't say anything about Mickey Marcantonio, either.

His lawyer—and Victor's—Tom Vangelis, moved that Judge Hartigan be recused from his son Angelo's rape case, and earned himself a hanging judge, the Honorable William D. Meacham, who wound up giving Angelo five to seven in the Allen Correctional Institution in Lima.

Cornelius McCardle not only made the Irish sports pages, but his death was front-page news. He was given a funeral befitting royalty: a monsignor conducted the mass, and judges and politicians from both sides of the Cuyahoga were in attendance, including the mayor, three U.S. representatives, and Judge Maureen Hartigan. The police even closed off West Sixty-fifth Street in front of Saint Colman's to all traffic for the better part of an afternoon to accommodate the crowds.

The media people were on the scent like hungry wolves—but the only one I'd talk to was Ed Stahl. I owed him that much.

It took Maureen Hartigan and Hugh Cochran almost a year to reclaim the items that Bill Poduska had stolen from them—the boots, the neckties, and the jewelry from Maureen's mother. The money was never returned, nor was Judith Torrence ever reimbursed.

The county prosecutor wanted to nail Donalene Poduska for what is known in Ohio as aggravated murder—i.e., murder one. But they never found a way to make that stick. On the advice of her attorney, Donalene finally copped a plea to murder in the second degree by reason of temporary insanity, and having drawn a judge who was sympathetic to her betrayed-wife story, was sentenced to twelve to fifteen years in prison, the first two of which were to be spent in a secure mental-health facility. There's a possibility she'll be paroled after seven more.

I didn't see Cathleen Hartigan very much after it had all died down. Too much had happened between us; too much had been said.

After calling Victor and telling him the whole story, including my keeping my mouth shut about Marcantonio and Dante Ruggiero, we didn't see much of each other for quite a while, either. Our friendship, or whatever the hell it was, didn't end exactly, but it cooled down considerably. Six months later I sent a big bouquet of flowers to Giancarlo D'Allessandro's eighty-fourth birthday party, to which I hadn't been invited. The don called personally to thank me, and that seemed to thaw things out. But there were no more dinner invitations forthcoming. I had crossed some sort of invisible line with them, I think—maybe just by one toe—and fences would eventually have to be mended.

I never did find out what happened to my car, but I imagined that James had disposed of it quickly, and that it had been chopped up and sold for parts even before the Lorain sheriff turned me over to McHargue. Gone with it were the Glock pistol I used to keep in the glove compartment, my handy camera, and my cellphone. The insurance company cheerfully replaced the car, and then raised my rates. There is no winning with an insurance company—you're betting against yourself in the first place, and if you happen to win, they whine about paying off. If anyone tried to gamble like that with the D'Allessandro family, or even in legitimate places like Atlantic City, they'd wind up at the bottom of the nearest deep body of water.

I bought another Sunbird, a shiny black one this time, and told the Pontiac dealer on Mayfield Road that at the rate I was buying cars, he was going to have to start giving me a fleet discount.

Three days after Donalene's arrest I got a call from Bob Matusen.

"When are we going to Johnny's?" he wanted to know.

"What?"

"You told me you didn't think we had a female perp in the Poduska case, and you said if you were wrong, you'd buy me lunch. Remember?"

"I guess I do," I said. "How does tomorrow look?"

"If nobody gets themselves killed on my turf between now and then—which is always a dicey proposition—it sounds fine."

I met him at noon at the elegant eatery in the Warehouse District. Most of the judges who had been at the McCardle funeral the day before were having lunch there, too.

"The lieutenant is ripping mad at you," he said after we'd tucked into our lunches.

"Just a little more so than usual."

"I kind of am, too."

"Why's that, Bob?"

He shook his head. "Milan, you gotta get it into your head that Marko Meglich isn't around to cover your ass anymore. You keep making McHargue look bad. That doesn't sit too well."

"McHargue is a good cop," I said.

"I know. She eats raw meat with her fingers, though."

"I can accept that . . ."

"Sure—you don't work for her."

"But she gets locked into certain ideas, Bob, and she won't give them up until she's proved wrong. She was looking hard at the Hartigans for the Poduska killing and wouldn't extend herself to look anywhere else. She has a closed mind."

"She sure does where you're concerned."

I shrugged. "I can live with it."

"I'll be honest with you," he said. "If it had been me running things, I would've been liking the wife for it from the beginning."

"Why?"

He poured the rest of his beer into a glass. "I don't know; there was just something about her. She seemed so beaten down, so whipped. Guys treat their wives bad like that, resentment builds up quietly, and then something happens to push them over the edge and you've got a dead husband on your hands."

"Your instincts were better than hers, or mine, too, then. You're a good cop, Bob."

"I just know that marriage isn't easy."

"Yours isn't?"

"I didn't mean that. Mine is good—it's just not easy, that's all."

"And yet almost everybody wants to get married eventually."

He nodded. "That's because nobody wants to die alone, Milan."

I thought about that when I got back to the office. In the end, we all die alone—it's just the way things are set up, and there's nothing we can do about it.

Living alone, though—*being* alone—that was another story.

I got out the phone book and looked up City Hall. I had to be transferred to five different people before I found the one I wanted.

"Jinny," I said, "this is Milan Jacovich. I'm calling to apologize."

"No need to," she said. "I read the papers. It made me feel lousy."

"Why?"

"Because I was sitting home after our interrupted dinner that night—thinking what a rude, thoughtless shit you turned out to be. And all that time you were close to getting killed."

"I forgive you," I said. "Enough to want to have dinner with you again. On me this time."

"Do you promise you won't go running off in the middle of coffee to shoot somebody?"

"It doesn't happen all that often. But I can't really promise. I'm in a peculiar line of work."

"I'm a civil servant, Milan," she said. "Peculiar beats hell out of boring-as-shit anytime."

"Is that a yes? We're on?"

"*Dinner* is on," she said, and I was amazed at how pleased I was to hear it. "Anything else after that, well—we'll just have to wait and see what develops."

That seemed eminently fair, I thought as I hung up. Seeing what develops—that's the way of life.

ACKNOWLEDGMENTS

WITH GRATITUDE

William F. Miller of the *Plain Dealer*

Miriam Carey

Patricia Britt, Cleveland City Council

Michael Dugan, chief of police, Independence, Ohio

Debi Buettner, my "computer fairy" and Webmistress—which isn't as kinky as it sounds

Richard Gildenmeister, my "bookie," for twelve years of friendship and support

Nick Orlando and Uncle Carmen Palumbo, for their memories

The Greater Cleveland Police Emerald Society

Ruth Cavin, my editor—and the eighth wonder of the world

Dominick Abel, my agent—the *ninth* wonder

Dr. Milan Yakovich, and Diana Yakovich Montagino

And Holly Albin, for her love, patience, and understanding on the dark, frustrating days

A NOTE FROM LES ROBERTS . . .

Since <u>The Irish Sports Pages</u>, I have not written another Milan Jacovich novel.

I love Milan. He's been a close friend and constant companion since 1987, when I wrote my first Jacovich novel, <u>Pepper Pike</u>. But after thirteen of them (as well as six other private eye books), I needed to write different kinds of stories. Like most authors, I wanted to use some "writing muscles" I hadn't exercised before, and to take more chances. My new books are mysteries, but they don't fit the Cleveland private eye format.

So in the past few years I've written another novel—a chase story set in about ten different cities (including, of course, Cleveland). I've written my own nonfiction memoir, <u>We'll Always Have Cleveland</u>. And, I've begun a historical mystery, set in Germany during World War II. Where to next? Perhaps Milan will make another appearance one of these days.

I appreciate your joining Milan Jacovich and me, and I'm grateful for your support and encouragement. Find me again, if you can.

Happy reading!

-- Les Roberts

PEPPER PIKE
Introducing Milan Jacovich, the private investigator with a master's degree,
a taste for klobasa sandwiches, and a knack for finding trouble. A cryptic
late-night phone call from a high-powered advertising executive leads Milan
through the haunts of one of Cleveland's richest suburbs and into the den of
Cleveland mob kingpin Don Giancarlo D'Allessandro.   1-59851-001-0

FULL CLEVELAND
Someone's scamming Cleveland businessmen by selling ads in a magazine
that doesn't exist. But the dollar amount hardly seems worth the number of
bodies that Milan soon turns up. And why is Milan being shadowed at every
turn by a leisure-suited mob flunky? One thing's certain: Buddy Bustamente's
fashion sense isn't the only thing about him that's lethal.   1-59851-002-9

DEEP SHAKER
Ever loyal, Milan Jacovich has no choice but to help when a grade-school
chum worries his son might be selling drugs. The investigation uncovers a
brutal murder and a particularly savage drug gang—and leads Milan to a relic
from every Clevelander's childhood that proves to be deadly.   1-59851-003-7

THE CLEVELAND CONNECTION
The Serbs and the Slovenians traditionally don't get along too well, but Milan
Jacovich makes inroads into Cleveland's Serbian community when an appeal-
ing young woman convinces him to help search for her missing grandfather.
Hatreds that have simmered for fifty years eventually explode as Milan takes
on one of his most challenging cases.   1-59851-004-5

THE LAKE EFFECT
Milan owes a favor and agrees to serve as bodyguard for a suburban mayoral
candidate—but these politics lead to murder. And the other candidate has
hired Milan's old nemesis, disgraced ex-cop Al Drago, who carries a grudge a
mile wide.   1-59851-005-3

More . . .

THE DUKE OF CLEVELAND
Milan dives into the cutthroat world of fine art when a slumming young heiress hires him to find her most recent boyfriend, a potter, who has absconded with $18,000 of her trust-fund money. Turns out truth and beauty don't always mix well—at least in the art business. 1-59851-006-1

COLLISION BEND
Milan goes behind the scenes to uncover scandal, ambition, and intrigue at one of Cleveland's top TV stations as he hunts down the stalker and murderer of a beautiful local television anchor. 1-59851-007-X

THE CLEVELAND LOCAL
Milan Jacovich is hired to find out who murdered a hotshot young Cleveland lawyer vacationing in the Caribbean. Back in Cleveland, he runs afoul of both a Cleveland mob boss and a world-famous labor attorney—and is dealt a tragic personal loss that will alter his life forever. 1-59851-008-8

A SHOOT IN CLEVELAND
Milan accepts an "easy" job baby-sitting a notorious Hollywood bad-boy who's in Cleveland for a movie shoot. But keeping Darren Anderson out of trouble is like keeping your hat dry during a downpour. And when trouble leads to murder, Milan finds himself in the middle of it all. 1-59851-009-6

THE BEST-KEPT SECRET
Milan takes the case of a college student falsely accused of rape by campus feminists, angering police and university officials. His investigation raises questions that stir up the real culprit and cast a harsh light on campus political correctness. 1-59851-010-X

THE INDIAN SIGN
A corporate espionage case gets much more complicated when Milan also investigates the murder of an elderly Native American man and the kidnapping of the man's grandson by a local mobster. 1-59851-011-8

THE DUTCH
A distraught father hires Milan Jacovich to investigate the apparent suicide of his daughter. What Milan uncovers isn't pretty—and involves a sinister web of lies and sordid behavior. 1-59851-012-6

THE IRISH SPORTS PAGES
Milan is hired by a wealthy judge who has a serious problem that she wants kept quiet. Things get noisy, though, when a dead body turns up, and it becomes Milan's job to find the killer. 1-59851-013-4

GET THEM ALL AT YOUR FAVORITE BOOKSTORE!